FEATHERS

and

THORNS

FEATHERS
and
THORNS

N. J. RODMAN

ENTHEAS
THORNCR
PATRIVAH
PINLAS MOR
TEMPLE OF VEDAS
BRAEXMIRTH
OLECASTO
ELI
STELONBRIAR
IREFELD
OBSIDIAN SEA

N
W
E
S
NURAKA
SAIPEI
XIAN DAO EMPIRE
ILASTEAD
TELAR
DRAESTEL
VREVERN
VAKARI DYNASTY
DHAMTRA

*For those of us who were forced to become
the heroes in our own stories.*

CONTENT WARNINGS

This book contains depictions of mental illness, with a particular focus on anxiety. Other adult themes include fantasy violence, gore, character death, grief, extreme torture, a sexual assault flashback involving a minor, profanity, and sexually explicit scenes.

PROLOGUE

Enara's and Baztien's bodies were crushed together under the snow, the oxygen almost depleted. They had minutes left.

"Baz, I'm scared," Enara whimpered as she tried to shift, stopping when snow filled the space she had just been occupying.

"Look at me," he said, giving her a small smile. "I won't lie to you; we may not get out of this, but if we don't, I'm glad I'm here with you. If we're lucky, it will be like falling asleep."

"I love you," she whispered quietly.

"I love you, too."

Silence.

Death wrapped her arms around them in a frozen embrace. They closed their eyes, pressing their foreheads together and took their last shallow breaths.

"I'm coming, guys. Hold on," Jai yelled from above.

They did not respond.

He clawed at the snow, his thin gloves doing little to protect his hands from the icy shards. They sliced into his fingers like pieces of shattered glass as he dragged the frozen ground away from the tip of Enara's staff, which had embedded itself vertically from where they sat, barely protruding above ground. He was lucky to have spotted it.

"Guys, I'm almost there!" he yelled again.

"Jai?" Baz asked weakly.

"Yeah, buddy, I'm coming!"

"Thank the Maker!" Enara cried.

Jai dug down another foot or so then let out a sigh of relief when his hand brushed against Baz's fingertips. He was lying on his side with Enara next to him, his hand extended, holding onto the staff's handle.

Jai widened the hole to allow them to breathe, and they sucked in the frostbitten air, thanking their lucky stars. Then he got Baz up into a semi-seated position to help move the snow around. After about twenty minutes, they both crawled free.

The avalanche had carried them into a tree well. A few more minutes, and they would have suffocated.

"Well, now we're even," Jai said, slapping Baztien on the back.

"Don't mention it," he replied, rubbing his shoulders to fight off the chill.

"How did you escape the avalanche?" Enara asked, blowing warm air onto her hands.

The tracker pointed to an overhang jutting up near the cliff's edge. "It was terrifying. I almost didn't make it. I pushed off the log and grabbed on right before it went over the edge. All the debris crashed right over me."

"That's crazy," Enara said, eyes wide.

"There's something else, too. We're closer than I thought. I saw kestrels circling over there"—he pointed—"just past that ridge. We should check it out."

"I'm with you, man, but we should regroup first," Baz replied.

"Yeah," Enara agreed. "My pack ripped off when I was holding on to Baz. Most of our med supplies are gone. All we have left is some antiseptic and a few bandages that I stuffed into yours."

"Shit." Jai kicked a chunk of ice and watched it roll down the hill. "Okay, let's take a moment to rest then get to the ridge. We can make a plan from there."

Baz and Enara nodded, and then Enara handed them each a piece of dried fruit from Baztien's pack. They would need the energy, but it was tough to chew, making their jaws ache.

"You know, I'm sick of Mother Nature trying to kill us," Baz commented, flashing back to their time in the tunnels.

"I think that's something we can all agree on, man," Jai replied, straightening his jacket as they trudged toward the ridge.

"It does seem like she has it out for us," Enara said thoughtfully.

"It's karma," Baz replied.

Enara's eyebrows pressed together in confusion. "What do you mean? What did we do to piss off Mother Nature?"

"Well, the Oculus holds the power of all creation, so it stands to reason that, if used, it could upset the balance of things," he replied simply. "Messing with it at all was sure to have some consequences."

"I mean, I think you're right," Enara said, huffing in annoyance. "I just wish the powers-that-be knew we were the good guys."

"Good guys always finish last," Jai said as they reached the ridge and peered over.

Enara and Baz shared a look that meant they would ask him to explain that statement later. Then they joined him to take in the view below.

At the base of the valley, they could see a manor house. The grey stones were stacked neatly in a U-shape, surrounded by walking paths that met near the back of the house and opened up into a large courtyard. The lake below looked like a shattered mirror, jagged chunks of ice floating this way and that. It had undoubtedly been disturbed by Mother Nature's wrath. It was still too far to make out too many details, but they could see black things moving by the entranceways—no doubt kestrels guarding their master.

Jai grimaced. "There's no way down from here. It's too steep. We're going to have to head down near our last camp and take the entrance to the valley."

"Every time we get closer, it's another step back," Enara said, frustration filling her voice.

"We've got this," Baz reassured her. "That's an evil fortress if I ever saw one. Castle, check. Evil minions, check. Isolated, check. There's no way Soren isn't in there."

"Yeah," she sighed. "I guess you're right. So, what is the plan, then? We can't stay up here. If they fly any higher, they will see us."

"Then we hide in plain sight," Jai replied.

They pushed back down toward the valley entrance and formed a makeshift igloo by digging into the mountainside. They used the shelter to stay out of view and settled in as the sun began to set behind the largest peak.

"I don't like the idea of sleeping in here," Enara said, looking around at their hovel, shivering.

"It's not ideal, but it will keep us from being spotted," Jai replied, giving her a sympathetic look. He understood the fear ebbing below the surface of her skin. This morning, the mountain had almost become her tomb. "Try to get some rest. I imagine tomorrow will be more physically demanding than any of us would like."

He was being nice. They all knew what tomorrow would bring. They would have to battle the kestrels again, and Enara couldn't help but worry for her small group. Their supplies were low, and they couldn't risk a fatal injury here—they would never make it down the mountain in time to get to a healer.

She blinked the unshed tears from her eyes as Baz snaked his arm around her middle, pulling her to him. She forced the negative thoughts from her mind in an attempt to get some sleep.

"Goodnight, beautiful," Baz said softy.

"Goodnight," she whispered.

They woke up to find dawn fighting with the mountain's shadows and peeked out from their shelter, scanning the white landscape for black feathers. Finding none, they loosed sighs of relief and began the trek down into the valley. Their pace quickened with determination to get their friend home.

"Man, I don't know how you do it," Baz said, directing the statement at Jai.

"Do what?" the tracker asked.

"Risk your life to find other people's treasures. It hardly seems like the payout is worth it."

"Some things are worth more than others."

"But seriously," Enara cut in, "this isn't going to be like fighting off some bandits hoarding gemstones. There is a good chance one of us will not make it out of here today."

Jai gave a noncommittal shrug. "Then, so be it."

"Just ready to die, huh?" Baz asked, patting Jai's back.

"No, I'm ready to live," Jai said, eyes sparkling, "Without Adaryn, I felt I had no purpose. I became a lowlife, a cheat, bound to roam the underground for the rest of my days if Patrivah's alliance with Xian-Dao went well. Now, I can at least feel like I did something for the world before I go. I don't want to go back to a life of shadows. So, like it or not, I am with you until this is finished."

"Hey"—Baz smiled—"if you're willing to die on this hill, then so am I."

They attempted to preserve every last ounce of their energy as they descended into their impending battleground.

After a disagreement with Enara, who was now on a warpath to get her friend back, Jai convinced them to wait about half a kilometer back from the manor while he scoped the place out.

He stayed out of sight, his footsteps silent. He could not risk being seen now, or they would lose the element of surprise. He stalked in a semi-circle around the property, noting windows and entrances and also the kestrels perched within a few feet of each one. *How the hell are we going to get in there?* he thought. *It's a damn fortress.*

He nearly jumped out of his skin when one of the beasts flew around the side of the manor, this one looking differ-ent from the rest—more human than animal. It flew up and motioned with its wings. At once, all the creatures surround-ing the building headed toward the frozen lake and over the mountain range on the other side.

Not trusting the creatures had left for his convenience, he circled back toward the entrance of the house and waited. He remained hidden as a young woman walked through the open gate and headed straight down the narrow path, in the direction of his companions. He followed behind her, glad the snow muted the sound of his footsteps. When she paused to tighten her bootstraps, he acted, running up behind her and pulling out his bowie knife. He held the blade to her throat as she struggled against him.

"What the fuck?" she growled, and he nicked her neck in warning.

"Where is your master?" he asked viciously.

"Are you thick in the head? I don't answer to anyone. Who the fuck are you?"

"I'm the one asking the questions." He put more pressure on the blade than necessary, and a small trickle of blood slid down her neck, pooling between her breasts.

"Asshole," she gritted out.

"Who are you?"

"Wouldn't you like to know?"

The sarcasm in her voice was so thick that he rolled his eyes in response.

Seeing that he wasn't getting anywhere, he decided to try a different approach.

"I'm going to back away now. Please refrain from doing anything stupid."

"Then don't give me a reason to," she retorted.

He removed the blade, pushing her forward in the same instant so she wouldn't have the chance to get the drop on him.

"Seriously!" she exclaimed. She had landed on her hands and knees in the snow. Standing, she pinned him with a glare.

"So," he said haughtily, "you going to tell me your name?"

She brushed the white flakes from her cloak before answering.

"My name is Soren."

CHAPTER ONE

"Shit," Jai exclaimed, taken aback. "I am sorry. I didn't know it was you. They said Soren had blue hair."

"Yeah, well, the facilities didn't provide hair dye. This is my natural color. Wait—who are *they*?"

"Baz and Enara."

Soren cried out, her heart bursting with happiness. "They're alive? Where are they? Why did they send you? Who are you? Are they okay?" Everything came out in a rush of words so quickly she forgot to take a breath. So, she guzzled in air, waiting for an answer.

"Yes, they are alive. They aren't far from here. I am a tracker. The name's Jai. They hired me to find you."

"Take me to them," she demanded, not giving a flying fuck who he was.

He laughed at her demanding tone. "They said you were a fiery one. Follow me."

Soren had to resist screaming with joy when she embraced her friends. They fell to the ground in a riotous heap, laughing and crying, and laughing some more.

"Maker, I am so glad that you guys are okay," she said, blinking away the moisture that had collected at the corners of her eyes.

"*Us?*" Baz breathed. "What about you?"

"Woman, I thought I would never see you again," Enara said, cupping Soren's face.

"It's been a hell of a time," Soren said, sitting back on her haunches to catch her breath.

"Have you been here this whole time?" Enara asked.

"Yeah, I have been his ..." She hesitated at the word *prisoner* because it wasn't quite accurate. "Well, I couldn't leave voluntarily, but I had free rein of the house."

"Why were you taken? How did you get out?" Enara continued peppering her with questions.

"It's a long story."

Soren recounted the events of the last few weeks, pausing to let her friends and their strange companion take it all in. She left certain parts out, not knowing how much this guy, Jai, knew, but Baz assured her that he was all good, and she trusted his opinion. So, she shared everything she had learned while in the manor, including how the relationship between her and Rook had grown and ended with the devastating discovery that Rook had murdered her father.

"Oh, Soren ..." Enara shook her head in disbelief. "Hon, I am so sorry."

"I feel so lost," she said solemnly. "Can we not talk about it anymore? I want to know what happened to you guys. Tell me everything."

"What do you want to know?" Baz asked.

"Well, for starters," Soren replied, eyeing their interlaced fingers, "you two seem more … comfortable with each other."

Enara blushed. "Yeah, you missed a lot, too." Her friend shared the stories of their travels and how she had saved Baz's life.

"Maker, I am so glad you're okay, Baz," Soren said, her stomach twisting at the thought of anything happening to him.

"And after a few well-played hands of joker's gambit," Enara finished, "we bumped into Jai and hired him to track you down." She purposely omitted the spicier details of her and Baz's newfound relationship. She would reserve those for a later time … when they had a moment away from the guys.

They embraced again as relief filled them. The trio was finally together again.

They settled on a plan for getting home, falling into old routines, finding comfort in each other after all the craziness of the last few weeks.

Soren was doubled over, laughing at a joke Baz had said, when her chuckling was cut short.

The four of them jumped to their feet as General Corvus walked into their camp, causing them all to reach for their weapons of choice.

"Well, isn't this cozy?" he mocked. "The master won't be pleased to see you tried to escape. He already killed my brother for nearly letting you drown. We can't have that now, can we?"

"You have two choices," Soren threatened, raising one of her blades. Evelyn had given her a set of throwing knives as a parting gift, but they felt strange in her hands. They didn't quite fit, almost as if her body was rejecting them. "Leave now," she warned, "or we will string you up, pluck out your feathers one by one, and leave you here to rot."

He smiled wickedly, and she resisted the urge to loose her daggers. Even unbalanced, she was confident she could have one through his skull before he flapped his wings.

"I was hoping we could do this again," he said, smiling.

The false grin made her feel sick to her stomach as his features contorted to bare his too-white teeth.

"I'm going to enjoy this," Enara said, standing firm beside Soren.

"Don't be a fool, girl," Corvus mocked. "My flock has been training; you won't stand a chance."

"Try me," Enara replied, her threat laced with venom.

As if it were the response he had been waiting for, General Corvus let out a loud whistle that resembled a broken bird call. A moment later, several kestrels dropped to the ground, shaking loose snow from the evergreen branches.

"Shit," Baz said, tightening his grip on his sword, trying to gauge which beast to attack first.

"They must have been resting in the treetops," Jai growled in frustration. He was angry at himself for being so distracted. He had one job, and he had failed to alert them of the danger. His heart beat painfully against his ribcage. Because of him, they were all going to die.

General Corvus looked all too pleased at their surprise and directed his gaze to Soren. "Sure you don't want to change your mind?"

"Oh, I'm sure," Soren replied through clenched teeth.

Corvus smirked, taking a step forward. He then fanned out his wings and simply said, "Goodbye, Miss Nightsong."

Then, his birds descended upon them.

JAI WHIPPED AROUND, RELEASING HIS BOWIE KNIFE IN AN ARC TOward the kestrel at his left. The blade sunk halfway through its disfigured head, and it screeched as the snow was dyed black. He ran at the creature, grabbed the hilt, and tore the knife out of its face, leaving it to bleed out on the ground, wings thrashing violently.

Corvus advanced on him, infuriated that one of his own had been bested by this insignificant fool. He lifted off the ground, flapping furiously so the snow and dirt lifted, blinding the tracker. Jai found shelter behind a tree and cleared his vision, swinging back around its trunk to join the battle.

Enara was struggling to release her staff from the talons of one of the beasts, her arms straining with the effort. She leaned in and kicked it in the gut, wrenching her weapon free and swinging the staff down like an axe, burying it in the creature's shoulder. It howled angrily and pulled the weapon out, tossing it to the side as the magic burned its skin, then slashed out with its claws. Enara ducked, running under its wing, and kicked it again in the back, causing it to fall face-first on the ground. It recovered quickly, pushing up and swinging its onyx wing into her chest, throwing her back into the base of the evergreen with a sickening *thud*. The wind was knocked out of her, and she struggled to stand, begging her lungs to take in air.

The kestrel loomed over her, ready to deal a killing blow, when one of Soren's knives sunk into its claw, and it doubled over. Enara gave her friend a nod of thanks and grabbed the knife out of its hand, thrusting it upward into the bottom of its jaw.

Soren was caught in a deadly dance with two more of the beasts. She twirled her arms, slashing this way and that, parrying and blocking blows while dealing her own in return. Her daggers glinted dangerously as blood splattered the trees. Her cape had been torn to shreds, and her arms were covered in thin ribbons of crimson.

Jai and Baz were fighting Corvus, side by side, while three kestrels watched, waiting hungrily. The general's fighting skills were impeccable. It was obvious why Adriel had chosen him to lead his ranks in Entheas.

Baz swung his sword, aiming to behead the creature, but the general spun out of the way and the blade embedded itself in a tree. Baz struggled to pull it out when Jai ran in to protect his back, catching the creature's forearm with his blade, only infuriating the enemy more.

Corvus slashed toward his chest, and Jai jumped back, but the claws still marred his skin. He hissed as the hot liquid seeped from the wound but swung again, catching a piece of Corvus's thigh.

The three onlookers jumped in as their general stumbled back, hissing profanities.

"Filthy human."

"Weakling."

Baz had heard enough. He swung his sword, slicing its beak off, the bird effectively silenced. He finished it off by cutting open its chest as it tried to lift itself off the ground.

The other two had Jai by the arms and were trying to carry him toward the canopy while he slashed at their ankles. They shrieked like banshees and dropped him toward the forest floor, their feet nearly removed from their feathered bodies.

He fell through the evergreens, reaching desperately for something to hold on to. The bristles scraped his face and arms, and he was knocked out by one of protruding branches. His body landed with a hard *thump* at the base of a tree.

On the other side of the clearing, Enara had jumped in to help Soren and received a few gashes herself. They worked together to knock one of the winged creatures onto its stomach, and then Enara brought her staff down, removing its wings. She smirked triumphantly as they fell, twitching to the ground.

The creature cried out as it crawled on its hands and knees, and Soren finished it off with her dagger. Its brother flew forward, knocking her to the side then grabbing Enara, whipping her body sideways at a boulder. She was out cold, blood trickling down her face.

"Enara!" Soren cried, running toward her friend. The kestrel blocking her path was down in seconds, a knife between its beady eyes.

Baz ran to Soren's side, and they looked around. The ground was soaked in blood, the snowy landscape transformed into a macabre painting of red and black.

Soren was down to one knife, and her body was rejecting any form of movement. Baz held steady to her side, his vision clouded by blood seeping from a cut above his eye. Their enemies had regrouped.

Corvus landed in front of them, his two best and brightest flanking either side. He assessed them, looking around and clucking his tongue. "Seems such a waste," he said. His voice was unsettling, making Soren cringe. He flicked his black eyes to Baztien. "If you leave now, I will spare you. We only need the girl."

Before Baz could tell him where to put that remark, another voice rang out from the trees.

"Touch her, and I will slit your throat where you stand."

CHAPTER
TWO

Their heads whipped right, their ears burning.

Rook stepped out from behind a large evergreen, and Soren inhaled audibly.

"What is he doing here?" Baz whispered.

Soren couldn't respond. She hated the way her heart lurched at the sight of the man who had broken it to pieces.

"Hold your tongue, boy. We have our orders," General Corvus said.

"And you have mine," Rook replied, the gravel in his tone relaying that he would not back down. He took a step forward, placing himself in front of Baz and Soren.

"You insignificant boy. Your orders are of no consequence to me when they do not exemplify your father's," Corvus said, scowling.

Rook grimaced. He understood the chain of command and had the internal scars to prove it.

"I don't give a fuck what his orders are. If you make a move toward her, I will not hesitate to kill you," he said, lifting his curved sword. The black metal seemed to absorb all light.

"I trained you your whole life; do you really think you could beat me?" Corvus glowered. "Don't be stupid, boy. I don't want to hurt you, but I will."

Rook barked out a laugh. "You have tortured me my entire life. That ends now." He slashed out at Corvus, meeting him blow for blow as the other kestrels descended on Baz and Soren. The pair weren't as well versed in each other's combat skills, but they managed.

Soren dug her blade into one of their wings, sending feathers flying all around them, and took it down with three quick jabs to the chest. Baz had lost his sword and tackled the second one to the ground, knees pinning its arms at the wrist to immobilize its hands. Its wings flapped helplessly, unable to lift Baz's weight as he laid into its face with his fists. Soren finished it off with her blade as Enara struggled to get her legs under her. She touched her head, her fingers coming back red.

"Hey, are you okay?" Baz asked, grabbing her face and making her wince. "Shit, sorry."

"It's okay," she replied, leaning into his palm before they broke away to join Soren, who was helping Jai to his feet. He was clutching his ribs and looked a little worse for wear.

"You okay, man?" Baz asked.

"Never better," Jai replied.

"If it helps, you still look as handsome as ever." Baz winked.

"Thanks, brother," Jai said, smiling weakly.

A crash from the trees had them turning as Corvus and Rook came back into view.

They fought immaculately. They knew each other's fighting styles down to each footstep and were well-matched. Soren considered throwing a knife but didn't want to risk hitting Rook, though Maker knew he deserved it.

Corvus's sword caught on a low-hanging branch, throwing him off balance, and Rook took the opportunity to land a blow to his leg, just missing the artery. The bird man swore and spun in the opposite direction, taking Rook by surprise, slashing his talons deep into Rook's flesh. Rook yelled and doubled over momentarily, dropping his weapon.

"I told you this wouldn't end well. Now look at what you made me do," Corvus chided. The creature limped in a slow circle around him, taunting, "Your father will do much worse. You will answer to him now."

Not able to watch any longer, Soren let her knife fly. The general predicted her attack, however, and batted it away with his wings. He looked back at the group of them, contemplating whether or not if he could take them all on at once and decided against it. He spat at the ground where Rook kneeled and spewed venom with his words.

"He's your problem now."

The comment had been directed at Soren, who glared at him, her eyes burning into the back of his skull as he flew out of sight.

She rushed over to Rook to inspect his injuries. Corvus might as well have subjected him to death by a thousand cuts because his entire body was covered with tiny slices. He hadn't been trying to kill him, Soren realized. He had wanted to teach him a lesson.

"Little bird," Rook rasped. His voice was a tiny stream of air that flitted into her ears.

"I'm here," she responded automatically, moving to his side.

"Soren, come on," Enara said, waving toward the path. "We have to get out of here before he comes back with re-inforcements. Leave pretty boy and let's go." She made to pull Soren to her feet, but Soren drew away from her out-stretched arm.

"I can't."

"What do you mean, *you can't?*" Enara asked, her tone matching the cold weather that surrounded them. "He killed your father. He kidnapped you. His creatures almost killed us … twice." Enara grabbed her arm firmly, but Soren wrenched it away, refusing to leave Rook's side.

"It's not that simple, and you know we won't make it far. The kestrels' poison will take effect soon, and I only have one anti-venom."

Enara looked as though she were about to start yelling, but before she could, Baz interjected.

"She's right; we need to be smart about this." He reached forward to touch Enara's shoulder, the simple act seeming to calm her slightly. "Let's hear Soren out," he said, softer this time.

Enara loosened her clenched fists and nodded. "Make it quick," she said, gesturing to Soren.

"The house is practically an apothecary," she replied matter-of-factly. "We can regroup there, but I will need your help to carry him." Without waiting for confirmation, she unrolled a bandage and wrapped it tightly around his torso to stop the bleeding.

"I'll second that motion," Jai said, hobbling toward them.

"All in favor?" Baz asked, trying to lighten the mood.

Everyone but Enara put up their hand, and she sighed.

"Fine," Enara replied but made no move to assist Rook.

Soren tried not to panic as the bandage changed color, and she willed her friends to move faster. They were only a kilometer away from the manor, yet it felt like a marathon. Even with their combined strength, the four of them struggled to get his body down the snow-covered path. Behind them was a trail of crimson that seemed to be following them like a shadow.

The adrenaline had worn off, and they were all feeling the results of their brush with the kestrels. Enara's head had stopped bleeding, and she had stuffed snow into her sock, using it as an icepack. Jai tucked one of Rook's legs under his arm and held his ribs with the other, fairly certain that at least two of them were broken from his fall through the trees. Baz had miraculously come out pretty unscathed, all things considered, with a few scrapes here and there. Soren's arms closely resembled the rest of Rook's body, some of the defensive wounds deep enough to require a stitch or two.

She looked at Rook's broken body, and tears welled in her eyes. Somehow, this man had struck a chord in her heart, and she sent up everything she had to the universe in the hopes that he would survive this. All their best moments from the last couple of weeks seemed to erase the bad ones. He had known pain and suffering beyond imagination, and she understood why he would do the things he had done to save himself, no matter how temporary the reprieve was. The things he had gone through—she shuddered—anyone else would have broke.

The group stumbled over some buried branches and almost dropped him, but they regained their composure and continued. The blood was dripping from the bandage now, and they were breathing heavily, the puffs of white a continuous cloud around their heads.

"He better be worth it," Enara grumbled half-heartedly as they came within sight of the manor.

"He is." The response was automatic, and Soren mentally kicked herself before adding, "I think."

They burst through the front door, blood streaking the floor of the foyer as they carried Rook's limp body through the house to the dining room. They laid him on the table, and then Soren ran out, promising to return with help

She sprinted to the servant's quarters in search of Meena and Evelyn, startling them with the state of her appearance.

"Rook … he's hurt … Come quick!" she shouted, darting back out toward the hall, knowing they would follow.

Soren sobbed internally as they patched him up. His chest was barely rising, and she could hear the steady *drip, drip, drip* of his blood pooling on the floor.

Enara held her hand, and Baz put his head on her shoulder. Jai stood to the side, unsure of his place in all this. They might not have understood Soren's compassion for this man but they respected it, nonetheless.

After a few minutes, Enara gave Soren a once-over, dealing with the worst of her cuts, and then she took the boys to retire to the next room to nurse their wounds.

"We will be right next door if you need us," Enara said gently. "We love you."

Soren stayed with Rook all night, dozing on and off, sleeping fitfully. Multiple times, she woke up with tears on her face, having dreamed he hadn't made it out alive.

"You should get some rest," Evelyn said when she came in to check on her as the first day's light started to enter the room. "He's settled now."

"I couldn't leave. I needed to know he was okay. I mean … I don't even know what this is … but I just couldn't go … I care … I mean, I don't want to … but I do. I told them we'd go after sunrise." Her eyes were red, and the dark circles were extensive.

"He cares for you," Evie said softly. "You know … in his own way."

"I know," she said, squeezing his hand. She swore she thought she felt him squeeze back but dismissed it due to the lack of sleep. "Can you give this to him for me?" She held out a piece of parchment. "And … could you … could you tell him that I'm sorry?"

"Yes, hon, of course."

"Thank you." Soren wiped her face and stood from the dining chair that she'd spent the night in.

"Soren?" Evie called as she reached the door.

"Yes?"

"We enjoyed having you here. You will be missed."

"I'll miss you guys, too," Soren replied as a sad smile whispered across her face.

As Evelyn departed, Soren looked at Rook one last time, thinking, *A few more weeks, and I could have tamed you.*

CHAPTER
THREE

"I still can't believe you slept with him."

The disgust in Enara's voice made Soren want to pitch herself off the cliffside. She ignored the quip as she narrowly avoided another tree well.

They had departed Thorncrest Manor two days ago and were near the bottom of the mountain range. Their travel was slow due to the heavy snow and debris left behind by the avalanche. Soren had nearly fallen into a tree well not once, but three times. The entire group had taken to using walking sticks for the remainder of the hike, swinging the wooden poles this way and that as though they were blind.

Soren couldn't have been more thankful when the white landscape finally gave way to dusty browns and grays. She breathed in the cool fall air and shed her thick cloak. She would rather have left it behind at the manor, wanting to rid herself of any memories of the place … and its owner. She folded it into her pack just as she mentally tucked away all fond thoughts of Rook. She filled the now vacant spaces in her mind with dark fantasies of how best to kill him should their paths ever cross again.

Baz's voice cut through Soren's murderous thoughts. "Guys, we have a problem."

Jai, Enara, and Soren all gave him a quizzical look.

"The four of us won't fit in that canoe."

Jai scrubbed a hand over his face. "He's right. The extra person would have been fine, but with the addition of our gear, there is no way we will stay afloat."

Enara groaned and sat down on a nearby boulder, her frustration mounting. She pulled the weathered map out of her ruck, searching for the quickest route home. "If we follow the river to the falls, there is a bridge near Murkwall. We can cross there and make our way south to Draestel."

Soren's ears perked up at this, and she shook her head vigorously. "I don't think we should go to Vreburn."

Enara's gaze shifted from the map to her friend, and she noted the resigned expression on Soren's face.

"I thought the goal was to get you out of there and get you home," Jai stated plainly, plucking invisible lint off his collar.

"It is … I mean, it was …" Enara started. She looked to Soren for answers.

Soren took a steadying breath. Enara could tell she was feeling guilty about something. After years of friendship, Soren's expressions were as familiar to her as the countless scars that ran down the length of her back.

"Care to explain, lady? Why wouldn't we want to go home?"

"Because," Soren replied, "we still have to find a way to destroy the Oculus."

"PULL IT OUT, AND I'LL TAKE A SWING AT IT," BAZ SAID, LOOKING for any excuse to use his sword.

Soren bit her lip to hide her smirk as she turned down the offer. "Sorry, Baz, but brute force isn't going to get us out of this mess."

"It's worth a try, isn't it?" Jai asked, grasping his own weapon.

Enara rolled her eyes at the cloud of testosterone forming in the air. "Simmer down, you two, and let her explain." She turned to Soren. "In your talks with this Rook guy, did he betray any information on how to destroy it?"

Soren picked at her fingernails, wishing she had a concrete answer. Her idea was a well-placed guess, at best. "Apart from bonding with Rook and using it to destroy itself, there is only one other potential solution."

"And that is …?" Jai asked, pushing for an answer with a wave of his hand. He had never been a particularly patient man and wanted to get a move on.

Soren narrowed her eyes at him before she continued, "We may not be able to completely destroy the artifact, but we can at least make it impossible for Adriel to make use of it." She looked to each of her friends then flashed a smug look at the tracker. "I think we should take it to Braexmirth."

THE TRIO HELD THEIR BREATHS AS SOREN EXPLAINED HER PLAN. They would require the heat of a thousand forges for there to even be a possibility of breaking down the strange metal. Olecastor was their best chance at succeeding in their mission. Once the Oculus was melted down, they would form it into droplet-sized pieces and spread them all throughout Entheas. Considering how long it had taken to find the Oculus when it had only been split into two sections, they figured it would be many ages before Adriel would be able to find it were it split into many. It was not a perfect plan and rested solely on them making it to the capital of Braexmirth before getting stopped, not to mention the capabilities of Olecastor's forges.

They all had their doubts, but a questionable plan was better than no plan at all.

With the new destination in mind, Enara mapped out the best route from their current location. They would travel southwest to Blightfall then cross both the Hazelbrooke and Claymore rivers. The trade paths would be easier to follow and keep their supplies well stocked while giving them the opportunity to ask locals about recent goings-on within the provinces. They would stay a night in Murkwall before crossing the final river into Braexmirth.

"It will take us about a week's time to reach the border," Enara estimated.

Baz kissed the top of her head, smiling. "Hey, I'm just glad this route is on flat ground."

"On that, my friend, we can agree." Jai clapped him on the back. "Let's let the ladies catch up. You can help me get the camp set up."

Baz looked to Enara and Soren then backed away slowly. He had felt the tension bubbling between them since they had first reunited in Thorncrest and knew better than to get involved. "Right behind you, buddy."

The moment they were out of earshot, Enara stood and rounded on Soren. "How could you get romantically involved with that monster?" She scolded her friend like a mother would, her voice so taut it was at risk of snapping.

"It's not like I planned any of this, Enara," Soren shot straight back, fuming.

"He nearly killed me and Baztien!" Her hazel eyes flashed a dangerous shade of viridian.

"You think I don't know that?" Soren snapped. "It just happened!"

"Is your solution for everything to climb into bed with someone?" The moment the words left her mouth, she regretted them.

Soren stepped back as though Enara's words had struck her. She kept her voice low as she glared at her friend. "I don't fucking need this, especially from you." She started to stalk away, needing a minute to calm herself.

Enara made to stop her but thought better of it. She slumped back down on a stone, clenching her fists in frustration. After a few deep breathing exercises, she went in search of the guys. She would check on Soren once she had calmed down.

She found Jai chuckling at Baz as he attempted to light the fire. His fingers were not as deft as the tracker's with the flint and steel. "Sure you don't want me to take over?"

"I got it," Baz replied with a look of intense determination visible between his thick brows. After two more attempts, he managed to spark the thin strands of wood pulp that Jai had scraped up. His face lit up as a tiny flame bloomed from between the pieces of kindling. He waggled his eyebrows at Enara. "See? I am a great provider."

"My hero." She smiled at him affectionately and sat beside Jai on the remains of a fallen spruce tree.

Jai's dark eyes scanned the space behind her, looking for Soren, his left brow lifting when he could not find her.

"She needed some time," Enara said. "There is no use talking to her when she's like this." She wrung her hands together, feeling guilty for picking a fight. She had just gotten Soren back—she should be happy—but every time she pictured her wrapped up in the arms of that vile man, she wanted to wretch.

The memory of Soren being dragged to him in the dimly lit hall below the temple had her blood boiling. Her efforts to fight against the taloned grip of the kestrels had been futile. Watching the stranger take Soren from her had made her feel every bit the helpless child she had been, cowering below her father's fists.

"You okay?" Baz asked as he sat down, taking her hand in his. He knew she was thinking of her father by the vacant look in her eyes. With his free hand, he gently guided her chin to face him. "Hey."

The clouds faded from her vision, going into hiding until the next storm hit. She nuzzled into the warmth of his hand, looking into his gold-flecked eyes. "Hey back."

HOW DARE SHE? SOREN'S ANGER WAS PALPABLE, AS THOUGH IT WAS a living, breathing monster, threatening to remove every ounce of goodness from her soul. She let out the rage in a half-yell, half-scream that had nearby animals skittering for their burrows. *Because I wanted to develop an attraction to my kidnapper.* She sat on the ground with her elbows resting on her knees. *And my father's killer.*

She dropped her head into her hands as a vice wrapped itself around her trachea. She had managed to put the events at Thorncrest Manor to the back of her mind as they had made their way down the mountain pass. The frigid temperature, combined with the pain shooting through her body from the fight with the kestrels, had offered a welcome distraction from her mental turmoil. Now the dam had come loose, and the tears that fell painted a sad abstract of heartache on the dirt floor of the walking trail.

Images of the past few months flashed through her brain like a distorted puppet show. News of her father's death, his lifeless body mottled with scars, the letter, the poems, the stars, the temple, the manor, Rook. The necklace holding her mother's ring felt heavy and cold against her skin, but it was the only piece of her that she had left, apart from the statue, so she cherished it. However, it was a double-edged sword. Every shift of the gleaming metal was a reminder of the love her mother and father had shared, but it was also a reminder of Rook's betrayal.

Unbidden images of him flashed through her mind. His bare chest glinting in the moonlight the first time he had dream-walked to her, stopping her from plunging off the cliff, his snowy hair sticking up like icicles as he held her to the door. The scent of him—the needles of the winter pines and sweet grass.

She choked back a sob as the bombardment continued. When he'd said he was sorry, the little drawing of a chess piece, the snowball fight, her birthday dinner, the library, his mouth at the apex of her thighs. All the enjoyable moments were now tainted with the undeniable truth that he had killed her father.

She watched as dark, thick blood seeped through the memories, forever staining whatever joy they had originally brought her.

She wiped her face with the sleeve of her white tunic then stood, brushing the dirt from her dark brown trousers before straightening the matching vest. They had been hand-picked by Evelyn.

Another rush of sadness flowed through her. In the short time she had known them, they had touched her heart and shown her kindness. For that, she would be forever grateful.

A rustle from behind had her turning. She was relieved to see it was Enara.

"I'm sor—"

"Stop." Soren held up her hands in defeat. "You don't have to apologize."

"Yes, I do." Enara rushed in and hugged her tightly, a few tears of her own slipping loose from their confines. "I never should have said that. I was angry, and it was stupid."

"It's okay. And believe me; you can't be more mad at me than I am at myself."

Enara released her, a smirk forming on the bow of her lips. "So I heard. I hope you're not planning on hunting tonight."

"Oh, you heard that?" Soren turned away, ashamed. She hated when her feelings got the better of her.

"I'd be surprised if the people of Murkwall didn't hear that. Come on. I told the boys they had to wait for us before eating."

Soren let out a soft chuckle. "I'm sure Baz loved that."

She took her hand, and they walked back to camp together, all hard feelings left in the dirt behind them.

THE BOYS AND ENARA HAD SCROUNGED TOGETHER A MEDIOCRE dinner of rabbit stew. Since Soren had scared away every edible creature within a half-mile radius, they had resorted to using salt-cured rabbit meat. Not wanting to waste any more water, they all contracted shriveled tongues due to the high sodium content. The only respite from the attack on their tastebuds was the slight sweetness the carrots provided.

As the evening winded down, they pitched the canvas that Soren had brought from the manor. The fabric was water resistant and would provide decent protection from the elements. They allowed the fire to dull to a warm glow amongst the trees as the night bathed them in a myriad of hazy blue light. The solstice breeze shook the trees around them, and gooseflesh erupted on Soren's skin. She pulled the heavy cloak from her tattered ruck in an effort to suppress the cold. Then she reached in further, searching for the woven wool socks that she planned on wearing to sleep when she froze.

Jai observed her change in posture across the low flames. "You all right?"

She jumped from her seat on the fallen tree and threw the cape sideways, no longer caring about the frigid temperatures.

Jai stood, sauntering over as she ripped items out of her pack, throwing them this way and that. He dodged to the side as a bar of soap zipped past his head.

"Guys!" he bellowed to Enara and Baz, who had taken a moment to themselves a little ways down the path. He waited as their silhouettes formed into concerned faces as they reached the fire.

"What's wrong?" Enara asked, immediately rushing to Soren. Her friend was screaming in frustration, shaking her upside-down rucksack.

"It's gone!" she yelled, throwing the bag into a near-by bush.

The boys looked to Enara then Soren, waiting.

"Soren, take a breath. What's gone?" Enara asked quietly, trying to calm her.

The confession fell from her friend's mouth as though she were vomiting. The regret and discomfort was clear on Soren's face. Her voice wavered as tears flooded her eyes and trailed down her cheeks.

"The Oculus … it's gone."

CHAPTER
FOUR

Two Days Prior - Anistera

General Corvus dragged himself through the gate, breathless from the duel with Rook. He would report with haste the betrayal of his master's son.

He had to hand it to the boy; he had taught him well. The insignificant child had even managed to land a few slices here and there.

Ichor still coated his wings, and he shook them off, black rivulets splattering the floor. *I'll get one of the privates to clean that up later,* he thought.

He paced back and forth before mustering up the courage to knock on the commander's door. He rapped his talons on the heavy wood then moved to the side. His wings sat flat against his back, and he stood as stiff as a board, knowing he would likely be punished for the outcome of the day's events.

The door creaked open, and Adriel beckoned him in. "General," he said, taking note of the blood on the floor before shutting the door behind them. "What have you to report?"

"Well, you see, sir, there have been some … shall we say … developments."

Adriel's brows pinched in frustration. "Out with it then."

Corvus ruffled his feathers, preparing himself for the inevitable. "We lost the girl."

"*What?*" Adriel's voice felt as though it would burst his eardrums, and Corvus cowered before him. His master grabbed him by the throat and pinned him against one of the nearby pillars. "How could you let this happen?" Adriel seethed through gritted teeth.

General Corvus's black eyes bulged, and his wings twitched helplessly at his sides. "Sir," was all he could choke out beyond his masters iron grip.

Adriel loosened his hold just enough for Corvus to suck in a haggard breath. He leveled the general with a glacial stare. "Explain yourself."

"He let her go," Corvus replied tightly.

An inferno blazed behind the ice in Adriel's eyes. "What do you mean, *he let her go?*" His tone was clipped and felt as harsh as sandpaper dragged across bare skin.

"There was an avalanche, and she fell through the ice. By the time I returned, one of my men was dead, by your son's hand, and she was back at the manor."

Adriel released his throat, waiting to hear the rest.

The general continued his recount of events, "As I circled the property, I watched her walk right out the front door, sir, without any trouble. It seems your son ordered the rest of my flock away. Naturally, I and a few of my most loyal followed her."

Adriel's brow lifted. "Go on."

The general shuffled nervously, wringing his talons together. "The couple from the temple had acquired the services of a tracker to find the girl, and they meant to escape, so we intervened. As I was about to bring the girl back to the manor, your son stopped me."

"A betrayal, you say? From my own son?" Adriel towered over him, his shadow bathing him in a wave of darkness.

"I would not have believed it if I had not experienced it firsthand, sir."

"Is he dead?"

"No, sir, I left him intact to carry out the mating."

"And the girl?"

"She took Rook back to the manor—he will be out for at least a week. She departed again the following day."

Corvus's head whipped sideways from the force of Adriel's fist, and ichor coated the insides of his cheeks.

"And you just let her leave?" His anger was an active volcano, on the verge of erupting and destroying everything in the outlying area.

The general shook off the blow, knowing better than to turn away from his master. "I was outnumbered, and I would not have made it back to you had I stayed."

"You have failed me." Adriel's words were thick with disappointment.

"Forgive me, sir. It will not happen again."

Adriel laughed. It was an unsettling sound, his sickly-sweet voice laced with pure malice. "I should think not. If you fail me again, I will strap you down and rip your talons out one by one before making you choke on them. Now, get out of my sight." The commander turned to leave as General Corvus dared to speak once more.

"One last thing, sir."

His master turned but said nothing, gesturing with his hand for the general to speak.

"I brought this."

Adriel's eyes lit with a dark satisfaction as his first in command held out his hand. A smirk played on his lips as a new plan began to form.

For between the beast's clawed fingers lay the Oculus.

ADRIEL TURNED THE METAL EYE OVER IN HIS HANDS. SOMETHING inside of it still awoke with his touch. He could sense that a part of it was still aligned with him. *At least the general had not been entirely useless*, he thought to himself.

He had since dismissed the general and had returned to the Architect's quarters at once to mull over his new plans. The girl was an unforeseen liability—there was no questioning that—but he was at a loss of what to do with the boy. *I have given him everything he could ever need, and this is how he thanks me?* Adriel scoffed. He debated idly if he should just have him killed, but the insolent child could still be of use.

He paced over the carpet in the living room. He had switched it out years ago, not wanting to be reminded of all the ways he and Celandine has christened it.

Something in his chest twinged, and he shook away the rogue thoughts. It had been over twenty years since she had broken their mating bond, and the only warm part of him had remained hollow ever since.

In all his years, she had been the only being he had ever grown to truly care for. Then her betrayal had only solidified that he was better off on his own. He would not make that mistake again. He was all he ever needed, and he preferred it that way. General Corvus was a trusted companion, but if he were to meet his end, Adriel would not mourn.

He had allowed himself one day to grieve the loss of his mate as he'd followed her to Entheas in search of the Oculus. He had assumed she had succumbed to the loss of her grace and had returned to Anistera after his initial search had come up dry. Day after day, he would send his ranks to hunt for the artifact, and even the beast of a horse, Obsidian, but his efforts had been unsuccessful. The creature had been tied to her life force, and he'd been happy to be rid of it, but that had still left him without the other half of the Oculus. He'd searched high and low for five years, chasing after rumors and hearsay when he'd finally stumbled onto Tarak Nightsong's property.

Celandine has been displaced during her fall and had not landed in the great stone reef of the Esinian Isles, as she usually would. The reef held secondary gates, inaccessible to humans, that opened up in hidden points in each territory's capital. A thoughtful invention from the previous Architect to allow for ease of travel in their limited time. Instead, he'd discovered she had been holed up in a handmade hovel on the outskirts of Vreburn on the mainland.

Adriel's fists clenched so hard that he cracked the arms of the chair he had sunk into at the memory.

When traveling through Estelar, he had heard a rumor of an archaeologist who had visited the great Tree City, speaking of a woman with Celandine's physique. He'd spoken fondly of her, as if they were more than acquaintances.

Adriel had acquired the information from a strange woman with white tattoos. She'd revealed little and had left immediately after their meeting, fearing him. He couldn't blame her. He'd let her live, if only for the entertainment of what stories she would spin upon future visits.

Seers were curious creatures and one of the few beings on Entheas whom he didn't want to constantly murder.

He'd found himself in the city of Vreburn, at a disgusting excuse for a tavern called The Crow's Nest. There, he had been able to gain information from a handsome council leader, who went by the name of Montgrove. He reminded him of himself, and the man was more than happy to share many personal details about the archaeologist. It seemed he had taken no time in learning about this stranger who lived in the middle of the woods.

Adriel followed the path out of town, directing himself toward the mysterious outlier. He let out a sigh of annoyance as a chill spread over his body. He hated the seasons here. One minute, he required a jacket, and the next, a thick layer of sweat would gather under his leathers. He was in a constant state of discomfort, which only gave him more of a reason to get this meeting over with. It had taken months to get to this point, and he only had a few hours left before he was to return home.

As he drew closer to the dwelling, he could hear voices. One was from a man—presumably the elusive archaeologist—but the other was female and decidedly young, a child. He hated humans as a whole, but most of all, he hated children. Mated pairs in Anistera bore children, but they grew up within days, not years, so the annoyance was bearable. In

Entheas, they endured the misery for what felt like eons, and Adriel loathed the puny, helpless creatures.

The tiny human bounded out the back door, her father close behind. She was carrying a metal watering can toward a bed of purple irises. *Celandine's favorite*, he thought idly. The unlikely coincidence halted his movements.

The man was obviously the girl's father, as they shared the same deep brown hair. She giggled as he tickled her side, causing her to slosh water onto her feet. She had been facing away from him, but the movement caused her to turn her head in Adriel's direction. His mind stirred.

It's not possible.

There was no mistaking it. The girl's face was a miniature copy of his late mate's, and his breath caught.

His shock was quickly replaced with fury as he realized the human man had procreated with *his* mate. He was seconds away from rushing the stranger and flaying every bit of flesh that had grazed his mate's skin before burying his body under the flowerbed.

His chest heaved, and he vibrated with the effort not to kill the man. *If I kill him, I may never find the Oculus*, he reasoned with himself.

A sudden movement from the corner of his eye had him turning. A black squirrel scurried up the trunk of the large cedar tree to his left, breaking him out of his rage spiral. *What a useless animal.* He rolled the tension from his shoulders and reverted his eyes back to the young girl. She was closer to him now, maybe fifty feet away.

A breath escaped him as an invisible thread in his chest gave a hard tug on his long cold heart. A whisper of the bond he shared with Celandine reignited. It was infinitesimally small but enough to spark a larger fire within him.

The girl shares her blood. He had never placed much thought into the human idea of luck. He assumed it to be something weaker men prayed for when times were dark. However, in that particular instance, he had to admit that favor had been well and truly placed upon him.

He had come up with the plan to destroy Entheas that same evening. He watched his mate's lover mourn her while the child was not looking. He prayed to the Architect that they would meet again, that they would be granted the same love the phoenix had shown the couple in the stars.

Adriel scoffed openly while Tarak sobbed. *Foolish man. Do not worry; your suffering will end soon.*

For, you see, Adriel already had the most important piece in his arsenal—Rook. The child he had never wanted, a bastard born to a bar wench from a small town in Southern Estelar. Rook had been alive not one traverse of the skies before he had been thrown to the wolves, so to speak. Adriel had not visited Entheas in nearly seven months, a blink in his timeline. When he had finally returned, he'd felt a magical pull leading him to a heavily wooded area outside the capital of Draestel.

He came upon a weaved wooden basket sitting in the woods. The cries coming from beneath the lid nearly drove him to slice of his own ears. Nevertheless, the tether drove him forward, and upon lifting the lid, he discovered an infant boy with hair so white it was as if all the pigment had been stolen away. There was no mistaking that this was his son.

He cursed himself for not being more careful. The child was an abomination. Bedding a human was of no consequence to him, but to create a child with one filled his body with disgust.

Before he could rid the world of his unwanted bastard, he made a discovery. In the mere moments he contemplated how to end the weakling's life, the umbilical cord had fallen off, the wound already healed. The puffiness surrounding his face and his misshapen head were suddenly morphed into a round, sweet face with piercing blue eyes, just like his own.

You should not mistake his hesitation for a change of heart. He did not want this child, and clearly, neither did the mother, but he needed to be sure he wasn't making a mistake by ridding himself of the burden too soon.

He slid his rapier from the side of his hip and, with a swift woosh of air, he nicked the child's shoulder. The inch-long cut was deep enough to require stitches but, to his surprise, the infant only cried for a short period before the wound healed itself.

A sinister smile played at Adriel's lips as he lifted the child into his arms. Then, as he disappeared into the shadows of the trees, he whispered in a menacing tone, "You may be of use to me yet, little one."

CHAPTER FIVE

Soren let out another howl of frustration as her eyes roamed over the contents of her emptied rucksack. "It was right here! It should have been right under my cloak and gloves." She slammed her fists into the ground, her body not yet registering the bite of the rocks as they embedded themselves into the soft flesh of her hands.

"When did you see it last?" Enara asked, gingerly lifting Soren to her feet.

Soren massaged her now throbbing hands and looked up at her with tear-stained cheeks. "I had it when I left the manor. I should have realized it was gone."

"You couldn't have known."

"I can feel when it's close," Soren explained. "Something in it calls to me … through my blood." She began retrieving the discarded items from her sack as she spoke. "I should have noticed, but between my injuries from the fight and the chill in my bones …" She looked down, the guilt of disappointing her friends weighing on her like the boulders that lined the mountain's peak.

"If any blame is to be placed, it is on those creatures, not on you or any of us," Jai's voice cut through the cloud of her self-loathing.

She did nothing more than nod as the group helped her find the rest of the items from her pack.

"So, what's our next step, then?" Baz asked. "It doesn't make much sense to go to Braexmirth without an artifact to destroy."

Soren bit her lip. "You have a point."

"They could still provide us with stronger weapons," Enara reasoned. "Plus, their lands would give us protection from Adriel's forces, should he attack again."

The tracker stroked the closely trimmed beard on his chin while contemplating their statements. "You are all formidable fighters; I have no doubt in your capabilities …" He sighed in a resigned manner. "Unfortunately, skill and well-honed weapons can only get you so far when facing an army."

"So, what do you suppose we do?" Enara asked.

There was a mischievous glint in Jai's eyes as he responded.

"We gather an army of our own."

"And how the hell do you suppose we do that?" Soren questioned, raising a brow—Baz and Enara had yet to fill her in on his true identity. "Last time I checked, we don't have an army in our back pockets. Besides, who would believe us? We have no evidence to convince people to join our cause."

"Well, it's a good thing I have confidence in the people enough for the both of us." Jai's tone was bordering on cocky, but before Soren could lay into him, he finished with, "I am the rightful heir to the Patrovian throne."

Soren started chuckling at his bad joke then quickly realized she was the only one laughing. She straightened herself, and Enara gave her a sympathetic look. Baz rubbed the back of his head, looking everywhere but at her.

Soren stared at the tracker, eyebrows raised up to her hairline.

He placed one arm behind his back, the other at a ninety-degree angle at his waist, and bowed.

Soren scoffed in disbelief. "Okay, say I believe you … what then?"

"Well, there are some necessary documents I require to prove my lineage. After that … we wing it."

THEY FOLLOWED THEIR ROUTE TO EDRAS MORA, TRAVELING south to Murkwall. Their haggard appearances helped them blend in with the locals of Thorncrest. The towns and cities that lay within the mountain range were home to the worst of people. Being so far north and without a leading body, Thorncrest was avoided by most folk. This was where the thieves, robbers, and murderers of Entheas chose to live out their darkest fantasies.

No one raised so much as a brow when the group sauntered in, looking worse for wear, to one of the many worn-down bars that lined the streets of Murkwall. The inside of the establishment smelled no better than the alleyways full of detritus that they had passed on their way here.

The entire town seemed to be encased in a ring of hush smoke. The mind-altering substance was derived from the sap of the white pines that were native to Thorncrest. The sap was melted down, formed into crystals, and mixed with the dried, fermented stalks of various hallucinogenic fungi to create a potent combination. Soren had to hand it to the person who had created the addictive substance. They were nothing, if not clever. Hush could be snorted, smoked, or even sprinkled into food, and the effect was always the same.

Soren took note of the many patrons in the establishment that were already under the drug's influence. Pupils were blown wide and unseeing, with their faces turned up into saccharine smiles. Hush was both a paralytic and a hallucinogenic, which allowed the user to enjoy its effects without pitching themselves off a cliff by accident.

Enara grimaced as she tripped over the foot of a burly man. "Sorry—" she started to say before cringing away from yet another inhumanly smiling face, unseeing eyes following her all the way to their table.

Baz let out a ragged cough, and Jai patted him on the back with a chuckle. "You okay there, champ?"

"Yeah"—he coughed a few more times—"just great." Coughing fit over, he sat down next to Enara and put an arm over her shoulders.

"You don't seem shocked by of this," Soren said to Jai as she gestured to the bar's drugged-out customers.

He barked out a laugh. "Well, as a tracker, I end up in some interesting situations. You should see the drinks they make in the Esinian Isles. I drank one once and swore I had an out-of-body experience."

Soren rolled her eyes. "Must be nice to be so well-traveled." The sarcasm in her tone was heavy.

Before he could reply, a barmaid in a tight, dirt-stained corset, with breasts pushed up to her chin, stopped at the table. "What'll yuh have?" she asked, her accent was so harsh that Soren thought she said "waddle."

"I'll have water, thanks," Jai replied.

The woman gave him a sensuous smirk, and he cringed at the crooked, yellow teeth that lay below her chapped lips.

She leaned in so close that her breasts were nearly grazing his shoulder. "There is much more I could offer yuh … later tonight," she said with a wink.

"I'm fine, thank you," he replied.

"You know where um at if yuh change your mind," she said, tracing his sleeve before turning to the rest of the group. "What about the rest of yuh?"

"Three of whatever ale you recommend," Baz said politely.

Soren and Enara just nodded in agreement.

"It's all shite, but I'll bring what we 'ave." She sauntered off, swishing her rather large hips behind her.

"I think I lost my appetite," Baz said once she was out of earshot.

Soren snorted, and Jai spat some of his water on the table.

Enara stifled a laugh as she looked him. "It's a miracle. Baztien Greymark, for once, is not thinking about food."

They all hid their smiles as the lady returned with their drinks. It wasn't her fault, really. She was doing what she needed to do to survive, just like the rest of them. They all felt a little guilty about laughing at her expense.

The trio took tentative sips of their ale while Jai looked on.

"She wasn't lying. This tastes like horse piss." Soren cringed before snatching up Jai's stein and downing the rest of the contents.

Baz and Enara made a few pained facial expressions before spitting the brown liquid back in their glasses.

In unspoken agreement, they stood and left, handing the barmaid a nice tip over the counter in thanks. She smiled her crooked smile and waved them off.

They found lodging two streets over in a ramshackle inn that was even less welcoming than the bar. Separate rooms were not an option, so the four of them agreed to split the night fifty-fifty, spending half the evening on the questionably stained mattress and the other half on the broken floorboards with the mice.

Enara spread out the canvas overtop the bedding and placed the three bedrolls they had previously acquired on the floor. She sat on the end of the bed, and Baz went to join her.

"Whoa, lover boy." Soren held up a hand, stopping him in his tracks. She nodded in Jai's direction. "You can sleep with Your Highness tonight."

"And I thought we were becoming the best of friends," Jai quipped back as he lay on the bedroll, leaning on his elbow, as if posing for a portrait.

Baz looked at Enara longingly before plodding over to Jai.

"I call big spoon," the tracker joked as Baz settled in beside him, shaking with laughter.

The girls climbed onto the bed, choosing to sleep in their clothes, and pulled Soren's cape over themselves. It was minutes before Baz's soft snores filled the room, Jai silently dreaming beside him. Enara couldn't help but smile as he murmured in his sleep.

"I'm happy for you two," Soren whispered from beside her.

Enara's cheeks warmed. "I wish I would have told him sooner," she admitted.

"He understands you wanted to protect him. I wish you would have told me, though."

Enara played with the leather cuff on her wrist that Soren had gifted her. "I thought you already knew."

Soren grabbed her hand and squeezed. "I did, but I was hoping you would admit it to yourself."

"What can I say? I'm stubborn."

Soren loosed a laugh before covering her mouth, worried about waking the boys.

Enara gave her a look, eyes glinting in the dying light of the singular candle that lit the room. "We both are."

"Thank you for finding me."

"You're my sister. Nothing in this world could have stopped me from coming for you."

"Enara?"

"Yeah?"

"I love you."

"I love you, too, Sor."

They embraced each other, allowing all the stress from the past few weeks to fade away as the flame died out and they drifted off to sleep.

Jai's ears perked up and his eyelids fluttered open when a faint scratching noise in the corner of the room roused him from a fitful sleep. His back was stiff as he sat up, rubbing his neck and shaking his shoulder-length hair from his eyes. Baz stilled snored beside him, blissfully unaware that something scurried in the shadowed corners of their current dwelling.

The tracker looked to the bed where Enara and Soren were affectionately curled around each other and decided not to wake them. At least three out of the four of them would get a half-decent night's rest.

He tip-toed to the tiny, circular window against the far wall and welcomed the cool air that drifted through. It was far from a fresh breeze, but it felt good against his skin. He kept his face in the shadows as he watched questionable figures slink down the streets.

Not long ago, he had been one of them—working in the shadows, ending up in all manner of dim, dark places. He would not allow himself to feel guilty for taking payment from those with more means than what they knew what to do with. The only job he had refused payment for was when Adaryn had been taken, but the king had insisted.

He played with the gaudy turquoise ring on his finger as he leaned against the side of the wall. The boards groaned beneath his weight, and he worried the whole decrepit building would collapse around them.

Behind him, Enara was muttering in her sleep. He couldn't make out the words, but there was a pained expression on her face.

Baz, who had remained catatonic until then, sat up, looking around the room. He gave Jai a nod before sliding one of the bedrolls over to the edge of the mattress. He tucked himself back in, reaching one hand up to entangle itself with Enara's dangling fingers. She stiffened at the contact then immediately relaxed, the bad dreams seemingly washed away by the touch.

Though Jai was happy they had found each other, the act reminded him of what he had been missing—a lover's touch. Not the kind you found in a brothel, but the kind that set your soul alight. He'd had that with Adaryn, and now, by his own doing, it was gone.

He mentally cursed himself for leaving the way he had. He hadn't even had the courage to tell her why. Knowing he would have to face her again struck more fear into his heart than fending off a thousand kestrels.

He blew through his teeth, pulling the window shut. The room had been aired out as well as it could, and he noticed Soren was shivering.

He removed his collared jacket and placed it over her shoulders from the head of the bed then shuffled back over on silent feet to the two remaining bed rolls. They were decently comfortable on softer ground, but the floorboards provided little in the way of cushion for aching joints. Even the snow-tipped mountain had provided more back support.

He lay sprawled out on his back, hands clasped above his waist, fingers resting on his ring, and accepted that sleep would not be joining him.

CHAPTER SIX

Soren was wearing nothing but a thin, white sleeping gown, her now faded brown hair drifting behind her as she walked down the city watch's dimly lit hallway. She was barefoot, and the wood plank flooring felt rough on the soles of her feet.

All the doors in the hallway were closed, apart from the one leading to the cold cellar. That was where they kept the bodies. She had been here before, the day they had asked her to retrieve Tarak Nightsong's body for the undertaker.

Soren hesitated momentarily at the doorway. A draft floated up the stairwell, carrying with it the stench of death. She covered her mouth with her sleeve, offended by the smell, though it did little to save her nostrils from their plight. Then she took the stairs one at a time, each step bringing her closer to the pinnacle of her nightmare.

The space opened up into a rectangular room. There were no windows, no place for the acrid stench of rotting flesh to escape.

Eight, long wooden tables were laid out in a grid-like formation across the stone floor. On each table lay a body, all different shapes and sizes, covered in thin, white sheets. Wooden buckets lined the wall on the far end, filled with red liquid and indecipherable shapes. Soren knew better than to look at what they might contain.

One of the sheets to her right shifted, and her breath caught in her throat. Eyes wide, she stared at the white cloth, waiting for it to move again. She sighed in relief when the body remained still, though the more she looked, the more the shape became one she recognized.

She moved closer to the table on silent feet, her heart hammering as though it were trying to forge a blade to protect her from what lay beneath. She reached forward with a shaking hand, her legs prepared to run, and slid the sheet off.

Her hand slammed to her mouth as she stifled a cry, not wanting to wake the dead. The fabric pooled at her feet like a pond of melted moonlight.

On the wooden slab, in nothing but a singular garment for modesty, was her father's body.

Tarak Nightsong looked as he had the last time she had seen him—brown hair, glistening against golden skin, and the mustache he'd favored in his older years peppered with specks of white. He looked peaceful, a serene image of how he should have been laid to rest.

Tears welled in her eyes as Soren reached forward to brush a lock of his hair when his golden-brown eyes suddenly opened.

The movement caused her to jump back, but then her heart rate slowed as her father sat up and gave her a lazy smile.

"Come here, my sweet girl," he said, swinging his legs to the floor and holding his hand out.

"Daddy?" The word snagged on the lump in her throat.

Though every sane part of her knew it was a bad idea, she couldn't stop herself from running into his arms. He felt the same as he always had—strong and sure. He smelled of spice, and parchment, and home. She wanted to nestle herself in the safety and warmth of his arms and never wake up.

They separated, and he squeezed her shoulders, giving her a smile.

"Daddy?" she said again as he wiped the tears from her cheeks.

"I hope you know how proud of you I am," he said.

"I just wish you would have told me," was her reply.

He gave her a sad smile and nodded. "There are so many things I would have done differently. I'm so sorry, my sweet girl."

She hugged him again, not caring about the mistakes of the past. "I love you tons, Daddy."

"I love you tons, too."

She took a step back to look at him again, wanting to soak in every last line of his face. However, something was wrong. His skin had gone pale and sickly. Then she watched in horror as his hair began to fall out in dark chunks and talon marks oozing black ichor appeared all over his body. He tried to speak again, but coagulated blood and black foam choked out his sentiment.

She stepped back, but her bare feet caught in the fabric of the sheet, causing her to crash to the floor. She landed hard on her tail bone, pain screeching up her spine as she looked up at her father's decaying body.

He was reaching out for her, and she gagged as his skin started to rot and putrefy. She pushed up off the ground, backing away as the dead skin, muscle, and sinew sloughed off in pieces to the floor. Soon, there would be nothing left.

A scream ripped from her throat as strange hands grabbed her shoulders from behind.

Her horror mounted when she turned to see a sheet-covered body at her back. She batted away the hands and ducked out of its grip, now noticing that the rest of the bodies were standing at attention.

The remaining sheets fell one by one to reveal the decaying bodies of her friends and loved ones. Baz, Enara, Celandine, Alondra, Laraline, and even Jai reached out to her with gnarled fingers. She shook her head, inching along the wall to the doorway, not able to take her eyes off of them.

A voice broke from the body to her right. It was larger than the rest, and she cowered against the stone as the sheet fell.

Adriel stood in all his perfected glory, a satisfied smirk on his face. "This is what will become of your heroics," he said. "Everyone you know and love will be dead, and the fault will be none but your own."

Soren shook her head, panic rising in her already clogged throat. She didn't know if she was going to sob or vomit. Before he could say anything more, she turned and ran up the stairs.

Her tears blinded her as she ran down the hall, toward the city watch's front door. She could still taste the decay, and bile rose in her throat. She dared a look back to see if the corpses had followed her, but the hallway remained empty.

However, she could hear Adriel's sick laughter rise through the floorboards.

She was nearly knocked out when she ran into another body, this one blocking her exit. She screamed, and punched, and kicked as hard as she could, but the arms held fast. She could feel its breath hot on her ear as she tried to push out of its grasp.

"Breathe, Soren."

Her whole body stiffened as the grip loosened enough for her to look up into Rook's sapphire gaze.

A smirk pulled up the corners of his lips. "Hello, little bird."

Soren's shock at hearing his voice was short-lived as images of her father's body ripped through her vision. The fear that, moments ago, had threatened to take over her entire being was quickly replaced with searing hot rage for her father's killer. She cursed herself for dreaming up such useless attire.

A quick glance around showed little for a way of escape.

Before he could spew more lies from those all-too-familiar lips, she twisted from his grasp and grabbed the nearest oil lamp. She used the glass encasement to knock him out cold before holding her open palm to the flame to rouse herself from the nightmarish hellscape her mind had created.

Soren's eyes flicked open. She could not yet move. The sleep hormones that usually failed her had decided to do their job for once, rendering her immobile.

Enara had rolled over, stealing her cloak and the warmth that came along with it, but another jacket had taken its place.

It smelled of wood and tobacco, smoky and mysterious, much like its owner.

The tracker was attractive, Soren had to admit, but he was hung up on another woman. *Too bad*, she thought. *He could have been a fun distraction.*

Her body still refused to grant her motion, so she resigned to settling her mind to hopefully rest for at least another hour or so. But then her father's decomposed body flashed across her eyelids the moment she closed them, and the fist around her heart tightened.

Panic in the form of darkness settled over her. A distorted figure of no discernible age or sex sat on her breastbone, crushing her below its impossible weight. It would suffocate her if she didn't do something.

She wanted to scream, but no sound came out. It was as though her lips had been sewn shut. She wracked her brain for anything that could save her, and the image of Rook standing over the beheaded kestrel came to the forefront of her mind.

He was a light amongst the shadows, cutting down the creature that had tormented her. She focused on the memory, and the black beast slowly slunk back to the dark corner of her mind that stemmed all panic and fear. The pressure on her chest eased, and oxygen returned to her lungs.

Her thoughts were still filled with images of Rook, and she cursed herself. She had been furious when he'd appeared in her dream like some white knight from one of her stories. She had wanted to douse him in the oil from the rest of the lamps and set his body aflame in the hopes he would never wake up again.

However, as before, in the mansion, something inside her broken heart had stilled her hand. The anger never retreated, and neither did her feelings for him, but she would not think of that now. Now, she would name all the constellations, mapping each star point as she created a galaxy in her mind. Here was where she could lay her head without the fear of bodies or betrayals. Here, she was safe.

CHAPTER SEVEN

Rook sat up, inhaling sharply as pain shot through his torso. His head was pounding from where Soren had accosted him in her dream.

I should check on her, he thought.

He looked down to see a cloth bandage covered in blood and began unwrapping it slowly. He hissed as he peeled it away, burgundy flecks falling onto his sheets as he tugged. He then set the fabric aside, revealing an angry gash about four inches long, marring his hipbone. He assessed it angrily, cursing his father for turning his creatures on his own flesh and blood. Thankfully, being half-immortal allowed him to heal quicker than most. A week from now, there would be no trace of it. He would have to rest in the meantime.

He struggled to shove his legs into a pair of loose trousers as more injuries from the encounter made themselves known.

Then he grimaced at his reflection, noting the thirty-seven cuts and gouges that marked his previously perfect skin.

"None of this would have happened if I had just followed my damn orders," he swore at himself.

He'd spent all of his formative years training for this and hadn't made it more than a few weeks before the little bird had crawled under his skin. She was insufferable, stubborn, and had the vocabulary of a scorned bar wench, yet she was beautifully broken, just like him.

Before he realized what he was doing, his feet had taken him down the hall to the door that separated them and knocked twice.

No answer.

He just needed to see that she had come out of the rumble in better shape than he had, and then he could go about healing in peace.

He knocked again.

Nothing.

Maybe she was in another room with her friends.

He not so secretly wished that the kestrels had taken them out. It would make everything so much easier without Soren continuously worrying about them.

He checked the other bedrooms, his frustration building with each empty space he came across. He was about to check the sitting room when Meena walked out, almost running into him.

"*Oof!*" She bowed, flustered. "Sorry, I thought you were still asleep. I was just coming to redress your wound."

"Where is she?" he asked firmly.

Her eyes widened. "Oh, um ... I'm sorry to tell you this—"

"Tell me what?" he growled, gripping her shoulders harder than necessary.

"I'm sorry, but Soren is gone. She left yesterday."

"I was out for over a day?" he snapped, his eyes burning with anger.

"I'm so sorry, Rook. Evelyn and I tried everything, but the kestrel's talons were ridden with poison, and with your injuries … the infection was immediate. It took a whole night just to get the fever down."

"And Soren?" He tried to hide the worry in his voice as he released her shoulders.

"A few stitches, but nothing major. They left at first light. You should know she did not leave your side until you stabilized. She gave Evie this and said to tell you she was sorry," she finished, handing him a crumpled piece of parchment.

He snatched it out of her hands, turning away from her, pausing before he walked away. "Thank you," he said, some of the anger leaving his voice, "for mending me."

"We would do it again. When you are ready, we will redress that for you," she said, eyeing the injury.

Rook nodded, and she left.

When she was a safe distance away, he turned back toward the sitting room and slowly lowered himself onto the sofa so as to not anger his body more. He sat in the dim light, breathing rapidly, and unfolded the parchment.

Wings flutter in a cage
Anger building into rage
Enter the cunning beast
Control relinquished, released
Dark secrets are hidden away

Her own heart did betray
A touch, a spark, a skipping beat
A hateful kiss
Burning with heat
A sin of lust, nothing more
A warm feeling
That did not exist before

He roared so loud that the chandelier above him shook. *This* was her goodbye?

He threw a nearby whiskey glass against the wall, shattering it, groaning as the movement put a strain on his injured stomach.

She was gone.

He hunched over, holding his side as he stalked back to his room and slammed the door.

And she was not coming back.

EVELYN BROUGHT IN THE MENDING KIT AND BEGAN TO REDRESS his wound. "You really shouldn't have angered it. You pulled out your stitches. They will have to be redone," she admonished.

"It wouldn't have happened if you hadn't let her leave."

"Don't put that on me. Soren leaving was based on your actions alone." She placed the antiseptic on his side, and he sucked in air angrily. It burned as if she had shoved a red-hot poker into his bare skin.

"That hurts," he ground out, the pain shooting to his groin.

"Don't pout," she replied before pressing the cloth back to his skin.

He glared at her. "Did she say anything else to you?"

She looked at him sympathetically. "She said to tell you she was sorry."

He let out a defeated breath then downed a glass of scotch before leaning back to let her begin stitching. The feeling of the thread weaving his skin together was as painful as it was unnerving, but the buzz of the alcohol helped.

When she finished, she cleaned the area again and wrapped him in a fresh bandage. Then she admired her handiwork. "Good as new."

"Thank you." He had to admit she was good at what she did. He realized now he often took the sisters for granted. He had gotten so used to them always being here that he had forgotten to show his appreciation for their loyalty.

"You and your sister deserve a better life than this," he admitted.

"You're not forcing our hand, Rook. We like living here. We love nature, the amenities help, and sometimes we even enjoy your company. Don't sell yourself short. We stay because we choose to."

"If you ever change your mind——"

"We know where to find you."

Meena walked in, carrying a tray of stew with a toasted baguette and some freshly churned herb butter on the side for dipping. "Lunch is ready." She beamed. "Glad to see you all fixed up."

Her positive attitude never seemed to waver. It used to annoy him, but the place needed something to brighten it up. She was like the sun—warm and inviting, always there when you needed it. He was thankful to have these two women to keep him company, and they had taken such good care of him all these years. He loved them like sisters and was thankful they chose to stay with him, as intolerable as he could be.

He spent the next two days resting, but sleep did not come easy. Every time he closed his eyes, he could see the look of betrayal on Soren's face. During the waking hours, he would look in the mirror, disgusted with what he had become. His father had taken a motherless boy and had turned him into a weapon. He had been trained, and tortured, and taught how to show women a good time. He didn't even really know who he was. His personality seemed fractured from everything he had endured.

He had grown up under Corvus's wing. His father had instructed that Corvus be in charge of his training, and the creature had reveled in it. He'd spent countless hours siccing the kestrels on him, allowing him to heal only long enough to start fighting again. He had been scarred a million times over, but to the naked eye, he was an untouched piece of art. Honed and crafted by a thousand taloned hands, he was ruthless and exuded danger. Even the girls were scared of him when his true temper broke through his cool façade.

With Soren, he had felt as though he was starting to find who he was. Little glimmers of who he wanted to be would spark and die out, but they had given him hope. The longer he'd spent with her, the brighter each spark had shone. Now he felt like the depths of the Obsidian Sea, where no light dared to enter.

Many times, he found himself pacing the halls, wondering where she had gone off to, and then he would return to his room when he realized she was gone. No one had explained what the absence of a person was like. They only said they would miss them, or that it hurt when they left. No one told you what it was like to enter their room and feel the emptiness they had left behind. The sheets still mussed, worn clothing laying in a heap on the floor, a water glass with barely the hint of a kiss on its rim. They didn't tell you what it was like to live in a mansion but know your home was somewhere else.

On night five, he got drunk. Evelyn had advised against it until his wound was fully healed, but he had disregarded her advice. He should have listened.

When he woke up the next morning, he discovered that he had trashed his entire bedroom, almost lighting the place on fire in his rampage to erase Soren.

He looked at the splinters left behind from the chairs and remembered the little game they had played. How could she have ever thought he didn't want her in that way? Her beauty could rival the late queen of Patrivah's, if it weren't for her smart mouth.

Her mouth, he thought. The things she could do with that mouth. He smirked a little, remembering a particularly enjoyable afternoon they had spent in the library.

He shook the thought away. Thinking about his body merging with hers only upset him further.

On the morning of the seventh day, he looked down to find the gash had healed and tested his flexibility. He was pleased to find that he was back to feeling one hundred percent.

He called a family meeting at breakfast, requesting the girls dine with him.

"I'm going after her," he stated bluntly.

Evelyn didn't hesitate to respond with, "Then we're going with you."

Meena nodded in agreement, her face serious.

"Absolutely not."

"Why not? You taught us how to fight, didn't you?" Meena complained.

"That was for emergencies only."

"Well, finding Soren seems like an emergency to me," Evelyn pushed, crossing her arms.

"You didn't think we would just wave you goodbye, did you?" Meena asked.

"I hoped."

"Sorry, you're stuck with us," she said, jutting her chin up in defiance.

They ate and packed, and then the girls left any perishable food on the grounds for the wildlife to enjoy and met him at the front entrance.

While they were outside, Rook had returned to the library to retrieve the Oculus. He loathed the object, but he needed it on hand so that he might find a way to destroy it. His father be damned.

He lifted the piano key, and the secret door popped open, the wood groaning. He stepped inside the small space, his eyes settling on the metal stand. "Of course you did," he said, his smile hiding his disappointment.

The space where the Oculus sat was empty, and Soren's journal had taken its place.

He flipped through the pages. It held details of their every encounter and her ways to cope with being trapped here, her thoughts and feelings about them and him. He had countless priceless books in his possession, but this was, by far, the most valuable.

He moved with intent, locking the library door and tucking the key away in its hiding place behind the face of the grandfather clock that sat in the entranceway.

The girls rounded the corner, and they walked out the door.

Giving it one last try, he asked, "There's no chance I can convince you to stay?"

"Nope," Evelyn replied.

"Not even a little," Meena confirmed.

"You realize how dangerous this is, right?" Rook asked, giving them a serious look.

"We understand. You saved our lives all those years ago, maybe we will get the chance to save yours … again." She smirked.

"We want Soren back, too," Meena chimed in. "But I do have one question."

Rook raised his eyebrow in response.

"What happens when your father comes back?"

He did not hesitate with his response.

"I'm going to kill him."

CHAPTER
EIGHT

Adriel stroked the Oculus as though it were a rare jewel. The artifact hummed, albeit quieter now, but it still called to him, nonetheless. He had missed the power that emanated from the item and chastised himself for ever letting it out of his sight. "I'll not part with you again," he said aloud to it, as though it were a sentient being. Though the sentiment was figurative, he still had trouble loosening his grip on the all-seeing eye.

He placed the artifact on the ornamental stand in the hall of worlds, amongst his father's things. He had not bothered to discard the previous Architect's possessions, as they could still be of value to him in the future. He was no fool.

With one last look at the all-powerful object, he turned to leave, but not before imparting some choice words to the two guards who stood at the hall's entrance. "If anyone apart from me attempts to enter, cut them down."

"Yes, sir," they replied.

Adriel's lips curled at their automated response. They would sooner die than defy his orders.

Over the last two and a half decades, Adriel had honed every citizen in Anistera into his own personal executioners. Well, almost every citizen. He had heard rumors of a possible uprising on and off over the years, but seeing as no action had been taken, he did not waste time fretting. Worrying was for the weak, and he was anything but.

He retired to the Architect's quarters, stretching out on the large, circular bed. Some days, he swore he could still smell the scent of Celandine on the linens. Though their bond had been broken, the remnants still remained. The moments they'd had together were something he still cherished and thought back to often, even as he took others to his bed. They had performed admirably, but bonding physically with a mate was not a feeling that could be replicated by another.

Adriel let out a growl of frustration as the bulge in his training leathers strained against the fabric at the thought of her astride him on the shores of the waterfall.

He stripped out of his clothes and took a cold shower. He would not give in to his bodily urges, not tonight at least. *You are pathetic to allow her to still have power over you*, his mind sneered.

He cut off the water stream, shaking the excess liquid from his hair, and dried off hastily. He donned a pair of white linen pants, poured himself three fingers of nectar, and sat back on the curved velvet sofa. He had yet to change out any of the furniture in the twenty-odd years he had lived in the Architect's quarters. He couldn't bring himself to. They were the last reminders of her.

He swallowed the golden liquid and savored the cool trail it left in its wake. It was like drinking the rays of the setting sun from a mountain creek. With every sip, he felt his grief slip away like the trickle of the stone waterfall.

He took one last look upon the grounds below before retiring to his room. He required rest, for tomorrow, he would move forward with the next phase of his plans, and the Oculus would hum for him once again.

THE TRAINING GROUNDS WERE LINED WITH THE CITIZENS OF Anistera. All of Adriel's little playthings standing at attention like the good little soldiers he had trained them to be. He smiled to himself, the edges of his mouth turned up in satisfaction at their obedience. *If only our father could see you now,* he thought.

He ordered the majority to return to their general duties but requested that all mated couples stay behind. If he could not use the original mated bloodline to unmake Entheas, he would use the blood of all the fated mates to bring it to its knees.

Out of the thousands of Celestials in Anistera, there were approximately fifty mated couples. Some had been mated for eons, others for decades, but no matter. The power of one hundred blooded mates was sure to give Adriel what he needed.

He'd had the blooding table moved to the center of the training ring in a similar set up to the day Obsidian had been made. The Oculus was perched on a stand in the middle of the stone slab with the ceremonial dagger at its side. The Celestials formed circular rings around their leader, their hands intertwined with their mate's.

Adriel smoothed his features before addressing them. "I have a very important task for you all." His eyes raked across the crowd, shining with mirth against the violet sky. "If you do this, Anistera will be saved from great peril."

The couples looked at each other then back to their leader, worry filling each of their hearts for the home they so loved.

"Lady Celandine has produced an heir in Entheas, and she plans to destroy us. Her name is Soren Nightsong, and she will be the death of us all."

The crowd erupted.

"The end of Anistera? It cannot be," an onlooker exclaimed.

"Surely, all will be well. We have outlasted countless ages," an older male reassured her.

The murmurs amongst the crowd intensified.

"What are we to do?" another male asked.

"I thought Lady Celandine died during the fall," his mate commented.

A few more beings nodded in agreement, and a stern-looking female narrowed her eyes at Adriel.

"You informed us of Lady Celandine's demise, yet you say she is alive. Speak truth, for I will receive no lies."

Adriel's jaw ticked at the tone in which she spoke, but he knew better than to make an example of her here. Therefore, he reassembled his mask and spoke once more. "Calm, dear ones, calm." He held up both hands in a placating gesture. "Do not allow panic and fear to distort your judgment. I, your

Architect, will share with you all that I know so that we may move forward."

The congregation quieted, holding their tongues so they might hear what their leader had to say.

"When I announced the loss of Lady Celandine, I spoke only truth," he said, his eyes boring into the errant female's, who crossed her arms, pressing her lips together in a fine line. "Until recent days, I thought her to be dead." He sighed, as though he bore a great weight on his back. "My troubled, lost mate has indeed met her end, though not in the manner we originally suspected."

The crowd gasped audibly, hanging on to his every word as though it were the very air they needed to sustain themselves.

Adriel folded his hands together and bowed his head, as though in mourning. "In my recent travels, I discovered that Lady Celandine survived the fall. How? I do not know. But she healed from the loss of her grace and mated with a human male." He brushed his hand through his inky black hair. "Their joining produced an heir who is half-celestial, half-human."

The entire assembly seemed to hold their breaths. Never before, to their knowledge, had a Celestial mated with a being from another realm. Father had expressly forbidden it. Anisterans were not meant to survive other realms, and to risk a child's life, not knowing if it would survive the world in which it was born, would be cruel.

"I have seen this child with my own eyes and could feel my mate's blood coursing through her veins," he continued. "I thought I could talk sense into this young creature, but alas, she has chosen another path. She has forsaken all of Anistera and turned the people of Entheas against us. Her warriors have already ended the lives of many of our faithful soldiers. She has no remorse and will bring on the destruction of Anistera."

The crowd fell into chaos. Screams and shouts rang off the stones of the colosseum.

"What will become of us?"

"Is there nowhere else we can go?"

"What would the Architect have us do?"

They all looked to their leader, at a loss for how to save their realm.

"My dear brothers and sisters," he addressed them with great reverence, "to save our world, I require but one thing from you all."

The air practically buzzed with their anticipation.

"Tell us, great one," an urgent voice broke from the crowd.

Adriel nodded in acknowledgment before speaking again.

"All I need is your blood."

Luscinia looked on as her brothers and sisters walked forward, one by one, and offered their palms to Adriel. He slid the blade across their skin, and they fisted their hands over the Oculus, coating it in each of their blood.

She leaned against her mate, Abraxos, who stood at her back.

He brushed her silver hair aside and kissed her affectionately on the neck. "All will be well, my beloved."

A single tear fell from her amber eyes as she turned to him. He brushed it away with his thumb and planted another kiss on the crown of her head. She nuzzled into his chest, her heart aching for what was to come.

"Celandine should be here." She sniffed. "She was so much stronger than I."

"You doubt your own capabilities. She was strong of heart; you are strong of body and mind. Whatever comes next, be it winds of frost or mountains of fire, I will follow you into the fold until I am no more."

Her heart constricted as she looked into her mate's soft gray eyes. "Until we are no more." She bowed her head.

"Until we are no more," he replied, embracing her.

His long brown hair brushed against her cheek as his strong arms enveloped her. Then their eyes turned back to the scene unfolding in the center of the arena. The final mated couple had returned to their original position as Adriel lifted the knife to his arm. He plunged the blade deep, slicing halfway from his wrist to elbow, bathing the Oculus in a scarlet pool. The act made Luscinia wince. How one could do that to themselves she would never understand. She silently thanked her father that her and her followers had been able to resist Adriel's orders.

Though they were made to obey the Architect, Adriel was unaware that demands could be resisted based on the way in which said command was worded. For instance, Adriel had asked all mated couples to stay behind; however, he had not specified where and for how long. This allowed Luscinia and Abraxos to remain in the shadows and avoid partaking in the horrific scene in front of them.

She held on to her mate tighter, forever grateful she'd had him by her side these last eighteen years. He was a few hundred years her junior, yet this was but a blip in their lifetimes. She had known more joy and love in these last eighteen years than she had since her creation.

He had found her during a particularly dark time and had brought her back into the light. If one were to gather all the poetry written in all the worlds combined, the words would still not be enough to describe how deep their bond was.

A sharp wind blasted around them, and Luscinia's eyes shot open. She had let her lids fall shut while nuzzling her mate, and her pupils dilated as she paid witness to what lay before them.

The mated couples stood still as statues, their gazes turned upward, awaiting their fate. Adriel stood atop the stone table, holding the Oculus upward, eyes closed, deep in thought. The artifact hummed so loudly that the entire arena began to vibrate. The excess blood that had pooled around the stone slab seemed to flow backward, absorbing into the metal.

Adriel's hands shook as he put his vision to the front of his mind. When his eyes opened, the whites were gone, leaving behind a black void.

The lavender sky was now a dark gray, and angry clouds rolled across the expanse above them, frothing like the mouth of a great beast ready to strike.

Suddenly, Adriel dropped the Oculus as though the metal had burned his fingertips. The silver eye sat face-up on the stone, waves of power flowing off of it.

Luscinia's sterling hair lifted as the first swell reached them. The couple turned to face it, eyes wide and hands clasped. The second wave brought with it the scent of old magic, of scrolls and parchment, of the lingering smoke after a candle had long burned out. The third crackled around them like an endless shower of sparks, making the hairs on their arms stand on end. The fourth and final wave nearly caused Luscinia to double over, for it brought with it the stench of death, of black magic pulled from the dark places of the world. Places long since forgotten.

Luscinia heaved, and Abraxos covered his mouth with the sleeve of his tunic, stifling a cough. They knew they should leave, escape from this place before what Adriel had decided would come to pass, but they could not look away.

The waves seemed to splash up the sides of the colosseum before cresting and falling back down, the power slowly ebbing back into the Oculus as though the tide was being pulled back out to its home at sea. Then everything went quiet.

All sound had been drained from the arena. Not a single breath or shifting of limb could be heard.

Adriel looked to the Oculus, his black eyes narrowed in frustration at the useless object. He bent slowly, reaching for his most precious artifact, when a bolt of blazing red light scorched past his face and into the stormy sky. The frothing clouds roiled and churned, the sight something akin to the cauldrons over which conjurers of other worlds would toil.

Adriel bellowed, holding his face where the bolt had struck, leaving behind an angry red scar that sat diagonally across his previously flawless skin. It did not heal. The Oculus, it seemed, had decided to remove his well-placed mask.

Thunder boomed in the distance, and the clouds spun, the eye of the storm forming where the Oculus's power had struck.

The couples, who had been silent up until this point, began to murmur, unsure of their next move. Their whisperings were cut short, however, when a bolt of black magic shot down, encasing Adriel in a blinding flash. They had little time to react as a barrage of lightning rained down upon them, each bolt striking its target as a viper would its prey.

Luscinia stared on in horror as, one after another, the couples fell.

"Luce, we need to leave," Abraxos warned from beside her, but she could not concede to his wish just yet. She needed to see what had become of her brothers and sisters.

She held her breath as the storm dissipated and the incessant humming finally stopped. It felt like hours before they witnessed any movement, though they now wished their siblings had perished. For, before them, rose beasts from which no weaver of nightmares could have imagined.

CHAPTER
NINE

It was early morning, and smog filled the dank room as the group rubbed their tired eyes. Soren handed Jai back his jacket in silent thanks, and then the four of them trudged downstairs to force down what was sure to be an unappetizing breakfast. They needed to get on the road as soon as possible if they were going to make it to Edras Mora in a timely manner.

"So, we camp out in Braexmirth's northern border and take your boat back over to Patrivah tomorrow?" Baz asked.

"That's the plan," Jai replied. "Should take about two days' time to reach the docks."

"Let's get going then," Enara concluded as she took a swig of water to choke down the rest of her stale bread.

They all stood, leaving their coin on the table for the barmaid.

"Enjoy yuh travels!" she called after them as they trudged out onto the road.

The cobblestones were uneven, and Soren tripped over a protruding piece of rock. Luckily, Jai's quick reflexes stopped her from full-on faceplanting.

"Thanks … again," she said, blushing with embarrassment. She noticed idly that he smelled of beechwood and tobacco leaves—warm and smoky.

"Happy to help." He gave her a wicked grin before quickening his pace to catch up with Enara and Baz.

"So, how's the king-to-be feeling this morning?" Baz asked, giving the tracker a side smirk.

"Oh, you know, might try to take over a country or something. Depends on my mood," he joked back.

"You two, honestly." Enara rolled her eyes. "You do realize how serious this is, right?"

Baz pinched her sides, causing a garbled yelp to escape her lips before she swatted him away.

"C'mon," he said, "you know we're only kidding. Humor is how we cope. Right, man?"

"He's not wrong," Jai said with a wry smile.

Enara craned her head back, noticing Soren had been uncharacteristically quiet. She let the boys continue on so she could check in with her friend.

"Hey, lady. You doing okay?"

Soren, who had been lost in thought, looked up at her friend and nodded. "Yeah, sorry, long night."

"You wanna talk about it?" Enara asked.

"Not really."

Enara sighed. She knew it was best not to push. Soren would tell her when she was ready. So, she linked her arm with her friend's, and they walked on silently, watching the guys chat animatedly.

Soren was happy Enara did not force her to recount her nightmare.

Before they reached the town's edge, she stopped in front of a rundown apothecary. "I'll just be a minute."

Enara nodded then yelled ahead to the guys to wait for them. They tilted their heads in question, and she shrugged in response.

Soren popped out a couple of minutes later, a cloth baggy of vials clinking beneath her fingers.

"Whatcha got there?" Enara asked, eyeing the cotton sack.

"Dreamless sleep tonic," was Soren's reply.

JAI BREATHED A SIGH OF RELIEF WHEN HIS ROUGH HANDS GRAZED the top of the wooden box. Before now, he had yet to be over a day's journey from them, and he prayed to the Maker that the documents had remained undamaged.

He brushed off the granules of sand that had stuck to the outside edges of the wood before lifting the clasp. The lid popped open to reveal that the rolls of parchment and Adaryn's photograph had come out unscathed.

He tucked the worn picture into the inside pocket of his surcoat, wanting to keep her close to his heart, and then shoved the box into the leather ruck he had acquired.

Soren cleared her throat to announce her presence. "Ready to go, Your Highness?" she questioned with a flourished bow.

Jai rolled his eyes. "You really don't need to call me that."

She shrugged. "Better get used to it if you're planning on claiming that crown of yours." She picked at her nails. "You ready to go?"

"Yeah," he replied. "Best to get the crossing over with. I recommend sitting at the back with me. Our friend has still yet to discover his sea legs."

Soren chuckled. "Oddly enough, he was the best swimmer in our final year."

"Really?" Jai asked skeptically.

"Yep, he just doesn't do well in open water. He does okay in shallow ponds and such, so long as he can see the bottom."

"Hmm … I can't say I blame him, given what happened to his parents."

"So, he told you, then?" Soren asked, surprised Baz had shared his childhood trauma with the tracker.

"Yeah, the three of us went through a lot to find you," Jai admitted, tugging up his collar as a brisk wind lifted the hairs on the back of his neck.

"I don't think I ever fully thanked you for all that you did"—Soren hesitated—"for putting yourself at risk for my friends and me."

"You are most welcome."

"I didn't say thank you yet." Soren scowled, hating feeling like she owed him something.

"Then thank me later," he said before planting a chaste kiss on her cheek and brushing past her toward the docks.

Soren stared after him, open-mouthed, and touched her hand to her face where she could still feel the warmth of his lips. Then she shook it off and followed his sandy footsteps to the dock, where Enara was mentally preparing Baz for the crossing. She gave Jai the side-eye as they set sail and thought, *I'll deal with you later.*

Enara rubbed circles across Baz's muscular back as he heaved the last of his breakfast over the side rail of Jai's boat.

"Hey now, watch the paint," Jai warned.

"Hey, leave him alone," Enara rebuked and turned back to Baztien, who had turned and slunk to the floor of the vessel.

"Sorry, man," Baz said, wiping his mouth then taking a sip of water from the canteen Soren had handed him.

"I was just bugging you, brother." Jai patted his shoulder before jumping onto the dock to tie off the ship.

Soren handed him the ropes from the bow and joined him in making sure everything was secure. She had to admit he was a half-decent sea captain.

He helped Baz and Enara offboard, and then the group headed for the seaside shack to get out of the midday sun. Jai, like Soren, rarely burned, but Enara's fair skin had reddened during their crossing.

"It's so warm here," Soren observed, tilting her head back to watch the clouds wisp across the clear blue sky.

Jai watched her, appreciating the way her hair flowed down her back to rest on the base of her spine. The soft skin of her neck peeked through the strands and, for a moment, he itched to brush it aside. However, he pushed the thought to the back of his mind. She was beautiful—there was no use in not admitting that to himself—but she was not Adaryn, no matter how much she reminded him of his lost love.

He had not so much as touched another woman since they had parted ways. A few had tried, but he would always find a reason to avoid garnering an invitation to their beds.

As they entered the shack, the four of them shook the sand from their boots and took a seat on the wooden floor. The color had returned to Baz's olive face now that he was no longer at sea.

Enara looked at the trap door, fear creeping into her bones at what had almost happened to them in the tunnels. "Are we traveling to Edras Mora through the underground?" she asked.

"I thought we would stay topside this time around," Jai replied, pulling some hardened cheese and baked crisps from his pack and passing them around.

Soren's stomach grumbled as she took them gratefully. It might not have been the type of food she'd had back at the manner, but something was better than nothing.

"So, what's the plan when we get there?" she asked. "It's not like you can just waltz in waving those papers of yours."

"I know a guy," Jai replied, his voice muffled by the food.

"Uh-huh." Soren gave him an incredulous look.

"The stable hand has been my best friend since child-hood," Jai explained, swallowing. "Everett will help us, no questions asked."

Soren considered this and conceded. She couldn't fault him, as her faith in her friends was also unwavering.

"We will rest here for a moment longer then head to Driedon. We can stop there to break again before heading to Amerus, then take the tunnels from there into Edras Mora."

The trio muffled their agreeance, and the four of them settled in for a short power nap. They had a long night ahead of them.

Gaining entrance to the castle grounds was easier than they had expected, especially considering it was well past twilight. The group had donned servant robes to cover their training gear, leaving their packs and larger weapons in a hollowed-out tree just beyond the edge of the estate. They had debated if Jai should just go alone, but arriving as a group made them less suspicious, oddly enough.

The first set of guards barely gave them a second glance as they shuffled through the gate. They bowed their heads low and scooted past onto the property. Palm trees and cacti decorated the area in patches of soft white sand, a few of them sprouting bright pink flowers. Cobbled paths made of white stone splayed out before them, heading in this direction and that, and all the spaces in-between were filled with well-groomed bushes and low-cut grass.

Jai directed them toward the stables, explaining in a hushed tone that Everett's living quarters were located above the horse stalls.

They walked with purpose, not so fast as to look rushed, but not as though they were up to some kind of mischief. The few guards patrolling the grounds paid them no mind, most likely under the assumption they were a group of servants returning from some much-needed downtime.

In the northernmost corner of the grounds sat a large stable. Enara guessed it was big enough to house at least two dozen horses, if not more. She was in awe, as the farms in

Vreburn could only house two horse stalls, maybe four if the owner was well off. The wood was white-washed with navy accents, and it had a dark brown roof. It looked as though it had just been erected, as there was not a single fleck of paint to peel.

"You all stay here. I'm going to run up and get him," Jai said before disappearing through the side door that they had not yet noticed until now.

The trio stood shivering. The evenings in Edras Mora were not cold per se, but the wind held the chill of the autumn tide after the sun went down.

"You guys are sure we can trust him?" Soren asked, nodding toward the closed door.

"I swear it on my parents, Sor," Baz said sternly. "I know it's hard for you, but I promise we can." His tone softened as he reassured his friend.

"He's one of the good ones, Sor," Enara confirmed, giving Soren's hand a quick squeeze just as Jai walked back out with the shaggy-haired stable hand. He had dusty blond hair and kind brown eyes, with a smattering of freckles across his nose and cheeks.

"Hey, I'm Everett," he said in a warm voice.

"Nice to meet you, man." Baz extended his hand.

"Soren," Soren said with an awkward wave. "And this is Enara." She gestured to her friend.

"Nice to meet you," Enara said in a hesitant tone.

Baz stepped back and laced his fingers in hers. She welcomed his warmth, knowing the gesture was meant to inform the newcomer of their relationship and not intended to stake a claim on her.

Everett's eyes twinkled with humor as he gazed down at their hands. He let out a soft chuckle before saying, "You don't have to worry about me, my friend. I'd rather have you in my bed than your beautiful partner." He gave Baz a playful smile, and Baz let out a laugh in response.

"Sounds like you've got some competition." Baz wiggled his eyebrows at Enara.

She nudged him playfully before looking to Everett. "Hey, you can have him."

"Or I would invite the both of you, if you were feeling so inclined." Everett winked.

Soren and Jai watched the interaction, enjoying the look on Baz's face.

"All right, all right," Jai said, trying to return to the task at hand. "Now that we're all more acquainted, can we get a move on?"

"Always in a rush," Everett replied, putting his arm around Jai's shoulders. "Come; I'll bring you in through the servants' quarters. One of the family rooms was recently vacated when the king found out their daughters stole one of Princess Adaryn's crowns."

"Those poor girls probably didn't know any better. I feel sorry for them," Enara said, shaking her head.

"Don't be," Everett said. "Princess Adaryn gifted it to the girls in secret. Unfortunately, her father found out and fired their parents, but Princess Adaryn insured they had a sack of gold before their departure. I am told they bought a sizable farm in Stelonbriar."

Jai's heart warmed at this. *Same old Adaryn, always putting others before herself.*

Everett led them down a short flight of stairs to a wooden door at the base of the castle. The hinges whined as he pushed it open, and then he led them down the narrow torch-lit corridor.

"I apologize in advance that it won't be a particularly comfortable sleep. The servants never rest—there is always something that needs done or doing."

"Anything will be better than that shack in Murkwall," Soren said.

"Agreed," Enara replied.

"I didn't think it was that bad," Baz said, shrugging.

"You don't count, Baz," Soren retorted. "You could sleep through an army of kestrels marching right past your tent."

He laughed. "Okay, you got me there."

Everett tilted his head. "What's a kestrel?"

The trio went quiet.

"I'll explain everything later, my friend," Jai said, coming to their rescue.

The childhood companions shared a look, and then Everett replied, "All right, I'll leave you be … for now. We will talk more tomorrow." He stopped in front of one of the many doors that lined the dim hallway. "You can stay here. If anyone asks, you are here to provide extra hands for the wedding."

"You didn't say anything about a wedding," Soren said, looking to Jai.

"What wedding?" he asked through gritted teeth.

Everett gave him a pitying look. "I assumed that was why you were here," he said, sucking in a breath.

"What wedding?" Jai asked again, his eyes boring into the stable hand's.

His friend replied in his soft tenor, as though trying to calm a caged animal, "Princess Adaryn is set to wed the Duke of Stelonbriar, by the week's end."

CHAPTER
TEN

Luscinia stood in front of the waterfall, needing a moment to steady herself. She had never intended to become the leader of the rebellion, yet here she was, preparing to rally her own troops against Adriel's new army.

The rebellion members were some three-hundred strong, and it had taken years to organize them all while avoiding Adriel's ever-watchful eyes.

"Come, my beloved," Abraxos coaxed. "It is time to move forward with our plans."

She nodded, taking his large, strong hand in hers and walking through the flowing blue curtain. The waterfall hid a narrow cave entrance. A few hundred feet in, it opened up into a large cavern. Celandine had discovered it on one of her many rides with Obsidian and had decided to keep it a secret from Adriel. She had, however, shared it with her best friend.

For those few short months after their Joining, she would meet with Celandine here to gossip, or to simply enjoy being hidden away from their responsibilities. Now, it had become the meeting place for all those able to resist Adriel's spoken word.

The cavern was shaped much like a teardrop. It had a wide, round arc at the back and tapered to a point near the entrance. The entrance itself was a cliff edge that sat above the rest of the subterranean room, giving Luscinia a perfect view of all the goings-on in the deep. It was also where she shared news of the outside, for many of the members had not left the safety of the cavern in years for fear that Adriel would somehow sense their loyalty had waned.

The underground city bustled with life before her. The entire area was lit with enchanted torches they had acquired from Entheas, along with small orbs filled with bioluminescent moss to light their paths while others slept. Thankfully for them, the moss did not require sunlight; the heat from the torches was enough to make them glow.

The back of the cave had been fashioned into humble living quarters. The stone rooms had been carved out of the wall itself and followed the natural curve of the stone. There were five levels that had been inset to the wall with a narrow path leading from one to the next. A diagonal stairway bisected them all, protruding from one corner to the other.

Luscinia could see from the moss glow that Horath and Malik had returned from Entheas. She would meet with them later to discuss their next weapons run.

She waited at the cliff edge while Abraxos took the few steps down to join the others, spreading the news that there was to be a meeting. Within minutes, the entire rebellion stood before her, having funneled out of their sleeping quarters and other makeshift huts and hovels.

They looked at her expectantly, as they always did. For many of them, this was their only way of knowing what was happening on the outside, apart from their trips off-world. Thankfully, time worked differently in some of those places, so they could have an extended reprieve from their stone prison.

Celestials were not meant to live in the dark. They were meant to bask under lavender skies, sipping nectar to their heart's content. The guilt of taking this from them weighed heavily on Luscinia's shoulders as she addressed the crowd.

"Bothers and sisters, I come with grave news." She pressed her lips together as they readied themselves for what they were about to hear. She felt it best to not whack at bushes, as the humans liked to say. "The time has come that we must act. Adriel has declared war on Entheas and has cursed all those with mated bonds to an unimaginably horrid fate."

Gasps and shouts rang out as she recounted the details of what her and her mate had witnessed in the arena.

"Can we not just end his life and spare the war?" came from a deep voice in the back of the crowd.

"Brother Enok, we have discussed this. Any attack on the Architect risks the lives of all of Anistera. If we were to fail, Adriel could order our brothers and sisters to turn their swords against us, or worse—on themselves. He would not take kindly to betrayal."

The male huffed and crossed his arms but said no more.

"I know you are angry," Luscinia continued, her voice strong and unwavering. "So am I. For too long have we hidden in the shadows. For too long have we masked our true selves for the benefit of an unfit leader. It is our time now. Will you join me, brothers and sisters? Will you join me to spare the lives of the innocent? Will you join me in freeing Anistera from Adriel's grasp? Speak now and let all of the worlds know that we, like the phoenix from stories of old, will rise from the ashes of Adriel's deceit and burn him to the ground!"

The crowd loosed their war cries, their voices ringing off the walls of the cavern. The air was charged with their might.

War was coming, and they would be ready.

"You have a way with words," Abraxos whispered softly. They lay in her mate's sleeping quarters on the ground level of the cavern.

She sat up, wiping her hands down her face with an exhausted exhale of breath. "I never wanted this," she admitted.

He grabbed her hand and brushed a featherlight kiss across her knuckles. "That is exactly why it should be you."

She gave him a look of apprehension, not quite understanding his meaning.

He smiled against her knuckles before explaining, "You have such power, yet you do not lust after it. You are humble and kind. Your heart does not waver in its quest to save all. You are the leader this rebellion needs, and the only one who *can* do this."

She nuzzled her head under his chin, allowing his shorn beard to tickle her scalp before she spoke again. "Until we are no more?" she asked.

"Until we are no more, my beloved."

When Abraxos's breathing slowed to a soft snore, Luscinia untangled herself from his arms and padded out of the cave. She nodded to a few of her compatriots who were still milling about and pulled at the strings of her cloak nervously.

Before retiring for the evening, she had followed her speech with the plans she had set in place for the rebellion. Once everyone knew what part they had to play, she had adjourned the meeting. But what they did not know was there was still one last part of the plan she had not informed them of. There was one task she herself would complete, a task she had not even confided to her mate. She was going to steal the Oculus.

Luscinia knew that if she told Abraxos of her plan, he would either try to stop her or join her, and she would have none of either. It was a suicide mission, she knew this, but she had to at least try.

She made her way across Anistera. Her steps were not hindered, as all the other Celestials were obediently obeying Adriel's imposed curfew. Everyone was to be in their quarters within two hours of the sky darkening, to ensure they were properly rested and ready to serve. This left Luscinia and the two guards that Adriel had stationed in the Hall of Worlds to watch over the Oculus.

Her goal was not to kill them but to disarm and silence them long enough to grab the artifact and flee. She did not relish the idea of harming her brethren.

She summoned her strength, praying to her father that she might be as brave as Celandine had once been.

She had known from the moment Adriel had announced her death that he had been lying. She'd tolerated him for Celandine's sake, but she had always known he was a snake. She had worked the forge where all the weapons and armor were crafted for Anistera's army. On occasion, she would join her brothers to assist with large deliveries to the training grounds. She had used that time to observe how Adriel led his troops and had noticed more than a few questionable interactions. She had wanted to warn Celandine but understood that her concerns would fall upon deaf ears once her friend had mated the foul male.

What Adriel did not know was that, before her supposed betrayal, Celandine had told Luscinia of her plan. Her friend had begged her to save Entheas in the event she failed to keep the Oculus safe.

Luscinia had tried to find her in Entheas, knowing she was alive—she could feel it in her marrow. One did not keep a friendship for centuries and not feel the loss of their life, no matter the distance. So, once a month, she would travel down in search of her friend, only finding rumors and half-truths of a saint. For years, she'd searched for Celandine, until one day, she'd felt it. There had been a sudden hollowness in her heart, as though a piece of grace had been plucked from her very soul. It was in that moment that she had known that Celandine was gone.

She'd mourned in silence for over a year. There had been no words of comfort that could have helped her bear the weight of that loss. She still mourned her even now, but she tucked away her grief in a pocket at the back of her mind. She had to focus on the task at hand.

She drew strength from happy thoughts of the years of memories they'd had together and coated her spine in steel. She would not fail on this night. On this night, she would fulfill her promise to her ages-long friend.

She threw off her cloak and brandished her double axes that had been hidden beneath. With sure steps, she stalked into the Hall of Worlds, not bothering to hide her face. The smile on her lips when she approached the guards was all teeth, for when and if they spoke again, she wanted Adriel to know it was she who would be his downfall.

CHAPTER ELEVEN

ook, Evelyn, and Meena stood at the edge of Vreburn's town center that had been all but burned to the ground. Smoke filled the sky in large plumes from the still-raging fires, and the air smelled of burned wood and tasted of ash.

Meena stifled a horrified sob as they walked past a pile of bodies to the left of the market square, all blackened beyond recognition.

"These poor people," Evelyn whispered, taking in the scene before her. A young mother had her son propped on the well, tending to a large burn on his thigh, while her own back was mottled with scorch marks. Evelyn could see that the fabric of her cotton shirt had melded to the skin and grimaced. *She must have carried him out, using her body as a shield to protect him from the flames,* she thought.

"Stay close," Rook said. "We don't yet know what happened here. We must tread carefully."

Meena gave him a pointed look. "These people need our help."

"As much as I appreciate your bleeding heart, we need to make sure this is not a ruse intended for us to let our guard down. Corvus would have reached my father by now, and we all know what he is capable of."

Meena backed off, but only slightly, and the three of them walked further into the square.

Rook's face was a cool mask. He refused to allow himself to show the anguish he felt inside every time they passed another pile of bodies, praying to the Maker that none of them were *hers*.

The journey to Vreburn had been done out of necessity. He would rather be anywhere but back in Draestel. Unfortunately for him, Soren had found a way to block him from entering her dreams, which made her impossible to track. Though he was a man of means, his pride prevented him from paying someone to find her for him.

Logically, he assumed she would return to her place of origin, which had led him here, to an inconsequential town in southern Draestel. The road had been long, but he'd had good company when Meena had learned to still her ever-moving mouth. He knew she had just been trying to pass the time over the course of their journey, but the girl really did not know when to shut up.

He looked to his companions, seeing their internal struggle to help all those they passed on the way to the town center. They had visited Soren's family home first but had found it to be empty. He'd thought she might not have been comfortable resting her head in the home her father had built and had altered their course toward the irritating Xian-Dao boy's home.

Being out of town, Soren's home had avoided getting caught in the crossfire and remained undamaged. The same could not be said for her friends' homes. Every building within the city limits had been burned asunder, with few survivors, from the looks of it.

Something unfamiliar in his chest ached when he spotted a head of long, brown hair hanging limp over a lifeless body's face.

He ran to the smoking pile of flesh without a second thought, startling Meena and Evelyn in the process. His heart nearly burst as he reached a trembling hand forward to brush the hair from the woman's eyes. *It can't be*, he thought. *Not my little bird.*

It wasn't. Cloudy gray eyes looked back at him from an unfamiliar face, and he released the breath that he had caged between his ribs. *It's not her. Thank the Maker it's not her.*

He replaced his stoic mask and returned to the girls, who looked at him expectantly.

"It's not her."

"Oh, thank the Maker!" Meena exclaimed, hugging him in relief.

He patted her head awkwardly before detaching her arms from his torso. "Just because that body does not belong to Soren, does not guarantee she is alive," he said coldly. The thought made his stomach roil, as though he had eaten something rotten, but he was trying to be pragmatic.

"Why do you do that?" Evelyn asked, her tone sharp.

"Do what?"

"Pretend like you don't care for the girl."

Rook shrugged in an effort to look indifferent. "I never said I did not care. I'm simply being realistic."

"Whatever you say, *master*." Evelyn rolled her eyes before grabbing Meena's hand and stomping a few yards ahead.

Rook cringed at the title—*master*. The word disgusted him. His father had instructed the girls to call him that, stating they should respect his generosity toward them. They only ever referred to him as *master* when his father was around, for fear of repercussion. He had requested to be called by his real name in all other instances.

Every time they had said it when Soren had been at the manor, he'd wanted to correct them, but he'd allowed it for their safety, knowing his father was set to arrive. After a week of hearing the term over and over, he had finally requested they stop referring to him in that manner. That was, of course, once he had known Soren would not say anything to Adriel. He would not risk the girls' safety. They were the closest thing to family he had.

"Lift!" a husky female voice yelled from across the square.

Rook was pulled from his thoughts of Soren to see two men and a woman attempting to lift a fallen beam from atop another woman's leg. She was screaming in agony, and her green eyes were brimming with tears. He watched on as they attempted to remove the obstruction, but the weight was too much. The woman screamed again.

They all cursed, and the men wiped their brows as the husky-voiced woman kissed the green-eyed woman's forehead. He knew he should ignore them and stay on task, but the other injured had already been tended to, and this woman was actively in trouble. He sighed his annoyance and pushed up the sleeves of his shirt.

"Try again," he said, wasting no time on introductions.

The husky-voiced woman looked away from her partner and dashed the tears from her eyes. She did not question the help, and her, along with the two men, joined Rook. They gripped the beam and, with a final heave, released the green-eyed woman from her ashy prison.

Meena cheered from the background, and Evelyn smiled.

"Lonny!" the green-eyed woman sobbed out as she slid herself from beneath the beam and hobbled to embrace the other woman.

"It's okay, Lara. You're okay."

Rook observed the rings on their hands and deduced they must be married.

Lonny smoothed her wife's hair and placed a soft kiss on each of her tear-soaked eyes. "Come," she said. "Let me take a look at you."

Rook watched on as Lonny tugged up Lara's trouser leg to reveal a nasty bruise, though he thought it miraculous that her bone had not snapped.

They would have needed another three men to bear the weight of that post if he had not arrived. His shoulder had dislocated in the process of pushing his body past its limits to release her.

He sauntered over to Evelyn and stated plainly, "I need you to reset my arm. It's dislocated."

She raised her brow but quickly maneuvered his limp arm back into its socket with a sickening *pop*.

Meena, who had been cheering silently about Rook helping the woman, cringed at the sound. "You know, one of these times, something isn't gonna heal right."

"Well, let's hope, for all our sakes, my father is dead before that happens."

The girls opened their mouths then closed them, unsure of how to respond to his bluntness. Then, before either of them could muster up what to say, a comment from the female couple stilled their tongues.

"Thank the Maker Baztien wasn't here. I can't even think of it."

The statement from the woman named Lara grabbed Rook's attention, and he stalked over to them with renewed purpose. He stood over her expectantly. "What did you just say?"

Lonny put a hand on his chest and pushed him back a step. "That's close enough. I appreciate you helping my wife, but that does not give you any right to invade her personal space."

He held up his hands in faux apology. "I'm sorry. I just heard the name of someone I know. I'm looking for him. You did say *Baztien*, did you not? Do you know him?"

Lonny laughed as if it were the most ridiculous question in the world. "Baztien is our son."

ROOK WOULD SAY HE COULDN'T BELIEVE HIS LUCK, BUT REALLY, the chances of him finding Baz's parents were statistically pretty high, considering the location and circumstance.

Rook and Evelyn sat across from the two women at Soren's dining table while Meena finished preparing dinner. She was sure the meal would be bland without any fresh produce but was pleased to find that the cold cellar provided more than ample supplies for heartier fare.

They all nodded in understanding as the two women explained that they were Laraline and Alondra, Baztien's adoptive mothers. Laraline then told them of the letters Baztien had been writing throughout their journey. She had been getting worried when she had received no news for over a week when, just yesterday, a letter had arrived from Murkwall. He had said they needed to leave for their own protection and that they were on the road to Edras Mora.

"The details were a bit stingy," she admitted, "but we packed our rucks with haste. We were just resting for a couple of hours before departing when the fires broke out." Her voice cracked at the mention of the fires, and Alondra gave her fingers a squeeze before continuing for her.

"We know we should go, but we figure the worst has already happened, and we can't leave the town like this. I ran the apothecary, where you found us, and they will need my skills here. I may not be a fully schooled healer, but my knowledge base is vast, and my hands are steady."

Rook was secretly glad. He hadn't wanted to acquire more traveling companions, especially when the two he already had were not even supposed to be there. "I will find them and assist with their journey as best I can," he said in the hopes his words would soothe their worries.

Alondra did not seem to trust what he said, but she relented. "We will do what we can here and join you in bringing them home once we get these people back on their feet," she said with finality. "Come, Lara; let's get you to bed. We need to elevate that leg." She extended her hand to her wife then gingerly led her up the stairs, retiring to Tarak Nightsong's old bedroom. It was the biggest room in the house, and they had all decided it was best they have it.

Meena called out, "Goodnight," just as the door clicked shut and joined her sister and Rook at the table. "So, what's the plan?"

Evelyn clasped her hands on top of the wooden surface and loosed a breath. "Well, at this point, I think we should stay here. Rook is more than capable of traveling alone to Edras Mora, and our skills are not meant for combat."

Meena bit her lip and nodded. "I was thinking that, too." Then, looking at Rook, she said, "Are you sure you won't need us?"

He quirked one of his rare smiles as he replied, "What's that saying? Separation makes the heart grow fond?"

ROOK GRIMACED AS HE TUGGED A HONEY-BLOND STRAND OF HAIR off his face and stepped out of Meena's arms. He was not used to familial affection and gave her an awkward smile as he backed away.

Evelyn patted his shoulder and gave him a contented look that said this was only goodbye for now and took Meena's hand. "Come, sister; we are needed elsewhere."

Rook watched on as the girls followed Laraline and Alondra back into the heart of Vreburn, wishing them well. They were resilient, and he knew they would be fine on their own, but he was glad that Baz's mothers could provide them with additional care and support.

As they faded out of sight, his thoughts returned to Soren, and something in his rib cage ticked painfully. He had stayed in Soren's room that night, hating the thought of anyone else being closer to her than he was. Enveloped in her earthy citrus scent, he had fallen into a deep sleep, disappointed once again upon waking that he had not been able to locate her in her dreams.

He re-entered the house and strapped his blade to his hip, relief filling him that he no longer had to guard Meena and Evelyn as his journey continued. He had avoided as much human interaction as possible on the way to Vreburn to keep them safe, but now nothing stood in his way. He would leave for Edras Mora and find Soren. He would explain what had happened with her father. And Maker help anyone who stood in his way, because if they did, he would teach them a whole new meaning of the word suffering.

CHAPTER TWELVE

The trio stood at the counter of the servant's kitchen, filling their bellies while they waited for Jai to return. After Everett had broken the news about the wedding, Jai had stalked off without so much as a word. After an hour, Jai's freckled friend had returned to the stables, promising to come back first thing in the morning. When Baz and Enara's flirting had become too much for her to stomach, Soren had waved them off to their room, saying, "You have thirty minutes before I come to bed, mid-tumble or not."

"You don't need to tell me twice," Baz said as he nuzzled Enara's neck, causing her to giggle.

His girlfriend raised a brow at him and smirked. "I love that you think you'll last that long."

"Why you—"

Before he could finish his sentence, Enara had turned and run from the kitchen, leaving his jaw on the floor. He swiftly picked it up, giving Soren an impish grin, and ran after her.

Soren shook her head, and a smile spread across her lips, but her happiness was short-lived. Though she was delighted her friends had finally come together, she could not help but feel the absence of a certain man with snow-white hair.

Before her thoughts could linger, Jai sauntered into the room and stopped in surprise when he saw her. "Sorry, I thought you would all be asleep by now."

"Baz and Enara needed some alone time, if you catch my meaning."

"Ah," he replied, leaning back against the counter. A smile played at his lips as he said, "So, they should only need five minutes, then?"

Soren burst out laughing. *So the tracker's got jokes.* She unstoppered the bottle of whiskey that Everett had so graciously given them and made to pour him a drink, figuring it might take the edge off of Jai's internal struggles.

The tracker gazed down at the glass, the amber liquid swirling menacingly as he twirled it around. Soren had poured him two fingers' worth before proceeding to press the rest of the bottle to her lips, drinking deeply.

She tilted her head in question when he placed the glass back down without taking so much as a sip. "Not up to your standards, Your Highness?"

"I quit drinking a year ago," he stated plainly, effectively shutting her up. "I went into a dark place for a while after leaving Adaryn, and it got me into some trouble. So, I decided to clean my act up."

"I'm sorry, I shouldn't have offered," she said awkwardly and snatched his glass off the table, draining the liquid.

He chuckled at her, the corners of his lips turning upward. "I can stand to be around it, Soren; I just don't drink it because I don't know how to stop when I do."

Soren contemplated this for a moment. She had the same problem when it came to alcohol, but she was not about to tell him that. Instead, she asked, "How are you feeling?"

"Not great," he admitted. "I knew they were set to marry, but I hadn't realized the date was so soon."

"So, this duke … What's his name? Is he so bad?" she asked tentatively.

Jai brushed a hand through his wavy brown locks and loosed a sigh. "Not at all. That's the worst part. Duke Erick visited a few times a year when we were growing up. He is kind-hearted and always treated Adaryn and I with the utmost respect. I hear he has shown signs of being a great leader." He hesitated before tacking on the last sentence, "There couldn't be a more perfect match for her, for the crown."

"I'm sorry," Soren said empathetically and took a step closer to him, placing a comforting hand on his arm.

He blew out a breath and chuckled mildly. "It's no fault of yours. It was my own stupidity that got me here. I thought I was protecting her."

"You're a good man," Soren said, repeating the sentiment Enara had spoken to him previously. She stood in front of him now. Even slouched against the counter, he still stood a few inches above her.

"I am a coward," he said, bowing his head in defeat.

Soren's brow furrowed, and she pressed both palms to each side of his face, willing his eyes to meet hers. "We all make mistakes, Jai. Some worse than others. It's how we learn from them, grow from them, that matters."

It was the first time he had noticed the gold ring that encircled her irises, like two tiny halos gazing up at him. His hands met hers, and they felt so soft and small in his.

Soren looked at him expectantly, a whisper of a breath escaping her parted lips. If he were a worse man, he would let this play out, but it would not serve either of them well in the long run.

Gently, he removed her hands from his face and said, "You are something to behold, Soren, and I want you to know I understand the closeness you crave, but we cannot do this. As much as we may want to, I am not him and you are not her."

As much as she wanted to lash out at the rejection, she knew he was right. It was her turn to bow her head, embarrassed for even entertaining the idea of kissing him. "I know."

"Come here," he said, pulling her into his arms.

Her body stiffened at the unexpected embrace, but her muscles quickly uncoiled, and she rested her ear against his chest. "I'm sorry."

"So am I," was his response as he rested his chin on top of her head.

Neither of them knew exactly what they were apologizing for, but in the early hours of the morning, they had found a comfort in each other that most others would not understand. A mutual mourning of two hearts breaking over lovers they could not have.

"Jai?" A soft alto voice drifted from the doorway, causing the tracker's body to stiffen.

Soren turned to see a young brunette woman with tanned skin a few shades lighter than her own. The stranger's gaze shot flames in her direction as she took in the sight of them. Her doe-like eyes narrowed to angry slits, her body wound so tight with anger it looked as though she would snap at any second.

It took Soren a moment to realize who this was, and she muttered, "Oh shit," under her breath before moving to the other side of the room. She wished she could scurry into the mouse burrow she had noticed earlier in the stone wall.

She had just reached the other side of the kitchen when the woman stormed forward, stopping within a foot of Jai's body, and punched him squarely in the jaw. To his credit, he took the hit without flinching and lifted a hand to rub his chin where the blow had landed before grabbing the girl's wrist. He caught her mid-swing before she could strike him again. His grip was firm, and she growled, trying to pull her hand away. He let her go, holding his hands up in surrender. Then he spoke softly, as if to a wounded animal.

"Hello, Adaryn."

"I KNEW IT WAS YOU!" THE WOMAN SCREAMED.

Soren took the opportunity to try to slink her way out the door but was stopped by the next words that flew from the girl's mouth.

"And after everything, you come here with some whore!"

Jai responded calmy, "We are just friends, Adaryn. Her heart is with someone else."

Adaryn scoffed. "You expect me to believe that? You were embracing her but a moment ago!"

"That was not as it looked. Let her go, and I will explain." He waved Soren off, and she left gladly, not wanting to be caught in the middle of a lovers' quarrel.

She ignored the shouts coming from the kitchen as she walked down the corridor to their sleeping quarters and hesitated at the door. She had guessed that only twenty minutes had passed but shrugged and entered, anyway.

She covered a laugh with her hand as she entered.

Baz was out cold, snoring away, and Enara lifted her head lazily as she walked in, clearly on the verge of sleep.

"I know that look, Soren, and yes, it was short but rather enjoyable, thank you for asking."

Soren pinched her lips together and tugged off her boots, tucking them into the far corner, then untied her vest.

"Jai's back," she whispered.

"Is he okay?" Enara asked.

"He is with Adaryn."

"Oh?"

"She walked in on us hugging."

"Oh … So, that's a no to him being okay?"

"A big no."

"*You left*!" Adaryn's voice was shrill as she laid into him. "Without a single word, you left! No explanation! No goodbye! For two years, I have hated you! I mourned the loss of you! And now you waltz back in here as though it is your rightful place, and all you have to say is *hello*?" She beat her hands on his chest until she was sobbing uncontrollably in his arms.

"Would you rather I say *good day*, instead?"

"You are an idiot."

"Yes, but I'm your idiot," he said, brushing away a loose hair that had glued itself to her tear-stained cheek.

She looked up at him with those big, round eyes that he knew so well, and he placed a single kiss on the soft flesh of her heart-shaped lips.

She returned the kiss momentarily before pushing at his chest to look him in the eyes. "I still hate you."

He gave her the side smirk that she loved, and she reached her hand up through his shaggy hair and pulled him down for another kiss. It was like the last two years had left them starving. They devoured each other with such fervor that it left them both breathless.

Adaryn sighed between kisses, fumbling with the clip of the belt that held up Jai's black trousers. He pulled her hands away, mumbling against her lips, "Not yet."

Before she could complain, he lifted her and turned one-hundred-eighty degrees, planting her firmly on the counter. He slid her closer, hoisting her skirts up and parting her legs, taking a moment to admire what lay before him. Her head lolled back as he worshiped her, and her back arched painfully as she climaxed against his mouth.

"I missed you," she breathed between shudders as he re-surfaced.

"I promise, I'll make it up to you," he replied, kissing her neck.

"Show me."

And he did.

He made quick work of his belt, tossing it on the counter beside her before releasing himself from the confines of his trousers. Adaryn reached her legs forward, pulling him to her impatiently. Not wanting to keep her waiting, he thrust into her in one swift motion.

"Jai."

The sound of her voice calling his name that way nearly caused him to finish right then and there, but he slowed his movements to calm himself. He would not disappoint her today. He pumped in and out of her achingly slow until she couldn't take it anymore.

Their chests were pressed together, and their breathing was loud and labored.

"If you do not stop teasing me, I will have you sent to the dungeons, and I'll have my way with you there," she growled, giving his ear a sharp tug with her teeth.

"As you wish, My Lady." He kissed the soft space between her breasts as he laid her back down on the counter. Then he hoisted her legs onto his shoulders, kissing the arch of each foot before burying himself back into her. He pumped faster now, and a thin sheen of sweat formed underneath his clothes. Adaryn was biting her hand to keep from crying out, and by the trembling of her legs, he knew she was going to come soon. He picked up his already feverish pace, willing his hips to move faster.

"I'm so close," she whimpered.

He leaned forward, pressing Adaryn's knees to her chest, kissing her hard. She moaned into his mouth as she climaxed, her body coiling, as taut as a bowstring. She tightened around him as he spilled into her, and their tongues danced until he stopped pulsing.

They stayed like this momentarily, foreheads pressed together, limbs locked and breaths ragged. Adaryn broke first.

"Um ... we should probably ..." She paused midsentence.

"Yeah," Jai replied, slowly removing himself from her. He grabbed a couple cloths from a nearby cupboard and used one to clean himself and Adaryn off. Then he scrubbed his hands in the sink and used the other to clean the counter. He tossed the rags in the wicker laundry hamper just as Mrs. Ferndale waltzed into the kitchen to start baking the morning breads.

She startled when she noticed the two of them, having expected the kitchen to be empty. Then she lifted her brows and crossed her arms, taking in the sight before her.

"Anyway, I should get back to my room before my lady's maids report me missing to Father," Adaryn said, briskly brushing past Jai.

"Yeah, I should try to get some rest. It's been a long night of travel," he said as she rounded the stout woman and left the room.

"Mrs. Fern"—he nodded—"nice to see you again." It was no use playing dumb. This woman had washed his soiled diaper rags—nothing was getting past her.

"Jai," she said with reverence. He knew by her tone that he was about to get one of her lectures. Something that had occurred all too often for his liking in his childhood. "Don't you go and do anything stupid now, you hear? You have put that poor girl through enough as it is."

His tail sat firmly between his legs. "I know."

Her face softened, and she pulled him in for a quick hug, patting his back. She had been like a second mother to him growing up. "I've missed you, dear. Now, run along and get some sleep. You look like hell."

Jai couldn't help but laugh. "I missed you, too, Mrs. Fern." He gave her another quick squeeze then headed for the door.

"Oh, and Jai?" she called from behind him.

"Yeah?"

"Your trousers are still undone."

CHAPTER
THIRTEEN

Soren rolled off her cot in a daze. The dreamless sleep tonic had worked wonders, but it left her groggy and out of sorts when she first awoke.

She pulled on yesterday's trousers, dawning fresh socks and undergarments before slipping the brown, long-sleeved shirt over her head. She slid the black vest under her bust and tightened the strings before strapping on her boots.

She noticed the tracker had joined them at some point in the night after he had reconnected with Adaryn. She silently thanked him for having self-control over what surely would have been a disastrous exchange of physical intimacy. She couldn't imagine how awkward waking up this morning would have been if he hadn't stopped himself from kissing her. Let alone if Adaryn had walked in on something *actually* happening.

She shook her head, annoyed with herself, and popped out the door in search of Baz and Enara, who had already vacated the premises. She found them in the kitchen, assisting a kindly older woman with wiry red hair that had begun to whiten at the roots. She was full-figured and was waving a hand in exasperation as she spoke to Baztien.

"No, no, no." She pressed a palm to her forehead, leaving behind a trail of flour. "You have to sprinkle flour over the surface first or the dough will stick!"

"Oops," Baz said as he held up the dough that had somehow weaved itself between all ten of his fingers. He tried shaking it loose, causing a chunk to fling sideways and affix itself to Enara's cheek.

She laughed it off, wiping her face, and assisted him in trying to save the unfortunate-looking food item. It was then she looked up from the counter and greeted Soren.

"Hey, lady, how did you sleep?"

"Not bad. A little groggy. I'm gonna have to get more sleep drought soon. I only have a few days' worth left."

"Maybe we can run into town and get some," Enara offered.

"Where's Jai?" Baz asked, blissfully unaware of Soren's interaction with the tracker from the night before.

She shrugged nonchalantly. "He had a late night. I figured we should let him rest."

"Fair enough," Baz replied.

Soren poured herself a large mug of coffee and observed as he continued to work on his dough under the watchful eye of the servant lady.

The lady turned to Soren, her large hips swaying back and forth as she approached. "And who might you be?" she asked as a way of introduction.

"Uh … I'm Soren," she responded quickly. She needed to act like she belonged here, just another servant to offer a helping hand before the wedding. "Soren Nightsong, from Amerus. I heard they were hiring extra help for the princess's wedding and I jumped at the opportunity."

The woman let out a boisterous laugh. "My dear girl, save your folly for the nobility. Your friends already told me you arrived with Jaideep Ashwood."

Soren nearly choked on her coffee about being caught so obviously in a lie. She cleared her throat and eyed her friends, who had momentarily paused their baking venture. "Maker, you two. I thought we were supposed to be inconspicuous!"

"It wasn't our fault, Sor," Baz clarified. "She saw right through our story, too."

Soren looked at the woman nervously. "If you know, why haven't we been arrested?"

The woman spoke clearly. "Because I trust Jai. I have known that boy since he was running around here in nappies, trying to steal my loxberry tarts."

Soren relaxed her shoulders before the woman continued.

"But don't think that gets you out of helping." She pointed a finger at each of them. "No one sleeps and eats for free, you hear me?"

"Yes, ma'am," they replied in unison.

"You may call me Mrs. Fern. Now, let's get cooking."

A few hours later, Jai woke and joined the rest of the hoodlums, as Mrs. Ferndale would call them, in the kitchen. By the looks of it, she had set them straight to work. The entire space was filled with bubbling pots, crackling oven flames, and the mouthwatering scent of—

"Are those loxberry tarts?" he asked, reaching a greedy hand toward the cooling tray on the counter.

Mrs. Fern swatted it away with a swing of her ladle. "Hands off."

The trio laughed as the tracker tried to dodge his childhood caretaker's wrath.

"Some things never change." Everett's voice was filled with humor as strode over to them.

Jai used the momentary distraction to snatch a tart and shoved the entire thing in his mouth, chewing aggressively.

"Insufferable child," Mrs. Ferndale admonished. "Get him out of here before he devours the whole tray," she told Everett. "And take his friends with you."

"Are you sure?" Enara asked, knowing their tasks were far from finished.

"Not to fret, dear. If I need you, I will find you. There isn't a hidden hallway or room in this castle that I am not wholly aware of," she said, her eyes shining.

The girls trailed after Everett and Jai, with Baz taking up the rear.

Jai looked at him, gobsmacked as he noticed he held a tart in each hand. "How did you—"

"She said I was her favorite," Baz replied with a shit-eating grin then shoved both tarts in his mouth at the same time.

Jai's glare could have lit a pond on fire. "Bastard."

Enara was overjoyed when they walked into the stable to find that Everett had saddled up five horses so they could travel the grounds. They were all thankful for the opportunity to speak openly and express their ideas and concerns away from curious ears.

"We exercise them daily, so no need to worry about looking suspicious," he said, tightening a strap on the underbelly of a speckled pinto. "This hear is Baymont."

"He's beautiful," Enara gushed, petting long strokes down the horse's thick neck. "Is he yours?"

"No, they all belong to the king, but my strongest bond is with the gray thoroughbred in the corner there. Amadeus is the fastest of the king's herd."

"Good thing we aren't racing then," she replied. Her attention shifted as another horse reared up on its hind legs in excitement as Jai approached it.

"Whoa, whoa, boy," he soothed, his arms raised. "I missed you, too," he muttered softly, kissing its snout as it sniffed at him happily.

"And that's Casper. He has been Jai's mount of choice since childhood, and his partner, Soliel, in the next stall is Adaryn's."

"Their horses are mated?"

"Yup, the symbolism of it all is eerie, isn't it?"

"I think it's sweet," Enara replied, chuckling as Baymont nuzzled into her hand.

"I think you're sweet," Baz chimed in, plopping a wet kiss on her forehead.

"Gross," Enara complained, wiping the spittle off with her sleeve.

He held the reins to another thoroughbred. This one had a white diamond on its forehead and a shiny brown coat.

Baz patted her flank, stating, "She's no Ellie, but I'm sure she will do a fine job."

That struck a chord in Soren's heart, as she was reminded of the black Friesen she had traveled with from Vreburn. She was disappointed that she had never had a chance to name him. She sent up a prayer to the Maker that the old man by the river was taking good care of them before hopping into the saddle on the cream-colored quarter horse that Everett had assigned to her.

The rest of the group mounted their noble steeds and followed Everett out the back gate, onto the sandy trails that lay beyond the iron bars. They gave the guards a tilt of their heads, and they nodded in return, seemingly unconcerned.

"The lack of agency in the king's guard is mildly disappointing," Enara observed.

"Well, considering there hasn't been an attack for over two hundred years, it's not all that surprising," Everett explained. "I think anyone would become complacent after that amount of time."

"Fair point," she replied, and they journeyed on.

With the horizon in front of them and the saltwater winds at their backs, Enara felt at peace.

They rested on a large blanket on the sand, the horses tied to a small grouping of palm trees at the edge of the tropical forest. They ate sandwiches of roasted pheasant and orange cheese smothered in a thick white sauce made of vinegar, egg, and plant oil. It was delicious.

Soren swallowed the last of it down with a guzzle of water and broke through the small talk the rest of the group had been making. "Hey, guys, I know this is nice and all, but we have to get a move on. What's our plan?"

Jai had filled in Everett on the major details—an all-powerful being, who had an army of bird-men, intended to destroy Entheas, and they were his main target.

Everett had asked a few questions for clarification but, to Soren's surprise, he did not balk or claim them to be liars. His faith in Jai was astounding. He took his every word at face value and vowed to help his brother in his mission to gather the forces of Patrivah to fight this new threat.

"I still can't believe you're going to be the king of Patrivah." Everett's concern regarding that fact was palpable.

"Well, believe it, brother, because the hierarchy around here is about to change."

After returning to the stables, they continued planning well into the evening, thankful that Mrs. Ferndale had not called on them again for assistance. There were many working parts and so many unknown factors, but they had finally decided on where to go from here.

Enara, Baz, and Soren would head to Braexmirth with the second copy of Jai's lineage documents, while the heir of Patrivah and Everett would stay in Edras Mora and try to convince the king to amass his troops.

The goodbyes were short-lived, as they planned to return to Edras Mora in one week's time, hopefully having convinced

King Elias to join the fight. The forges of Braexmirth might not be able to destroy the Oculus, but the bladesmiths of Olecastor would surely provide them with weapons stronger than any of the other provinces. The ores they had access to were tougher and lighter than any other mineral in Entheas. This, at the very least, would give them a better chance against Adriel's forces.

Luckily for them, Everett allowed them to take the horses. He told them the king would never know with all the wedding preparations distracting him.

They packed and mounted their four-legged companions then clopped through the gates casually, mentally preparing for the few long days of travel ahead.

JAI WATCHED THE LAST OF THE HORSES PASS THROUGH THE GATES and breathed out a sigh. They were off to do their part. Now it was time to fulfill his side of the bargain.

Momentarily, he wished to be back in his boat, on another self-serving mission to fill his coffers, but he knew that was not where his heart truly yearned to be.

He had avoided coming back here because he knew if he did, he would crash the wedding and ruin Adaryn's chance at happiness. But he was here now. And so was she. And Maker damn him, but he would rather face down Adriel's whole army of beasts alone than to let Adaryn marry Erick.

A new sense of calm and purpose filled his veins, lighting a fire in his belly. He stood taller and spoke with regal authority.

"Come, brother, I have a kingdom to claim."

JAI AND EVERETT TRAVELED THROUGH THE CASTLE WITH CAU-tion, though most rushed past, carrying fine china from one room to the next while the royal event organizer barked orders.

"That tapestry is sideways!" A woman clicked her teeth and scribbled notes on a parchment pad that she held in her hands, the jar of ink dangerously close to spilling. "No, I said appetizer plates, not dessert plates!" Her voice was shrill as she lay into one servant after another to get the castle ready.

The guys stifled their laughter as they snuck past, not wanting to get pulled into the fray.

"She seems delightful," Jai commented.

"She's not like that all the time," Everett assured, his tone implying they knew each other on a more intimate level.

Jai let his eyebrows ask the question for him.

Everett shrugged. "What? It was only once or twice. I just help her to relax after the big events."

"And the palace footman?" Jai asked.

"Oh, he got removed from the staff. Apparently, they caught him pick-pocketing the nobility as he helped them into their carriages." He let out a disappointed sigh. "Too bad. He was a fun roll in the hay, too."

"You have no shame," Jai said as they turned the corner to the next hall and his heart skipped a beat.

The corridor was empty apart from Adaryn, who stood at the end of it. She wore a gown the color of autumn leaves, and her hair was pinned up on one side, a tiara of woven gold sitting squarely on her head. She looked every bit like the princess of Patrivah.

Jai's brows furrowed when he noticed that her arm was nestled comfortably through the elbow of the Duke of Stelonbriar, and he stifled a growl. This was no longer the young boy they had known since childhood; this was the man she was set to marry.

CHAPTER
FOURTEEN

The road to Braexmirth was surprisingly beautiful. After making the crossing from Patrivah, Soren, Baz, and Enara found themselves in the wide-open expanse of Braexmirth's flatlands. This section of the province was where the inhabitants raised their livestock and grew certain crops that could survive their harsher climates.

They had arrived in the early evening, and the sun was beginning to fall past the large mountain range in front of them. The farmlands were set ablaze in dark oranges, reds, and yellows that reminded Enara of the heart of a sunflower.

The sunset contrasted the colors of the first set of mountain ranges. The warm tones swirled and melted with the charcoal grays, greens, and blacks of the stones, like paint on woven fabric. Their school texts had always spoken of the great mountains of Braexmirth, but they had always assumed them to be drab and gray since no pictures had been provided.

They camped out at the halfway point to Olecastor, choosing to sleep under the stars. As evening turned to dusk, and the golds faded to silver, they settled onto their bedrolls, staring up at the stars for a while when Baz broke the silence.

"Hey, Sor?" he asked, his tone hesitant.

"Yeah?"

"I think your dad would be proud of you."

The admission caused her throat to constrict, and she looked at him tearfully. "I hope so," was all she could muster before the drop fell.

"I know so," Enara said from beside her. "Not many would still be standing after all you've been through, lady. You don't give yourself enough credit."

"Thanks, guys."

"We love you, Sor. Let's get some rest."

Baz yawned and curled his arms around Enara's waist. "Love you," he murmured against Enara's neck.

"I love you guys, too," Soren replied then whispered up to the stars, "I love you tons, too, Dad."

THE ENTRANCE TO OLECASTOR LAY AT THE APEX OF THE ROCKY expanse. The city itself spanned the entire mountain range, but the royals resided in the castle built into the eastern side. The cliff faces loomed up ahead of them, and their pace slowed as they reached the large stone door flanked by a guard on either side.

Soren could not help but feel intimidated. These were not the simple guards of Tree City. These men were huge, and the early morning sun glinted off their armor. Soren held up her hand to shield her eyes as they approached, unsure of what to expect.

As they reached the threshold, the guards shifted, lifting their long swords into the ready position and holding out their hands to halt them.

"Speak your business."

It took Soren a moment to respond. Their accents were harsh, and their voices were so low that she struggled to take their meaning. She opened her mouth to reply when Enara came to her rescue.

"We have come to hold court with King Elias."

The bearded guard to her left raised a brow, eyeing the group with suspicion. "What business do you have that would require a meeting with the king?"

"We have news from the House of Drekar, King of Patrivah." Baztien's voice was strong and firm, and Enara blinked at him in surprise.

The guards seemed to consider this and exchanged a look. Then the bearded one nodded, startling them by yelling, "*Kedaestach!*" in his native tongue.

They braced themselves as the twenty-foot-high door shifted open, the stone grinding against the massive metal hinges.

The two armored men stood aside, and the second one spoke in the common tongue. "You may enter." Then he nodded to his bearded comrade. "Callan will go with you."

"Thank you," they responded and rushed after the man named Callan, who was already ten strides ahead of them.

Soren quickened her pace to match the lumbering giant and looked up at him. He was younger than she had first thought. His dark blond hair held a reddish hue, and the front pieces were pulled back from his face in braids and twists affixed with small metal clips. The length of it fell just past his shoulders, and his beard was fashioned to match.

"How long have you guarded the gate?" Soren asked, curious about these people she knew so little of.

Surprised at the question, he looked down at her with eyes the color of a cornflower field. He cleared his throat before responding in his deep baritone, "This is not my normal post, but the secondary guard's wife is birthing their youngling and requested his presence."

"You speak common tongue well," Soren observed.

"Yes, my father forced lessons upon us all."

"What is your normal post?"

"You ask a lot of questions," he said in annoyance.

She was about to continue when Enara grabbed her sleeve, pulling her back to where her and Baz had followed behind them.

"What are you doing?" she asked in a hoarse whisper.

"What? I was just curious," Soren replied.

"We have to keep these people happy if they are going to help us. We have to tread carefully."

"Yeah, okay, I guess you're right." Soren looked down, as if scolded, and picked at her fingernails.

The trio followed Callan along the narrow valley floor until they reached a secondary door. The guards there took one look at the large man and opened it immediately, bowing low as they walked past.

The trail opened up into a wide valley that connected multiple mountain ranges. There was a river of the clearest blue flowing down from the farthest one, cutting through the thick rock and trailing out the base of the castle built into the cliffside.

The air tasted of iron and smelled of molten metal and crushed stone. Plumes of smoke drifted from deep within the walls of rock, no doubt stemming from the forges that lay beneath.

Everything in the city seemed to be carved out of stone, from the houses that snaked back and forth up the mountainsides to the castle that looked like it was part of the range itself. All harsh lines, and thick walls, the greens and grays were the only color amongst the black rock.

Callan led them up a large, curving staircase to the front gates of the castle. The guards again bowed to him as they let them pass.

The trio was left speechless upon entry, for the entire room and the hallways that lay beyond were as black as the midnight sky, an unworldly beauty. Though most would imagine it to be foreboding, the walls spoke of a quiet strength rather than darkness to be feared.

Emerald rugs lined the floors, and sconces made of hollowed-out fire opal refracted mischievous patterns on the obsidian walls. There was little in the way of artwork, but the few pieces they did see had been formed out of differing metals, melded and arced together in a fantastical array of golds and silvers.

As they reached the end of the west hallway, Callan brought them down another twisting staircase then a short, wide corridor that ended at a set of double doors made entirely out of jade. The entrance towered above them and was covered in intricate carvings, depicting kings and battles long since past. Soren struggled to keep her emotions in check as she gazed upon it. *Dad would have loved this.*

"When you enter, you will speak when spoken to," Callan's voice broke through the thought of her father.

"Easier said than done," Soren muffled.

Callan gave her the side-eye before loosing a breath. "Just let me do the talking."

Baz and Enara nodded in agreement, and then Callan called out, "*Kedaestach, brathairs,*" which meant, "*Allow entry, brothers.*"

They walked through the entryway, keeping their heads bowed, unsure of the customs required in meeting the King of Olecastor, but a booming voice from across the room greeted them.

"Lift your heads, friends. Hold them high, for you are welcome here."

The voice came from the obsidian throne that lay on the other side of the large room. Atop it sat a large man, clad in armor that matched the guards, with kind blue eyes and a long beard. His previously blond hair was fading to silver, and his face was battle-weathered.

He was flanked by two more men holding long, onyx staffs, the tips forged from xethriel, the strongest ore in Entheas. The men themselves were tall and lean, every muscle toned and pulled taut against their dark skin. Their coarse hair was twisted into long, ebony locks that were pulled back in an intricate weave, the sides shaved to their scalps. They had serious, deep-set brown eyes, full lips, and were identical in their looks. The only way to discern between the two was a pale scar that lay across the left one's scalp.

The king assessed them once more before speaking again. "So, tell me, why has my son brought you here?"

Soren looked to Callan, whose stony expression hinted at a smile before untying her tongue to speak.

"Sir," she started, "we have come to request aid for Patrivah. We have news from the House of Drekar."

"My dear girl, we have already heard of the goings-on in Edras Mora. Tragic, really."

A look of confusion passed between Soren and her friends before she said, "I'm sorry, I don't catch your meaning."

"Not to worry yourself, young one. My scouts have already informed me that the king is dead."

"WHAT?" SOREN COULDN'T HELP THE SUDDEN OUTBURST. "What do you mean, *the king is dead?*"

The leader of Braexmirth chuckled. "I thought I had learned the common tongue well, but I guess not. Is there another term for the end of life I should know?" The beginning of his Rs rolled slightly and ended as if something caught in his throat.

"Father," Callan spoke, "I believe the word you're looking for is *murdered.*"

"Ah, yes, that's the one."

"That can't be possible," Enara said, shaking her head. "We were just there not but two nights ago and had heard news of no such thing."

Baz put a hand on her lower back, just as confused as she was. "What exactly did your scout report?" he asked hastily then added, "If you don't mind me asking?"

The king ignored his question, noticing the sword at his back. "Bring me your blade."

Baz stiffened, worried he might have offended the man, but he brought forth his sword and bent on one knee to present it.

"I know this blade," the king said, taking in the blue sheen of its length. "This sword has been passed down through generations of the McKenna family. Now, tell me, boy, how it is that you have come to possess such a weapon?"

"It was passed to me, from my grandfather. He fought with Draestel during the war, and Lord Krikseth gifted it to him for taking out Bao Ren's commander." Baz waited as the king contemplated his response, stroking a hand through his long beard. A nervous sweat settled on his brow, and it felt like an eternity before he spoke again.

"Yes, I seem to remember hearing something of this, though I am surprised to find that you yourself are of Xian Dao heritage." The king beckoned him to stand, handing the sword back.

Baz swallowed thickly. "I was adopted," he explained. "A couple from Draestel took me in after my parents died trying to flee the country, and Byron Greymark was my mother's, Laraline, father. He left the sword to her, and she passed it on to me."

"Ah, that explains it, then. I myself am an adoptive father of sorts. Found these two"—he nodded toward the guards—"along a mountain pass at the age of five. They said they came through a portal from the Esinian Isles." He smiled fondly at them. "Kids, I tell you. I raised them as my own, along with Callan. He is my blood son."

"They are lucky to have you," Baz acknowledged.

The king chuckled again and stood, clapping Baz hard on the shoulder. "They might not tell you that, though." He gestured to the three of them, his eyes twinkling, "Come; we must celebrate that the heir to such a great ally has come to visit us."

"But, sir, we have much to discuss, and you haven't told us what happened in Patrivah," Soren said, exasperated.

"All in good time, my dear," the king replied, already heading for the doors. He turned to Callan and said, "Prepare them for the festivities. We can discuss more serious matters in the morning."

"Yes, Father," he replied, bowing.

"But—"

Callan caught Soren's arm as she tried to interject.

She glared up at him, wrenching her fist away. "I wasn't finished speaking with him," she said sharply.

Callan smirked. "Well, he was finished speaking with you. And take it from me, he will talk when it pleases him, not the other way around. You would do best to try to enjoy the evening, and you will have your answers in the morning."

"We have friends in Edras Mora who would be greatly affected by the king's death," Soren said, worry for Jai filling her heart.

"If it puts your mind at ease, your friend is not in any danger. I do not know the details, but my father did inform me that the perpetrator has been caught and has been sentenced to death."

She pressed her lips together and looked to Baz and Enara. "What do you guys think?"

Baz spoke first. "I think Jai is one of the most resourceful guys we know. He can make it a day or two more without us."

"Yeah," Enara joined in. "Besides, this may be a good way to show the king we mean well. I say we join in the festivities."

"Okay, then." Soren nodded then looked to Callan. "I hope you know how to throw a good party."

CHAPTER
FIFTEEN

Callan took Baztien to get ready in his quarters and left Soren and Enara with a lady's maid named Saoirse. She had piercing green eyes and wild red hair that curled out from the top of her head in a large mane. Her pale skin was flawless, and her long legs had her towering above even Enara by a good six inches.

"I can not wait for tonight," she said with a large grin splayed across her striking features. Her voice lilted like a song but was made rougher by her thick accent. "Hallival is the best event of the year," she continued. "You are lucky to have arrived on this day." She practically skipped as she led them down a hall and into a large dressing room.

"What exactly are you celebrating?" Enara asked as she took in the cream-colored pouffes and large mirrors that lined the left wall.

"Oh, I'm so glad you asked," she said with a mischievous grin. "Come; bathe with me, and I'll tell you the history of Hallival."

Without warning, Saoirse stripped naked and padded to the large bath that ran from wall to wall at the back of the room. She immersed herself in the steaming water and beckoned them to join. After a moment's hesitation, they did.

Communal bathing was not common practice in Vreburn, but Soren and Enara had gone skinny dipping on more than one occasion, so how different was it really? At least this water was warm.

The large bath was filled by a hot spring that flowed from further up the mountain. The water traveled over the rock that had been heated by the molten lava below, resulting in a luxurious bath that never cooled. Enara marveled at the ingenuity.

They scrubbed away the previous days' travel as Saoirse began explaining the origin of Hallival.

"Hallival, or Festival of Dathan—or color, in the common tongue—has been celebrated in Braexmirth for over three centuries and is always held on the final day of the autumn tide. In the old days, the men would set out to hunt at the start of the autumn tide, wearing only white to show their prey who their masters were."

"That had to be nearly impossible," Soren said in awe. "They would be seen from a mile away."

"Exactly." Saoirse nodded. "This is what made the hunt so exciting. They had to earn the trust of the animals over the course of days and weeks before making the kill."

"That's kind of sad, isn't it?" Enara asked. "Making the animal feel safe before ending its life?"

"I could see how you would feel that way, but their deaths were quick, better than any they would have received in the wild. No part of the animal was wasted, and any beast younglings were off limits. When the hunt was over, they would come back wearing the pelts of their chosen familiar and celebrate. They would eat sweets and drink until their hearts' content, dancing under the stars as the last of the leaves fell from the trees."

"That sounds beautiful," Soren said.

Saoirse let out a soft chuckle. "I imagine it was, though traditions have changed over the years since we no longer need to hunt for survival. Now, the celebrations are held in a more symbolic way, to honor our ancestors. We still dance under the stars. Everyone dresses in white, with masks depicting different animals native to our lands, and we eat and drink until our minds are fuzzy and our hearts are full."

"Well, I am all for it," Enara replied, wringing out her hair.

"Only one problem," Soren said, wrapping herself in a hemp towel. "We have nothing to wear."

Saoirse's eyes twinkled. "I think I can help you with that."

BAZ STOOD AT THE BASE OF THE WINDING STAIRS THAT LED TO the throne room, his face half-covered in a mask designed to match the features of a mountain lion. Callan stood beside him, and they waited in awkward silence for the girls to join them. The event, he was told, would be held in a cavern near the edge of the mountain, and they would travel the pathways carved through the castle to get there.

Baz shuffled back and forth nervously, tugging on the white linen that hung from his hips. It wasn't like he was ashamed of his body. Though Callan was larger than him in stature, Baz matched him muscle for muscle and couldn't help but be pleased with himself. He was simply used to wearing a cotton suit rather than the white fabric that was little more than a loincloth wrapped around his waist and stopping just short of his knees.

A breeze drifted through the landing, causing Baz to jump as it drifted to places it had no right being in.

Callan chuckled though his wolf mask as the poor boy adjusted the little fabric he had on. "Leave it be, lad. You'll not be the only one showing a lot of skin tonight."

Baz was about to ask what that meant but stopped short when he heard familiar voices floating down from the stairwell. Almost as if Callan's comment had summoned them, Enara, Soren, and the redheaded lady's maid appeared.

All three of them wore white clothes that left little to the imagination. The fabric was draped and knotted in all the right places to accentuate every one of their curves while somehow keeping their personal bits covered. Their makeup was minimal; all they had done was add some charcoal to their eyes and salve to their lips.

Baz swallowed thickly as they descended the stairs. The redhead came down first, taking Callan's arm, excitement bubbling from all of her pores. "Don't they look great!" Her smile was radiant beneath her mask; her animal of choice being a rabbit. The ears from her mask popped up playfully against the blazing inferno of curls that was her hair. Baz had to admit the creature seemed to match her personality.

Soren followed, her mask that of a fox, which Baz thought complemented her small features nicely. Her hair had been redyed and shone a radiant midnight blue, and the sides had been twisted back from her face and secured with pinched clips of silver.

She patted Baz's muscular arm as she stood beside Saoirse and said, "Try not to get too excited."

"I make no promises," he responded, staring in awe at Enara.

Her brown hair was tied back in a series of connected ponytails that had been tugged gently to splay out like a beautiful main to the back of her head. Her mask was that of an owl, which conveyed a sort of quiet strength. The minimal fabric covering her body made his mouth dry, and he resisted the urge to adjust himself.

He held out his arm as she approached, and she took it, smirking at him. "You can pick up your jaw now."

He blushed under his mask, not realizing he had left his mouth hanging open, panting like an excited dog. "Sorry." He laughed nervously, and she planted a kiss on his already parted lips.

"All right, the two of you," Saoirse said, cutting the kiss short. "You'll have plenty of time for that later. Let's get a move on."

Just as she spoke, the doorway swung open to reveal the king, his beard peeking out from under his bear-shaped facial covering, trailed by the twin guards who wore identical elk masks, complete with dangerous-looking horns. The king wore a tunic along with his loincloth, and Baz could see the glint of white metal underneath, no doubt as a precaution. The guards had also swapped their gray armor for white, the light tones making their skin look velvety and rich, their dark eyes mysterious.

"You lot could almost pass for locals," the king complimented. "Now, let me show you how we in Braexmirth celebrate."

THEY FIRST HEARD THE DRUMS AS THEY FOLLOWED THE TUNNEL deep into the mountain. The deep booming radiated through their bodies, and Soren could feel the hair on her arms lift. The energy was palpable, and though she was worried about the goings-on in Edras Mora, she couldn't help but let some excitement wash over her. *This could be good to get my mind off of things.*

She'd had some time throughout their travels to do a deep dive into her own psyche and had come to two conclusions. One, it was okay to continue to grieve her father, but she needed to find less destructive means of coping. And two, as much as she wanted to deny her feelings toward the man who had killed her father, a sliver of her heart still beat for the Prince of Ravens.

A twinge of guilt stole the breath from her lungs, and her panic creeped forth from the dark recesses of her mind. *He killed him. You disgrace his memory by admitting your feelings for that monster.*

Images from her nightmare flashed before her eyes, and she grabbed a hold of the wall to fight back a wave of nausea. Her mind did not relent its attack.

You are a terrible daughter. Your father would be ashamed.

She swallowed against the knot in her throat and inhaled deeply.

The rest of the group was ahead of them, apart from one of the twins, who took up the rear.

"Are you all right?" he asked, speaking above the music. His tone was surprisingly gentle, given his tough exterior.

"Yeah," she spat out. "Must be the change in altitude."

Seeming to accept that answer, he smiled and said, "We are almost there. Have some water and sit for a moment, and you'll be as good as new."

She returned his kind smile, albeit half-heartedly, and took a few more calming breaths.

As they traveled, Enara had been working with her to manage her panic better so she wouldn't succumb to it like she had back at the manor. Anytime her panic arose, Enara would walk her through the five senses to help her regain her composure and practice deep breathing until she was well enough to speak again. But Enara would not always be there, and she would not submit herself to being their third wheel for the rest of her life.

Idly, her thoughts popped back to her home in Vreburn and the little jar of pills in her bedside table. She had never liked taking them in the first place and only had when it seemed absolutely necessary. She was determined to heal on her own without the need to supplement herself.

She waved the guard off and tried to put up her mental shield to fight against the intrusive thoughts.

You are a disgrace, the voice in her mind sneered at her, the same voice that filled her with regret and self-doubt, but she fought it back.

I did not know of his actions until after my feelings developed. It is not my fault.

You are disgusting for still caring for such a beast.

Feelings don't just go away, even if you hate someone.

You should have killed him.

Killing him will not bring my father back.

The last retort seemed to silence the demons in her mind and gave her the reprieve she needed to steady herself. Her senses came back into focus, and she let the drums replenish her energy stores. She could still feel the voice nagging in the back of her mind, but it was far away, muted by the cacophony of music that surrounded her.

I will not let you win today, she thought to herself as she placed a firm wall up to block out the last of her negative thoughts. *Today, I will enjoy myself fully and not seek out meaningless pleasure.*

With that in mind, she walked around the final curve of the carved-out tunnel and took in all Hallival had to offer.

THE CROWD BEFORE HER WAS SO LARGE THAT EVERY CITIZEN IN the province had to have been in attendance. Thousands of bodies swayed back and forth, moving to the rhythm of the massive drums that sat on a platform above the fray.

The cave was naturally occurring, but stoneworkers had carved out staircases and platforms to make the space more usable, working with the naturally formed pillars. The stalagmites and stalactites were so large that they connected floor-to-ceiling, and a bright teal pool sat in the far corner. An assortment of every sweet Soren had ever deigned to think of sat atop a large flat stone on the right-hand side of the room, and a grouping of people milled about happily. She noticed Baz shoveling the goodies into his mouth at an unhealthy pace and laughed. *Good thing his mask doesn't cover his jaw*, she thought.

She jumped as a hand encircled her wrist but relaxed when she realized it was Enara.

"Hey, lady, thought I lost you there," she said, out of breath from running up the stairs. "Ori said you needed a moment to yourself. Are you okay?"

"Who?" Soren asked distractedly.

"Ori, the guard. His brother's name is Ikei."

"Oh, gotcha. Yeah, no, I'm okay. Was just overwhelmed for a minute, but I'm good now."

Enara's hazel eyes bore into her brown ones from beneath her mask.

"I promise," Soren said. "Now, go have fun."

"Okay, but it's crazy down there. Meet at the bottom of this staircase when the night's over if we don't find each other before then?"

"Yeah, yeah. Now, go!"

As she turned to leave, Soren smacked her on the butt, and Enara gave her the finger.

"Have fun," her friend yelled then added, "But not too much!"

Soren laughed and made her way down the stairs. Enara had already dragged Baz into the crowd before Soren had reached the sweets' table. She popped a mini chocolate ball into her mouth and relished in the mix of sweet and bitter that played on her tongue. She tasted a few more delicacies that could not easily be found in Draestel, including a tart made from elderfruit, before washing it all down with a full glass of bliss. Soren thought the name odd, but it looked delicious. The liquid was like molten silver but went down like cool water and tasted of vodka and sweet cream. She reached for a second glass, but a voice to her left stilled her hand.

"I wouldn't," a man in a badger mask said. "Not unless you want to end up in bed with someone before the party really starts."

"Excuse me?" Soren asked. She would have responded with a, "*What the fuck did you just say?*" but she was the guest of the king.

"Sorry," he said, yelling over the music. "I just mean that it is an aphrodisiac. It is weak, but if you inhale it like you did the last glass, your actions may not be entirely your own."

"Oh, thanks, I guess," she replied, putting the empty goblet down and opting for a glass of crisp cider instead.

He then surprised her by asking, "Do you want to dance?"

She took a moment to decide if it was a good idea or not. *He seems nice enough. I mean, if he was trying to get into my pants, he would have poured me another glass.*

Seeming to make up her mind, she finished the cider in one breath and said, "Sure, if you think you can handle this."

He chuckled, gray eyes glinting. Then he held out his arm and led her into the chaos.

SOREN HAD TO ADMIT THAT BRAXTEN WAS A GOOD DANCER, AND an appropriate one at that. He only let his hands roam when Soren took the lead and did not press their bodies together until she made a joke about him dancing as though he was back in primary school.

He was friendly, and happiness radiated from behind his mask. He had light brown curls that bobbed up and down with the music, and his presence put Soren at ease. He was muscular, as were all the men from Braexmirth, she had noticed, but on the smaller side. He was still larger in comparison to her small frame but a few inches shorter than most of his brethren.

She could feel the effects of the silver drink kicking in, and her cheeks flushed. Thanks to Brax, as he preferred to be called, she was a comfortable level of aroused. Her skin tingled, and the closeness of his body to hers gave her a faint buzz, but she was not overwhelmed with the need to jump him in one of the side caverns.

As one song flowed into the next and their bodies melded together, he nuzzled her neck affectionately as they swayed. Soren let herself enjoy the rapture of it all.

She had seen Enara and Baz a few times throughout the night. They had all even danced together at one point, but Enara had not gotten the warning about the bliss, so they had "retired early." Baz had been all smiles.

Braxten paused their dancing and left to get her some water.

This was exactly what I needed. She danced by herself, sharing smiles with the other attendees who were all grinding and gyrating around her. It was animalistic and exciting, and you could cut the sexual tension in the air with a knife.

The stars peeked out from the large hole in the roof of the cave, which also served as an escape for the smoke rising from the excessive amounts of torches lining the space. Despite the amount of bodies, the air was cool, and it felt heavenly against her oversensitive skin.

She smiled as an arm snaked around her and Braxten pressed his body back against hers. His breath tickled her ear, and a faint smell of pine needles wafted into her nose, reminding her of …

No. It can't be.

And then his voice was speaking ever so softly into her ear, a voice like velvet drifting over her, enveloping her like cold flames, and her body stiffened.

"Hello, little bird."

CHAPTER
SIXTEEN

Two Days Prior - Edras Mora

Jai had been actively ignoring Princess Adaryn's upcoming betrothal, but upon seeing her arm wrapped in her husband-to-be's, he could ignore it no longer. His blood boiled, and his heartbeat pounded in his ears so loudly that he had not heard them announce their presence when they had crossed paths in the hallway.

"Jai?" Adaryn's voice cut through the haze, her big brown eyes large with concern.

"My Lady," Everett replied, bowing low. "We were just on our way to consult with the king about the horses for the wedding entrance."

Jai couldn't be more thankful that his friend was quick on his feet.

"Yes, we just have a few final details to go over with him," Jai added, mirroring Everett's bow.

For some odd reason, Adaryn burst out laughing, and neither Jai nor Everett could figure out why. They lifted their brows at each other, waiting for her to compose herself.

"Oh, you two, you can stop with the disingenuous formalities," she said, still giggling.

Duke Erick looked at her, humor also painting a smile on his narrow lips. "Should we put them out of their misery?"

"Yes"—she nodded—"I think we should."

Everett and Jai looked as confused as ever, so the duke clarified for them by crossing the menial distance between where they stood and planting a passionate kiss on Everett's unsuspecting lips. Then he ran a hand through his perfectly coiffed golden-blond hair and flashed a smile of perfect teeth. "I missed you, farm boy."

"And I you," Adaryn said, following suit and giving Jai a smooch before tucking herself against his chest.

His heart was beating rapidly against his rib cage, and when she feared the shock might be too much for him, she explained further. "The marriage was strictly to help strengthen each of our countries. The duke and I are good friends."

"And Erick and I are more than good friends," Everett said, his blush almost matching the soft pink of his lips.

"You didn't think to mention this earlier?" Jai grated out, obviously feeling left in the dark.

"I, like you, didn't want to risk causing issues with the wedding," Everett replied.

"Right," Jai said, running a hand through his long hair and stepping back from Adaryn.

"And you did not want to mention this to me last night?" he said with a raised brow.

She shrugged off the quip. "If I recall correctly, we were otherwise occupied."

Jai nearly choked on the breath he had been trying to suck in and looked to the duke, gauging his response.

He clapped Jai on the shoulder, chuckling. "C'mon, Jai, we've known each other since childhood. I would never come in and steal your girl. Though, I do have to say: what the hell were you thinking leaving her like that? I had to do damage control for months!"

Jai didn't even bother arguing because he knew Erick was right. Instead, he tried to change the subject.

"And what about you two?" he asked, looking to Everett. "How long has this been going on?"

"Well, there was that one time when we were about sixteen, and then we rekindled things when he began to court Adaryn."

"And you were okay with this?" Jai asked her.

"Of course," she replied, as if it was the most ridiculous question in the world. "Who am I to stop our friend from finding his own happiness. Besides, I was heartbroken. The last thing I needed was Father parading me around in corsets and petticoats in front of all the eligible bachelors."

"I see," Jai replied, scratching at his beard. He was due for a trim soon. "And what about when it came to producing an heir?"

Adaryn was surprisingly unruffled by the question and waved her hand as she responded, "We were going to deal with the semantics later, but I do believe it would have involved an item used for basting pheasant."

At this, they all burst out in laughter, finally breaking the spell of awkwardness that had settled over them.

"So, now that we have all that out of the way, care to explain why you're back?" Adaryn said then added a fiery, "Because I know you didn't come back for me."

Taking that as their cue to leave, Erick and Everett sauntered back down the hallway, toward the stables.

Jai shifted from foot to foot, not knowing where to start. "Maybe we should head to the gardens. You'll probably want to sit when I tell you why I'm really here."

She nodded, letting him lead the way.

The gardens were located in a central courtyard, in the middle of the castle grounds, and housed an array of beautiful plants and shrubs. Her seat of choice was an intricately carved wooden bench, and Jai joined her, taking care to sit an appropriate distance away.

"So, I guess I'll just start from the beginning …"

THE AMOUNT OF EXPLETIVES THAT SHOT FROM ADARYN'S MOUTH had to be some kind of record. She paced back and forth in front of the bench, going through a new wave of emotion with every piece of the puzzle Jai laid out before her—shock being the main reaction. If the servants were surprised by her behavior, they didn't show it. Adaryn was known to be feisty, so they all just skittered by, not wanting to be caught eavesdropping.

"So," she said, trying to gather herself, "you are to be king, then?"

Jai sighed loudly. "I guess so. I mean, unless you feel like leading Patrivah into a war that cannot be escaped where everyone is likely to die."

She shook her head violently at the thought. "Absolutely not," she said with finality. "You are the blooded son of the king—it has to be you." Adaryn was usually one to balk at tradition, but when it came to responsibilities to the crown, she had always done what was necessary for the benefit of her country.

This is why you would have made the perfect queen, Jai thought.

Adaryn took his hand, momentarily forgetting herself, and then released it, smoothing her skirts to cover the action. She looked around, hoping no one had noticed the affectionate exchange. "I should warn you," she said in a hushed tone. "Father has not been well."

"What do you mean?"

"He has been losing weight for weeks now. He can't seem to keep anything down. He grows weaker by the day."

"Where is he?" Jai asked, concern etched between his brows.

"In his rooms. We have a healer on site who checks in twice a day, but he has yet to discover what is wrong."

Jai stood, his face a mask of newfound resolve for his mission.

"Take me to him."

ADARYN HAD BEEN GENEROUS WITH HER DESCRIPTION OF THE state of the king's withering body. The healer had just been leaving as they arrived and gave Adaryn a small, sad nod, no doubt a silent confirmation that his status had not improved.

They entered the chambers, and Adaryn dismissed the guards stationed at the doors. "Jai and I wish to speak to my father alone," she told them. It was not a request.

When she heard the door click behind them, she rushed to the bedside and took the king's hand. "Papa," she said quietly, tears blurring the edges of her vision.

When there was no response, Jai stepped closer and placed a reassuring hand on her back.

"He is in and out of consciousness most days." She sniffed. "Today must be a silent day."

"We will figure it out together," he said, unsure of how else to provide her comfort.

"Papa," she said, trying again. "Papa, I have brought someone to see you." Her voice was like a child's. "Jai has returned to us."

The words seemed to pull the man from the precipice of death, and his once bright eyes flitted open to reveal murky brown irises. He opened his mouth to speak then waved a hand toward his night table. Adaryn rushed to poor some water into his parched mouth, and he began to speak through cracked lips.

"My son," he said, his eyes landing on Jai, "you have come back."

"Yes," Jai said, needing to get to the point quickly in case the king's consciousness slipped again. "I have come to take my rightful place as heir to the throne. I will ensure Adaryn's safety and well-being, but there is a war coming, and we need an army." It was a lot to drop on a dying man, but he wanted the king to know he would keep his promise to protect Adaryn at all costs.

"Slow down, son," the king wheezed out, waving a hand for more water.

King Otis had always been on the heavier side, having had access to the finer things in life, so seeing him in such a state made Jai's chest ache. He had to have lost nearly eighty pounds, and his once overstretched skin seemed to lay limp on his bones. His eyes were sunken, and his hair seemed to be falling out. It looked as though he had aged thirty years in a matter of months.

The king flicked his tongue out of his mouth to wet his lips then spoke again. "I am sorry I was not the father you needed, but I am thankful you became the son I always wanted," he started. "I have no doubt you will take care of Adaryn. I only ask that you treat her better than I treated her mother and the late queen. If the last few months have taught me anything, it is that life is short. The riches I have spent my lifetime accumulating mean so little now. A stack of gold isn't going to come to my bedside, saying how much it's going to miss me." He was overtaken by a coughing fit, and when he placed the cream-colored handkerchief back on the bed in front of him, Adaryn and Jai noticed it was speckled in blood.

Adaryn's lip quivered, and she bit it to keep from wailing. Jai grabbed her hand and squeezed it tightly while they listened. He had never felt particularly close to the man who lay before him, but in that moment, he couldn't help but have sympathy for him.

"Did you ever find my great-great-grandfather's lost treasure?" King Otis asked wistfully.

"Sorry to disappoint," Jai replied, "but no, I did not."

"I think you did," the king responded, smiling fondly at Adaryn. "Looking back, I think he created those tunnels to protect his most valued treasures—his family."

Adaryn was openly sobbing now, tears flowing in solemn rivers down her face. "You'll get better," she choked out. "Once the healer figures out what is ailing you, we will fashion a cure."

The king reached up a shaky hand and wiped a tear from her face. "My dear girl, I have accepted this is my time. You must do so, also. Jai will need a partner as fierce as you if he is to win this war that is about to come."

"We don't know how to lead a country," she said, defeated. "We need you."

"Adaryn"—he lifted her chin to meet his eyes once more—"you have been running the country alone for months now."

"I would hardly say that. I—"

The king used a hand to cut her off. "You have done more for Edras Mora in the last few months than I did in all my years on the throne. Trust yourself and trust each other." He looked to Jai. "You are the leaders of this province now."

Adaryn stood and wiped her face, letting his final words fill her with strength. She would keep it together. If not for her dying father, or Jai, but for this kingdom.

Finding her fortitude, she cleared her voice and spoke for them both when she said, "For Edras Mora."

To which the king replied, "For family," and took his last breath.

Fifteen minutes later, Adaryn finally released her father's hand and walked to the wash basin to clean her face.

She was still a bit shaken at his sudden passing, but more so that if it weren't for Jai's unexpected arrival, he would have passed without her being by his side.

She walked over to him one last time and kissed his forehead. It was still surprisingly warm. The sensation unsettled her.

She stood back as Jai walked forward and touched the king's feet over the blanket, pressing his fingertips to his forehead as was accustomed in Vakari. He was preparing to say his last words to his father when the door to the chambers creaked open.

"We are not finished!" Adaryn yelled, assuming it was one of the guards getting nosy.

When the door continued to move, her mouth parted to yell again, but she stopped short when her uncle walked in.

"Now, what have we here?" he asked, looking at Jai hungrily. "The tracker has returned. Our hero," he sneered. The wretch of a man had yet to even notice Adaryn's red-rimmed eyes or the fact that his brother's body was now devoid of life.

"August," Jai said, clenching his fists.

"Why the hostility?" he asked with a saccharine smile, revealing yellowing teeth. "Aren't you happy to see me?"

"No," Jai growled angrily. He took a step toward the man, grinding out every word in the sentence that followed. "I am not happy to see the man who tried to have me murdered."

CHAPTER SEVENTEEN

Hallival, Present Day - Braexmirth

Soren turned in slow motion, ice filling her veins. The shock on her face was evident even below the keen features of her fox mask. Eyes the color of glaciers met hers, and her breath was momentarily stolen from her lungs.

Rook's eyes roamed up and down her body, obviously appreciating her current outfit. He, of course, wore a raven mask.

How fitting.

"What the fuck are you doing here?" Her voice was clipped. She threw out each syllable as though it were one of her daggers, pinning him in place with their pointed edges. She tried to ignore the fact that he was shirtless as she waited for an answer. The knowledge that she still found him unimaginably attractive vexed her to no end.

He cleared his throat to speak, and it was then she realized she had been ogling him for a solid minute. She tore her eyes away, returning them to his icy stare.

The smirk that peeked out from below his mask confirmed that he had noticed her staring. She was thankful he could not see her blush, at least.

"After you left …" He started again, all traces of humor erased from his expression. "I needed to explain."

To his surprise, Soren laughed, but it was not a humorous laugh. Her voice was strained, as though her psyche were moments away from cracking. Her resolve was like a porcelain glass crashing to the floor and breaking into a thousand little pieces.

"What possible explanation could you have to give? You murdered my father. You should be lucky I don't cut you down where you stand." The fury in her eyes showed she would follow through with her threat, though he noticed the hint of sadness behind the golden halos.

"I did not kill him in cold blood," Rook started, but she cut him off.

"It doesn't fucking matter how you did it, Rook!" Her voice was shrill, and she was thankful the music was loud enough to hide their quarreling. "My father is dead because of you. Now get the fuck away from me." She quickly moved past him, slipping through the crowd to one of the dozens of small tunnels and caverns that veered off the main cave.

The panic had returned, and her heart raced as she sucked in rattled breaths. Her mind was in emotional turmoil, and she struggled to rein in her feelings. Though she would never admit it to him, even after everything, something in her chest had still warmed when she'd first realized it was him.

Until the memories had returned.

Her father's body, covered in hundreds of marks. Burying him. The trauma of being hunted and kidnapped. The fear, anxiety, and heartbreak of finding her mother's ring. It was too much. It was all too much.

She clawed at her throat, unable to inhale the amount of oxygen she needed to keep herself going. The edges of her vision began to blur, and she slammed a hand to the wall in a poor attempt to steady herself.

"Hey, are you okay?" Braxten asked, miraculously appearing out of nowhere. He placed the two goblets down and rushed to her side when she didn't answer. "Did that guy say something to you?"

When she didn't respond, he continued, chuckling nervously, "I thought he may be a friend of yours when I saw you talking from across the room and didn't want to interrupt. You looked upset when you walked away, so I followed you."

His rambling had allowed Soren's mind to clear enough to slow her heart rate, and she managed to squeak out, "Ex-boyfriend." Though the label was not exactly correct, it was the only way to explain the situation to an outsider in as few syllables as possible.

"Oh ..." he said, dragging the word out. "Are you okay now?"

"I will be," she replied, eyeing the goblets. "Could I have one of those?"

"Oh, yeah, sure, no problem," he said, his sheepish grin returning.

His smile was infectious, and she couldn't help but return it as the water cooled her.

She finished the contents, and Braxton put both glasses in one hand and held out his arm for her. "Let's get back out there and show him what he's missing."

Now that, I can do, she thought, linking her arm with his, and then they headed back toward the party. It was almost midnight, and she didn't want to miss the surprise that Saoirse had spoken about. Mercifully, Rook was nowhere to be seen. She hoped, for her sanity, he had taken the hint and left.

How is he even here?

She shook her head to remove the thought. She was here to enjoy herself, and she was not going to let that asshole ruin her night.

Braxton handed the goblets to one of the many servants milling about and took Soren's hand, pulling her into the center of the crowd. The energy was palpable as they resumed dancing with Braxton's hands grasped firmly on her hips.

A mane of red hair to her left caught her attention, and she noticed Saoirse and Callan locked in what looked to be a rather sensual embrace. They were facing each other, both of his hands firmly grasping her buttocks as they pressed their bodies against one another's. Her hands were draped around his neck, and it was apparent they would be leaving together.

For a moment, she thought it odd that the king's son would be so outwardly affectionate with the royal staff. She just figured the people of Braexmirth followed different rules than those in Patrivah.

If it were even possible, the energy in the room seemed to expand even more. The entire cave pulsed with the ebb and flow of bodies mingling amongst the sounds of the drums, and Soren followed the gaze of the crowd as they lifted their hands to the sky. It was then Soren noticed the tiny rings of metal wires encircling the opening at the top of the cave. They were attached to small orbs that were affixed to the roof. She watched in awe as one of the servants stood, waving a torch on a platform at the far end of the room.

The music stopped abruptly, and the king was led up the dais with his guards in tow to make an announcement.

"Happy Hallival!" he started boisterously.

The crowd whooped and cheered, falling silent again as he held up a large hand.

Soren leaned back against Braxton's chest as she listened.

"In a few moments, the autumn tide will end, marking the 317th anniversary of the hunt. May the next season bring you all warmth and joy." He paused here, giving a signaling nod to the servant who brought the torch to the wall. Much like the explosive powder back in her mother's temple, Soren watched as the flame lit an invisible path up the wall leading to the dangling orbs.

"I hope you're ready," Saoirse whispered.

"Ready for wha—"

Her question was cut short as the flame reached the metal rings and the orbs began to explode overhead. Each one had been filled with a different colored powder to represent the changing of leaves between seasons.

Saoirse let out a squeal of excitement as everyone re-moved their masks and allowed the powder to cover their bodies. Soren followed suit, placing her mask in the hands of another servant who was making their rounds and let the pow-der wash over her.

The entire crowd was soon a live painting of the autumn tide. Faces and bodies were covered in deep oranges, dark bur-gundies, and golden yellows as the powder fell.

The drumbeat picked up again, and the dancing continued.

Soren turned to Braxton, whose face was now half-red, half-orange and couldn't help but smile. She couldn't imagine how she must look to him in that moment, but the heat behind his eyes showed her it couldn't be all that bad.

He used the pad of his thumb to wipe a small mound of powder from her cheek, and she found herself leaning into the touch. She was not looking to bed him, but when he leaned in to press his lips against hers, she allowed herself to enjoy the sweetness of the moment.

The kiss was short-lived when Braxton's lips were ripped from hers by a fuming Rook.

"Touch her again, and I will break every finger that has graced her skin," he growled. His white hair had been dyed red from the colored granules, and his chest was smattered with lines of dark purple. His rage was palpable, and Braxton couldn't help the surprised look on his face. To his credit, he ignored Rook completely, meeting only Soren's eyes.

"The ex?" he asked.

"Unfortunately," she replied.

"Do you want me to do something about him?" Braxton asked sincerely.

Rook scoffed, "I'd like to see you try."

Soren's heart twinged that this man, who barely knew her, would so readily come to her defense, and not to display male dominance but because he genuinely cared. However, as much as she would have liked to see him land a solid punch to Rook's face, she knew that, ultimately, he would lose. She didn't want to be responsible for him getting hurt.

"It's okay, Brax. I'll take it from here," she said softly.

He looked at her with sad disappointment that their night had been cut short but respected her wishes and walked away without another word.

"What the fuck is wrong with you?" Soren yelled, stomping away before he could answer.

Before she knew it, her anger led her up the stairs and down the winding halls, back to her room. She could hear Enara's faint moans drifting from behind the door next to hers, and she suddenly wished she was deaf.

She made to slam the door shut to announce her presence to her noisy neighbors, but it stopped short when it reverberated off Rook's palm. Soren huffed in annoyance as he overpowered her hold on the handle and pushed into the room.

"Will you just leave me in peace!" she yelled, suddenly exhausted from the night's physical exertion.

"He kissed you," Rook said, his eyes wild, like a cornered animal. He clenched and unclenched his fists as he replayed the image of Soren's lips meeting the other man's.

"And your point being?" Soren asked, flailing her arms in annoyance. "You do not own me, nor my body, and I will do with it as I see fit."

"You. Are. Mine!" he snarled, his nostrils flaring.

"I. Am. My. Own!" she retorted, responding in the same indignant tone.

"So what? You just let anyone lay their hands on you now?" he asked, inches from her face.

She balked at the insinuation and slapped him—hard. Then she wound up for a second hit, but he caught her wrist, bending it painfully and using the backward momentum to push her into the wall beside the door.

She swung out with her non-dominant hand, yet he caught that, too, pinning both arms above her head as she bore holes into his eye sockets through her own.

The silver drink had worn off, but she was still uncomfortably affected by his proximity. The scent of sweet grass and pine needles surrounded her in a heady cloud, and her breath quickened. His eyes darkened as he noticed the effect he was having on her, so she hardened her mask and slammed her protective walls back into place.

"Let go of me, you bastard," she said, struggling against his grip.

"Not until you hear me out," he replied.

He was so calm that Soren wanted to scream in his stupid face, but she stilled her tongue, not wanting to alert Baz and Enara to her current predicament.

"You killed my father, called me a whore, and now you want me to *hear you out?*" she asked incredulously. "Do you hear how idiotic you sound?"

He deserved that. Seeing her with the other man had brought out the beast in him.

He pressed his eyes shut, pushing away the anger, and then reopened them, willing Soren to see the sincerity behind the wall of ice.

"I am sorry for what I said. He had his hands on you all evening, and when he kissed you, I snapped."

She stared at him, open-mouthed at his admission, before spitting out, "So that gives you the excuse to label me a whore?" Her brows bunched together angrily before she added, "I wonder what Meena and Evelyn would say if they heard that."

As the shock of her words hit him, his grip on her wrist loosened enough for her to pull them from his grasp and shove him away.

"Get the fuck out," she reiterated, fuming.

"It was a mercy kill," he blurted out.

"I don't believe you!" she cried.

"Then don't, but it is the truth."

She wanted so badly to scream at him, to hit him in his stupidly attractive face until her fists came back bloody. As she looked at him, however, she felt nothing more than pity, which made her heart ache.

Her blood cooled, and she dared to ask, "What happened?"

Rook explained that her father had pre-emptively come to see him prior to hiding the Oculus. Tarak had been looking for Adriel when he stumbled upon the manor. He had begged Rook to show Soren mercy if he failed his mission. He had given him the ring to prove that Soren could trust him, which had coincidentally done the exact opposite.

"Corvus arranged the attack," he continued. "Apparently, one of the kestrels had overhead my exchange with your father and reported back to him. He sent the whole unkindness after him. He didn't stand a chance."

Soren's throat collapsed in on itself at the last sentence.

"I'm sorry. If the details are too much, I can stop," he offered.

She shook her head. She wanted to hear everything. She needed to.

"I found him not far from Vreburn, his pulse so weak that most would have assumed him already dead. Unfortunately, he had not been that lucky. He must have laid there for hours, his life slowly leaking out of him from the infected wounds the kestrels had inflicted."

Soren wiped the tears that had trailed down her cheeks, and Rook wanted so badly to embrace her but resisted.

"His eyes were swollen, but he managed to say a few words as I approached. He said to protect you, that you spent your whole life in a cage of your own making. He loved you very much. He asked me to end it for him. I refused at first, but he used the last of his strength to place his hunting knife in my hand."

Soren pressed her eyes together, knowing what was coming next.

"I refused the knife, not wanting to create a murder investigation, and offered him an alternative. I carry a small vial of hellebore root on me at all times. It's tasteless, dissolves instantly, and kills the host the second it enters the bloodstream. It's painless and untraceable. My father forced me to keep it on hand in case he needed me to assassinate anyone. Few people know of its existence, and I want you to know he went quickly."

As he had spoken, Soren had slowly made her way across the room and sat in silence on the bed. It was so much information to take in at one time, and the tears fell freely as her mind went into a tailspin. *Dad is dead. Rook killed him. No, Corvus gave the order. But he poisoned him. He was showing him mercy.*

Noticing the signs of an impending panic attack, he moved toward her slowly.

She surprised him by asking, "If all this is true, then how is it you did not know my name?"

"He never spoke your true name to me. He only used various terms of endearment."

"Is that why you call me little bird?" she asked.

"Yes," he replied, daring to wipe the tears from her cheeks. "Because he wanted you to fly."

CHAPTER
EIGHTEEN

Enara detangled her limbs from Baztien's and stretched her tired muscles. Last night had been something else. Soren would have blamed it on the mysterious silver liquid, but Enara would have had her way with Baz regardless of the aphrodisiac. Her only regret was that they hadn't made it until midnight to witness the surprise that Saoirse had kept saying they *had* to see.

She couldn't help herself. After a few hours of being pressed against Baz's hard muscles, her need to take him to bed had overpowered all rational thought. They had barely shut the door behind them before Enara was throwing off her mask, untying the knot from his waist, and taking him into her mouth. The white fabric of his outfit still lay in a heap by the door.

She reminisced about how his hips had shuddered and bucked as she'd swallowed the length of him. His hands tangled in her hair as she appreciated every inch of his olive skin.

It had only been a few moments before he'd been begging her to stop through clenched teeth.

"If you keep going, I won't have time to return the favor."

Her smile was hungry as she stood to lift his mask off his face and kissed him. "Well, we can't have that, can we?" she whispered in a sultry voice against his lips.

"My turn," he growled as he lifted her up in one fell swoop and dropped her in front of the blazing fireplace. They had forgotten to light their oil lantern before the party, and he wanted to see her.

Without a word, he began untying the few knots that held the fabric of her outfit together and tossed the material aside. He beckoned for her to sit on the lounge that faced the fireplace, and she complied.

Enara was not shy about her body, apart from the scars on her back, and so she leaned against the cushions, opening her legs for him. His mouth went dry, and he swallowed thickly as he kneeled before her.

He wasted no time, diving into the apex of her thighs like a man starved. He devoured her as she rolled her hips against his mouth. She made no effort to stifle her moans, and the sound made him even more ravenous. It wasn't until her legs were shaking and he had lapped up the rest of her juices that he gave her what she really wanted.

He lifted her into his arms and, with her legs wrapped firmly around his waist, eased himself into her. Once he was fully seated, he adjusted his grip on the soft flesh of her ass and began sliding in and out, slowly picking up the pace.

His breathing became ragged, and Enara's moans turned to screams of pleasure as he pounded into her. She had a vice grip around his neck, leaning her head back in ecstasy, her long brown hair falling in waves behind her.

The firelight danced off her skin as the warmth from the flames heated them. In that moment, he thought he had never seen anything more beautiful.

He could feel that she was about to climax by the way she tightened around him, and he turned, bringing her mouth to his and pressing her back against the stone wall. He moved with ferocious intent as their mouths clashed.

"Baz, don't stop," she whispered as her orgasm crested.

"Never," he replied, resuming the amorous kiss.

She cried out as she came around him, her nails digging into his shoulder blades as one wave of pleasure after another rolled over her. That pushed him over the edge, and he nuzzled into her neck as he spilled inside of her, pulsing each time her muscles clenched.

They both sighed heavily, and Enara brushed away the hair that was plastered to Baz's forehead before kissing the tip of his nose. "I love you."

"I love you, too."

It was the best sex of her life, and heat pooled low in her belly as she glanced over at the lounge. Their room was one of the fancier ones in the castle. She would have to thank the king later for his generosity.

She tightened the strings on her navy leather vest before slipping on her boots. Then she gave the still-snoring Baz a quick kiss on the temple before exiting their quarters. She had heard Soren speaking with a man in her room last night and wanted to investigate.

She closed their door and shuffled the few steps to Soren's, hesitating at the threshold. She debated knocking but decided to say fuck it and walked on in.

"Rise and shine, bitch!" she yelled loudly, smiling at her quip. Her grin quickly faded, however, when her eyes landed on the bed.

A surprised Soren sat up, rubbing her eyes. "What the fuck, Enara? Are you trying to give me a heart attack?"

But Enara was too busy staring down the white-haired man in Soren's bed.

She couldn't control the rage that flowed through her veins. Rook had shattered Soren's heart into a million pieces. This was the monster who had killed the only person in her life who had deserved the title of *father*.

"How dare you come here!" Enara's nostrils flared, and she saw red as she stalked toward him.

Soren, realizing her friend's intent, shot up from the bed to stand between them. "Enara, stop!" she demanded, holding up her hands. "Let me explain."

Enara flicked her eyes to Soren then returned them to the enemy sitting nonchalantly on the edge of her mattress. "How is he even here, Soren? How could you let him into your bed after everything?" Her voice was balanced on a cliff's edge, walking a tightrope on the verge of snapping.

"If you used your eyes, you would see that we are fully dressed," Soren said, gesturing to the white outfit she had obviously slept in.

Enara scoffed. "Like that would stop you!"

Enara regretted the words as soon as they flew out of her mouth and immediately began apologizing, but Soren held up a hand to stop her.

"You're not the first person to insinuate that in the last twenty-four hours," she said, pointedly looking in Rook's direction.

To Enara's surprise, he looked genuinely saddened, but that didn't make her want to kill him any less.

How dare he call my best friend a whore!

"You asshole, I should chop off your dick for saying that to her."

The amused grin he responded with only infuriated her more.

"Enara, stop. As entertaining as that would be to watch, we don't have time for this. The king will send for us soon, and I don't think he would take kindly to you committing attempted murder under his roof."

"Fine," she grumbled, smoothing out her hair. "But I don't trust him, and neither should you."

Soren gave her a serious look. "I don't, but we may need him. He knows our enemy better than any of us, and we would be stupid not to use that knowledge."

"Fine," she said again, stalking toward the door. "But we're keeping him on a short leash. And Rook"—Enara turned her attention directly on him—"if you hurt her again, I will flay the skin from your body piece by piece and feed it to the wolf dogs."

Rook chuckled to himself as she slammed the door behind her. "Your friend has quite the way with words."

Soren turned and smacked him hard on his bare shoulder. "You didn't need to go and rile her up. If you haven't forgotten, you're the one who needs to earn our trust, not the other way around."

She sighed heavily and rubbed her hands down her tired face. She was still exhausted from all the revelations from last night and had fallen asleep against Rook's shoulder. Sometime in the night, he had lifted her fully onto the bed and covered her in the blanket. He had intended to sleep in the small reading chair by the hearth but, in her sleeping, drunk state, she had beckoned him to lay with her. She vaguely remembered him crawling in beside her, the heat of his skin pressing into her back, and him wrapping his arms around her waist.

"You're going to hate me in the morning, little bird," he'd whispered against the nape of her neck.

"I already do," she'd replied and pulled him closer.

It had been the first time a man had ever stayed in her bed without sex being involved. Even so, the men she had bedded only stayed the night when they were too liquored to make it home safely. She hadn't wanted to give anyone false hope that they would share breakfast in the morning, but she also hadn't wanted to be responsible for someone's son getting lost in the woods and eaten by some wild animal.

Even back at the manor, Rook had always slipped out before she'd woken, seeming to understand the invisible boundaries of their "relationship." But she had to admit that, for the first time in a long time, a man other than her father had made her feel safe.

She clasped her mother's ring that still hung on the chain around her neck. She hadn't taken it off since that day back in Thorncrest. It was a miracle she hadn't lost it in the lake.

"Soren?" Saoirse called from the door. "Soren, are you awake?"

Before she could get to the door, Saoirse turned the handle and walked on in, her eyebrows shooting up to her hairline when she noticed Rook, who was still perched at the end of the bed.

"Does nobody understand doorway etiquette in this province?" he asked, rolling his eyes.

"Sorry, I didn't realize you had company," Saoirse said, addressing Soren.

"It's fine. What did you need?"

"The king has sent for you."

"Okay, we just need to change, and we will be right down."

Saoirse nodded and gave her a quick hug before exiting the room. "Don't forget to say goodbye before you head back to Edras Mora."

"I won't," Soren replied then turned back to face the man who had her in constant emotional turmoil. "You should go."

"And I was so hoping I could stay and watch the show," he said, his eyes shining.

Soren rolled her eyes. She knew he was kidding, but it did seem kind of silly to kick him out when he had literally seen every inch of her naked body.

He hopped off the bed and stood toe-to-toe with her, heat radiating off his skin as he looked her up and down.

"What are you doing?" she asked breathlessly.

"Saving a mental image. You look delectable, and I find myself wishing last night would have gone differently."

"If you think last night means you're getting anywhere close to this again," she said, gesturing to her lady bits, "think again."

"We'll see, little bird," he replied, booping her on the nose before exiting the room, leaving her blinking like a doe in the torchlight. "Meet me in the stables when you're done," he called back to her.

"I hate you!" she yelled after him.

"I know!" he yelled back from somewhere down the hall, and she couldn't help the smile that graced her lips.

THE TRIO STOOD NERVOUSLY BEFORE THE KING, WONDERING what news he had for them regarding Edras Mora. The distractions from the previous evening had now subsided, and their chests filled with worry for their tracker friend and his lover.

"Come. Sit. Eat," King Elias commanded, gesturing to the empty chairs that surrounded the large gray table. It was made of carved stone that speckled as though stars had been trapped within the dark rock.

"Thank you, Your Majesty," they replied in unison. They ate in a rush, wanting to get a move on as early as possible and fidgeted with the remnants of their breakfast as the king wiped stray toasted wheat breadcrumbs from his beard.

"So, back to business," he said, placing his elbows on the table after the servants had removed his plate and clasped his hands together.

"Yes," Soren said. "You mentioned something happened to the King of Patrivah. We were hoping you could share with us whatever details you may have."

"You seem like wonderful folk, but there is only so much I can reveal to commoners," he replied. "Protocols and such."

"That is why we brought this," Baz said, handing the King Jai's heritage documents, still sealed from the late King Otis.

King Elias broke the seal and read the contents, stroking his beard thoughtfully. His large brows furrowed, and the group held their breaths, unsure of what he would say.

"I have corresponded with King Otis many times during my reign in an effort to heal what our grandfathers damaged all those years ago, and I recognize this to be his writing and royal seal. But one detail is of concern to me."

"And that is …?" Enara asked, her mouth dry with worry.

"He names Jaideep Ashwood as the true heir of Patrivah, but unless there was some confusion with my informants, it also matches the name of the man arrested for his murder."

CHAPTER
NINETEEN

The Previous Day – Edras Mora

August continued to stare at Jai, a lecherous grin revealing yellowing teeth. His eyes were the color of watered-down mud, and his shoulder-length brown hair hung in greasy tendrils around his face.

"After all this time, the prodigal son finally returns," he said, his nasally voice grating on Jai's nerves.

"So this, the whole time, you knew," Jai said. It was not a question but a statement. "You knew who I was when you ordered that archer to take me out," he growled.

Adaryn, who had thought the injury was caused by their escape attempt in Idatia, slapped her hand to her mouth in shock. "You. Did. What?" she asked, pinning the haggard man with narrowed eyes. They normally held the innocence of a fawn, but at the thought of her uncle intentionally hurting Jai, they filled with barely contained fury.

"Yes, why don't you tell her how you paid off an assassin to take out your own nephew?" Jai continued, coming to her side.

"I am quite offended that you would insinuate such a thing. Especially considering, since our sweet Princess Adaryn over here is unwed, I will be labeled steward, which makes you a traitor to the crown."

Adaryn had heard enough. She shook the rafters when she yelled, "Guards!"

The two guards stationed outside the king's quarters came rushing in, swords raised, expecting the worst.

Adaryn was about to have August arrested, but he spoke first.

"Arrest this man," he said, pointing to Jai.

The tracker scoffed. "On what grounds?"

His uncle's lips curled, as if hearing the punchline to a joke that only he understood. "For illegal tracking ventures and the assassination of the king."

"He lies!" Adaryn screamed in Jai's defense, unable to control her temper.

"The poor girl is distraught. He is her lover, you see. She has been seeing him behind the duke's back and is no doubt an accomplice to her father's murder."

"You're insane!" she spat as the guards moved to make their arrests. "He tried to kill Jai during my kidnapping. He was probably the one who had me kidnapped in the first place," she said as they pinned her and Jai's arms behind their backs.

"We will find a way out of this, Addy. Save your fight for later," Jai said softly. He could have easily taken out the guards and cut down August himself, but what would that get them? It would leave Patrivah in political duress, and they would live a life on the run.

He turned his gaze to August and, to his uncle's surprise, he smiled. "Maybe not tomorrow, or the next day," he said, his voice eerily calm, "but you will receive everything you have ever deserved. I can only hope I am around to see it."

And with that, they were removed from the room, stealing final glances at their late king, knowing they would not lay eyes on him again.

FRUSTRATED, JAI SLAMMED HIS FISTS AGAINST THE STONE WALL OF his cell until his knuckles bled. Finally, after unleashing all his anger toward his uncle on the stone, he sat down next to Adaryn in the ten-by-ten-foot cell.

"I wish you wouldn't have done that. Now look at you," she said, using a strip of fabric torn from the hem of her dress to wrap his injured hands.

"We need to get out of here," he said through gritted teeth.

"Everett will come; you know he will."

Jai's plan had solely depended on the trust he had built with his childhood friend, and he was frustrated that Everett had yet to come to them.

"Well, you look like shit."

The couple turned to see Everett and Erick standing next to the cell, holding a torch.

"About time you showed up," Jai said, grinning. It had been a day and a half since they had been tossed into the dank cell with nothing but some hardened bread and water to satiate themselves. The chamber pot in the corner had been a whole other ordeal.

"We had to wait until everything settled down a bit. The entire castle is in an uproar, as you can imagine."

Jai nodded. "I assumed as much. Now get us out of here."

"I can't." Everett's words were almost a whisper. "Your uncle made strict orders that he be the only person with access to the keys to your cell until you meet the noose."

"Why has no one come to tell us we have been sentenced to death?" Adaryn asked, horrified.

"Your uncle seems to think you should not be provided such niceties," Duke Erick answered. "He has turned our wedding day into a public execution. He plans to hang you both in the main market square to make an example of you."

"How do you know all of this?" Adaryn asked.

"He seems to think I would be angry with you for committing adultery before our nuptials," he said with a smile.

"So, where does that leave us?" Jai asked, pacing the cell.

"I have a plan, but it is risky," Erick said. "The execution is set for three past noon, and they have decided to continue with the grand reception as a sort of celebration in the king's honor."

"Of course he did," Adaryn scoffed. "Because why would anyone want a moment to mourn their king before going to a royal party?" She had been wringing her hands so hard that the knuckles had turned white.

"Mrs. Ferndale also received correspondence from Braexmirth that your friends are due to arrive sometime before lunch tomorrow. She had the letter burned, wanting to keep your uncle from knowing you have backup coming."

"What about the letters of heritage? Do they mean nothing?"

Everett pressed his lips together, wishing he had better news. "Your uncle is the only one who can currently confirm or deny their legitimacy, and he is saying you had them crafted so that you would be named king upon the death of your father. He is saying it was all an elaborate plan."

Jai groaned loudly, rubbing his hands down his face then grasping the bars of the cell. "I'm going to kill him!"

"And rightfully so, brother," Everett replied. "But not before we get you out of here first."

Jai's eyes grew wide as Everett held up a baggy of questionable powder. "Is that what I think it is?"

"The cleanest batch you've ever seen."

Jai wiped the smile off his face before admonishing his friend. "I thought you quit when I stopped drinking."

"Yeah, well, I had to find some way to pass the time after you left."

"Well, thank the Maker for your lack of self-control." And just like that, their plan was set in motion.

Braexmirth - The Following Morning

Soren, Baz, and Enara were still shaken from their meeting with the king. They had struggled to hide their concern for their friend, not wanting to be seen as accomplices. News of Jai's arrest had hit them all hard, and they could feel their hope dwindling.

Their concern for saving Entheas was multiplied ten-fold when a short, stout man came huffing and puffing to interrupt their breakfast with terrible news. Their hometown of Vreburn had been burned to the ground, and three other attacks had occurred across the provinces. Dhamtra had been leveled to nothing but a pile of rubble and sand, and the Esinian Isles had been ravaged by black beasts that no one could seem to describe.

"I worry, sir, that we may be next," the informant said through a fit of coughs. "The attacks seem to be moving west. It won't take long for the scourge to reach us once they enter Estelar."

"I see," was the king's surprisingly simple response. "Thank you, Odhran, I will handle it from here. I recommend you stay with your family for the time being."

The informant nodded and said, "Yes, sir. Thank you, sir," before scurrying off.

The whole table had fallen into an uncomfortable silence as they waited to hear what the king had to say.

He eyed them one by one before he spoke. "Why do I have a feeling these attacks have something to do with you showing up on my doorstep?"

"Well," Baz started, "there is no use beating around the bush now." He stood, crossing his left fist over his chest and kneeling before the king. "I know I am a commoner to you, born to the country of one of your enemies, but there is true evil coming that does not care where we are born. They seek to destroy us all, and we have come to ask for your help."

With impending war, the time for secrets was over, so the trio launched into a recap of everything they had experienced since the death of Soren's father then held their breaths as the king seemed to contemplate their story.

By some miracle of the Maker, he sensed the truth behind their eyes and placed a large hand on Baz's shoulder. "You are brave, son, just like your grandfather. Where you hail from is of no consequence to me. If our world is at stake, you can count on my soldiers to fight with you as your grandfather did for his people all those years ago. I'll have Callan ready your horses. He will accompany you, along with Ikei and Ori. They are three of my finest soldiers, and you may need their help to free the new King of Patrivah."

"Who will stay to protect you?" Soren asked, not wanting to leave the King of Braexmirth at a disadvantage.

He gave her a sly grin and responded, "My dear girl, if I can survive my wife, I can survive this."

The trio laughed at his candor.

"My forges will rage once more. Give my metal smiths the week then return with your army. If we are going to face gods and monsters, we will do it with the strongest of armors and the sharpest of blades." With that final statement, he waved them off, his twin guards trailing close behind.

They swiftly grabbed their belongings from their rooms and, along with Callan, the twins, and Saoirse, who refused to be left behind, they headed for the stables at the base of the mountain.

Their chattering stopped short as they entered the building.

"Well, this is a welcome party I wasn't quite expecting," Rook said, his blue eyes glinting.

Callan went to unsheathe his sword, but Soren stepped between them, halting the soldier's attack.

"It's okay," she said and, to Rook's surprise, followed it up with, "He's with us."

"THINK SHE WILL EVER STOP STARING DAGGERS INTO THE BACK OF my head?" Rook asked as they clopped along down the dirt road toward the ferry.

Over the course of the previous day's travel, Enara had threatened Rook's life no less than eight times, and Soren had to hold Baz back from punching him out twice. She couldn't blame her friends for their reaction to him. She was still debating on smothering him in his sleep herself.

"Well, if you stopped antagonizing Baztien, she might hate you a little less," Soren said with a pointed look.

Rook gave her that boyish smirk that filled her mind with frustration and other places with heat. "It's not my fault the guy is a walking joke."

The comment made Soren bristle. "At least he has a sense of humor, unlike someone I know."

"If I recall, I made a few well-placed one-liners back at the manor."

Soren snorted. "Oh, please, you have the humorous capacity of a chamber pot."

"Did you just make me the butt of a joke?" Rook responded, the corners of his lips curling up into a smile that Soren couldn't resist returning.

"Okay, fine, that was mildly funny."

They rode on in companionable silence as Saoirse chatted animatedly with Callan.

Ori and Ikei had surprised everyone by being the most loquacious of the bunch. Throughout the morning, they had regaled the group with the story of how they had ended up in the king's care. The beginning of their tale was hazy due to the fact that they had only been five when the events had started. They had a hard time remembering details of their parents, though they mentioned they had a sister who was two years their senior.

"They all think we are crazy," Ikei said.

"The kids in Patrivah are another thing," Ori continued. "They are not laughing now, though." He grinned at his brother.

They had apparently excelled so highly in their combat training that they had been sent straight to the king's guard after graduating, and then guarded the king himself after the previous men had aged out.

They had not been demoted, per say, but put into a position better suited for their skills. They had become trainers and teachers for the new recruits to the Patrovian army.

Loyal to the king and with a skill level to match their intellect, Ikei and Ori went on about growing up in the castle with Callan. They seemed forever grateful that the king-to-be was so accepting of his new adoptive siblings.

"My mother was no longer able to bear children after having me, so I was happy to gain two new brothers," he explained.

Saoirse, it seemed, had joined the Olecastor boys six years prior when she'd joined the castle staff as a chambermaid, but her positive attitude and work ethic had gotten her promoted to head of house within two years. She had become fast friends with all three of the boys, but Callan was the one lucky enough to have gained her affections.

"I still think I could have you, if I didn't feel so bad for my brother's lack of courting skills," Ikei said, leaning forward on his horse to poke Callan with his staff.

"You wish," he replied, turning swiftly, causing Ikei to lose balance and fall off his horse.

"Are you just going to stand there?" Ikei asked, looking at his brother through the dreads that were blocking his view from the ground.

"No, I think you got this," Ori replied, trotting onward.

Something inside Soren warmed as she looked at them. They reminded her of her friendship with Baz and Enara and, in some aspects, even Jai. Each its own group of misfits brought together by sheer chance and ended up being closer than any blooded family.

Her heart sank when her gaze fell back on Rook. Even with the explanation of what had happened to her father and the feelings she had been trying to ignore, she was still having a hard time trusting him. She worried that if they ever made it through all this alive, whatever their future held, it would not be this. It would always be them and him. She knew that it would never work, because if she had to choose between her friends and the man who stood before her, she knew what her answer would be. She would rip her own heart out and bury it in the sand before giving up on her family.

"What's wrong, little bird?" Rook asked, his sapphire eyes searching hers.

"Nothing," she replied.

He gave her a look that said he knew better, but he did not ask again.

ENARA HUFFED OUT ANOTHER BREATH AS HER AND BAZTIEN trudged along behind the rest of the group. She preferred to have everyone in her line of sight, *especially* Rook.

What does she see in him? she thought angrily.

"You know, I can practically see steam coming out of your ears," Baz chirped.

"I want to trust her, Baz—you know I do—but I think she has a blind spot when it comes to him. I'm worried about her."

"And that's okay," he said, reaching a hand across the space between them.

She reached back, giving it a squeeze before returning her grip on her reins.

"You're allowed to worry," Baz continued. "But you also have to let her make her own mistakes."

"But if she makes a mistake now, it affects all of us," she said in a resigned tone.

"Don't forget that I have eyes, too. If there is anything, we will figure it out together, okay?"

She gave him a soft smile and nodded. "Okay."

"We should probably also discuss what Rook said about Vreburn," Baz prompted, brushing his hand through his hair nervously. It wasn't a topic he wanted to bring up, but they were getting close to the provincial crossing, and he wanted to know Enara's mindset going into the next stage of their journey.

She looked off into the distance for a moment to gather her thoughts. Rook had informed them of the fires that had ravaged their homes and that there had been few survivors. Baz thanked the Maker that his mothers were okay and that they had received his most recent letter, but Laraline and Alondra had also shared that the entire Montgrove clan, apart from her mother, had perished. Mrs. Montgrove had escaped their house with a broken arm and a few other scrapes and bruises, but Altair and Enara's brothers, Rayden and Hawk, had been at the tavern. The Crow's Nest had not had a single survivor.

Baz waited patiently for Enara to mull over her thoughts and was surprised when she said, "I don't feel anything."

This concerned him, as he had assumed she would be relieved to know her abuser was no longer living.

"I just mean, what difference does it make?" She fiddled with her reins as she fought to voice her feelings. "I thought I would feel a weight off my shoulders, but I don't think I realized he already couldn't hurt me anymore. The power he had over me was lost years ago when I moved in with Soren. The tether that bound us had already been cut."

She released her breath slowly as she went on. "I don't feel much for my brothers because we both know they would have ended up just like him. I pity my mother, and I don't know how I will approach her if I see her again, but I wish her well. Will I be thankful that I will not have to see my father's face again if we make it home? Yes. I am happy for that, I suppose, but Altair has been dead to me for a long time." She shrugged. "At least now I don't have to attend the funeral."

"I'm proud of you, you know," Baz said.

"Why?"

"Because you are an unstoppable force, Miss Montgrove," he replied seriously. "You have lived a life of abuse and mistreatment from those who should have protected you the most. Every time he beat you down, you came back stronger and proved them all wrong by never giving up. You are beautiful inside and out. You are who I strive to be—unbreakable, unyielding, a force stronger than the sea. You are the hero of your own story, and now you are also the hero of mine."

Enara brushed the tears from her cheeks and stifled a sob. "I love you," she whispered.

"I love you, too."

CHAPTER
TWENTY

Edras Mora was in an uproar when they entered the city. Well-dressed townsfolk hungry for blood stood in the town center, awaiting Jai's execution. They formed a tight semi-circle around the wooden platform that butted up against the inner city's wall. An executioner stood next to one of the wooden posts in a black tunic, dark brown trousers, and leather boots. He was using a knife to pick at his teeth and was ignoring the many shouts from the townsfolk.

It was close to three past noon, and the group had but minutes to come up with a plan to save Jai from the hangman's noose.

Soren gulped back the lump in her throat as she looked to the perfectly knotted section of rope that hung limply from the crossbar, knowing her friend would soon be dangling below.

She had never witnessed an execution. They had been outlawed in Draestel centuries ago for their inhumane nature. She was disgusted as she listened to the crowd.

"How long do you reckon he lasts?"

"He's not a large fellow; I'd give him a few minutes at least before his legs stop kicking."

"I'd wager three and a half," a robust woman chimed in.

"I'll take that bet," another man holding up a handful of bronze said.

"You're on," the woman replied, smiling.

Soren grimaced. *These people have no humility.*

"They should be disgusted with themselves," Enara commented, falling into step with her as they pushed closer to the front of the crowd.

"Yeah, well, the rich get bored, I guess. Let's just try to stop the show before we find out which of them is right."

Enara nodded as she squeezed her way through another handful of people.

The group had agreed it would be best if the men stationed themselves at the perimeter of the crowd, using their height to give them a better vantage point. Meanwhile, Saoirse was strategically placed in the center of the crowd, waiting for the opportune moment to provide a distraction. But Rook, being the lone wolf, had decided to scale one of the sidewalls to perch on the roof of a fabric shop. Soren had reluctantly given him her bow as a backup plan to split the rope in case their efforts were unsuccessful.

As Enara and Soren reached the front of the throng, the crowd began to fall silent. They stopped just short of the raised platform as a nobleman dressed in navy and gold addressed the crowd.

"Great people of Patrivah, I want to thank you for your attendance this afternoon. Our late king would be proud that all of you showed up in his honor to witness the execution of his murderer."

The entire crowd bellowed, "King Otis, may he rest in peace," before the man continued.

"I am saddened to inform you that Jaideep Ashwood and his accomplice, Princess Adaryn of the House of Drekar, have decided to follow up their act of treason with cowardice. Rather than face all of you, they took their own lives sometime in the night."

The bloodthirsty crowd shouted their disappointments that all bets were off. The citizens' unrest rang out all across the square.

"We want justice!"

"We came to see someone hang!"

"Justice for the king!"

The man raised his liver-spotted hands to hush the crowd. "I know many of you feel slighted by their actions, so in an attempt to placate you, I have brought the traitors' bodies with me."

The crowd fell silent once more, their hunger temporarily satiated by the man's words.

"I think that is the uncle Jai spoke about," Enara whispered. "The one who had him attacked."

"It would make sense," Soren replied. "The king only had one brother, and without Adaryn to fill her role as queen, he would be made steward."

"How do you know so much about court politics?" Enara asked.

"Books."

Their conversation was halted when the palace guards walked forth, carrying two limp bodies. Enara's and Soren's mouths gaped open in horror, as there was no mistaking that mop of dark hair.

The first body belonged to Jai. Enara could even make out the turquoise ring on his finger, which could only mean that the long-legged woman dangling in the guard's arms next to him was none other than Princess Adaryn.

There was no mistaking the way their bodies thumped heavily as they were carried up and dropped onto the floor of the platform. The girls flinched as they watched their friend get dragged across the wood, a splinter catching on Jai's embroidered jacket. The guard pulled harder, and the fabric gave with a loud tear. They propped Jai and Adaryn back-to-back, the center post sandwiched between them.

Their heads lolled forward, and their hair covered their faces. But, for a moment, it almost looked to Soren as if Jai were smiling. She brushed it off as a trick of the light. She knew what a dead body looked like—images of her father's plagued her mind on a daily basis. In that moment, she knew her friend was dead.

She bit her lip to hold back the tears that welled in her eyes as the steward spoke once more.

"To pay homage to our king, we will leave the bodies of his betrayers in the square as a reminder of what happens when you forsake the crown. In this way, we will honor my brother and cleanse our lands of this treasonous blight. Thank you again for your attendance today. I hope that, as steward, I can continue to make Patrivah as bountiful as ever."

"Here, here!" someone jeered.

"Maker rest the king!" another chimed in.

Soon, the whole crowd was yelling, "Maker rest the king!" and the steward waved his goodbyes, making to return to the safety of his castle.

The crowd had started to disperse just as an explosion rang out west of the gate. A large cloud of black smoke billowed into the sky, turning the once-white clouds a nasty shade of gray. People started screaming and running in all directions, pushing past each other in search of safety. Soren and Enara jumped up onto the platform that was now free of guards to get a better view.

The twins, Baz, and Callan were moving slowly in their direction but making little headway against the current of bodies attempting to leave the square. Soren deflated when she noticed Rook was no longer at his post above the fabric shop. *Fucking coward.*

A voice from the crowd caught her attention as Saoirse screamed for help. She was being pulled back toward the east entrance by a wall of people who were unwilling to let her pass.

Enara was about to jump down to assist her, but she spotted Callan switching directions, no doubt having heard his lover's cries for help. She also noticed that Rook was nowhere to be seen and scowled before turning back to Soren.

"What now?" she yelled over the noise.

Another explosion rang out from the opposite side, which caused the crowd's panic to rise even higher.

Somewhere to her left, a child was screaming, and Enara watched, heart-stricken, as the mother shielded her son from the swarm of bodies that were now pushing them the other way.

She turned again to Soren, who had yet to answer her, but she was no longer at her side. Enara whipped her head around to find her kneeling by Jai's and Adaryn's bodies, and her stomach twisted painfully at the sight. She joined Soren, placing a comforting hand on her shoulder, and closed her eyes, tears starting to form.

Jai had been a loyal friend, and she felt partly responsible for his death, and Adaryn had been unfortunate enough to be caught in the crossfire.

"Enara," Soren said, grabbing her attention, "I don't think they're dead."

"What?" she asked, wiping away her tears to get a better look.

Soren had brushed Jai's hair out of his eyes and tilted his head back to reveal that his mouth was set in a wide grin. Normally, the sight would have been unsettling, but in this case, she couldn't have been more relieved.

"Is he—"

"Drugged?" she finished for her. "I think so."

"That stuff they were smoking in Murkwall?"

"Looks like it," Soren said, feeling for a pulse to confirm her suspicions. She found nothing in his wrist, so she moved to check the left side of his neck. She remembered from a medical text that the left side of the carotid held the strongest pulse. She nearly jumped for joy when she felt the minuscule throb of blood pumping against her fingertips.

"He's paralyzed, but he's alive," she confirmed before rushing around the post to check on Adaryn. "She's good, too," Soren said just as the twins and Baz hopped onto the platform. Callan had reached Saoirse and was following close behind. She was disheartened to see that there was still no sign of Rook.

Two more explosions came from the north and south ends of the square, which meant the attack was now coming from all sides.

"We have to get their bodies out of here!" Soren yelled.

The rest of the group looked at her in confusion, and she rolled her eyes.

"They are still alive. I don't have time to explain. Now help me!" she ordered as she untied Jai and Adaryn from the post.

Baz, who knew better than to question Soren when her mind was set on something, grabbed Jai's body and threw him over his shoulder. Callan grabbed Adaryn, and the twins were pulling everyone else's weapons out of the two large bags they had been carrying. They quickly equipped themselves with matching duel tonfa knives that ran the length of their forearms.

Enara hurriedly attached Baz's sword to his belt and stole a swift kiss over his free shoulder. "Hey," she said.

"Hey back," he replied, and then they started heading east, toward the castle.

Just short of the gate, they were stopped by Everett.

"Thank the Maker," he said, huffing in a breath.

"We need to get them somewhere safe," Soren said, adjusting the thigh strap that housed her new set of daggers. She had refused to give Rook her father's bow without some form of collateral.

Everett swallowed thickly and nodded. "I know a place. Come on." He took off in the other direction.

"I thought we were going to hide him in the castle!" Enara called after him.

"We can't," he called back. "The steward has the whole place on lockdown. No one is allowed in. I had already left to come check on Jai, so I'm stuck out here, too."

They followed him around a couple of side streets until they hit a section that Enara and Baz recognized. They pushed through the iron gate and ran through the tombstones to the mausoleum. The group barely fit into the small space where everyone took a moment to catch their breaths.

When Baz could speak again, he chuckled and looked at Enara. "No one bothers the dead."

"We have to keep moving," Soren urged, ignoring their obvious inside joke. "Vreburn was burned to the ground in a matter of hours—we are not safe here."

"I agree with Soren," Callan said, his large hand entwined with Saoirse. "Besides, we have no food or water here." The group had finished the last of their sustenance on the road and had planned to restock after their attempt at heroics.

As if in agreement, Jai groaned from the corner of the room where he was propped up.

Baz scooted over and gave him a slap on the back. "Welcome back to the world of the living, man."

Jai let out a dry cough. "Thanks, brother." As if remembering what had happened, he stiffened and turned to Adaryn, his eyes wide with fear. "Is she ...?" he asked, his voice a low whisper.

"Don't worry," Soren said. "She's alive. If you took the same dose, hers may take a little longer to wear off since you weigh more than she does."

"Thank the Maker," he breathed and ran a hand through his unruly hair. "Now, does anyone want to explain to me why we are in the crypt?"

"There was an attack," Saoirse said.

"Not to be rude," Jai replied, "but who are you?"

"Oh." She giggled. "Sorry, I am Saoirse, and this is—"

"I am Callan McKenna, Son of Elias McKenna, King of Braexmirth," he said, grabbing Jai's forearm in greeting. "And these are the strongest members of our guard, Ori and Ikei."

The twins nodded in greeting, keeping their knives firmly grasped along the metal cuffs that protected their dark skin from their blades' wrath.

"They came to help us," Baz said as a way of explanation. "The king accepted your lineage papers after hearing our story. He is making weapons and armor as we speak."

"So, now we just need an army?" Jai asked, the mischievous glint returning to his dark eyes.

Baz smiled. "Now we just need an army."

CHAPTER TWENTY—ONE

Saoirse and Callan agreed to stay behind with Everett to protect Adaryn. Jai resisted at first, not wanting to leave her side, but if he was to lead this country, he would have to set an example. He would not be like his uncle and cower in the castle while his people suffered. He tightened his grip on his longsword and followed the rest of the group out of the cemetery.

Smoke filled the sky, and screams rang out all across the city. They planned to start in the market's outer rings and work their way in, hoping to remove whatever threat was placed on the city before too much damage was done.

The twins split off, hoping to cover more ground, and vowed to meet back at the cemetery. Jai led Soren, Enara, and Baz through the alleyways and side streets, stopping short halfway to Edras Mora's outer walls.

A group of locals had barricaded themselves in a tavern, where a large, black creature was hacking away at the door. The thing had to be almost eight feet tall and looked to be the kestrels' much scarier cousin. It had the same elongated face, with hollow pits for eyes, and the sound that escaped its mouth was a thing of nightmares. Instead of wings protruding from its back, two large appendages burst out from each of its shoulder blades. They were akin to a second set of arms, but the ends tapered into points resembling a scythe. It had elongated taloned feet, and their knees bent back at an awkward angle.

Jai hesitated for only a moment before running at the creature in an attempt to catch it off guard. Seconds before he slashed his sword, the monster shifted out of his blade's path and swung out with one of its pointed arms. Jai turned just in time to block the blow but was thrown to the ground by the force.

Baz ran in, yelling, to take the attention off his fallen friend. "Hey! Ugly! Over here!" he shouted as he circled the creature.

The beast seemed to take offense to that comment and ran in Baztien's direction.

Baz ducked as it swung at his head but was thrown back as the creature's large fist connected with his chest. Baz coughed and wheezed as he tried to recover from the blow to his solar plexus.

Enara was about to join in, but Jai jumped between the creature and his friend, blocking the killing blow it had no doubt planned to land.

Jai had learned from his first attempt and managed to keep his footing. He twisted his sword away, throwing the beast off balance, and sliced into its thigh. Black blood spurted from the wound, and the creature let out a horrific screech that was something between the wail of a banshee and a man's yell. It was truly unsettling.

Baz had gotten to his feet and stood next to Jai, readying himself for the next onslaught. The creature was now angry and came at them in full force.

They dodged and swung, trying to cause any damage they could. Baz bent backward at the waist just in time to watch a scythed arm swing overhead. He straightened and slashed out as the beast finished turning and sliced into its side.

It rounded on him, and Baz cringed under its hollowed gaze. It made to attack then stopped short as Jai's blade cut through its body in one swift swing. The tracker had sliced the creature in half, having dragged his blade from in-between its legs and up through its skull. The beast's body split in two in slow motion, like the fabric of a curtain being parted by a soft breeze, and fell to the ground with a *thud*.

"Nice one!" Baz said, smiling as Jai helped him to his feet. Both were covered in black blood, but neither were injured.

Their celebration was short-lived as the creature shifted behind them. Baz's smile dropped into a frown, and Jai could not suppress his shock.

"That's not possible."

Amidst the puddle of ichor, the creature stirred. As the two halves of its body stood, they rippled and shifted. The appendages that protruded from their backs seemed to slide through their bodies and became their second arm and leg. Their skin seemed to soak up the ichor and rippled again, filling in their damaged skulls and healing their wounds. Each head was left lopsided with one black eye in the center, like two separate pieces of a monstrous puzzle.

"Well, that's not good," Baz said, turning to the rest of the group. "Get out of here!"

He could see the determination on Enara's face as she replied, "I'm not leaving you!"

"Come on, Enara," Soren said, pulling on her arm as Baz and Jai squared off with the black beasts.

"I won't leave him," she said through gritted teeth, wrenching her arm away.

Soren's face softened as she spoke again. "They are some of the best fighters we know. They will be okay."

Enara looked at her momentarily, considering her words.

"Look around," Soren continued. "These people need us more than they do."

Enara hesitated one moment longer as she looked at Baz and seemed to make a decision. Then she grabbed Soren's hand, and they ran.

WITHIN A FEW MINUTES, THE GIRLS HAD REACHED THE OUTSKIRTS of the city. Charred bits of rubble and bodies littered the streets. They slowed their pace as they came up to the city's main gate. They pressed their backs against the stone as a few unfamiliar voices drifted from just outside the wall.

"Tabbris, report."

Soren clapped her hand over her mouth to hide her surprise. She would recognize that voice anywhere.

General Corvus.

Her eyes widened as she looked at Enara, who motioned toward an empty doorway. They shuffled across the cobblestones and hunkered down under a shattered window.

"The castle has been blown asunder, sir," a deep voice that Soren didn't recognize replied.

"And the king?"

"The king has apparently gone to the after, according to some of the more open-lipped townsfolk. His brother was named steward. I confirmed his death myself, sir."

"Well done, Sergeant. Gather the troops; we don't have long before you must return to Anistera. Tell your men to enjoy the nectar while it lasts. Big things are coming."

"Yes, sir."

They heard a large flap of wings as Corvus departed and held their breaths as the sergeant marched down the path toward the inner city.

Enara peeked through the doorway after him. "I'm going to take him out," she said as she made to stand, but Soren grabbed her arm.

"We will—together," Soren told her. "I'm not going to let you have all the fun."

"Together," Enara said, sneaking out of the doorway.

A smile curled at Soren's lips. "Let's make these fuckers pay."

"Maker, that stinks," Baz said, fanning his hand in front of his nose.

"Fucker caught my arm," Jai commented, peeling off his leather jacket that was now no more than shreds.

"Here." Baz opened his pack, handing him a vial of the healing pool's water.

Jai swallowed it quickly then swung his arm back and forth, testing it out. "Good as new. Thanks, brother," he said, grimacing as the smell of burning flesh mixed with rot filled his nostrils. "Maker, you weren't kidding." He covered his face with his torn jacket.

"Well, at least we know fire works." Baz kicked at a hunk of monster leg that was sizzling on the ground before him. It stuck to his boot, and he shook his foot violently until it splatted back onto the cobblestone.

"Thank you! Thank you!" A man wept as he ran toward them.

A group of people slowly filed out of the tavern, looking dazed.

"How can I ever repay you?" the man asked sincerely then paused. "Wait—do we know each other?"

"Jai Ashwood," Jai said, holding out his hand.

The man took it, contemplating the name for a moment before realization struck. "You're the man who they said killed the king. You're supposed to be dead."

The rest of the people who had been held up in the tavern slowly formed a circle around them, eyes narrowed.

"Is that true?" a teenage boy asked.

"It must be!" another cried. "The steward caught him in the act!"

"He killed the king!" a middle-aged man in a fine trader's suit yelled.

"Let's get him!" another person cried.

The crowd began to close in around them, and Baz and Jai shared a worried glance around. They did not want to harm these people.

"Please, allow me to explain," Jai said, placing his sword down and beckoning Baz to do the same. "I did not kill the king," Jai continued as the crowd grew closer. "Augustus framed me and Princess Adaryn to take the crown for himself."

An older lady cackled at this. "And why would we believe you?" she sneered.

"Because, Agatha, he speaks the truth."

The crowd turned to find Princess Adaryn flanked by Everett, Erick, Mrs. Ferndale, Callan, and Saoirse, along with a handful of royal guards.

"Well, if it isn't the traitorous princess herself," the lady crooned.

"That is Princess Regent to you," Adaryn said, rising to her full height. "The steward was killed in the attack."

The lady looked her up and down with dull blue eyes. Her graying hair was a mess of tangles tucked beneath her cloak. "How do we know *you* didn't kill him, like you did your father?"

"Because I am not his daughter."

The admission seemed to silence the rest of the crowd.

Adaryn pushed through the throng and placed her hand in Jai's. "This man is the true heir to the Patrovian throne, and before any of you naysayers disagree, we have the evidence and witnesses to prove it," she said, nodding to Mrs. Ferndale and one of the guards.

"It's true," Mrs. Ferndale began. "I delivered Jaideep as a babe, myself. His mother worked in the castle, and the king had a long-standing affair with her in the early years of his marriage to the queen."

"I can confirm these remarks," the guard said. "I was on duty the night Jai was born and the eve on which the king sealed his lineage papers."

Agatha looked at them skeptically, as did the rest of the crowd. "And let me guess, these papers were destroyed in the attack on the castle."

"We had them, I swear," Baz interjected.

"Had?" the crone asked, lifting a brow.

"My father, the King of Braexmirth, has them now," Callan replied for him. "Our forges are working to make weapons and armor as we speak."

"You all don't really believe this, do you?" Agatha asked, addressing the rest of the congregation.

The tavern owner bowed his head slightly. "I'm sorry," he whispered, looking at Jai. "Thank you for ridding us of that awful creature, but I remain loyal to our king, and a debt must be paid to honor his death."

"Enough!" Adaryn's raised voice split through the crowd. She then gestured to the guard. "Gareth, would you please show the crowd the papers?"

"He," Agatha said contemptuously, pointing to Callan, "just said the papers are no longer at our disposal."

"*His* copy, sure," the guard said, pulling a roll of parchment from a tube on his hip. "The king was rather clever, you see. He made a third copy that only his most trusted were aware of, in case of his untimely death."

The man held the scroll toward Agatha, who snatched it out of his hands greedily. She fingered the wax that could not be mistaken for anything but the king's royal seal and cracked it, unfurling the parchment.

Her eyes roamed the page as she muttered under her breath. Then she lifted her gaze to the guard, flicked her eyes to Adaryn, and finally turned to Jai. It was obvious to him that she had a penchant for violence but was unable to fight the truth.

"What does it say?" the tavern owner asked.

The crowd waited with bated breath before she spoke.

"The scroll confirms their stories," she spat angrily. "Jai Ashwood is indeed the king's son and heir to the throne. However," she said, taking a step toward Adaryn, her teeth glinting, "Adaryn is not the princess we all thought. It says here she was the daughter of a lowly stable maid, paraded around as a princess. She is no one."

The woman's face whipped sideways as Adaryn's palm made perfect contact with her cheek.

"I don't know what happened in your life to make you so hateful, but the next time you talk down to me, just remember that I am sleeping with your king-to-be." Adaryn then turned on her heel, leaving the woman to ponder her life choices.

AS SOREN ROUNDED THE FINAL CORNER LEADING BACK TO THE city center, she flung an arm out to halt Enara from barreling forward. They had planned on dispatching the sergeant but wanted to get a better idea of how many enemies were still in the city.

"What is it?" Enara asked with Soren's hand still pressed against her chest.

Soren peeked around the corner again to get a better look. "There are three more of them, and they aren't alone. There are two kestrels with them, and another one of those horrible creatures Baz and Jai were fighting."

"What are they doing?"

"It looks like they are rounding up stragglers," Soren said then gasped. "I think they plan to execute them."

"Let me see," Enara said, pushing aside Soren's hand to peek around the edge of the stone wall.

Soren had been right. The four men, if she could even call them that with their beautiful, inhuman skin, were lining up citizens and pushing them to their knees as the kestrels and their larger counterparts stalked back and forth in front of them.

"Where is Soren Nightsong?" the sergeant bellowed.

A chill creeped over Soren's skin. *They are looking for me.*

He spat through his too-perfect teeth, "Speak!"

"We don't know!" a man replied in an attempt at self-preservation.

"Then you are useless to me," the sergeant sneered then nodded to one of the kestrels.

Before the man could defend himself, the creature thrust its taloned hand through his chest, causing a ripple of fear throughout the crowd. The man fell to the ground, sputtering, and bled out in seconds.

Soren had seen enough. Before she could talk herself out of it, she ran forward into the square. She couldn't let any more people die on her account.

"I am Soren Nightsong," she said, her voice sounding surer than she felt. "You have found me. Now let these people go."

A cruel smile formed on strong features, and the sergeant's green eyes shone in the late afternoon sun. The smoke from the explosions had dissipated, and the sun's rays glinted like flames licking off the gold accents of the city's walls.

The sergeant spoke then. "You have caused the commander much trouble, little girl."

The comment stoked Soren's temper, a spark igniting the fuse of her barely held together resolve. "Let them go," she ordered through gritted teeth. "I will come with you if you leave them unharmed."

"You are in no position to be barking orders, tiny human," the sergeant sneered. His eyes then flicked behind her, and she turned to follow his gaze.

"Let go of me!" Enara shrieked at a kestrel that had its talons wrapped around her biceps. Soren hadn't noticed that one of them was missing from the square, and her heart dropped into her stomach cavity.

"If you so much as scratch her, I will cut out your eyes and feed them to you," Soren spat. Her anger boiled like a tea kettle, the steam rising, a pressure filling her chest that made her feel as though she would explode.

A laugh escaped from the sergeant's mouth. He clearly was not taking her threat seriously, so she sought to silence him. She would not risk throwing one of her knives. If she missed, she could harm one of the bystanders.

She palmed two of the blades and gave them a spin, relishing the way they felt like an extension of her hands as she lunged for his throat.

The sudden attack took everyone by surprise, and Enara used it to her advantage. With the heel of her boot, she crushed the bones in the kestrel's foot and turned to land three swift blows with her fists. It sickened her as the two blows to the creature's chest sounded hollow, but she followed the jabs with an uppercut to avoid the sharp angles of its face. The beast fell back, flapping its wings angrily.

Enara reached for Coraxis, her bladed staff, which was still affixed to her back. She was thankful that the incompetent bird had not removed it and braced herself.

The kestrel flapped its raven wings, lifting itself a few feet off the ground, ready to attack. Enara tightened her grip, ready to impale the ungodly creature, but before it could bridge the gap between them, an arrow whistled past her temple and embedded itself into its head.

Enara turned to see where the arrow had originated and exhaled a sigh of relief when she saw Rook's lithe form running across the rooftops. Then her breath caught when she saw Soren locked in combat with the sergeant. She ran to help her friend but was cut off by the kestrel's larger companion.

She ducked as it swung two of its pointed arms above her head in an attempt to decapitate her, and then she ran. She did not doubt her fighting skills, but she was no idiot. *I'll lead it to the narrow streets where I can constrict its movement. Then I will strike.*

Soren watched the beast trail after Enara through a small entryway just as the sergeant swung his blade at her feet. She jumped, narrowly avoiding losing her ankles, and slashed down with one of her daggers. She caught him across the side of the neck, and he hissed, taking a few steps back.

"You'll pay for that!" he shouted, spittle flying from his mouth.

She smirked at him and wiped the blood from the dagger on her trousers. It had not been a killing blow, but it was a start. *If he can bleed, he can die.*

Their fight continued as his rage fueled him forward. He swung and hacked at her with his sword, but as quick as she was, he was overpowering her. His armor had few weak points, and she was struggling to fight back.

She cried out as his blade sliced into her calf, and she fell hard onto her tailbone. Blood seeped from the wound, surrounding her lower leg in a pool of crimson. She hobbled to her feet, knowing the end was near. She would not die cowering on the ground; she would go down swinging.

She gripped her daggers, her hands slick with blood, and lunged again. He dodged and landed an elbow to the back of her head, making her see stars. He was playing with her now, knowing the fight was won.

Her eyes cleared, and she turned again to face him, limping weakly on her uninjured leg. They had moved away from the crowd now and, in a last-ditch effort at survival, she threw both daggers in quick succession, both aimed for his head. He blocked one with his sword, and the second grazed the side of his temple, cutting off the tip of his ear. Soren watched as a tiny piece of his shaved hair floated to the ground.

He stalked toward her, eyes blazing, and placed the tip of his blade at the hollow of her throat. She would not give him the satisfaction of closing her eyes. Instead, she smiled up at him with a look of defiance and waited for the end, but it did not come.

The next thing Soren knew, she was covered head to toe in blood that was not her own, the sergeant's body lying lifeless at her feet. The taste of iron coated her tongue, and she struggled to see through the red haze.

Her body sensed him before she could see him, muscles tensing in fear and excitement all at the same time. When her vision cleared, she met his eyes. The familiar icy stare warmed a little as she took him in. She knew how she must look— hair in tangles, bathed in blood as though she were a creature resurrected from the depths of hell. To her astonishment, a smirk played at the corners of his lips, and what Rook said next caused heat to pool low in her belly.

"I like you in red."

CHAPTER TWENTY-TWO

It was hard not to appreciate Rook's body as he stood before her, covered in the blood of her would-be killer. He looked every bit the weapon Adriel wanted him to be. Corvus had trained him well.

When she didn't respond to his quip, his look of satisfaction shifted. His brows pinched together, and he sheathed his weapon. "Are you all right, little bird?" he asked, searching her gold-rimmed eyes.

Her mouth had gone dry, and she swallowed thickly, nodding, taking in the rest of him. She had never doubted his capabilities as a fighter and had watched in awe when he had fought General Corvus back in Thorncrest, but this was different. She could practically *feel* the danger ebbing off of him, like little bolts of lightning whipping and crackling against her skin. She knew it was an absolutely ridiculous moment to be reminded of her deep attraction to him, but she couldn't help it. She was thankful then for the rush of pain that rolled through her nerves, washing away all her lustful thoughts.

"Soren."

She looked up when he said her name, as he rarely used it. It was then she realized he had closed the distance between them and was cupping her face.

"I need you to talk to me."

Her eyes flicked back and forth, taking in their surroundings. It was then she noticed the bodies. Two kestrels and three more of Adriel's soldiers were laid out before the captives, an arrow through each of their skulls. She met his gaze then, her eyes wandering to the tip of her father's bow peeking out from behind his back before widening. *He killed them all.*

The townspeople had gotten to their feet but made no sudden movements. They seemed unsure if they should thank Rook or run from him in the hopes of avoiding his wrath.

Without looking at them, he growled, "Leave. All of you." It was not a request.

The crowd shuffled away quickly, leaving them alone in the large square.

She licked her lips, tasting the tang of blood, and then pushed through the lump in her throat to croak out, "I think I'm okay."

He released her face and brushed a knuckle down her cheek. "You've lost a lot of blood." His tone was strained. "I need to get you somewhere safe."

Before she could stubbornly reject his offer, he bent and lifted her into his arms, taking care not to brush the large gash on her leg. She could feel the warmth radiating off his chest and allowed herself to lean into him.

Even covered in blood, he smelled like the snow-covered trees that surrounded Thorncrest Manor. She nuzzled in closer, inhaling his scent as her mind swam from the loss of blood. She closed her eyes and let her thoughts drift as her body went limp in his arms.

SOREN SAT UP, SHIELDING HER EYES FROM THE MIDDAY SUN. SHE blinked, allowing her pupils to adjust, and used the momentary blindness to take stock of her body. She rolled her shoulder and could no longer feel the pain that had just radiated there. She dared to look down at her leg, worried she would see a flap of skin hanging limply from bone. To her surprise, the muscle was intact.

She bent her knee and stretched it forward a few times, deeming the appendage fit to participate in a marathon.

"You'll still need rest." Rook's voice drifted over her like a soft blanket. He stood before her in a field of wildflowers, wearing his finest black tunic. His eyes matched the forget-me-nots that she pressed between her fingertips.

She was no longer in a blouse and trousers, but in a white cotton dress that fell to her knees, the soles of her feet pink and bare. Her brown eyes were as rich as the soil between her toes, and her blue-stained hair swayed gently between her shoulder blades.

"I thought I told you to stay out of my head," she said, picking at her somehow perfect nail beds.

"I thought you might forgive the intrusion, considering I saved your life," he replied, stepping toward her.

She held her breath as he approached, not daring to move, like a bronze sculpture she had once seen her father uncover.

"I thought you could enjoy a moment of peace before we return to the havoc my father unleashed," he said in his soft tenor. He brushed her cheek again, and she allowed herself to lean into his hand.

"What happened?" She remembered fighting Corvus's sergeant, but everything else had gone hazy.

"You passed out from blood loss. I brought you to a fabric shop."

"You left," Soren said flatly, her anger returning. She would not treat him like a hero when he had ditched them all at the first sign of real danger.

"You were well guarded," was his clipped response.

"The whole point was to have cover from higher ground!" Soren lifted her hands in exasperation.

"I did not want to leave you."

His admission surprised her but did not excuse his actions. She opened her mouth to say as much, but he continued, cutting her off before she could begin to berate him.

"I saw some of my father's men attacking a group of women outside the square—a mother and two daughters." He paused, unsure of how to word the next part eloquently. "Anyway, I dispatched them," he said, clearing his throat.

Soren just looked at him, her mouth opening and closing like a beached fish.

"I came back for you as soon as I could," he said, his tone softer now. "I should never have left." He shook his head. There was a pain behind his eyes that she couldn't quite register.

Soren looked at their surroundings. It was so peaceful here, calm. She understood then what he was doing. This dreamscape was a kindness.

"I'm dying, aren't I?" Soren asked quietly, her brown eyes searching his.

The question caught Rook off guard, her blunt words nearly knocking him off his feet.

"Your wounds are deep," he replied cryptically, avoiding her gaze. "I stitched your calf to the best of my abilities with the store's supplies, but I foolishly used the last of the healing vials on the woman's youngest child." He ran a hand through his hair, looking to the ground beneath his feet. "I will never forgive myself for the pain I have caused you."

Soren knew he was referring to more than her current dire situation. She could see the battle he fought within himself to express his meaning.

"I never wanted to cause you harm. I only wanted to escape Adriel. I was selfish and should have never kept the truth of your father from you."

Soren's throat tightened like the hangman's noose Jai had just barely avoided, and she looked at him through misty eyes.

She could feel the life slipping from her, like an autumn leaf detaching itself from its home tree, only to drift away on a soft current to places unknown.

She stepped forward, taking in the lines of Rook's face. He inhaled sharply as she reached up to run a hand along the exposed section of collarbone peeking out from the neckline of his buttoned tunic. The skin was warm beneath her fingertips, and she longed to kiss it like she had so many nights ago. Their life together at the manor had been endlessly infuriating and terrifying, but somehow, it was simultaneously some of the best moments in her life.

What they had was volatile and dangerous, a cruel fate and a wicked trick, but it was theirs.

Soren often wondered if the Maker above had enjoyed playing with his creation's emotions. Placing slivers of hope into their little black hearts to bring them back to life, only to cut away every ounce of happiness with the precision of a healer's blade.

"Little bird," Rook whispered softly, shoving away her negative thoughts with a steady hand. He reached up and clasped her palm in his, and the back of her hand was pressed against his rapidly beating heart. Soren knew this was still a dream, but it felt so real. *He* felt so real.

Her eyes drifted from his hand to the hollow of his throat, to the sharp line of his jaw, landing in the cold winter of his eyes. It was in this moment that she knew she loved him. She loved every battered, bruised, and broken part of the dark soul that he had kept hidden from the world. She saw the truth of him behind his perfect porcelain mask. She saw the boy who had longed for his father's acceptance, the teenager who had lived through unimaginable horrors, and the man who fought every day to cage his demons.

She saw a light in him that his father and Corvus had tried so hard to snuff out. The single beat of a new star shining through the black of night. She saw the kind soul and warm heart that had, for many years, been buried in a shroud of ice. Every moment, every touch, every quiet whisper curled up together in their library had slowly melted away his frozen walls.

She had hated him, had wanted to kill him even, to smother him while he slept to escape her bounds and save her friends. He had once been the bane of her existence yet had somehow become her reason for living.

The grief from her father's death had turned her into a hollowed-out version of her previous self. The loss had snuffed out all joy and color from her life, leaving her to drown in an ocean of gray.

Day after day, night after night, she had gone through the motions to get by. She had shut out her friends and had become selfish and uncaring. She had closed herself off from feeling for other people to protect her own heart. The more she cared, the more she had to lose, and she did not think she would survive another loss like the one of losing her father. Baz and Enara had been so patient with her and had tried everything to get the old Soren back, but they didn't understand that the old Soren had died along with her father.

Rook had challenged her in a way they could not. Her words and actions had pushed her friends away while they seemed to only make him gravitate closer. In the beginning, she had been trying to escape her circumstances, but by the end, she had known she was only trying to escape her true feelings for the man she was supposed to consider the enemy.

She could feel his soft breath caress her cheek, followed by the faint metallic tang of blood mixing with the soft pines of his own scent. She looked into his sapphire eyes, letting herself get lost one last time in the fractured shards of crystal that lay behind his long lashes. She willed herself to be brave and use these last moments to show him where her heart truly belonged.

She pressed her lips to his in the sweetest of kisses. It was a kiss that said, "*I wish we had more time.*" It was a kiss of love and longing, and hope and heartbreak. It was goodbye.

Before their mouths parted, Soren whispered against his lips. She spoke so softly that the words would have been carried away before Rook had even heard them, had there been a breeze. Three words that would forever change them both.

"I forgive you."

CHAPTER
TWENTY-THREE

"I forgive you." Those three words were like a balm to all of Rook's unseen wounds. When she'd nearly died in the frozen water those long weeks ago, he'd assumed she would hate him forever.

He pulled her tight against him and could feel the wetness of her tears dampen his chest. She was fading. He could feel his grip on her mind slipping. The world he had created around them started to shimmer. He reached one hand down, tilting her chin upward, and stole one last kiss.

"I hate you," she said, giving him a sad smile.

He smirked and brushed his thumb down the apple of her cheek. "I love you, too, little bird."

The words had slipped from his tongue before he could stop them, but he did not regret the admission. If he was to truly lose her this time, he was glad she knew.

The shock on her face was evident, but before she could say anything more, the dreamscape wavered again, and his hold on her world ended.

ROOK WAS BACK IN THE FABRIC SHOP, HIS HAND FIRMLY GRIPPING Soren's as she lay on the crafting table before him. The sewing needle and thread he'd used to mend her injury lay beside her leg, along with the strips of cloth he had used to staunch the wound. The blood on his hands was beginning to dry and flake off like pieces of ash from a dying fire. It was still sticky where their palms met, and he kissed her knuckles before separating his fingers from hers. She had minutes left.

He pressed his lips to her forehead, not caring that her hair was matted to her scalp with the blood of the enemy. Before he could whisper his last goodbye, however, the door burst open. His weapon was in his hands, and he was poised to strike.

Before he could swing his blade, the female Celestial donning the armour of the enemy held up her empty palms and said, "Wait—I can help."

"I sincerely doubt that," Rook ground out. His teeth were pressed so hard together he feared they might crack.

"Let me save her," the woman said softly, not taking her eyes off his sword.

"*Save her?*" He let out a sickening laugh. "It is your people who have done this."

"I know, but I am not here for them. Please, let me heal her."

Rook looked at her, and then at Soren, whose breathing had slowed to a dangerous rate. He flicked his eyes back to the strange woman, and something in him said to trust her.

"Fine, but if you try anything, I will remove the hands you say will heal and show you what the true meaning of pain is."

To his surprise, she quirked a smile and said, "I would expect no less."

The woman had an intense look of determination in her golden eyes as she moved to Soren's side and placed her hands over her calf. Her palms glowed with a soft violet light that seemed to soak into Soren's tanned skin and snake through her veins. Within seconds, her whole body glowed violet as the woman's power took hold.

When she was finished, she backed away, breathing heavily, and sat in the chair Rook had been previously occupying. His blade fingers itched as she then traced her index finger along Soren's face. What she said next took him by surprise.

"She looks so much like her mother."

"You knew Celandine?" Rook asked, still wary of this stranger.

The smile she gave him made her look as aged as all the years she had been in existence. Then she nodded, wiping away a stray tear. "She was my best friend." She held up her hands. "She was the only one, until my mate, who knew of my ability."

"How does it work?" he asked, lowering his blade. If she was going to attack him, she would have already done it.

He rolled the tension from his shoulders and waited for her to answer.

"My father liked to experiment, you see. The Maker of all things got bored, and making different versions of his children brought him joy. Adriel was gifted the power of healing himself, whereas I was gifted the power to heal others, though mine is finite. Father must have known I would use my gifts on the people of Entheas and did not want me to upset the balance of nature here."

"What is the cost?" Rook asked.

Her brows pressed together in confusion. "I'm sorry, I did not catch the meaning behind your question."

"If your power is finite, like you say, what does it take from you?"

"Years," she said simply. "I have lived a long life, you see. Each time I heal, I age backward. Since I am the only one of my kind, it is hard to guess what would happen should I empty the well, but I would imagine I would just cease to exist."

"Thank you," he said, nodding toward Soren, "for giving a piece of yourself to save her."

"I would give her the last of me, if I had to," she said honestly. "Her mother was a light in my life, and I would die happy knowing I saved her child."

Luscinia jumped in surprise when Soren's hand squeezed hers, and she looked at Rook with wide eyes. "She is coming back to us."

Rook tried to ignore how the word *us* made him feel coming from this stranger's mouth. She was *his*, and he did not relish sharing her with anyone else when he already had Baz and Enara to contend with.

He tucked his jealousy away and walked over to take Luscinia's place at Soren's side, replacing her hand with his.

Soren's petite hand flexed in his, and he was happy to notice that the warmth had returned to her fingers.

Her eyelids fluttered open to meet his. The browns and golds in her irises met the cloudless skies of his.

"You love me?" she asked breathlessly.

"Always, little bird."

Before she could articulate how those words made her feel and what she wanted to say in response, her body stiffened. She sat up swiftly, the fingers of her free hand searching for her dagger as she glared at the soldier in the corner.

Rook placed his hands on her shoulders, dragging her attention back to him. "She is a friend," he said in a calming tone. "She healed you."

Soren narrowed her eyes at the woman, still hesitant to trust someone who bore the armor of Anistera. "Why did you heal me?" She had a feeling that the woman's actions would have a cost, and she wanted to know what bargain had been struck while she had drifted between the living and the lasting.

"Because you," Luscinia started, looking to the both of them, "are the only ones who can defeat Adriel."

"Not anymore, not without the Oculus," Soren said, the cool hands of guilt crawling under her skin like a cluster of spiders waiting to catch her in their webs. "It was stolen in the battle to leave Thorncrest."

"Fucking Corvus," Rook growled, baring his teeth.

Soren nodded. "I'm sorry," she said, disappointed for letting that happen. "I didn't know it was taken until it was already too late."

"I know, little bird, it's okay," Rook told her. "We will find another way."

She gave him a small smile. She liked this softer side of him. She did not see it often, only in glimpses so small she usually thought the moments were imagined. His entire life, he had been trained to be strong, to not show emotion, and to endure pain without flinching. Now, he was free to feel what his heart had fought so valiantly to hide, and it warmed her from tip to toe.

"There is no need for that," Luscinia said, reaching behind her.

Rook placed himself between the woman and Soren, fingers inching toward his weapon, just in case. He didn't want to be unprepared for any surprises.

The woman noticed his change in stance and chuckled lightly. "I believe this may help," she said, holding the metal artifact in her palms.

Soren's eyes widened, and she gently pushed on Rook's hip to move him aside so she could take a better look. The metal eye peered up at her from Luscinia's fair hands, and she could feel the buzz of energy that emanated from the otherworldly metal. She was surprised she hadn't noticed the sensation before. The loss of blood must have temporarily muted her body's response to the item.

Soren hopped off the table, feeling better than she had in weeks, and took the artifact for her own as Luscinia offered it to her.

"What did you say your name was again?" Soren asked.

The woman chuckled again, her gilded eyes glinting. "It is Luscinia, but you may call me friend."

Luscinia hurried down the alleyways that led to the outskirts of Edras Mora. She was running out of time. If she stayed in Entheas any longer, she risked sending herself to the afterlife.

Before leaving Soren and Rook with the Oculus, she had outlined the basics of Adriel's plan. She would have given anything to stay a few moments longer, but she would be of little help if she were dead.

She flew through the doorway of an abandoned home on the edge of the city and padded down the cellar stairs as swiftly as her armor would allow. She weaved through the random items that had been stored there over the decades and pushed aside the tapestry that hung on the wall to reveal a portal. The golden light shimmered as she stepped through and felt a sharp tug behind her navel as her body was displaced.

Her feet landed firmly on the soft, white sandy beach of the Esinian Isles. The gates to all eight province capitals, as well as the larger gate to Anistera, lay before her in a circle.

She ran for the archway, feeling the seconds winding down until her time was up, and hoped her tardiness did not raise suspicion.

Luscinia walked through the blinding light and onto the rocky cliff in Anistera. She schooled her features into a stony mask when she arrived to find ten of her brothers and sisters, all Adriel loyalists, surrounding the gate.

Adriel, who stood in the center of the group, took a step forward, his lips turned up in a satisfied grin that said, "*Gotcha.*" She wanted to smack the smugness right off his face.

"Running a little late, aren't you, sister?" he asked.

"Just dealing with a few stragglers," she replied nonchalantly.

"The orders were given to return to Anistera three hours ago," he stated plainly. "Care to explain how you deliberately disobeyed a direct command?"

"Must not have heard it," she said, her hand tightening on her blade.

"Funny how you happened to stay in the same city Soren had been spotted in," he mused, looking at his well-groomed fingertips.

"If you look up the meaning of the word coincidence, it may help you to understand things better," she replied with a bright smile. She was sick of pretending she agreed with this monster.

"Enough of these games," he spat, gesturing to the guards on his right.

They parted to reveal Horath and Malik, their skin showing obvious signs of torture. She resisted the urge to run to them.

"What have you done?" She was seething now and could feel the anger rippling beneath her skin, her hatred clawing at her willpower to demand justice for her friends.

"You see, I knew something had been off with you recently," Adriel explained. "So, I thought I would question a few of your friends regarding your recent whereabouts."

"We are sorry, Luscinia!" Horath cried.

"We didn't mean to tell him anything!" Malik finished for him.

Luscinia's eyes went dark, hatred for her wayward brother filling in all the gaps where light might have slipped out.

She softened her gaze when she looked to her friends. "All is forgiven. We will find a way through this."

Adriel laughed at the sentiment. "Kill them."

"No!" Luscinia shrieked, running toward her friends.

Two more of her siblings stopped her in her tracks, and she tried to get through to them. "Nakir, Ansell, please don't let him do this! Don't you see this is wrong?"

Their eyes were blank, no emotion resting behind their gaze. The siblings she had once known were gone, replaced by Adriel's dark influence.

She looked on, horrified, as Horath's and Malik's throats were slit and they slumped forward, blood gathering at their feet. She continued to watch as the crimson pool expanded and bathed her armored boots in waves of red.

"You are a monster!" she screamed. She managed to shift out of her siblings' grip and lunged for Adriel, slashing out, her sword catching him on the cheek.

"You insolent bitch!" he bellowed, grasping at his face. "Throw her in with the rest of our traitorous family." The cut was already healed, but his face was still marred by the Oculus scar, which made him look even more menacing, but Luscinia did not balk. She would not give him the satisfaction of cowering before him.

"You know, I was happy when I thought Celandine was dead," she spat. "Because at least I knew she would finally be free of you."

Luscinia's world was rocked when Adriel's fist connected with her face, shattering her jaw.

She smiled through the blood in her teeth. "You're too late." She started coughing, choking on her own blood. She spat toward his feet to clear her throat.

"Get her out of my sight—*now!*" Adriel's voice was filled with malice.

Luscinia laughed wildly as she was taken away. Before she was fully out of sight, though, she yelled back one final time.

"You will soon know what our father felt—the betrayal of a son."

CHAPTER TWENTY—FOUR

"Soren!" Enara's worried voice carried into the shop from the square. "Soren, where are you?" Her throat bobbed as she choked down a sob. Her mind was racing at all the terrible things that could have befallen her friend in her short absence.

She was covered in black from head to toe, and it took two vials of healing water from her pack to stop the spread of the new creature's venom.

"We should start doing building checks on the ones that are still standing," Ikei said.

"Yes, maybe she had to run for safety," his brother finished.

She shook their head, not bothering to look in their direction as she scanned the blood-soaked ground for any signs of Soren. "She wouldn't run from a fight."

"You got that right," Soren said, bursting out of the door of a tailor shop.

Relief washed over Enara like the cool water of the Boreal River, healing her slowly breaking heart. Before she knew it, she was running and lifting Soren into the air, nearly squeezing the life out of her. Tears pricked at her vision, and she blinked them back, giving her best friend a once-over. Her eyes widened when she registered just how much blood covered her body. She looked like a scene out of a horror play they had once seen back in Vreburn.

"What happened?" she asked, rounding on Rook. "And where the fuck were you?" She jabbed his chest with her index finger, her disdain for him circling her like a dark cloud.

Soren stepped between them, gently removing her friend's finger from his chest. She could feel the heat of his body seep into her back as she tried to stop Enara's rampage. She knew that look, and if the sparring dummies were any indication of what was to happen next, Rook didn't stand a chance, healing powers or not.

"The blood's not mine," she said. "Well, most of it, anyway. He saved me."

"He ditched us as soon as the attack began! How can we even begin to trust him?" Enara was practically foaming at the mouth.

Soren debated wiping the spittle from her lip but thought better of it. When she was angry, she was like a rabid dog, and she did, in fact, bite.

"You don't need to trust him," Soren said simply, catching Enara's hazel eyes with her own. "You just need to trust me."

Enara stared at her for a long moment, and an unspoken conversation seemed to pass between them before she flicked her eyes back to Rook.

"Fine. But I'll be watching you." If glares could kill, Rook would be nothing but a pile of ash.

Soren turned to notice him fighting the urge to smile. Luckily, Enara had not seen it, already walking in the direction of the mausoleum.

Soren's brows pinched together, and she shoved his shoulder. "You are not helping," she whispered angrily.

"Would it be any consolation if I said I liked her?" he asked.

"No," Soren said but suppressed a smile of her own.

THEY TRUDGED AFTER ENARA, JUMPING AND SIDESTEPPING OVER and around chunks of stone and other fallen debris on their way back to the agreed meeting point. The cemetery gate, along with the first couple rows of tombstones, had been blown to bits. Fortunately, the caskets remained mercifully underground.

The group deflated when they reached the doorway, only to find it as devoid of life as the rest of the burial grounds.

"*Ugh!*" Enara yelled, clenching her fists in frustration. She had been hoping Baz and Jai would have found their way back by now. And where were Callan, Saoirse, and Adaryn?

Before anyone else could offer a suggestion, she stormed past Soren, the twins, and Rook, taking special care to knock him in the shoulder on her way out of the cemetery.

"Where are you going?" Soren called, running after her.

"To find them."

Soren grabbed her arm, whipping her around to face her. "Don't be stupid."

"I came back for you, didn't I? Don't ask me not to go after him," she said, clearly frustrated.

"I'm not saying don't look for him," Soren reassured her. "I'm just saying, it's going to be dark soon and splitting up is a terrible idea."

Enara knew her friend was right and swung her fist into the nearest wall in frustration. The skin of her knuckles turned red and angry, and shock waves of pain reverberated up her wrist. A moment later, the pain was gone, and the scratches had healed over, thanks to the remnants of healing water in her system.

"He could be bleeding out somewhere, or worse ..." she verbalized, not wanting to finish the thought.

"You know we need to give him more credit." Soren placed a hand on her friend's back. "He's strong and resourceful, not to mention Jai's fighting skills aren't anything to scoff at, either."

Enara wiped the stray tears from her cheeks and straightened her back. "At first light, we go search," she said with finality.

"Agreed," Soren said, pulling her in for a hug.

"Thanks for talking me off the ledge, lady," Enara whispered against her cheek.

"Anytime."

"Those tears aren't for me, are they?"

From down the path, Baz's voice lifted their spirits.

"Baz!" both girls yelled excitedly.

He sauntered toward them with a huge grin plastered on his face. "Don't tell me you were planning my funeral already," he joked as Enara ran into his arms.

"Hey," she whispered into his ear.

"Hey back," he replied, pulling away just enough to kiss her forehead.

"Don't mind me," Soren said, scooting Enara out of the way to give Baz a hug of her own before ruffling his hair.

"Hi to you too, Soren," Baz said, punching her shoulder playfully. "Now, what did I miss?"

AFTER THE TWINS PULLED BAZ OFF OF ROOK, THEY ATTEMPTED A more civilized means of conversation. Apparently, he had also noticed Rook's lack of attendance at Jai's almost-hanging and had wanted to say a few words … with his fists. To his credit, Rook had allowed him three good hits before he had started dodging blows.

"*Will you two stop it?*" Soren screeched as Ori and Ikei pulled them off of each other. Soren was ready to tear her hair out.

"Hasn't there been enough bloodshed today?" Ikei asked as Soren wiped a crimson streak off the side of Rook's face. His eyebrow had been split, and though it was already healing, it had bled a lot.

Rook licked the last of the blood from the corner of his lip as he stared into Soren's eyes.

She gave him an incredulous look back that said, "*Now is not the time for flirting,*" before facing her friends.

"Look, you don't have to like one another, but if you hurt each other, you hurt me. So, can you at least attempt to get along?"

"Fine," Enara repeated her sentiment from earlier.

"All right, Sor," Baz said, seemingly calmer now that he had at least punched the smirk off of Rook's pretty face.

"As you wish, little bird," Rook replied.

Ori's laugh broke through the awkward exchange. "And we thought *we* had a weird family dynamic."

"You and me both, brother," Ikei replied.

"Yeah, yeah, we're all a little fucked up," Soren said, brushing off the comments. "Moving on ..." She looked to Enara. "You first, what happened with the kestrel wannabe? Did you kill it? I saw it chase you out of the square."

"I ran for as long as I could, but it caught me at a dead end where one of the buildings had collapsed. If it weren't for these two"—Enara gestured toward the twins—"I wouldn't be standing here. You should have seen them."

"Aw ... you give us too much credit," Ikei said.

"She already had him halfway dead when we arrived," Ori finished.

"Yeah, but if you guys hadn't torched that thing ..." Enara tried to continue, but they held up two sets of hands to stop her.

"The life taken is not what matters," Ori said.

"What matters is the life saved," Ikei finished, pointing one of his tonfa blades toward her. "When we were assigned to you, you became our new family. You may not be the sister we once had, but we will protect you as if you were, all the same."

"Thank you," Baz said, holding Enara a little tighter, "for being there for her when I couldn't."

"No problem, brother. We are all in this together," Ori said.

"This fight is for all of Entheas. Our home provinces no longer matter. We are all family now," Ikei added firmly.

"So, does that make me the reclusive uncle?" Rook asked.

Soren raised a brow at him. "We seriously need to work on your humor."

"*Ahem*," Baz coughed out. "I believe the role of handsome jokester is already filled, but you could try out for family asshole."

Soren cringed at the comment, waiting for the next round of insults to start. To her surprise, Rook just laughed. His real laugh that she had yet to hear. It was the most beautiful thing. She wished she could bottle it up and put it on a shelf to listen to when times were dark.

She took in the bright smile that crested his cheeks and felt her breath hitch. Brooding Rook was handsome as hell, but smiling Rook was the stuff of stories, a beauty unmatched by those living in the mundane world. She guessed she should thank Adriel for that, but then she realized, apart from his eyes, they didn't look much alike. She assumed he took after his mother, and then she suddenly felt a pang of sadness that he had never been able to meet her.

"All right, your turn," Enara said, looking to Soren then glowering at Rook. His laughter, it seemed, had yet to win her over.

Soren explained how the battle had gone with the sergeant, and Rook filled in the details about patching up Soren's leg and Luscinia showing up to offer her healing skills. Soren was thankful he did not tell them about the dream or how close she had been to dying. She was fine now, and there was no need to worry Enara for nothing.

"So, before she left, she gave us this," Soren said, pulling the Oculus out from a satchel she had stolen from the tailor shop.

"Oh shit!" Baz exclaimed, and Enara gasped, "How?"

"She stole it from Adriel to return to us. She said we are the last hope of defeating him," Soren answered, her voice shaky.

"So what?" Enara asked. "You guys have to magically fall in love or something for it to work?"

"Maker, Enara, no!" Soren replied, cheeks flaming.

"The mating bond is much more complex than that," Rook replied matter-of-factly.

"This is more of a backup plan, anyway," Soren said, wanting to move on from this topic. "The biggest thing is Adriel can't make anymore creatures without it. To secure a mating bond, we would need more time, and that is something we no longer have."

"What do you mean?" Enara asked.

"Luscinia stated that my father plans to attack the rest of Entheas in one month's time," Rook answered, fiddling with his rapier. "They plan on hitting Braexmirth and Stelonbriar last. Xian-Dao has pledged themselves to Adriel's cause and has already helped them devastate the Isles. Dhamtra is all but leveled, and Draestel, Estelar, and Thorncrest have already been demolished."

"Did she say if anything was left of the Esinian Isles?" Ikei asked, worried for him and his twin's homeland. They might not have lived there since they were children, but they had hoped to visit one day.

"Did Queen Lilianna survive?" Ori added.

"I am sorry," Rook replied, shaking his head. "She did not specify; she only said they had used a set of targeted attacks to create earthquakes, which in turn caused tidal waves and volcanoes to ravage the islands. Bao-Ren's forces were already in Estelar when the attacks happened. His men were willing to die for the cause. I guess they figured being blown up was better than bleeding out on a battlefield."

The twins bowed their heads, unsure of how to respond to the news that their homeland was all but buried under flame and water.

"So, we have one month?" Baz asked, trying to wrap his head around all the new information.

"Yes," Rook said, "we have one month to save Entheas."

THEY PICKED THEIR WAY BACK TO THE TAVERN AFTER BAZ HAD explained what had all happened with Jai and the king's guard providing his proof of lineage. Jai had sent Baz to meet with them at the monastery while he dealt with the townspeople.

The tavern owner welcomed them with open arms, and they joined the rest of their crew for a meager meal of vegetable soup with day-old bread.

Mrs. Ferndale was running around, clearing tables and assisting the tavern owner as best she could, not being able to sit idle. Jai gave the woman a kiss on the cheek when she brought him a wooden stein of water, and she patted his head before scolding some kids who were getting a little too rambunctious.

The few king's guards left stood against the wall, eyes shifting back and forth, searching for any potential attackers to their new king-to-be. Jai had told them the worst was over and that they should take a break, but the one who knew him since birth had simply said, "Your enemies are not resting, and neither will we."

Jai did not want to push, but he did see Mrs. Ferndale force him to eat a piece of dried meat, so he called that a win.

"Glad to see you all made it out with your skins intact," Jai said. Then his eyes heated when he saw Rook. "And I see the deserter has returned."

Soren held up a hand in protest. "Don't. We have been through this twice now. Yes, he left his post. He did it to save a mother and her kids. He came back and helped save my life. Can we move on? I have news."

Jai gave her a big smile that showed a little too much affection for Rook's liking. "All right, let me have it."

Soren took the lead, reiterating everything that Luscinia had told them about the attacks and Adriel's timeline to finish off the rest of Entheas.

Once Soren had concluded, Jai scratched his beard in thought. It had grown a little unruly over the last few weeks and seemed to age him. He was silent for a moment then startled them all by calling out, "Who here is the fastest rider?" He scanned the crowd. The tavern was full of people who had no homes to go back to.

A young boy with wild brown hair stepped forward.

"What is your name?" Jai asked.

"It's William. I won the dune races this past summer." The dune races were held once a year. The competitors started on the eastern tip, riding the whole way around Patrivah, and finishing in Edras Mora. The winner was gifted a large bottle of healing waters and a place in the king's court. The race was grueling on both rider and animal, and Jai couldn't have asked for a better young man.

"I need you to take a message to Braexmirth. Timing is of great importance."

"Of course," the boy said, bowing. "Anything you need, Your Majesty."

Jai chuckled softly. "You don't need to bow, young one, nor call me that just yet. I was not so different from yourself once." Jai reached forward and squeezed the boy's shoulder. He couldn't have been more than sixteen. "Ride hard and return to us as soon as you are able. Mrs. Ferndale will ready a pack for you, and Everett here will ready one of Patrivah's finest steeds."

The boy nodded, seemingly grateful for the opportunity, and allowed himself to be dragged off with Mrs. Ferndale.

"Malcolm," Jai called out to the barkeep. "I am in need of a quill and parchment."

"Not a problem," he replied. "I have some in my back quarters." The townsman shuffled away, quickly returning with the items.

"Thank you," Jai said, and then he began to write to the King of Braexmirth.

King Elias,

I am Jaideep Ashwood. You do not know me, nor do you have reason to trust me, but I am hoping these words find you well. I am sending this correspondence to inform you of the most recent attack on the capital of Patrivah. The king's brother perished in the onslaught, leaving me to lead in his stead. I cannot say I am sad for his passing, as it was discovered he had been slowly poisoning my father. Please know that I have been proven innocent and only want what is best for my people. Edras Mora has faced great evil this past day, and the worst is yet to come.

We have been given information on good authority that the being in charge of these smaller attacks plans on coming for Braexmirth and Stelonbriar next. The Duke of Stelonbriar left this afternoon to warn his people and gather his troops. I suggest you amass your forces, as well.

My companions have relayed to me that your people have been working on weapons and armor for the cause. For this, I thank you. I have heard of the master forges of Olecastor and humbly request that you meet us on the fields of Stelonbriar in one week's time with as many weapons and plated armor sets as you can.

I know our people have not always seen eye-to-eye, but for the good of all of Entheas, we must put our differences aside to face an even greater threat. Please be aware that Bao-Ren has joined with the enemy.

I will be sending riders to rally other fighters from across Thorncrest, Estelar, Draestel, the Esinian Isles, and Dhamtra, but I have doubts there will be many left to fight. Our source shared the details of the other provinces' devastation, and I fear we may be all that is left.

I ask that we, along with the people of Stelonbriar, join forces to save our people and this world that we all hold most dear. Every able-bodied son and daughter in Entheas will be requested to fight, apart from those who are with child or are responsible for a child. Duke Erick will have his people set up camps all over the fields of Irefeld, where we will begin training our forces.

War is coming, and I am hoping to meet you on the front lines as friends and equals to fight for us all.

Jaideep Ashwood of the House of Drekar, Prince Regent of Patrivah

Without his father's signet ring, Jai decided to use his turquoise ring to seal the folded piece of parchment. Using the ivory wax from a nearby candle, he pressed the smooth stone into it until the engravings around the stone embossed the seal. Before the wax fully dried, he proceeded to borrow Adaryn's smaller signet ring and pressed it into the center. Then he looked upon the parchment, pleased with himself. If they survived, he would have a proper seal made. For now, he would settle for the melding of their two rings to match the melding of their hearts.

With the letter complete, he walked over to Everett and handed it to him. "Make sure the boy has the fastest mount," he said sternly.

"Are you sure?" Everett asked, knowing well that King Otis's steed was the fastest of the royal horses.

"Yes, I'm sure. Amadeus will ride true. We are running out of time."

"Can do, Your Majesty." Everett said, bowing with a flourish that had the rest of the group stifling a laugh.

"Yeah, yeah," Jai said, giving his shoulder a shove. "Get out of here."

They watched him go, sending a silent prayer to the Maker that the boy would relay the message in time.

CHAPTER
TWENTY—FIVE

In the week that followed the attack on Edras Mora, Jai had ordered a grouping of other messengers to gather the troops from all around Patrivah. Callan and Saoirse, along with the twins, parted ways to reach out to the other provinces, spreading the word of what was to come. Jai could only hope that some of the smaller military groupings across Entheas had survived.

Within the first few days, every available soldier in Patrivah, and anyone else willing to fight, was loaded into the wide array of ships in the south harbor to make the crossing to Stelonbriar. They had decided it would be faster to travel by water than to attempt traversing the mountains of Braexmirth. Jai had to trust that Erick would have followed his instructions and started setting up in the farmers' fields.

He looked around at the inhabitants of his larger ship and guilt settled in his stomach like a bowl of rancid meat. They had numbers, sure, but he did not relish the idea of sending young women and boys to their deaths with little to no combat training.

The ships were filled to capacity with packs, bedrolls, canvas sheets, weapons, targets, armor, and as much food and water as they could scavenge. Luckily for them, the larger food stores were not located in the city's capital but evenly dispersed around the province.

He laughed when he noticed Enara rubbing Baz's back as he leaned over the railing. They hadn't even started moving yet, and the poor guy was already fifty shades of green. Jai hoped for his sake that he had eaten a light breakfast.

"We are ready to depart when you are, Your Highness," the captain barked from the helm.

He was still not used to people referring to him in such a formal way, but he did not correct him. "Onward to war, then," he said, and the captain gave the order to unmoor from the dock.

"I still can't believe he's back," Adaryn said to Soren, her gaze locked on Jai from across the deck.

"I'm surprised you let him off that easily," Soren poked. "You know, besides his whole handsome, saving-the-world bit, two years is a long time to disappear without a word."

"I thought you two were friends," Adaryn said, eyes flashing defensively. "Besides, two years is nothing in comparison to knowing him my whole life. I wanted so badly to be mad at him, but when I saw you two in the kitchen, all I could think of was how much I missed him." She paused to give Soren a side smirk. "And how much I wanted my knuckles to meet your face."

Soren chuckled again. "I mean, that's fair. You should know that nothing happened. I thought I wanted to kiss him, but he let me down easy. He has only ever had eyes for you."

Adaryn blew out a breath. "Well, I can't really blame you, now can I?" she jested, her gaze drifting to her lover. "I mean, look at him."

The girls giggled as though they were school-aged again, chatting about their most recent flames.

"I hope you know I have all the respect in the world for the two of you," Soren started, needing to clear the air. "I was lonely, and he was there. There was never anything real between us."

Adaryn held up her hand. "Do not worry; Jai already told me everything. You two have been there for each other. I understand, and I harbor no ill-will toward you."

The knot around Soren's heart loosened a little. "Friends?" she asked.

"Friends," Adaryn replied with a smile. "Now, I am going to go see if Mrs. Ferndale needs a hand below. We have many mouths to feed, and I don't see how this boat will stay on course with two hundred hungry soldiers." She turned on her heel and disappeared below deck with Soren smiling after her.

She gazed out over the dark water, wondering if this would be the last time she would look upon its large expanse. She could make out the dock in the distance, and her heart clenched when she was reminded of all those they had sailed away from. She had watched as fathers said goodbye to their babies, children said goodbye to their mothers as their injured fathers cried silent tears. Her sadness crested as teenagers left home for the first time with no guarantee of coming back. The whole scene had been absolutely heartbreaking.

Oddly enough, she found comfort in the fact that all of her closest friends were with her, even if they were sailing toward death.

She clutched the ring at her neck and thought of her father. *I love you tons, Daddy. Please watch over us all. I miss you. Say hi to Mom for me.*

She couldn't be sure, but she swore she felt a warm breeze wrap around her, protecting her from the cold spray of the ocean as the ship bobbed along the waves. In her heart, she knew that he could hear her.

It took three days for the whole fleet to land in Irefeld. As grueling as the trip had been, Soren was thankful for it. Turned out that Rook was also not fond of the water, so him and Baz formed a sort of unspoken kinship while they continuously hurled over the side of the boat. Mutual seasickness seemed to spark a comradery between them, and even Enara had shown a sliver of sympathy for Rook by the end of the second day.

Erick welcomed them all with open arms as they sauntered down the wooden plank and onto dry land. Everett blushed as Erick winked at him before turning to lead them away from the bustle of the trading docks.

Stelonbriar's shipping arrangements with the rest of the provinces kept them busy year-round. In-season produce, and freshly butchered and preserved meat products, were their main exports, thus resulting in a wealthy province.

"I am glad you have made the journey safely, my friends," the duke said. He nodded to a few of his townsfolk as they crossed the square and headed for his manor.

"I had hoped you received my correspondence in time," Jai said. "I was concerned it may not reach you before we arrived."

Duke Erick nodded grimly. "I did, in fact. And I also happened to run into a few friends of yours," he said cryptically, looking to Rook.

Before Jai could ask what he meant, a fury of honey-blonde hair came barreling into the group, catching Soren and Rook in a tight embrace.

"Nice to see you, Meena," Rook said through a choked breath.

"I can't believe you're here!" she said, her voice cracking like weathered paint. "I have a bone to pick with you," she said, turning a frustrated gaze on Soren. "If you ever leave us alone with him again"—she pointed a thumb in Rook's face—"I will personally hunt you down and chain you to the table myself!"

Soren's mouth hung open for a moment before she clacked her teeth together in a smile. "I missed you, too, Meena."

"And what about me?" Evelyn's calm alto drifted from behind Meena's bubbling frame.

"Yeah, I guess I missed you, too," Soren replied, welcoming her in a gentler embrace.

Evie placed a hand on Rook's shoulder before saying, "I am glad you are all right." Her eyes misted, but she blinked back the tears as she took in the small army in front of her. "You all look like you could use a drink and a hot meal."

"You've got that right," Adaryn said, rushing forward to shake Evie's hand. "I'm Adaryn, the king-to-be's partner, and I am famished." Apparently, helping Mrs. Ferndale maintain the crew with half-decent meals on the ship had left little time for Adaryn to enjoy a hot meal to herself. She had spent the three-day journey eating cold leftovers and crunchy bits scraped from all but empty pots and pans below deck. She, of course, had not told Mrs. Ferndale this, for fear of being reprimanded for not eating properly. She had spent years in the castle overindulging and thought the least she could do was offer her portions to those who required a little more sustenance.

"Well, Adaryn," Evie replied with a kind smile, "I think we can help with that."

After stuffing themselves with some cabbage stew and salted ham, Soren excused herself from the makeshift table of the large mess tent. The massive piece of fabric was stretched over evenly spaced poles that created a tarped-off area that was one hundred feet long and forty feet wide. As they had entered, Erick had explained how this was where the soldiers and fighters would congregate to eat and also to discuss training schedules and have instructions relayed to them from their group leaders.

Soren looked at the barren field before her and couldn't ignore the sense of foreboding. The attack on Irefeld had occurred while they had traveled. All the great fields around the Stelonbriar's capital had been burned to the ground. Luckily for them, the city remained greatly untouched, and most of the residents had extensive cellars filled with canned fruits and vegetables that could last them until they rebuilt. *If there is any-thing left to rebuild.*

Soren pushed the negative thought from her mind as her gaze drifted over the flat, black landscape. It reminded her of an unfinished painting. It was almost as though the artist had lain out a black tapestry in the hopes to add bits of color but was stopped mid-brushstroke, leaving behind a foreboding black hole.

Her attention shifted as she heard Baz's laugh carry from across the room. Somehow, he and Rook had ended up in a strong-arm contest, and from the angry look on Rook's face, Baz had won.

Retreating from the smoke-filled air, she returned to her seat beside Enara.

"You good, lady?" Enara asked, having noticed her temporary absence.

"Yeah, just wanted some fresh air," Soren replied, picking at a limp piece of cabbage that had affixed itself to the side of her wooden bowl.

Enara scrunched up her nose. "And how did you enjoy the smell of burned vegetables?"

"About as much as I enjoy Baz's dad jokes," Soren replied.

Their conversation halted for a moment before they burst out in laughter at Baz's expense.

"You're not wrong," Enara replied, still laughing.

A hand reached for her face, and she flinched, the joy in her eyes swiftly replaced by fear as she folded away from the stray limb.

"Hey, it's just me," Baz said from beside her.

Enara looked up to see Baz lift his hands in a calming gesture. She visibly relaxed and reached for his wrist to pull him into her.

Soren sat in silent understanding, letting the exchange play out.

"Oh, hey," Enara said, her cheeks heating with embarrassment. "Sorry, I didn't realize it was you."

Baz cupped her cheek and kissed her forehead. "Never apologize for protecting yourself," he said, his lips tickling her hairline.

She pushed back far enough to look into his dark eyes. "I thought you were—"

"I know."

"I'm sorry. I'm being ridiculous. My father is gone, and I still freak out anytime someone makes a sudden movement." She wrung her hands in her lap, before playing with the strings of the corseted vest she wore.

"You"—Baz kissed her nose—"are not"—he then kissed her temple—"ridiculous." He finished by planting a firm kiss on her lips.

"You're right," she replied, her fear chased away by his touch. "*You* are ridiculous." She chuckled before kissing him again.

"Get a room," Soren joked, her brown eyes glinting in the lamplight.

"*We* already have one," Enara said, winking. "And I wouldn't comment on our sleeping arrangements unless you want us to inquire about yours." Her eyes flicked to where Rook still looked unimpressed at the adjacent table. Meena was speaking animatedly with Everett, who sat next to him.

Soren sighed, deciding she had lost this one. "Fine, but seriously, we should all get some sleep."

"Agreed," Enara said, pushing up from the bench and looping her arm through Baz's. "Meet you in the morning?"

"Yeah, I'll be here," Soren replied.

"All right, lady, sweet dreams."

"Sweet dreams."

Jai watched as Enara and Baz slipped through the folds of the large tent, no doubt turning in early to prepare for the day to come.

He had been impressed with the duke's military prowess and sauntered over to commend him on his efforts.

"You've done well, brother," he said, clapping Erick on the back.

"Anything to help," he replied solemnly. "Anyway"—he stretched—"I'm going to retire for the evening. I have a few more things to go over, and it has already been a long day."

"Of course," Jai replied, moving out of his way as Erick pushed up from the wooden pew. The long table comprised itself of ten smaller square tables, borrowed from the local tavern, and was lined with the pews from a nearby church.

"We will reconvene in the morning to begin training," Erick said, his eyes drifting over to where Everett was seated. "Until then, make the most of this evening. It may be one of the last peaceful ones we have."

CHAPTER
TWENTY—SIX

"And that's how Jai and I ended up on dish duty for a month."

Meena giggled into her wine goblet as Everett droned on about some childhood story of him and the king-to-be.

How Meena found anything he said humorous, Rook would never understand. He wanted to find a way to exit the conversation, but Meena was having fun, and Maker knew the girl needed it.

He often felt bad that they had chosen to stay in the castle with him. He had offered them more money than they could ever need to start over somewhere else, yet they had always turned him down.

He wished they didn't feel indebted to him. The whole point of him taking out Madam Elvira's men was so they could be free. He had seen two girls, with no parents, struggling to make it in the world, and couldn't help but intervene.

He had been sent into Wrathbrook to follow a lead on Celandine. It hadn't been often that his father would permit him to leave the manor, and he had relished in his temporary freedom. After beating the information out of a lowlife hush dealer, he had allowed himself a walk about town to clear his mind, frustrated that the lead had turned out to be one he'd already heard before. *Saint Celandine lives.* He had scoffed to himself before trudging down the cobbled road, toward the tavern in search of a drink.

Shrill voices from a nearby alley attracted his attention, and he flattened himself to the brick wall and peered around the corner. A much-younger Meena was curled up next to an open cellar door as Evelyn tried her best to shush her. Rook could just barely make out their conversation amongst the other less savory sounds that drifted from the above windows. The alley backed into Madame Elvira's pleasure house, for those seeking the comfort of a woman's touch, and Rook cringed as the sounds of unrequited orgasms filled the air.

"I can't, Evie. Please, I can't do it anymore."

"Shush," Evelyn said, trying to comfort her younger sister. "I know, I know. Only a few more months, okay? Then we will have enough to get out of here."

The statement caused Meena to sob even harder, and she blew her nose into a stained handkerchief.

"Everything okay here?"

The girls jumped at the sound of Rook's voice, no doubt in concern he would rat them out to Madam Elvira.

He held up his hands to show he meant them no harm. "I'm sorry. I didn't mean to startle you."

"No, sir," Meena replied, wiping her tears away. "It is us who should apologize. Please, come inside and allow us to entertain you."

Rook grimaced. "As beautiful as the both of you are, I prefer women who bed with me willingly."

"Oh," Meena said, unsure of how to continue the conversation.

"Who are you?" Evelyn asked.

Rook couldn't help but give her a devilish smile. "Someone who can help."

He told the girls he would come back in one week's time, but Meena and Evelyn decided to make a run for it that same night. He was shocked when they showed up on his doorstep, half-frozen from the frigid mountain temperatures.

He surprised the girls by paying their dues to Madam Elvira and offering them temporary work in the manor until they felt safe enough to travel elsewhere.

Rook had not admitted it to himself then, but he enjoyed their company. Evelyn and Meena brought warmth to the cold walls of Thorncrest Manor.

The girls were with him for two weeks when Meena mentioned she felt like they were being watched.

On their next trip into the city to buy goods, Rook decided to ignore his father's wishes to stay in the manor and instead watched over the girls. Sure enough, he noticed some unsavory characters eyeing them from across the street, trying to act nonchalant. He couldn't say he was surprised when they started following Evie and Meena past the city limits.

He gave them credit where it was due. They stayed close enough to follow, but far enough back not to be seen. Any movement could be easily mistaken as snow sifting through branches or a stray animal going about its daily business.

Rook used his stealth to get close enough to hear their plans. He would never repeat their words to another soul. The insidious thoughts of these men had come from a place so dark that not even he could fathom. He was not surprised to find out they had been sent by Madam Elvira herself, no doubt in a fit of anger for losing two of her most attractive indentures.

His gaze flicked to the girls in the distance and the manor looming just past the next treeline. He knew it was time to act.

He struck them down as they separated to relieve themselves, and while the girls slept, he delivered their heads to Madam Elvira's private residence with a singular message.

The next attempt will be your last.

The following morning, he went about business as usual until the girls sat down at the dining table while he thumbed through some shipment receipts. He raised an eyebrow in their direction, beckoning them to speak, as they usually took meals in the servants' quarters to maintain the appearance to Corvus that he was their master.

"We know what you did," Evelyn started, resting her forearms on the table and clasping her hands together.

Before Rook could confirm or deny anything, Meena blurted, "We followed you last night." She then covered her mouth as though she could shove the words back in, but it was too late.

Rook's jaw ticked, and he took a breath before asking, "What did you see?" His voice was dangerously low.

"We saw the bodies," Evelyn started.

"And the heads," Meena finished, looking a few shades paler.

"I see," Rook replied, fingering his glass. "And you're still here?"

"Well, I … Well, we …" Evelyn stuttered before clearing her throat. "We figured, if you meant us harm, you would have already done so."

Rook nodded to confirm her suspicions. He was not yet ready to admit he had grown fond of them.

"Anyway," Evelyn continued, "thank you."

"Yes, thank you!" Meena chimed in a bit too excitedly. The color had returned to her cheeks, and she beamed a grateful smile in his direction.

"Don't let it go to your heads," Rook said but couldn't help the smile itching to pull up the corners of his lip. "So," he went on, "have you decided where you will go?"

"Well," Evelyn started, "we talked about it last night, and we have decided to stay here … with you." Then she added, "If you will have us."

Rook did not outwardly show an emotional response, but if he was being honest with himself, he had wanted them to stay. Telling them that would have been preposterous, of course, so instead, he supplemented with, "As you were, then. Breakfast won't cook itself."

"Yay!" Meena cheered, breaking the awkward silence that followed Rook's less-than-sensitive statement. She then jumped from her seat and ran over to his side of the table, kissing his cheek before skipping back toward the kitchen.

Rook's face was an immovable mask.

"Sorry," Evelyn apologized on her sister's behalf. "I'll have a talk with her about personal boundaries."

"You do that," he responded as she slipped through the door after her sister.

He looked to the girls now, three years later, and couldn't help but be proud of how far they had all come.

Noticing a break in Everett's story, Rook took the opportunity to stand. "I am going to head out for the evening."

"Oh, okay!" Meena said at his abruptness. She started to stand, too. "Did you need me to——"

"No," he cut her off. She looked lost at his sharp response, so he continued in a softer tone, "You don't work for me anymore, Meena. Do not leave on my account."

"Are you sure?"

"I can walk you back to your tent," Everett offered, holding out his arm to her.

She looked at him, then to Rook, almost as if asking permission.

Rook gave her the most imperceptible nod, an unspoken confirmation that he approved of Everett's intentions.

"Sure," she replied happily and let Everett lead the way.

Rook shadowed them and watched as they approached Evelyn and Meena's designated tent. The stable boy bent low to kiss Meena's hand before wishing her goodnight then sauntered between the tents until he was out of Rook's line of sight.

He bent his head from side to side to loosen the knots of stress that had settled there before making his way to his assigned stretch of canvas.

He entered the tent and fumbled around, reaching for the oil lamp he had seen earlier, cursing as his knee collided with the cot. He sat on the edge of the thin bedroll and peeled off his tunic, giving his shoulders a stretch. He debated removing his trousers but decided against it just in case Adriel had any surprises for them

He inched his body down on the uncomfortable bedding, missing his lush mattress from the manor, and fell into a fitful sleep.

CHAPTER
TWENTY—SEVEN

oren walked through the rows of tents that lined the blackened fields and tried to remember which one was hers. It was nearing midnight, yet she still wasn't tired. It had been a big day, and her anxiety was clawing at her like a creature in the dark, waiting until her weakest moment to strike.

She retraced her steps from earlier in the day and finally found the tent she was looking for. She swore she had left the flaps open, but she was too tired to ask questions. So, she undid the wooden hook and loop clasps and stepped inside, taking care to seal it behind her. She did not want any more of the dead crop air to fill her nostrils.

She reached around, looking for her pack; the lamp would be no use if she couldn't find the matches to light it. She silently cursed herself for not setting them out sooner.

Her fingers sifted through the contents of her pack and landed on a small metal tin. She could hear the matches tinkling around inside and smiled in the dark. She stood to find the lamp, and her breath caught as she found her back pressed against someone else's body.

Before she could react, a blade was pressed to her throat.

She dropped the matches, her hands shaking. Unable to move her head for fear of helping the blade's journey, she swung her elbow back, hearing a low grunt. The reaction loosened her assailant's grip long enough for her to push his wrist away and put some distance between them.

She wanted to run, but the man's shadow towered before her, seemingly unfazed by her assault. She opened her mouth to call for help, but she was cut off by the stranger's threat.

"I suggest you leave before this escalates."

The deep tenor of his voice caused goosebumps to ripple over Soren's skin. It took a moment before her shock let her mouth respond. She swallowed back the lump of fear that had made a home in her esophagus and finally spoke.

"Rook, what the hell are you doing in my tent?"

ROOK LOWERED HIS BLADE AS SOREN'S VOICE CARRIED THROUGH the short distance between them. "Little bird?" he replied in confusion. "This is *my* tent."

Soren scoffed loudly, and he imagined she was putting her hands on her hips as she responded with, "You scared the shit out of me." He could hear her voice wavering as her breathing sped up. The panic behind her words was clear. "I thought … I thought …" She began sucking in breaths.

He reached for her in the dark. "Soren, you need to breathe."

"I … I can't."

Rook caught her just as her knees buckled and she fell to the floor of the tent, her hands wrapping around her knees, forming a cage between them.

He shuffled around so he was behind her. With legs on either side of her shaking form, he pulled her back against his chest and kissed the back of her head before resting his cheek on her shoulder so he could whisper against the shell of her ear, "Breathe with me." He inhaled slowly, letting her feel his chest rise against her back, and when she sucked in a haggard breath, he said, "Good. Now out," then continued to exhale at the same pace.

She shuddered against him, and he could hear her let out a trembling breath.

"I'm here, little bird. I'm not going anywhere."

She nodded in understanding, trying to get her heart rate under control.

He did not know how long they sat like that. He could feel her hot tears as they slid from her face to rest on his bare arms. After a while, the tears stopped, and her breathing evened out enough for her to choke out, "Water."

Rook reached for his canteen and offered it to her.

She took it gratefully. The water cooled the frayed edges of her mind, washing away the rest of the panic.

He was kneeling before her now and brushed his knuckles down her cheek. "Come, little bird; let's get you to bed."

Soren's eyes adjusted to the dark space enough to make out Rook's bare chest in front of her. She took another swig of water before closing the canteen and setting it aside. She let him pull her to her feet then brushed her hands down her arms. She hadn't had a panic attack in front of him since the first day they had met. She felt stupid and weak.

He brought her over to the cot and coaxed her to sit. One by one, he undid the laces of her boots and pulled them off, followed by her socks. If the circumstances were different, she would have shrugged him off, but the anxiety attack had lowered her defenses.

She watched with wide eyes as his deft fingers undid the corset ties on her vest. He set the material aside then gestured for her to lay back. Her tunic had lifted, and the skin below her navel heated as his knuckles brushed against it before he undid the button on her leather training pants. He slid them down her thighs at an agonizing pace, leaving soft kisses in their wake. Then he folded her bottoms, placed them beside her vest at the foot of the bed, and stood to put his tunic back on.

"What are you doing?" she asked then followed up with, "Did you want to?" Her hands gestured to her half-undressed body.

Rook bit down on his lip to remind himself that it was not the time for sexual advances.

"As tempting as that is, I thought it best if you got some rest." He began pulling his boots on over his bare feet.

Soren sat up, her chest tightening. "Please," she said, struggling to articulate. Her next words were so soft, but they penetrated his heart with the strength of a thousand daggers. "Please, don't go."

He continued his steps in reverse, removing his boots then his tunic before scooting onto the cot beside her. She had turned toward the side of the tent so he could mold his body to hers.

"Thank you," she replied, nuzzling back into him, relishing in the heat that always seemed to radiate from his athletic frame.

"Do you want to talk about what just happened?"

"Ask me tomorrow."

"As you wish, little bird," he replied, allowing himself to bask in the lavender scent that drifted off her skin. Three days at sea, and she still somehow smelled just as he remembered.

"And Rook?"

"Yeah?"

"Stay tomorrow, too?" It was a question, not a statement.

Asking him to stay with her on a continuous basis was not something she was sure she was ready for, but she did know one thing—she felt better when he was around.

She waited nervously as he took his sweet time to answer.

"As long as you'll have me," he responded, kissing the soft spot where the curve of her neck met her jaw. "Now get some sleep."

"Always so bossy," she quipped with a lazy smile.

He held her tight as her breathing softened and her body fell into a rhythmic sleep. He stayed awake for a while, savoring the moment, for he did not know how many nights like this they might have together.

"I love you," he whispered, not willing to admit just yet how much he wished for her to say it back.

He allowed her dreams to be her own for the night and let his mind drift until sleep took him.

Morning came too soon, and Soren immediately regretted staying up so late. She stirred, opening her eyes, and found herself looking into Rook's sleeping face. *I must have turned over,* she thought. She ran her hands through his hair, enjoying the feel of him being so close.

His lids fluttered open, and his eyes met hers.

She couldn't help but grin at how cute he looked all mussed with sleep. His normally rigid demeanor was softened, and she enjoyed this was a part of him that no one else got to see.

"Good morning, little bird." he said.

"Morning," she replied, feeling suddenly awkward. She sat up, running her fingers through her tangled hair.

"Did you sleep okay?"

"*Eh.*" She shrugged and started picking at her nails. "Thank you for staying."

He turned to rest his head on his arm and grabbed her hands with his free one to stop her nervous habit. He brushed his lips along the curves and valleys of her knuckles and kissed each fingertip. "It was my pleasure."

The action sent a tingle of warmth to all her nerve endings, but she gently pulled her hands from his grasp. "I'm sorry about last night."

"What do you mean? The tent thing was an honest mistake. If you no longer want to share, we can confirm with Evelyn where the other tent is."

Soren gave him an incredulous look. "First of all, this is *my* tent. Second of all, I'll decide if I want to share depending on if I like you today."

Rook laughed at this, and Soren could feel the vibrations rumbling from his chest through the bedroll.

"That is not very promising since you hate me every day," he said, leveling her with that smirk she loved so much. Sometimes, she let herself forget how unbelievably attractive he was.

"I mean, true, but that's not what I was apologizing for."

He gave her a questioning look.

"I'm sorry for freaking out."

"You're apologizing for having a reasonable emotional response to what you thought was a stranger threatening your life?"

When he put it that way, it made her feel ridiculous for even broaching the subject.

"I just don't like people seeing that side of me." She looked down at the worn blanket but turned her head back to Rook as he pressed up from the cot to sit beside her.

"So, you're saying Enara has never seen you like that before?"

"No. I mean, of course *she* has, and Baz a couple of times, but it's not something I go sharing with everyone. I don't walk around Vreburn like, '*Hey, just wanted to let you know I have anxiety and debilitating panic attacks on a regular basis!*'"

Rook chuckled again, and Soren wondered why she hadn't tried to make him laugh more back at the manor. The melodic sound filled her soul with joy.

"I just mean to say your emotions do not make you weak. If anything, they are your strength. Your worry for your friends is what kept you going at the manor, and your love for your father is what brought you here. Your emotions are your armor, and you are the sword. They are your strength—do not forget that."

Tears welled in her eyes, and she choked down a sob. "I wasn't always like this, you know."

"What do you mean?"

"Something happened when I was young, and since then, I have always had trouble dealing with things rationally."

"Being emotional does not make you irrational … Well, sometimes," he said, giving her a playful smirk. "But go on."

"It's too hard. I'm not sure I'm ready to talk about it just yet."

"I understand, and I won't force you, but if you won't talk about it when we could all be dead in a couple weeks' time, then when do you think you will be ready to talk about it?"

Soren knew he was right. She also knew she didn't want to potentially go to her grave without someone knowing all of her. She always thought when she finally wanted to share the source of her trauma, it would be to Enara. She had tried so many times to tell her what had happened that night, but she never knew where to start. After a while, she had just tucked it away in a box at the back of her mind. She had even managed to forget about it for a few years … until memories started breaking back through from the buried spaces in her brain.

Her father's death seemed to have broken the dam that she had built inside to protect herself, and everything had come flooding back with one giant wave that threatened to pull her under.

She took in a steadying breath and said, "Okay."

"Okay?"

"I'm ready."

Rook waited quietly as Soren started to articulate what had happened to her. She went on to explain that, back when she was a child, she had a sleepover at one of her father's friends' houses. This had been before the incident with Altair, and he had known quite a few people in town. He had been celebrating a recent find and wanted to spend the evening with some friends from back home. So, he'd made arrangements with Mrs. Rouse and her husband to have Soren stay over at their place for the evening.

They had a daughter who was a year and a half older and a sixteen-year-old son. Soren had been eight. Tarak had been friends with the couple for years, and the kids had grown up together. He couldn't have known anything bad would happen.

Soren went on to explain how they would play games about rescuing princesses and capturing thieves, and how she had always loved spending time with them. The older brother, Marshall, would always be the conquering hero, and her his blushing bride.

Every time they finished a mission, he would say she had to give him a kiss to say thank you for saving her. She, of course, would oblige. Even at her young age, she had always thought him to be pretty and felt special that he wanted to kiss her. She had never realized how inappropriate his requests were until the memories came flooding back. The sister, Tilly, had never known anything was amiss, or if she had, she had never said so.

Soren remembered everything about that night. She remembered what they had eaten for dinner, what play they had acted out before they were tucked into bed. She remembered the nightgown she had worn when Marshall had snuck into the room. She remembered being surprised that Tilly hadn't woken from the bed next to her as Marshall slid below the blankets and pressed his body to hers.

Rook repressed his anger as Soren continued.

She explained how sometimes she could still feel the touch of his hands on her skin. The kisses he had planted on her neck and back that had made her child-sized toes tingle. The heat between her legs as he'd pressed his fingers into her body in a way that had felt so foreign but good in a way. The soreness she had felt afterwards as she had followed him to the kitchen.

She couldn't recall most of their conversation, but she remembered watching him take a bite of an apple and asking him if he should clean his hands. She didn't remember what had happened after that. She couldn't recall any other instances, apart from that one time, but that one time had changed everything.

She had always felt the need to be in control of things her whole life. When plans changed, or people were unreliable, she would take her frustrations out on those closest to her. Her personal relationships had always been strained, and her father had been none the wiser because she had never spoken about the events of that night with him. Instead, he had always been so patient with her and let her get her anger out with sports or combat training in school.

She never blamed him for not asking more questions. She knew she had hid her feelings from him well, and when she had lashed out, she had been so quick to apologize that he had chalked it up to growing pains. Not having her mother in the picture had given him a little bit of leeway in that regard. How was he to know what the teenage experience was like from the female perspective?

"I was so angry all the time," Soren continued. "I never sought help for my issues. I didn't even know how to ask for it until Enara came into my life. Then Baz suggested I speak to his mom about taking something to help with the panic attacks. Yet I still never told them exactly what had happened."

Rook had remained silent as she shared her story, building a mental wall around the anger that threatened to burst forth and burn the world to the ground himself to find this boy who had taken advantage of Soren as a child.

"You know you don't owe them an explanation, Soren," Rook said softly.

"I know, but how do you explain something like that to someone and share that it felt good while it was happening? Something inside me is wrong. How could I have found enjoyment in someone doing that to me?"

"You were a child, Soren. The actions of a grown boy, who was old enough to know better, were not your fault."

"So, you don't think I'm fucked up?"

Rook shook his head and pulled her close to him. "I think you were taken advantage of and didn't know how to ask for help. You owe the world nothing, Soren."

She sniffled and crossed her arms over her knees to hide her face. She muffled something, but Rook couldn't understand the words.

"Speak up, little bird."

Soren lifted her reddened eyes to repeat herself. "Sometimes, I feel like I am just as bad as he was."

Rook was taken aback by her admission. "Why do you feel that way?"

"After Dad died, I kind of went on a rampage. We both know I am no virgin." She laughed at this, but the sound was like a dead weight sitting in the pit of Rook's stomach. "I wanted to take my control back. Control over my own body and what men could or could not do with it. You would think, after being sexually assaulted as a child, that I would avoid that type of contact with anyone, but it was the opposite. I wanted to take back what he had taken from me, and I thought, by being promiscuous, it would give me back a sense of control. *I* chose who was allowed in my bed and when. *I* chose how far things went and if I felt like seeing them again. I could kick them out whenever I pleased because it was *my* house. But, like, who does that?"

"Soren, if you're expecting me to judge you for your previous sexual encounters, you're wrong. Well, apart from Marshall, who I am very much in debate on hunting down. As long as everything was consensual, it is really none of my business. We all have a past; I do not judge you for how you chose to cope with your heartache."

"So, you don't think I'm broken?"

"I think we are all a little broken," he replied softly. Then he folded her into his arms, and all the tears she had held packed away in that little box finally broke free.

CHAPTER
TWENTY—EIGHT

Present Day - Anistera

Luscinia's cheekbone shattered as Adriel dealt another excruciating blow.

"*Where is she?*" Adriel bellowed, spittle hitting her in the face like tiny disgusting raindrops.

She remained silent, as she had every day since he had placed her in the makeshift cell in the training hall. Adriel had turned an entire wing of soldier's quarters into a temporary jail for any betrayers he might find. All escape routes had been filled in with stone, and windows had been bricked up within inches of the roof to allow for minimal airflow. Everything else in the small space had been stripped bare, apart from a twin-sized bed. There was a bathing room attached to each suite, to which the door had been removed. Luscinia was a proud woman, but she had not cared to relieve herself in front of the guards when the choice had been taken from her.

The floor to her cell was usually clean but was currently speckled in varying shades of red from the continuous injuries Adriel had caused since her arrival. At least once a day, he or General Corvus would try to glean information from her through various means of torture. Thankfully, Malik and Horath had only betrayed Luscinia's whereabouts and had not given Adriel information on the hidden rebellion, which meant they were safe … for now.

On day one, they had kept their attempts pretty tame. Most of the assault had been verbal threats, finished with a few blows to her ribs. Day two, they broke two of her fingers and made a few incisions on her left thigh. Luckily for her, they were in this for the long haul and had not cut deep enough to require healing. She assumed the last thing Adriel wanted was to have her bleed out before she could give him the information he needed.

On day three, they had decided to remove all of her nails. She had made it to the eighth full avulsion before she'd passed out. When she had awoken a few hours later, she had observed how they had, indeed, removed the final two nails. *At least they will grow back evenly*, she had thought through a pain-induced stupor.

Day four, they had tried a different approach. All day and all night, the stationed soldiers kept poking and prodding her through the bars that had been installed between the stone. They would douse her in water and scream at her or sing songs repetitively. Every few hours, the soldiers would switch out for a fresh batch to elicit a new kind of auditory misery.

Today was day five, and Adriel was starting to become impatient.

\"*Look at me!*" Adriel screamed as he fisted her hair, pulling her neck back sharply to make her meet his gaze. His once beautiful features looked out of place next to his blazing red scar. She couldn't help but smile. The power of the Oculus had revealed his true self and the hideous creature that crawled beneath his perfect face.

"How many of you are there?" he growled. His straight teeth flashed in the low light that filtered in from the hallway.

Up until now, he had left her face untouched, likely to make it easier for her to relay information. Now it seemed the time for talking was done. She knew he wouldn't kill her just yet. Given their long lives, she suspected he could torture her for eons and never get sick of hearing her screams.

He twisted a knife around in his hand then held it to her cheek. "Let's see how quiet you are after I flay off a bit of that pretty face."

She again stayed silent, giving him a look that said, *"Do your worst."* The eye above her shattered cheekbone was beginning to swell, and it almost looked as though she were winking at him.

He spoke again, as if they were carrying on a conversation. "Have it your way then, sister," he sneered, pressing the blade to her skin.

Present Day - Irefeld

"When you are done with your allotted time in your assigned section, you will have a ten-minute break before moving to the next. Look to the soldiers for guidance—they are your mentors now, and anything they have to say may be the difference between life and death." Jai paused for effect before continuing his speech to the crowd before him. "Train well, and we will see you at dusk to debrief."

At this, the crowd dispersed to different training areas that had been erected on the perimeter of the largest field. The center had been left open for group training and coordination, with the outlying areas organized for specialized abilities. Jai and Erick had agreed that it would be best to give everyone basic fighting skills then work on each person's individual strengths. Since today was day one, everyone had to be tested.

They would go through each section of the training gauntlet five at a time and be rated on a scale of one to ten for overall ability in each skill. There were eight different sections to cover the basic groups required for ground attack and defense with some small changes made to accommodate for their enemies' aerial attacks. The sections included hand-to-hand combat, archery, basic healing, survival skills, melee combat, equestrian skills, leadership, and mind training. Each section played an important part to ensure them the best chance at survival.

Enara was assigned as group leader for hand-to-hand combat, alongside Callan, while Meena and Evelyn joined a few other men and women to lead in healer training. Soren assisted in archery, working below a gentleman named Kristoff who could sever the tongue from a frog from one hundred yards away. Survival skills and leadership training were led by a few of the duke's men, while mind training was left to a group of elders from multiple provinces.

Mind training was more important than most people knew. You could be the best fighter in Entheas, but if you lost your mind at the first sight of a dead body, you were about as useful as a bucket full of holes.

After some convincing, Rook was drafted alongside Jai and Baz to help with melee training. He might have grimaced the entire time, but Jai had to admit that his instruction points were valid, though his correctional manner could use some work.

"Again. But this time, *look* at where you are swinging your weapon." He dragged out the word "*look*" as though he were speaking to an infant.

Jai considered showing him a gentler approach, but they did not have time to perfect everything. He figured if they couldn't handle a little admonishment, they wouldn't last long in the field, anyway. Instead, he opted to give them all a positive pep talk at the end of each group's training session to help boost morale.

He was halfway through his pick-me-up speech when a familiar rider approached. It was the boy he had sent to Braexmirth before they had shipped off from Edras Mora.

"Your Majesty," the boy said, dismounting to bow before the king-to-be. "I have news."

"Rise and speak, young master," Jai said.

The boy looked around. "It may be best if we speak without audience."

If Jai was worried, he did not let it show. The last thing he needed was to panic everyone. Instead, he nodded and dismissed the group, commending them on their good work.

"Come; we will speak in the war tent," Jai said, grabbing Amadeus's reins and leading them away from watchful eyes.

The second they passed the canvas threshold, the boy blurted out, "Braexmirth was attacked."

Jai gripped the table at the center of the room that was covered in papers and maps marking known attacks and potential strategies. "Shit," he said under his breath. "And the king?" It was a loaded question. He did not know if Entheas would survive the loss of another leader so soon.

"Oh, sorry, sir, I did not mean to insinuate. King Elias is fine. He sent me to update you on goings-on across the border."

"Go on, then," Jai said, gesturing for the boy to sit in the armchair across from him while he leaned against the table.

"Olecastor, it seems, was a bit more well protected with its high walls and steep peaks. They are accustomed to fire and were able to contain most of the attack to a small area. It seems, in the enemy's haste, they did not do much research into the province's capabilities."

"Good news, then," Jai said, stroking his beard. "Did King Elias relay if his troops will be ready to fight?"

The boy nodded vigorously. "Yes, sir. He sent me ahead to inform you that they will arrive within a few days, weapons and armor in hand. Everything is as planned, though they were delayed due to the attack."

"You've done well, William," Jai said, grabbing the boy's shoulder. "Go to the healer tent in the training grounds and ask for Meena. Tell her Jai sent you for accommodations. She will set you up in a tent with the other boys your age and get you some food. Tomorrow, I want you to join the equestrian instructors."

Without question, the boy nodded. "Thank you, Your Majesty." As he leaped to leave, Jai's voice carried across the room.

"William."

The boy turned swiftly, his light hair turning auburn in the lamplight. "Yes, Your Majesty?"

"Remind me to knight you when all this is over."

The boy's eyes beamed with delight as a smile won over most of his gentle features. "Yes, Your Majesty." He stood there for a moment, unsure of what to do with the compliment he had just been bestowed.

"You may go, William," Jai said.

"Oh, yes. Sorry, Your Majesty. Thank you." And with that, the boy was off and running, no doubt to tell all his friends the big news.

Jai let himself have a moment in silence to melt into the chair before returning to the training grounds. He found himself reinvigorated.

With Olecastor by our side, we just might stand a chance.

CHAPTER TWENTY—NINE

Soren and Enara stood side-by-side, mouths open in awe as King Elias's forces arrived two days later. They marched in from the north, carrying flags of green and black and singing an old Braexian war song. They couldn't understand the words, but Saoirse translated for them as they marched closer.

Callan stood next to her, singing along in his native tongue, his deep voice melding with those of his brothers.

> *Let it be heard on mountains high*
> *The hammer of Olecastor sounds*
> *We march to our deaths readily*
> *Feel our might within the ground*
> *With metal and stone, we forge our way*
> *Through river and barren land*
> *We lay waste to those who oppose*

Bringing our wrath by steely hand

There is no need to die this day
Let us wash the blood away
Mercy is given to those who pray
Let us wash the blood away

Our anvils ring down in the deep
Creating blades of legend and myth
Our swords ring true
Be wary of those who come from the cliffs
Heed the warning of Braexmirth
That our daughters and sons shout
For they may be the last words you hear
Before your light is snuffed out

There is no need to die this day
Let us wash the blood away
Mercy is given to those who pray
Let us wash the blood away
Let us wash the blood away

Saoirse's voice quieted as her brethren approached. The king stopped before them to embrace her and his son before he gave Soren, Baz, and Enara a nod. Gone was the jolly king from Hallival, and in his place was the leader of Braexmirth, King Elias of Olecastor, Lord of the Forge.

He continued on to clasp arms with Jai and the Duke of Stelonbriar, speaking in hushed tones for a few moments. Soren could see Jai and Erick nodding slightly before King Elias turned to speak.

"In the past, our peoples have not always seen eye-to-eye. I will not ask you to forget those who have fallen before our blades, nor to forcefully befriend those you see as an enemy. All I ask is that you be willing, for the time being, to set those feelings of misgiving aside to help save our world. For in these dark times, we are no longer the enemy, but a willing party, hoping to find allegiance amongst your ranks." His voice boomed over the crowd with a calm authority they all seemed to respect.

"Your leaders and I have agreed that if any of you no longer wish to fight, then that is your right. So, those of you who want to leave, do so now. We do not have time to train the unwilling for what is to come."

A handful of people from different sections of the crowd made their way out of the throng, heads bowed. Soren recognized one of them as Duncan, a kindly tailor from back home in Vreburn.

She expected there to be an uproar of people, angry with the deserters for valuing their lives above everyone else. To her surprise, not a word was spoken.

King Elias watched them go, and once they were out of sight, he continued his address. "Now, I know that must have been hard for some of you. Maybe you are wondering now if you made the right choice. But if you take a moment to look at those who stand beside you, you now know that they will not desert you when things get hard. These people, from all different walks of life, chose you over themselves, and that is more valuable than long-standing hatred between people. We are no longer Braexians, Patrovians, and so forth. We are all of Entheas, *and they will hear us as we march forth to protect what is ours!*"

The crowd broke out in cheers and whoops as people from all the provinces clasped hands and embraced each other as equals. Soren couldn't help the tears that rimmed her eyes, and she squeezed Enara's hand.

Once the crowd had settled, Jai and Erick dismissed everyone for the evening. Meanwhile, King Elias's men awaited instruction on where to put their cargo. After a short discussion, it was decided that everyone would be outfitted first thing in the morning to begin training with the added weight of their armor.

Soren and her friends followed their leaders into the mess line that ran in rows down the tents. She appreciated the fact that Jai, Erick, and King Elias took their spot in line just like everyone else and did not pull rank to move to the front.

Once she had eaten her fill, she joined Adaryn and Mrs. Ferndale in cleaning the after-dinner dishes once the tables had been cleared. She was elbow-deep in dishwater when Jai walked in, flashing a smile at her before dipping Adaryn into a searing kiss.

Soren looked away, hoping to give them some semblance of privacy, as Adaryn let her hands roam over the tracker.

"Love, we have company," Jai reminded her, looking over to Soren. "Sorry, got a little carried away."

"Hey"—Soren held up her soapy hands—"don't let me stop your fun. I just didn't want to stare."

"I don't mind if you want to watch," Adaryn said, giving her a wink.

"I don't think so," Jai said, lifting her up and throwing her over his shoulder.

"What?" Adaryn whined as her hair fell in thick waves over her face.

He gave her a spank before admonishing her. "Save your fantasies for another night, love. Tonight, you are mine."

Adaryn giggled as Jai carried her out the back exit of the tent.

Soren gave her a wave as they disappeared into the night then rubbed away the sweat that had formed on her hairline.

"Are you okay to finish up here, dear?" Mrs. Ferndale asked.

"Yeah, no worries. I only have a few left, anyway," Soren replied, shaking an empty glass in her direction.

"Thank you, dear. Malcolm from that nice tavern invited me for a drink, and I was hoping to oblige."

"That's awesome!" Soren exclaimed with a little too much enthusiasm.

Mrs. Ferndale chuckled at her before waving goodnight. "Just latch the tent behind you."

"I will," Soren called after her.

When she'd finished for the evening, she snuck over to the bathing area. She had brought a fresh set of clothes to dinner and wanted to wash off the day's sweat before returning to her tent.

She did the best she could with cold water and a bar of oat milk soap before she tucked her light blue tunic, sans bra, into the tanned peasant skirt she had borrowed from Saoirse.

Her nerves kicked in the closer she got to the tent. The last few days that Rook had stayed with her, they had passed out from exhaustion and had barely talked after her heavy admission.

She was on a mission tonight, though she felt silly for being so nervous, considering their many trysts back at the manor. Tonight just felt more significant for some reason. She felt closer to Rook after telling him about her past, but nothing like the mating bond he had described.

She decided to not put so much pressure on their relationship. Keeping the Oculus out of Adriel's hands would have to do for now. In the meantime, she just wanted to explore her relationship with Rook and enjoy the time they had together, however short that might be.

She could make out his silhouette beyond the fabric, following every sharply honed edge of his body illuminated by the oil lamp. She hesitated at the threshold and took one more breath before walking in.

Rook sat propped up against the back wall of the tent, the fabric molding around his shoulders. He was shirtless with his ankles crossed above the blanket, reading a book she didn't recognize.

Their eyes met, and his pupils turned to question marks as she plucked the book from his hands and placed it gingerly on the small corner table. He then went to sit up, but she pressed her palm to his chest to keep him in place.

She lifted her skirt and climbed on top of him, letting the fabric pool at their hips. He sucked in a breath when he realized her breasts were bare under her tunic, and his eyes darkened. She could feel him harden under her and couldn't help the satisfied smile that pulled at the corners of her lips.

Without breaking eye contact, she leaned over to extinguish the oil lamp, twisting the gear to turn down the wick and blowing softly into the chimney until they were shrouded in darkness. Then she leaned forward and kissed along his collarbone.

"Little bird … what are you—"

"Shh," she cut him off. "Tell me to stop if you want, but otherwise, shh."

She took his silence as permission to continue her ministrations.

She let her tongue trail along his jaw, enjoying the rough feel of his stubble tickling her taste buds. Without the amenities back at the mansion, he had acquired a more disheveled look that only made him that much sexier.

She could smell the oat milk on his skin and deduced that he must have hit the bathing tent shortly before she had. Her suspicions were confirmed when she sat up and ran a hand through his still-damp hair.

She trailed her fingertips up and down his sides, delighting in the fact that he squirmed under her. He was ticklish, and he hated that she knew it, but she loved the way it made him press into her harder. She continued to kiss and nip everywhere but his lips and even dared to bite him just hard enough to leave a mark on his neck.

He took her closeness as an opportunity to flip them. He cradled her head and lifted his hips, using the momentum to get her on her back, then lifted himself with the opposite arm. He was now hovering above her in the missionary position, and he could just make out the look of surprise on her face.

"Now it's your turn to say stop."

He tortured her in the same way she had him. He kissed her everywhere but where she really wanted. He avoided her lips and kissed up the inside of her thighs, stopping short of where her underwear should have been. His hands circled the sides of her hips, coming up empty. He traced a finger along the joint where her hip and pelvic bone met, causing her to writhe. When he did, in fact, confirm she was not wearing anything under her skirt, he hardened even more.

Unable to take it anymore, he growled, "Naughty little bird," and crashed his lips to hers. When he broke the kiss to catch his breath, his eyes had gone black, his pupils blown out like she was the most beautiful drug. He continued trailing hot kisses down her neck and onto the bare flesh that peeked out from the middle of her tunic.

"Take it off," she said, her voice breathless. Then she sat up, fumbling with the small brown buttons.

He grabbed her hands and pressed them to her sides, keeping his dark eyes on hers. The swirls of midnight blue were like whirlpools in the Obsidian Sea.

He undid each button at an agonizing pace then gently pushed the fabric off her shoulders. He slid the shirt down until it reached her wrists then used the excess material to tie them together.

She looked up at him with wide eyes, her heart beating in her chest like an ancient drum.

A rumble of pleasure sounded from behind Rook's ribcage as he ran his fingers over her torso. Her nipples were a dusky rose and had formed into sharp peaks in the cool air of their tent. He purposefully avoided all of her most sensitive areas as his hands roamed.

"You are still in control, little bird." He grazed his teeth along her jaw and nipped at the soft flesh at the top of her chest. "The bonds are loose. You can free yourself at any time."

Soren put his words to the test and easily slipped a hand free from the knot he had tied. She traced her nails down the curve of his chest and up the back of his neck, pulling his hair lightly to place a kiss on the corner of his lips. Then she returned her arm to its position at her back and waited.

The lust coursing through his veins had Rook feeling like he was about to burst. He laid Soren on her back, pulled the skirt down over her hips, and then took a moment to drink in her naked silhouette before he undid the belt on his dark brown pants. He coiled it twice before setting it on top of his ruck.

"If it becomes too much, say *dreamer*."

Soren nodded, but he urged her to speak.

"Say it for me, little bird. What word do you speak if it becomes too much?"

"Dreamer."

"That's my girl," he praised.

She expected him to touch her then, but he reached toward the table. She watched with wide-eyed curiosity as he removed the chimney and wick from the oil lamp then lifted the jar of golden liquid out of its base.

Rook tested the heat of the castor oil by tilting the jar and letting a few drops hit the soft skin on the inside of his wrist. It was quite warm but cooled quickly and tingled afterward.

"What are you going to do?" Soren asked.

"I am going to make you feel so good, little bird." He could see her mouth form an *O* in the darkened tent and bared his teeth. "Under one condition," he said, letting a few drops of the caster oil fall between her breasts.

Soren let out a surprised squeak, and Rook reached forward to press his index fingers against her lips.

"You have to stay silent. We don't want to be waking up the neighbors, now do we?"

Soren sucked his finger into her mouth, nodding in understanding.

Rook bit his lip to distract his mind before he took her right then and there.

"If you do that again, this will be over quicker than both of us would like." It was the last warning he spoke before he massaged the oil over her breasts and toned stomach.

He continued pouring and massaging the warm liquid over her thighs and calves, kneading her aching feet before traveling back up to work the larger muscles at the top of her legs. She hissed in annoyance as his hand grazed the flesh next to her core teasingly.

"Rook," Soren ground out.

"Tell me what you want," he replied, kissing the top of her pubic bone.

"Touch me," she said.

His laugh vibrated against her core, causing another rush of heat to flood her center. He set the oil down before responding, "You will have to be more specific than that, little bird."

"Make me come," she begged.

He growled his approval and moved to lay his body atop hers. He was naked from the top down, and Soren could feel the heat from his chest seeping into her bones, warming her.

Their lips crashed together once more, and their tongues danced as Rook's long fingers found her center. He teased the bundle of nerves before slipping one finger into her wet heat, followed by a second. He curled his fingers upward, putting pressure on her G-spot, causing a few moans to escape her lips. Then he nipped he earlobe—hard.

"*Ow!*" she exclaimed.

"Quiet, little bird. If you make another sound, I will stop, and we will both go to bed disappointed."

She gave him a half-hearted glare but pressed her lips together, obeying his command.

He moved his fingers with increasing speed, pumping them in and out of her as she writhed against him. She kept her lips pressed together and squeezed her eyes shut. Her nostrils flared, and he could hear the small, stifled moans trying to escape. She was getting close; he could feel her tightening around him.

As she came apart on his hand, she couldn't hold it in any longer and cried out. He swallowed her screams of pleasure with his mouth as she rode out her orgasm.

"I need you—*now*," Soren commanded, lifting her lower back and removing her hands from the cloth manacles.

She undid his trousers and began pulling at the hem with greedy hands.

He tsked her as she rushed to try to undress him. "Always so impatient," he admonished as he finished removing his pants and kneeled between her legs.

"I have been patient," she clipped out, digging her nails into his forearms. "Now, fuck me."

"I thought you'd never ask," Rook said, lining up with her entrance. He pressed into her slowly, savoring the way she wrapped so tightly around him. He basked in the feeling for a moment before he obliged to her request, adjusting his grip, his hands digging into the soft flesh of her ass, lifting her hips to meet his. Soren let out a whimper as he sunk even deeper into her.

His voice was a husky whisper when he spoke next. "Don't forget, little bird—not a sound."

She nodded once more as he slid out of her before slamming back in, burying himself to the hilt. He continued at a feverish pace as Soren's nails cut into his forearms. He clenched his teeth together in an attempt to keep his beast at bay, nearly losing control as she clenched around him. His breathing was haggard, and the sounds escaping from behind Soren's closed lips were about to send him over the edge.

"Come for me, little bird," he ordered, pressing his thumb against her sensitive bud.

She bucked beneath him at the unexpected friction. Then she gripped his wrists, her climax peaking. Her legs shook as her internal walls tightened deliciously.

"Rook," the whispered moan escaped as she came around him.

Hearing his name on her perfect lips undid him. He grunted as he spilled into her, his chest glistening with a mixture of sweat and castor oil. To Soren, he looked like the outline of a god brought to life with quill and ink just for her.

He slipped off the bed and pulled his trousers over his hips, saying, "Be right back," before disappearing into the night.

Soren lay on the bedroll in post-coital bliss as she waited for his return.

He was back a few moments later with one of the washbasins and a couple of cloths.

He took his time cleaning her off, the cool water sending tingles across her overly sensitized skin. Once she was clean, he folded her dirty clothes, setting them aside, and passed her a fresh tunic from his own bag.

Her lip quirked upward.

"I like it when you wear my clothes," he mumbled as he removed his trousers to clean the rest of himself.

Soren just smiled as she shrugged the black shirt over her head, enjoying the way it smelled like him.

Rook donned a fresh set of undergarments then joined her below the blanket, wrapping her up in his arms. Her face was pressed against his chest, and his head rested atop hers.

"Get some sleep, little bird."

"Do you think anyone heard us?" she asked, slightly embarrassed.

"I hope they did."

"What?" she asked, incredulous. "You're the one who told me to keep quiet."

"That's just because I like telling you what to do."

"Bastard," she grumbled against his chest.

"Admit it, you love me," he said before he could stop himself.

"I—"

"You don't need to say it, Soren," he cut her off. "I already know. Now, go to sleep."

"Sweet dreams, Rook."

"Sweet dreams, little bird."

CHAPTER
THIRTY

The training grounds were a cacophony of sound and movement. Now that everyone had been assigned to their battalions, things were moving a lot smoother. All groups continued to do thirty minutes of instruction in each other section to ensure they were well-rounded, and the second half of the day was dedicated to specialized training.

Jai had to admit that everyone seemed to be in decent spirits. It helped that more soldiers from the outlying provinces had started to arrive, along with some other civilians, ready to fight. The untrained went through a condensed version of the gauntlet and were sorted into their battalions like everyone else.

"Brisk morning," King Elias observed as he joined Jai overlooking the main training area. Groups of soldiers marched and sparred in the empty field. The sound of metal clashing on metal rang out, breaking through the cool morning air. It was nearing the end of the autumn tide; winter would blanket these lands soon. If it weren't for the constant physical exertion, the cold would have seeped deep into their bones days ago. Even so, Erick had requested Irefeld's matriarchs to weave some heavier blankets, hats, and gloves to have on hand in case winter decided to rear its ugly head early. The last thing they needed was to lose able-bodied fighters to frostbite.

"Indeed," Jai agreed. "Your men seem to be faring better."

The king chuckled. "You should have witnessed them when we crossed the border. There was not a leaf nor branch unmarred by their stomach contents."

Jai allowed himself a laugh at the Braexian's expense. Braexmirth's soldiers were used to living high up in the mountains where the air was thin, so coming to Stelonbriar had forced them down to ocean level. The result was high altitude de-acclimation syndrome. The Braexians just called it "the drop."

"How many do we have?" the king asked, his gaze panning over the large expanse of farmland. Jai knew that he was, of course, referring to how many lives they would be risking in the coming weeks.

"Just over four thousand."

"Will it be enough?" he asked.

"It will have to be."

Enara waved off a cloud of smoke and shook her head at Baz. "Did you even listen to the instructions Ikei gave us?" She rolled her eyes and beckoned him to come closer so she could wipe the black residue off his face. The twins had taken all the group leaders aside to show them how to use the smoke bombs their brothers had delivered from Braexmirth. The small onyx orbs looked harmless, but when thrown with enough force, the chemical reaction of the powders inside caused a powerful explosion.

Baz looked at the twelve-inch-wide crater in the ground at his feet then gave Enara a sheepish look. "It was an honest mistake!"

"You almost blew your foot off!"

"I didn't mean to step on it. It was an accident," Baz replied.

Enara made another sound of annoyance as she finished wiping off his face. "Tell that to them!" She swept her arms around them at all the eyes that were staring in his direction. "What happens next time you're in the middle of it and that spot is one of us?"

Baz hung his head in defeat. "It really was an accident," he said quietly.

Enara scrubbed her hands down her face, immediately feeling like a piece of shit for berating him. "Hey," she said softly, cupping his cheek, "I'm sorry."

"No," he responded more firmly. "I need to do better, be better. I don't want it to be my fault that anyone gets hurt."

Enara shook her head. She hated it when he beat himself up. "I shouldn't have said anything. I knew it was an accident. I just … It's all starting to get to me."

Baz pulled her to him, wrapping her tightly in his arms. "We all feel the weight of what's coming. We just have to make sure we focus on fighting the enemy and not each other."

Enara sniffled against his shoulder, allowing herself a moment to feel all the emotions she had been holding in for weeks. Baz said nothing as she cried silently against him before she pushed off his chest and wiped a tear away.

"I'm sorry," she repeated.

He wiped away the final tear and kissed the apple of her cheek. "Everything will be okay."

"You can't know that," she whispered.

"No," he replied. "But I believe it."

JAI WATCHED BAZ AND ENARA EMBRACE FROM ACROSS THE FIELD and wondered idly what Adaryn was doing at that moment. Apart from sharing a tent and their daily rituals, they had barely laid eyes on each other.

Adaryn would wake early to help Mrs. Ferndale get breakfast started, and he would sneak into the kitchens to share a quick breakfast with her before starting training. They would sit down in the mess tent for lunch, asking about each other's days before separating again until dinner. He would leave her to join King Elias and Duke Erick to discuss strategy before turning in for the evening. Then they would come together before sleep in a tangle of teeth, tongues, and limbs, not caring if their moans were heard across the barren fields.

Adaryn was insatiable, and Jai was only too happy to concede to her in any way she wanted. Once, before dinner, she had ordered him to take her out back of the mess tent, their bodies crashing together passionately on the hard ground. He then returned to his seat by Erick and King Elias while she began filling serving trays with her hair slightly mussed and cheeks pinked.

If nothing else good came of this war, he would at least enjoy the fact that he could be with the woman he loved out in the open for all to see. Court etiquette had lost its place among the rubble that was now his kingdom.

War brought out a different side of people. The side that begged for blood to be spilled and for all those to relish in their dark desires as though they would die tomorrow. Because they might.

Jai adjusted his trousers, which had gotten uncomfortably tight due to his racy thoughts. He decided to check in on Soren and the old man, Kristoff, to see how they were liking their new bows.

He could hear the *swoosh* and *thump* of the arrows as they hit their mark, and he gave Soren a friendly wave when she noticed him approaching.

"How's it going?" she asked, trotting over to him. Her armor chinked lightly as she moved.

"Decent day. Only a few minor injuries from the younger crowd. Warwick dislocated his shoulder, but Evelyn managed to replace it without much trouble."

"*Oof*," Soren replied, grimacing.

"He's all right. Unfortunately, that means we are down another staff fighter. I'm glad we have Enara to pick up the slack."

"Yeah." Soren smiled fondly. Enara was definitely a woman to be reckoned with.

"Honestly, it's been hard to find people to spar with her," Jai said, rubbing the back of his neck.

"I'm not surprised. You should have seen the practice dummies back home." A shadow fell over Soren's eyes at the mention of Vreburn. Even though she knew her home was safe, it was hard to imagine what she would go back to if they survived the war.

Jai's thick brows furrowed in concern at her expression.

"I can only imagine how well it's going for the ones who do challenge her," Soren said, trying to brighten the mood.

"Oh, you missed out on a few good takedowns, for sure," Jai said, his eyes brightening. "Ori thought he could best her, and she had him on his back in less than thirty seconds."

"Go, Enara!" Soren whooped.

"Hey, I have an idea," Jai said, playing with the dark hairs on his chin.

Soren gave him a skeptical look. "I'm listening."

"Why don't we have a mini tournament? Maybe boost morale with some sort of prize."

Soren couldn't help the grin that spread across her features and crinkled the corners of her eyes.

"I'm listening."

THE CROWD CHEERED AS BAZ GRAPPLED ONE OF THE BRAEXIAN'S and threw him out of the circular ring carved into the ash-covered ground. He was coated in the black dust and breathing heavily.

Enara couldn't help but appreciate the way his large muscles strained against his tight training shirt. The leather molded to his skin in a way that made her want to take him right there in the training ring.

After Baz was named the winner of that round, the Braexian stormed off, kicking up a cloud of soot in the process and sending a few of the onlookers into a coughing fit.

"Someone's a sore loser," Enara said under her breath as she watched the mountainous man stalk off.

"He'll be all right," Callan replied from beside her. His arms were wrapped around Saoirse, who was looking at her with wild eyes.

"Be glad you weren't the one to take him out," she said, smirking. "That would have been a real temper tantrum."

"Why?" Enara asked. "Because I am a woman?"

"No," she replied, her smile getting larger. "Because Braexian men prefer to dominate those they wish to bed."

Enara looked at her, open-mouthed, unsure of how to respond to the comment.

"Julian was hoping he could win your affections by defeating Baztien," Callan explained.

Enara's mouth started working again as Baz returned to her side after finishing his victory lap.

"Then what? Did he think I would just leave Baz in the dust and jump into bed with him?" she asked incredulously.

"I mean, basically, yeah," Saoirse replied, suppressing a giggle.

"Braexians do many things to display our affections toward our intended. Fighting just happens to be one of them."

Enara huffed her annoyance in the direction of the beastly man who was talking with knife hands at a group of his brothers and sisters who seemed to be laughing at his expense.

Baz followed her gaze and asked, "So, do you mean to tell me that I was just part of a literal cock fight?"

Enara pressed her lips together and smacked his shoulder while Saoirse and Callan burst out laughing.

Baz reached forward and booped Enara's nose with his pointer finger, leaving behind a dot of black residue. She finally broke, and he was rewarded with a full belly laugh. The sound brought joy to his ears, and he used his sleeve to wipe off her nose before following it up with a kiss.

"Hey, save it for later. You're up, Enara," Soren yelled from across the circle where she stood with Jai, Adaryn, and Rook.

Soren had yielded in the third round to a wiry teenager from Irefeld. Enara knew she probably could have bested him, but Soren likely wanted to give him the confidence boost. It must have worked, considering he went on to win two more rounds after that, using his long limbs and speed to defeat two larger men.

Rook had looked furious the entire time Soren had been in the ring, and Enara could see his hand flexing around his rapier. She had also noticed how his whole body seemed to relax anytime Soren was in his presence. To her surprise, she had grown to find him somewhat tolerable. He had even won Baz over, though it irked her to no end that he made jokes at her lover's expense.

She shook her head, returning her attention to the task at hand, and entered the ring.

IT WAS OVER QUICKLY. SHE HAD MANAGED TO TRIP THE FEMALE archer to the ground and grappled her into an arm lock. The archer had fought valiantly but ended up tapping out.

Rook fought next, taking out his opponent with ease. Then Baztien lost to a woman from Estelar named Astrid. She was in her early thirties and took him by surprise, dodging as his arm swung for her ribs and used her own arm and his forward momentum to flip him onto his back, winding him. He popped to his feet quickly, but she burst forward in an onslaught that he didn't see coming. He landed hard on his hindquarters in the dust. He let her help him to his feet and shook her hand before saying, "Good fight."

They were down to the final four, which included one guard from Irefeld and the elder twin, Ikei, Enara, and Rook. Enara defeated the guard, but she had earned herself a bruised rib and a slight twinge in her left ankle.

She watched on as Rook and Ikei entered the ring, dying to know which one of them she would be fighting. The speed at which they moved was mind-blowing, reminding her of when Rook had fought off the beast, Corvus, in Thorncrest. She felt a twinge of sympathy for him as she remembered what he had looked like after losing against his mentor.

She heard Soren gasp as Ikei landed a punch and two swift kicks to Rook's chest and upper thigh.

Enara had to admit she was impressed with how well he was faring this far into the game. She had not been surprised when Ikei had made it to the top of the ranks after witnessing his fighting skills back in Edras Mora. His brother had only been defeated two rounds before by the same woman who had taken out Baz.

It was a long fight, and both men were limping by the end of it.

Rook had noticed that Ikei was favoring his leg and made it his new target, finally knocking him out of the ring. They shook hands, and he gave Enara a devilish smile that said, *"You're next."*

Rook was offered a fifteen-minute reprieve before entering the ring, which he refused.

Furious that he thought she needed to be given an advantage, she stormed right up to him to give him a piece of her mind.

"What the fuck do you think you're doing?" she growled.

"Only what is fair," he responded calmly.

"I don't need help or pity to claim king of the ring. Or in my case, queen," she pointed out.

"I was not trying to offend you," Rook said quietly. "I have an unfair advantage already, in case you forgot."

Enara's eyes went wide, and then she mentally smacked her hand against her forehead. "You heal," she hissed. She scanned the crowd, trying to decide if she should call him out, but the strategic side of her warned that it would not be a good idea to share his secret.

"The worse the injury, the longer the healing time," he continued in his lowered voice. "But if you want to make it more interesting"—he raised his tone so everyone could hear—"we could use blades. Give this crowd a real show."

"Is that a joke?"

"Not at all," he said, his eyes glinting with mischief. "First to draw blood wins. Sound fair?"

"Fine," she replied, turning to grab Coraxis from Baz's hands. "Don't worry," she said, assuaging his unspoken concern.

When her focus was back on the ring, Rook stood waiting, his rapier in hand. Normally, he brandished two, but Soren held the other tightly in her fist, her knuckles turning white with the effort.

"Let's do this," Enara snarled as Jai entered the ring.

It was decided that Jai, Duke Erick, and the king would not be allowed to fight in case of accidental injury. The leaders needed to remain in top shape with sound minds to lead them into battle, so they settled for cheering on the mayhem.

"The rules are as follows," Jai started, and the crowd went silent as he spoke. "First to draw blood wins it all."

"What's the prize?" an onlooker called out.

They had yet to announce what the winner would earn. There had been so much pent-up energy amongst the warriors that just the thought of a reward had them all signing up for the mini tournament.

"The winner," he continued with a dramatic flourish, "will get to enjoy a hot bath and … will switch accommodations with me for the next three days."

Oohs and ahhs sounded from the crowd.

It was amazing how something like a war could put things in perspective. Before the recent attacks, a bath and a larger, more comfortable bed would have been a disappointing prize when now both things were highly coveted.

"Maybe I should let you win," Rook said, crinkling his nose in disgust. "I'd be doing us all a favor—I can smell you from here."

Enara knew he was goading her, but she couldn't stop herself from giving him a smart reply. "At least, when I get laid tonight, it won't be because I had to kidnap my partner."

The comment effectively shut him up, and Enara let her lips curl into a satisfied smirk as she readied herself.

"On that note," Jai said, awkwardly gesturing his hands toward the ring, "let the fight commence!"

Enara and Rook circled the ring, sizing each other up. For a moment, it seemed as though they would never start until Enara got impatient and began swinging. She had paid close attention to his fights, looking for signs of weakness, and couldn't find any obvious openings, but as she dodged a blow, she caught a glance of Soren across the ring.

Her best friend stood with her hand over her mouth, watching the fight unfold, and Enara knew how to beat him.

As their weapons clashed, she muttered under her breath to him, "You will break her."

The comment threw off his concentration long enough for her to land a sharp elbow under his chin, followed by a swift kick to his forearm, causing him to lose his grip on his sword. The weapon went clattering to the ground, and Enara used the length of her staff to send it skittering to the other side of the ring.

She stood between Rook and his weapon, and the look he gave her could have leveled all of Entheas. His chest was heaving, and his breath turned white in the cool air. Evening had fallen quickly over the last few bouts, bathing them in silver light.

It was Rook's turn to make the first move. Knowing he was at a disadvantage, he wanted to be in control of his trajectory. He managed to fake her out since he was faster than her, but as he darted toward his weapon, Enara spun and swung out with the tip of her blade, catching his boot.

Rook let out a loud *oomph* as the air rushed from his lungs upon impact but was on his feet again, trying to inch his way back to his weapon. He caught Soren's eye and gave her a wink before turning back to Enara.

Soren had debated if she wanted to stop the fight between her best friend and her lover but ultimately decided it was about time they had it out. That didn't stop her from gasping loudly every time their bodies clashed or Enara's blade just missed a sliver of Rook's flesh.

In a surprising turn of events, Rook managed to land enough blows to make Enara drop Coraxis. She had not been so lucky as him in the fact that her weapon landed in the black earth at his feet, but she knew something he did not.

Touch it, she thought, willing him to attempt to use the enchanted weapon against her.

She exaggerated her injuries and pretended to struggle to get to her feet. Her face was etched with false pain while, inside, she smiled widely as he reached his bare hand toward her bladed staff. His long, white fingers grabbed the weapon eagerly, and she waited for him to cry out in pain, but the sound never came.

Her eyes widened as he strode toward her with purpose, and she stood as still as the great trees of Eldrin as he lifted the weapon and placed a featherlight nick on her right hand.

Her eyes flicked to Soren, and then to Baz, who seemed to finally catch on to what had just happened.

"I believe you dropped this," Rook said, holding the weapon out to her.

She grasped it lightly, as though it were now a foreign being, no longer designed just for her. Then she followed Rook's movements as he retrieved his sword and returned to the center of the ring to be congratulated by Jai.

The blood pumping in her ears was so loud it nearly drowned out the cheers of the crowd as Jai raised Rook's hand in the air.

Soren and Baz were immediately by her side as her mind tried to process the discovery she had just made. Somehow, impossibly, her and Rook were both able to wield her weapon, which could only mean one thing.

The thought was so jarring that a wave of nausea threatened to turn her body into a convulsing mess. She was not ready to speak the words out loud just yet, but they rested on the edge of her tongue, begging to be released.

The words repeated over and over in her mind, screaming against the edges of her skull until she felt it might crack in half.

Rook and I share the same blood.

CHAPTER
THIRTY—ONE

As the crowd dispersed, Rook stood with a confused facial expression as Baz, Jai, Enara, and Soren stared.

"But they look nothing alike," Baz stated.

"He can't be," Soren denied.

"The staff worked on me, though," Baz said, looking at his now flat fingertips whose prints had been singed off by the blood magic.

"Will anyone explain to me what's going on?" Rook interjected.

"Yeah, I'm going to let them take the reins on this," Jai answered, gesturing to the other three.

Enara, who had been silent up until that point, finally gathered the strength to speak the truth that her mind refused to believe. "It would seem that you and I are related."

Rook laughed coldly, taking her words as a sort of cruel joke. He had accepted a long time ago that he had no true family. The thought was ludicrous.

"But how?" Soren asked, still in shock at the news. She could not comprehend that the two most important people in her life, apart from Baz, of course, could possibly be related. Though, she had to admit that the thought warmed her. "It would have been before you were born. He's older than you."

Rook realized now they were not trying to play a trick on him and immediately rounded on Enara, questions coming out one after another as fast as arrows from an archer's bow. "Where did your family originate? Who is your mother? What was her maiden name? Did anyone in your family have hair like mine?"

"Slow down!" Enara snapped. "I know as much as you do, so take it down a peg, will you?"

"I'm sorry," he replied sincerely. "I grew up amongst animals. My father took me from my mother. I did not think of the possibility that I had other family members."

"What about you?" Enara asked, returning fire as she pinned him with questions of her own. "Where were you born? Who was your mother?"

"I never knew her name," Rook replied. "Adriel found me as an infant, in the woods, on the twenty-ninth day of the autumn tide."

At this, Soren placed a hand on his forearm, garnering his gaze. "You never told me that it was your birthday a few days ago."

"It hardly seemed important with everything going on," he replied quietly.

"You are important to me," Soren said, looking into his glacier eyes.

The ice in them melted slightly before Enara's comment broke through their moment.

She stared off into the distance as she said, "My brother was born that day."

"Enara," Baz said, pulling her close to him, "I thought you mentioned that your brother passed after childbirth."

"That's the story my father told my mother," she said, her voice sounding far away. "My mother lost a lot of blood. She was not conscious at the time."

"So, you have no proof that your brother actually died?"

"I don't know," Enara said, wringing her hands together. "I mean, there was a gravestone, and Mother said people in town attended the funeral."

"Wouldn't the city watch have to investigate?" Baz asked.

"Not if it was medical. They only investigate if there is just cause or reasonable suspicion."

"Did your parents have any other siblings? Could he be a distant cousin or something?" Jai asked, trying to help.

Enara shook her head. "Mother lost her sister when they were children, a freak accident with a runaway carriage, and my grandfather only ever wanted a son, so my father was an only child."

"Where did she live when this happened?" Rook asked.

"They lost him shortly after they moved to Vreburn. My father had received an offer for a position on the council, but they used to live in Southern Estelar."

Rook sucked a breath in through his teeth, and Soren could feel him go rigid beside her.

"That is where my father found me," he said, his voice a low whisper.

"So, that means ..." Baz started.

"You're my brother," Enara said, putting the pieces together.

"And you're my sister." The words fell from Rook's lips like droplets from a cloud. Then the pressure in his chest became so heavy that it finally burst into an emotional storm of rage and sadness.

"All this time!" he yelled to no one in particular. "All this time, I had a family and did not even know. All this time ..." His voice trailed off as his throat constricted with tears. He turned from the group to blink them away, allowing the anger for his father and his lies to twist the protective thorns back around his breaking heart, piecing it together like a dying botanical sculpture.

"Hey," Soren said, trying to push back the brittle wood and spikes. "Do not let him have this power over you." Then she locked eyes with Enara. "Or you."

Enara's fists were clenched, and Baz was hovering beside her, giving her some space to vent her anger. "Even in death, he still finds ways to hurt me," she said, grinding her teeth together.

"Try to look at it in a positive light," Jai said calmly.

"What is positive about this?" Rook snapped at him, his eyes like icicles—sharp and deadly.

"I think what he means to say is that you two have more in common than you realize. I know all of this is ... a lot. But maybe you can find some comfort in the fact that you both have been given a second chance at having a family. Your fathers did not cherish what they had with you, but we do.

We"—Soren gestured to the group of them—"are your guys' family."

Enara huffed and rolled her eyes, and Rook frowned.

"Look," Soren went on, "I don't expect you two to be best friends—siblings bicker all the time—but I think we can all agree we are bound together by whatever the Maker planned for us. We can waste our time fighting amongst ourselves and spending energy on past hurts, or we can choose to move forward. All of us … together."

Rook and Enara eyed each other skeptically, and Soren held her breath.

"I mean, I don't completely hate you," Enara said.

"Yeah, fine, you're all right, I guess," Rook replied.

"Group hug?" Baz suggested.

"Not a fucking chance in hell," Enara scoffed.

"Absolutely not," Rook said, grimacing at the thought.

"Well, kids," Jai concluded, "now that we have that sorted, how about we get us some dinner?"

THEY WERE ONE WEEK OUT FROM BATTLE, AND THE LAST FEW days had been awkward, to say the least. Rook and Enara had agreed to spend some time together to put aside their differences. They went into their conversations hesitantly but ended up sharing a mutual understanding of each other. They both knew what it was like to grow up feeling unloved and uncared for, and they both knew the sting of weapons and fists.

It was heartbreaking to Soren that their largest connection was the fact that they both had suffered extreme abuse from those who should have taken care of them, but she was happy that they were finally starting to get along.

She watched as Rook and Enara took a lap around the training grounds and couldn't help but let herself feel a little twinge of hope. If they got out of this, maybe they could eventually call themselves friends.

She scarfed down the rest of her jarred peaches before returning to her hand-to-hand combat session with Baztien. Her skills had improved, and she was feeling a little more confident about takedowns. Her joints were sore and aching at the end of each day, but she attributed it to the muscle she was building.

Her and Baz readied themselves for another bout just as Jai walked up, halting them.

"You two, come with me, and gather the rest of the group leaders," he said in his no-nonsense voice. "We have news."

"No problem," Baz replied, straightening.

"We will be right behind you," Soren confirmed.

The two split off in opposite directions, each taking a brisk jog to their half of the grounds.

A few minutes later, the leaders gathered in the war tent and took seats at the large table. Jai sat at the far end, flanked by Erick and King Elias. Their expressions were grave, and worry buried itself deep in the pit of Soren's stomach. She knew that whatever news they had to share would not be good.

Jai cleared his throat to silence the last of the chatter before speaking. "We have received intelligence early this morning from a resistance within the Xian-Dao dynasty. Bao-Ren's forces are on the move and will be upon us in two days' time."

The silence was deafening, and it felt like all the air had been sucked out of the room as the last words escaped his mouth.

"I understand this will come as a shock to all of you, but we have no time for weakness. We must relay this message to our ranks and ensure they are ready to fight. We should also assume Adriel's forces will be joining them. We need to be ready for anything."

Soren's voice broke through the silence, "When should we let everyone know?"

"As soon as possible," Jai replied. "We just lost a few days of what could be left of the rest of our lives. They deserve to decide how they will spend their final moments before battle."

There were muttered agreements throughout the small space, and then Jai dismissed them to gather everyone in the training grounds. He then ran to the mess tent in search of Adaryn, who could tell by the look on his face as he burst into the tent that something was terribly wrong.

"What is it?" she asked, her doe eyes as wide as the dinner plates she was scrubbing.

"Two days," he choked out. His resolve was slipping, and tears welled in his eyes. "I have to tell them all we have two days until they are upon us."

Adaryn didn't ask questions. She just dried her hands and held him tightly until he replaced his anguish with the stoic mask of a king.

"Two years or two days, we will make the time worth while," she said softly, running her fingers through the dark waves of his hair.

"I have to go," he said, nuzzling the skin at her neck.

"I know," she replied.

He took one last moment to drink her in. She smelled of grass and honeysuckle, and it comforted him. She felt like home. A home that he prayed to the Maker that they would eventually return to.

He pressed his lips to hers then walked out of the tent.

He allowed himself a breath as he approached the platform, the king and Erick by his side. He was unsure how he had ended up the leader of this war, maybe because he had the majority of the troops, but the responsibility of it all weighed heavily on his heart.

The crowd hushed, and he could see the false hope in their eyes. He wished he had good news for them. He wished he could send them all home to their families to rebuild in peace, but now was not the time for peace. War was upon them, and their days were numbered.

The words that came next broke his heart, but he had to say them; they had to know what was to come.

"We have been preparing these last few weeks to fight our enemies. I have watched over all of you as you learned new skills and accepted each other with open arms. I am happy to call you all brothers and sisters." He paused to gather himself.

"As your section leaders have been made aware, we received correspondence from a resistance deep within Xian-Dao. You may not know this, but our melee weapons trainer, Baztien Greymark, his parents were part of this resistance. Now, many years later, they still come to our aid. They have informed us that Bao-Ren's forces are on their way here this very moment. We were expecting the troops from Anistera to regroup at the end of the week, but our enemies will now be upon us the day after next."

He waited for the uproar. He waited for shouts of discontent, for screams and cries of upset soldiers, complaints that their final days were to be taken from them. Instead, he was met with silent resolve. This was what they had been training for, and their response told him everything he needed to know. They were ready, and they would not go down without a fight.

He gave Duke Erick and King Elias a quick glance before moving on. "For those of you who wish to touch up on certain aspects of your training, speak to the section leaders, and they will accommodate you. Otherwise, I suggest you all take the next day and a half to rest and write to your loved ones. Eat and drink to your heart's content and cherish those around you. Think not of the bloodshed to come but of love, and life, and family. May the Maker be with you all."

The entire army cheered as he finished his speech. Their energy was palpable, and he couldn't help but smile. His heart knew he might never see many of their faces again, but he took the moment to enjoy the comradery.

As he followed Erick toward the war tent, King Elias placed a large hand on his back and boomed, "Come on, lad; you look like you could use a drink."

"You know what," Jai replied. "I think you're right."

CHAPTER
THIRTY-TWO

Soren untangled herself from Rook's grasp and chugged water from the canteen on their nightstand. Her cheeks warmed as she looked at the oil lamp and stretched her sore body. She was naked, apart from Rook's short-sleeved shirt, which hung to the middle of her thighs.

She padded over to her ruck and changed into her training gear, deciding to sweat off her hangover. Then she trudged across the burned ground and tried not to let the smell make her dry heave. She had grown accustomed to it, as they all had over the course of their training, but her resolve had been weakened from the previous evening's libations. Her stomach did a little flip, and she took short breaths in through her mouth to avoid getting sick.

As she approached the training area, she noticed a few people hard at work. She guessed they, like her, had frayed nerves and couldn't sleep.

A voice from behind startled her, and she nearly tripped over a nearby sparring dummy.

"Hey, lady. How did you sleep?" Enara looked like she had been out here for hours, a bead of sweat running down her temple.

"I didn't," Soren replied honestly.

"I figured," Enara said, sighing. "Me, neither."

"I'm guessing Baz is still out?" Soren asked.

Enara chuckled. "Yeah, but I don't mind. I needed to clear my head."

"Same," Soren said. "I've missed you. I feel like we haven't talked since training started." She picked her fingernails as she continued, "I mean, I know I see you at mealtimes and stuff, but … I guess … I dunno. I miss just hanging out."

Enara hugged her hard, and Soren could feel the heat radiating off her body. "I miss you, too, lady. How about this? Why don't we train together this morning and have a girls-only afternoon?"

"Yeah," Soren replied somberly. "I would like that."

"Besides," Enara went on, "you smell like the floorboards of a tavern. We gotta get the rest of that alcohol out of your system."

"Oh, fuck off," Soren replied, shoving her.

"For the record, I hope you know I have seen the change in you." Enara's tone took on a serious edge. "I noticed you haven't been drinking as much and, apart from the stress of our circumstances, you seem to be handling things better than before."

"I don't feel the need to drink as much now," Soren replied. "It kind of lost its charm, I guess."

"Well, whatever it is, I'm glad." Enara gave her a comforting smile before giving Soren a hard smack on her butt.

"*Ow!* What the hell, Enara?" Soren screeched, rubbing her behind.

"Let's go!" her friend replied, flashing her teeth. "First to complete a lap and three takedowns has to give the other a foot rub."

"Oh, hell no," Soren replied, swiping a foot out and tripping Enara. She landed with an *oof*, and Soren took off running.

"You'll pay for that!" Enara yelled, chasing after her.

The two women spent the rest of the afternoon enjoying some much-needed quality time together. They talked about their favorite moments and memories, wanting to focus on happier times. When they pulled aside the canvas to the mess tent for dinner, their hearts were a little lighter.

Enara took her place beside Baz, and Soren took hers next to Rook. She wasn't sure what they had gotten up to all day, but she had seen the two of them training with Jai and Erick earlier.

"So, how is everyone feeling?" Baz asked, trying to break the ice. It was the elephant in the room. No one wanted to talk about the fact that they could all be dead tomorrow.

"I've been better," Rook replied between bites of his roast beef.

Mrs. Ferndale and Adaryn had gone all out for their final dinner before the fight started. There was the rosemary-crusted beef tenderloin that Rook was indulging in and seared pheasant legs for those who did not eat beef. Honey-roasted carrots and creamy mashed potatoes were laid out in large troughs atop the wooden tables. Soren couldn't believe that the vegetables had been from a jar by how well they were prepared. Her mouth had been salivating as she and Enara waited to fill their plates in the buffet line.

They scarfed down their food with such intensity that Baz and Rook gaped at them with open mouths. For once, Rook didn't admonish Soren for her manners. She guessed he figured manners didn't mean much in times of war.

They chased down their final supper with a pale ale from Erick's personal stores.

"It's a good thing they didn't bring this out last night," Baz remarked between sips. "There would be none left."

"I prefer something stronger," Rook replied, grimacing at his cup after taking a swig. "It tastes like dog piss."

"Well, sorry we don't all have your refined tastes," Enara jabbed, but it was all bark and no bite.

"Yeah, well," Rook replied, sitting back lazily against the pew, "we can't all be this perfect."

Enara raised her brow, and Soren and Baz burst out laughing.

"Yeah, okay," Soren managed between snorts.

"I didn't hear you complaining last night," Rook said, his eyes darkening. His voice was devoid of all humor now, and he looked hungry, but not for food.

Soren swallowed as a blush creeped up her chest to color her cheeks.

"Anyway," Baz said, cutting through the sexual tension that had been building between them, "anyone have final thoughts on how tomorrow is going to go down?"

Enara shook her head.

"I know Jai planned on organizing the battalions at first light so we can be ready for anything," Rook said, turning his attention back to the group.

"On the plus side, the kestrels will be at a disadvantage because we will see them coming from a mile away," Soren commented, trying to force down a few more glazed carrots. Her appetite had suddenly left her, and she shifted her food around on her plate.

"Yeah, I think Jai definitely made the right choice to wage the battle here instead of the mountains. They have no place to hide now," Baz said.

"Yeah, but neither do we," Soren whispered.

"We will manage," Enara said, sounding stronger than she looked. She had the same doubts Soren did but voicing them would only make everyone feel worse.

"Whatever happens, I love you guys," Soren said tearfully.

Rook couldn't help but shift in his seat at the sentiment. He felt slightly disappointed that she was not directing those words at him. He knew how she felt, but he had hoped that, with so little time left, she would say it. He would have begged on his knees to have her speak those three little words to him, but he also knew that when she did speak them, he wanted it to be of her own volition. So, he waited.

He did not regret saying *I love you* first. He had never spoken those words to anyone in his life before Soren, and he was glad for it. Those words belonged to her and no one else. He would stand by her on the battlefield tomorrow and fall before any sword in an effort to protect her. He would take every cut of a blade, every sting of an arrow, every crush of a fist, and every slice of a talon before he would let Adriel take her from him.

All the soldiers thought they were going to war with Adriel when, in reality, Adriel was going to war with him, and he would lose.

Soren dragged out dinner to spend more time with Baz and Enara. She had missed this. She had needed today, and she couldn't be more thankful that Rook understood that she required some extra time with them.

From her understanding, he had spent the afternoon with Meena and Evelyn, making sure they were prepared for what was to come. She knew he was scared for them, but he would never say it; she didn't think he had to. He loved them just as she loved Baz and Enara, in his own way.

As they left the common area, she gave Baz and Enara one last squeeze and let her fingers entwine with Rook's as he led the way back to their tent. She remained silent as they entered, the weight of what was to come sitting heavily on her shoulders.

"I have something for you," Rook said, beckoning for her to sit on the cot. "I should have given them to you sooner, but I was waiting for the right time." He reached into his pack and pulled out a roll of fabric. He laid it out on the blanket beside her then unfurled it to reveal four immaculately formed daggers.

"Rook, these are beautiful," she marveled, lifting one of the blades and taking in all the fine details. The handles were carved from the same white antlers that formed the chandelier at Thorncrest Manor. She traced a finger along the roses and vines that had been whittled into the animal bone, and her eyes misted. "You remembered," she whispered, twisting the blade around in her hand, testing its weight.

"A flower is only as good as its petals, so I thought I would give you some thorns."

"If I am the thorn, then you are the feather—strong in the harshest of winds, but the softest of souls."

"We could name them as such," he said. "If you wanted."

She nodded. "Name them as the parts of a feather so you can be with me out there."

"This will be Rachi," Rook named the blade in her hand then pointed to the other three, assigning their titles. "Then Vane, Quill, and Notch."

"They are perfect," Soren said. "Did you carve them yourself?" She traced the blade to its tip and then hissed when she nicked herself.

Rook reached forward to grab the injured finger and sucked it into his mouth to remove the crimson droplet from its end. "Yes, while I healed," he answered, keeping pressure on her fingertip. It was the tiniest of cuts and stopped bleeding almost instantaneously.

"Thank you," she breathed and turned to embrace him.

"You're welcome, little bird," he said into her hair. "Besides, I owed you."

She let out a soft laugh. "That you did."

"I am sorry," he said seriously.

"For what?"

"About making you lose your father's daggers. Had I known they were so sentimental, I would have—"

"Stop." Soren pressed her hand to his mouth. "I don't want to spend what could be our last night together dwelling on our past mistakes. I just want to be here with you."

He nodded, kissing the tips of her fingers before removing her hand so he could lean in to kiss her lips. She sighed against his mouth, and a hungry growl broke free from the back of his throat.

"Wait," she said breathlessly, and he pulled back, searching her eyes.

"Is something wrong?" he asked, his brow worrying.

"Not at all," she replied. "I just hope you know how much you mean to me."

"I know," he replied, twirling her hair between his fingers. The blue strands had fallen loose from their ties and fell in a soft curtain around her shoulders. Her dark eyes danced in the low flame of the oil lamp, and her skin glowed a deep bronze. He brushed her hair aside and trailed kisses down her shoulder, relishing in the way it caused goosebumps to rise on her arms.

He removed Rachi from her hand and placed it with the rest of the blades, rolling them up and setting them on the table. Soren was surprised when he held out a hand instead of rejoining her on the cot.

"Where are we going?" she asked as he shouldered his pack and led her out of the tent.

He held a finger to his lips and made a shushing sound.

They passed by the rest of the tents and made their way onto the open field. It was silent, and the late autumn air sent a chill up her spine. There was a slight breeze coming in from the west that seemed to clear away the scent of scorched earth.

"I have one last thing for you," he replied cryptically as he dragged her onto the wooden platform Jai had used to make his address.

She stood aside as he pulled a thin blanket from his ruck and laid it out on the platform, beckoning her to sit. He was leaning against the wood post, and she crawled to settle between his legs, resting her head back against his shoulder. The half-walls of the platform protected them from most of the elements as she let herself snuggle against Rook's warm body.

"So, are you going to tell me why we're out here?" she asked.

"No, I am going to show you."

As if the night itself had overheard their conversation, a meteor shot across the sky, its tail burning in a brilliant flash of white light.

"Oh, wow!" Soren exclaimed, awestruck by the phenomenon.

"I overheard one of the farmers saying there would be a meteor shower this week."

"How could he possibly have known that?" Soren asked as another bright flash streaked across the sky.

"His son owned a star-glass and could predict showers up to one month in advance."

"And if he had been wrong?" she challenged.

"Then the stars would have had to do."

"It's perfect," Soren replied, staring upward as more meteors lit up the night. "You're perfect." She turned, pressing her lips to his. He groaned as she climbed into his lap to deepen the kiss.

"You're … going … to miss it," he growled between kisses as his hands reached around to grab her from behind, pressing her closer to him.

"No, we won't," she replied, kissing down his neck and nipping him hard. She smiled at the little indent her teeth left behind.

"Little bird," he warned.

"Yes," she replied in a sing-song voice before tracing the shell of his ear with her tongue and doling out another sharp bite.

"Fuck," he groaned then commanded, "I want you on your back."

She did as he said and laid back, the blanket doing little to protect her from the wooden boards.

He moved quickly, stalking toward her on his knees, his eyes as dark as the sky above them. Then, wasting no time, he removed her bottoms, and she squeaked as the cool night air breezed over her sensitized skin. He tossed them aside but chose to leave her undergarments on in case they were interrupted. He didn't want to share this part of her with anyone. She was his.

He traced the lines of her panties, and she let out a little moan as he slipped a finger past the fabric and teased her core. She was wet and wanting, and he couldn't wait to taste her.

He stretched the fabric to the side and sucked at her sweet spot as he curled two fingers inside her. She bucked against him, moaning his name.

"Rook, please," she begged.

"Open your eyes, little bird," he ordered between licks.

She was so focused on how good he felt between her legs that she hadn't realized she had closed them. She let out another moan of appreciation, and her eyes shot open.

The entire sky was laid out before her from her new vantage point, and the meteor shower was in full force. Her mouth popped open in an *O* as he circled her clit and she cried out.

"Be as loud as you want, little bird. No one can hear you. I want you to scream my name to the stars as you come for me."

"Maker, Rook, right there," Soren moaned, grinding into him. "Don't you dare stop."

He was relentless, and the thread of pleasure that was building inside her was pulled so taut she feared she would snap from the ecstasy of it all.

The meteors blazed overhead as Rook ignited the inferno inside her. She exploded around him like a dying star, her orgasm going supernova as she screamed his name.

As she came down from her climax, he crawled up to her face to claim her mouth. She could barely breathe as his tongue danced with hers.

She fumbled to unclasp his belt, and he sucked in a breath as her hand slipped into his trousers to grasp his firmness. She stroked him from root to tip as he palmed her breasts, his breathing getting more erratic by the second.

"I can't wait anymore," she said, pushing his trousers past his hips and grabbing his length, pulling him toward her.

"Impatient little bird," he chided, reaching a hand down to guide himself into her. She was so wet for him, and he growled in appreciation, the sound rumbling low in his chest.

"Fuck, Soren," he groaned as he pushed in deeper. He grasped her hips hard enough to bruise and started picking up the pace. He leaned back to look at the stars as he pounded into her and she cried out in pleasure. The meteors streaked past in a stunning display, and he clenched his teeth together. He would not last much longer.

"I'm going to … Rook … please," she begged. "Come with me."

He could feel her tighten around him, and his eyes met hers. "As you wish, little bird," he managed as his climax crested. It was as if every nerve ending lit up at once, and the stars in his eyes matched those above.

After finishing, he collapsed on top of her, breathing heavily. Then, once he was able to catch his breath, he rolled off of her, using a corner of the blanket to clean her off.

She slipped her training pants back on, and they returned to their seated position with Soren between his legs to watch the rest of the meteor shower, bodies sated and hearts full.

"Rook," Soren said quietly into the night.

"Yes, little bird."

"I lov—"

She was cut off by an earth-shattering *boom* in the distance.

Both of them were on their feet in an instant, Rook grabbing the hunting knife he had placed in his ruck for emergencies.

The ground shook as more booms sounded, this time coming from all around them.

They took a moment to face each other. An understanding passed between them. Soren's eyes were wide with fear, and Rook's had iced over. They knew that sound. Soren had only heard it once before, but it was a sound that had haunted Rook's dreams since he was a child. The sound marked the arrival of a Celestial in Entheas.

As if needing to hear the confirmation herself, Soren looked at the field before them and said, "They're here."

CHAPTER
THIRTY—THREE

Soren's lungs ached as she and Rook sprinted down the rows of tents to gather their armor and weapons as they screamed into the night.

"The enemy is upon us!"

"Gather your weapons!"

They did not have time to make personal stops, and Soren's heart clenched. She wanted so badly to go to Baz and Enara, or Jai and Adaryn, but she would be no use to them without her weapons, and Rook's hunting knife would hardly be enough to fight off an army. She sent a silent prayer to the Maker and trusted that her friends would be able to fend for themselves.

They tore the fabric of their tent aside and assembled the thin metal plates as quickly as possible before Soren used her thigh sheath to arm herself with her new daggers. She tied back her hair swiftly then slung her bow and quiver over her back, the arrows rustling together. Rook was already in his armor, and he looked every bit the son of Adriel. A god.

He gripped his rapiers tightly in his fists and turned to her. "I hate you," he said, a smirk trying to make its way through his now stony features.

She gave him a swift kiss. "I hate you, too," she replied before they ran in the direction of the closest screams.

All the plans of formations and battle groups went out the window as they sprinted to the far end of the war tents. The ground shook beneath their feet as thousands of celestial bodies marched in the hard-packed earth toward them. The gate to Irefeld was close. They had planned to use it as a bottleneck to take down Celestials as they arrived, but she already knew this plan was folly.

They hurried back toward the training area to join the fray. The gate lay just beyond the next field, and by the time they made it back, their friends were already clashing swords with the enemy.

"Gather your horses!" Jai yelled to the group of riders who were fighting their way through a group of enemies whose armor bore the red sun of the Xian-Dao empire.

That's not possible, Soren thought as she nocked her bow and took out a man who was attempting to swing at Jai from behind.

The tracker gave her a nod of thanks before slicing down two more enemies.

The group of riders managed to make it to the stables and began mounting their horses. They shot out of the wooden gate with a war cry, cutting down enemies in their path.

Rook was a blur of black and silver streaking down the field, leaving a trail of bodies in his wake. Soren followed his movement with her arrows. She couldn't help but be impressed when she realized he was specifically targeting Celestials.

Her breath hitched as her hand reached back and came up empty. Then she felt the rush of air before a soldier's sword swung toward her face. She ducked low and swung her bow hard, the curved wood taking out the man's legs. He fell to the dark ground with a heavy grunt, and Soren turned on him. She swung her bow to the side and grabbed Rachi from her thigh. With one swift stroke, she dragged the blade across the back of his knees, slicing the tendons there. After rendering his legs useless, she plunged Rachi into the soft spot at the base of his neck, severing his brain stem. Then she leaned in close so her breath was against his ear. She did not care that she was speaking to a corpse when she whispered harshly, "That was for Baz's parents." She shoved him to the ground before following the line of bodies to where Rook was pulling his blade out of the chest of another Celestial.

"Have you seen Enara?" Soren asked through ragged breaths.

"No, but I just saw Jai go over the hill with Ikei and Ori's battle group," Rook replied, slamming a shoulder into a nearby Xian-Dao warrior. He fell to the ground, and Soren finished him off with Rachi.

They ran again, following the trail Jai had taken over the small ridge to where the rest of the battle raged on.

Soren noticed a crater to her left that had no doubt been made by one of the Braexian's powder bombs and gagged at the sight of the body parts strewn about the explosion site. She coughed, covering her nose with the cold metal of her plate armor, and carried on behind Rook.

"There!" Rook called out, pointing to the west side of the field.

Jai was fighting on foot, and King Elias was riding a brown horse with a black mane, swinging his sword wildly, lobbing off the heads of the Xian-Dao warriors. His form was impeccable, and he let loose a loud war cry as another head dropped to the ground.

His warriors surrounded him as best they could, but they were losing numbers fast. The Celestials were stronger and quicker than regular humans, and the field was a bloodbath. The once-black ground had a crimson sheen to it that looked sickly in the low light.

Shadows formed in the sky, inky black blots against the midnight blue, and Rook swore at the sight. "Fuck."

"Kestrels," Soren spat as she ran past him and onto the field. She had no idea where the rest of her friends were, but she needed to warn them somehow.

Rook quickly checked the strap holding the Oculus to his back below his armor and raced after her.

"Look to the sky!" Soren screamed. "The kestrels are coming!" She was halfway across the field when one of the winged beasts landed directly in front of her, cutting off her path and slashing forward with its talons. She tried ducking again but not far enough, and it caught the side of her face and shoulder. She let out an angry cry.

The creature laughed, but before it could attack again, Rook assaulted it from behind. His two swords shoved through the back of his ribs and out through his chest. The beast choked loudly before falling to the ground.

"You okay, little bird?" he asked, grazing the scratch on her cheek.

"Nothing I can't manage," Soren responded through gritted teeth. Her shoulder was unmarred, thanks to the armor, but the scratch on her face stung as the kestrel's poison entered her bloodstream.

Together, they cleared out two more Celestials and at least a dozen of Bao-Ren's men before they were able to reach Jai.

"About time you showed up!" Jai yelled, his sword landing in a sickening crunch into the shoulder of a Celestial. The tracker lost grip of his blade as the man stumbled sideways, bellowing in pain. Jai was on him quickly, removing the dagger from his boot and stabbing it up through the Celestial's jaw. The man's eyes bulged as he crumpled at their feet.

Jai wiped off the blade and returned it to his boot before planting his foot on the man's back, wrenching his sword free.

"Have you seen Adaryn?" he asked, his eyes filled with worry.

Soren shook her head vigorously. "No, I'm sorry."

"Fuck," he replied, running his hands through his hair. It felt sticky to the touch, no doubt full of other people's blood.

He pressed his eyes together, pushing his feelings into a box and hiding it away. When they opened again, he was a king personified, a true leader.

"We need to regroup. We will not survive separated like this."

"Agreed," Rook replied.

Soren slipped Notch from her sheath so she could dual wield. It almost felt as though the blades were humming in her hands, begging for blood.

Her armor dripped black, but her eyes blazed hot as she looked at their leader.

"Tell us what we need to do."

Enara wrapped the blade of her staff around the back of a kestrel's neck, bringing it to the ground. She placed her boot between its wings before bringing Coraxis up and planting the curved blade into its skull. Then she scanned the blood-soaked field, looking for Soren's blue hair.

It was still too dark to see. The sun was beginning to rise, but it had yet to crest the horizon. The inky black sky was slowly melting into pale blues and light golds, yet she couldn't bring herself to enjoy the sight.

Sunrises were supposed to be a thing of beauty, but there was nothing beautiful about this day. Bodies littered the field, the majority of which were people she had come to know over the last few weeks. Where most would have looked away to avoid the pain it would cause, she did the opposite. She looked into the dead eyes of the people she had called friends and etched them all into her memory. If she survived this, she would mourn every single one of them.

Her attention moved to where Callan and Baz were pushing back against a group of Xian-Dao warriors. Her heart squeezed a little tighter as the man, who held her heart, cut down his enemies. He was the epitome of goodness, and she would annihilate anyone in her path to get to him, which was exactly what she did.

Coraxis held no prisoners as she parted her way through the bodies like a stone parts a river. Enemies fell on either side of her as her warpath separated soul from body and blood from bone. She created a new kind of river, one that flowed like liquid rubies. By the time she reached Callan and Baz, she was smiling.

"Hey," she called to Baztien as he finished off the last of Bao-Ren's group.

"Hey back," Baz replied, returning her smile. Then he grasped her arm, pulling her in for a chaste kiss before refocusing on the battle. "Shit," he muttered angrily, and Callan and Enara followed his gaze across the field.

The sun had breached the pasture's edge and casted light over the space. It was a pure chaos. Their numbers had been greatly depleted. Most of the calvary lay in ruins, their mounts sprawled out in miniature lakes of crimson, their eyes unseeing.

Enara's heart broke a little more. Though she would mourn every life lost, the pain of losing an animal always hit harder. Their loyalty was unwavering, and they had not chosen to fight. They rode into battle on command from their riders and fell alongside them. In that moment, Enara promised to put them to rest, as well.

A cacophony of loud booms rattled the field, causing the fight to momentarily pause as everyone looked toward the gate. Adriel had arrived, and he was not alone.

A blast of power shot out from the gate, knocking anyone within a fifty-foot radius backward as the new Architect strode forth while the rest of his demons filtered in through the archway behind them.

"*Ach Fecknaff,*" Callan swore in his native tongue.

"Yeah, we're fucked," Baz agreed as more and more enemies marched forward.

Jai was using the temporary distraction to cut through some of the battle haze and regroup the troops they had left. Meanwhile, Soren and Rook were helping the squadron get into one large formation. There were so few of them now that Jai knew their best hope of survival was to stick together. Their numbers had dwindled down to a few hundred, and things were looking bleak.

"Humans!" Adriel's deep voice carried across the field.

A silence fell over everyone as the god-like man spoke. Even with the red scar etched angrily across his face, he was still inhumanly handsome.

"You have fought valiantly, and I want to show mercy to those of you who have looked your gods in the face and dared to stand against them." His eyes scanned the crowd, and the coldness in them made Enara shiver.

She now stood next to Soren and Rook, noticing how rigid her brother's stance had gotten. She knew the feeling well. The moments when her father's rage would cause her skin to tighten and her heart to race in fear. The nights she knew she would go to bed with blood loss and broken bones. Suddenly, she understood him.

Soren had shared stories of what he had gone through at his father's and General Corvus's hands, but seeing the outward effect it had on him made her soul ache. Now she felt connected with him in a way that went so much further than blood. Scars of the soul were just as binding as a mating bond.

She glared daggers at Adriel as he continued his speech.

"Bow before me, and I will spare you. You will be given free pass to Anistera, and all will be forgiven," he said, flashing his perfect teeth.

"He lies," Rook growled, his voice deep and angry. "Mortals cannot enter Anistera. He will execute us all if we surrender."

This caused Adriel to level him with a stare. "My son knows not of Anistera's magical capabilities. I let him believe he could not join us in the above realm to protect him."

There were a few mutters from the crowd from those considering switching sides.

"Do not be fooled by his charms," Jai continued where Rook had left off. "Whether you die in battle or by his hand, there will be no mercy on this day. Do you see any remorse for those who fought from the East? He cares not for their lives, nor yours. He wants all of Entheas to burn. Do not go up in flames with him!"

This seemed to steady the unrest, and Enthea's ranks solidified their place.

The change on Adriel's face was instant. His eyes turned to glaciers, and his features curled down into a disgusted grimace.

"Then so be it," he spat before his horde descended upon them.

CHAPTER THIRTY—FOUR

The Entheans braced themselves as Adriel raised his arm and beckoned his beasts forward. There had to have been nearly fifty massive black creatures crawling toward them while the last few kestrels circled hungrily in the sky. They preyed on the weak and injured as a vulture would, swooping down to strike their prey with their talons before returning to the clouds. The remaining archers had managed to take out a few of them when the fight had begun, but they were now out of arrows, and the ones they attempted to scavenge were broken or too difficult to remove from their previous targets.

"We need to take out Adriel!" Jai yelled. "With him gone, they may retreat."

"The general, too," Rook gritted out, looking to where Corvus circled above them.

They ran forth with the rest of their troops, heading straight for the beasts. They would have to work quickly. If they didn't burn the bodies of the fallen creatures, they would piece themselves back together, and then their efforts would be for naught.

Grunts and screams filled the air as the battle raged on, and Enara cried out in anger as one of the Celestials broke her nose with the butt of his sword.

"You'll have to do better than that," she scoffed before doubling the woman over with an elbow and finishing her off with Coraxis.

"Nice one, Enara," Soren called from where she was pulling a dagger out of the still-writhing body of one of the large creatures that Baz had helped her take down. He was swinging his sword skillfully, covering Soren as she grabbed a nearby torch from where it lay on the ground and set the beast aflame.

The ichor ignited like dry kindling. Soon, the sky was filled with black smoke. The body stunk like rotting meat and burning flesh, and Soren stifled a gag.

"*How dare you?*" a kestrel wailed from above her. It had used the smoke as cover to take her by surprise and grasped her shoulders before lifting her away from the group. The motion caused her to lose her grip on Rachi and the torch, her arms helpless in its grip.

"Let me go!" she screamed, thrashing her head and legs. She knew they wouldn't make it far, considering the extra weight her armor bore.

"Oh, I'll let you go," the beast sneered, "once I get high enough."

"Fuck you!" Soren screamed, her throat going raw.

"Soren!" Enara called, running below them, following their path.

Soren had never been afraid of heights, but when she noticed how small Enara's form was becoming, a knot grew in her stomach. She tried shifting her arms, but the talons caused pain to shoot down to her wrists and up her neck.

Not like this, she thought. *Not like this.*

She stretched her neck as far as it would go, deciding at once that if she was going to fall to her death, it would be on her own terms.

She bit the kestrel's foot—hard. The creature screeched and released his grip on her shoulders, and then she was falling.

"*No!*" Rook roared as he watched Soren fall from the sky. She was too high, and he was too far to try to catch her. But he ran, anyway. His blades moved at a blinding speed as he made his way to where she would land. He thought that maybe, just maybe, if he could catch her, his half-celestial body might be able to withstand the force enough that she would live.

He moved his legs, pumping them harder than he thought possible, and entered the landing zone with moments to spare. He braced himself for the impact, wishing they'd had more time. Wishing he could hold her, and kiss her, and tell her everything would be okay. To tell her that he loved her once more.

Her scream could have broken the sound barrier as she plummeted toward him. He planted his feet, his blades thrown to the side, arms held out to cradle her. Then he closed his eyes at the last second, not willing to watch what happened next.

The impact never came as a gust of air knocked him off his feet. He landed hard on his tailbone, blinking to remove the shadows from his eyes. He realized quickly that the shadow was a large, black body looming before him. However, it was not the body of a man, but of a horse. A great black creature with onyx wings stood before him with a breathless Soren upon its back.

He reached forward to brush a hair from her face, and the horse gave him a warning snort in response.

"Whoa, boy," Rook muttered, holding his palms up before speaking quietly to Soren. "Little bird, you can open your eyes now."

Soren's eyes fluttered open, and her death grip on the horse's mane loosened. "Rook," she groaned.

"Yes, little bird, I'm here."

She pushed up into a sitting position, wincing at the pain that shot through her shoulder blades.

"Drink this," Rook said, holding up a vial of healing water from a small pouch at his side.

She took it gratefully and, after a moment, attempted to roll her shoulders. They weren't fully healed, but the pain was manageable. She could feel the effects of the venom fading to a dull burn.

She allowed Rook to pull her down as the great horse chuffed again. Soren embraced Rook tightly before walking around to thank the majestic creature. She hugged the horse's thick neck, nuzzling into the softness of its coat. Then Soren pulled back to look into the creature's big brown eyes and whispered, "Thank you."

She continued staring at the creature for a long moment as the war raged around them, and something in her heart clicked. As if to confirm her suspicion, the horse stretched its wings wide before folding them in on himself. She was momentarily shocked as they seemed to disappear into his body, leaving behind a regular black stallion.

"It *is* you!" she exclaimed, hugging the horse again.

Rook was staring between the four-legged beast and Soren, obviously confused.

"He was a part of my journey early on," Soren explained.

"You didn't think to tell me that you rode a winged horse?" Rook asked, raising his brow.

Soren made to answer, but then grabbed Quill, threw it past Rook's head, and into the eye of a Xian-Dao soldier who had been trying to sneak up from behind them.

Rook turned to watch the body fall and couldn't help but be impressed by her arm. He reached down and turned the man over, removing the dagger with a sick, sucking sound. The eyeball came with it, and he plucked it off the end of the blade, tossing it behind him before handing Quill back to Soren with a smile on his face.

"Seriously?" she asked, and he just shrugged his shoulders. "That was disgusting." She grimaced.

"Would you prefer I delivered it to you in a box?" he questioned.

"No, nope, absolutely not," she replied, grabbing Quill and hopping back onto the stallion. "You coming?" she beckoned.

Rook hesitated for a moment before mounting up behind her as the creature's wings splayed out from the space between their legs.

"Does it have a name?" Rook asked as they lifted up into the sky.

"I couldn't find one that fit," Soren replied before her voice was swallowed by the wind. She did not know how this creature had come by its wings, but she set the confusion aside and went in search of more enemies to destroy.

"WE NEED TO GO," BAZ SAID AS JAI PRESSED HIS FINGERTIPS TO William's eyelids, shielding his gaze from the horrors around him. "C'mon, man," Baz urged, his tone sterner this time.

Jai ripped his eyes away from the rider and ran with Baz toward another group of men who were fighting off three of the kestrels' larger counterparts.

"He was just a boy!" Jai barked.

"I know," was all Baz replied before they sunk their blades into one of the creatures. Black blood sprayed everywhere, and then one of the Enthean's bent forward to set its body alight. The guys' eyes followed the smoke trail to the sky where Soren and Rook sat atop a great, winged horse, dropping the last of the kestrels with ease. They continued to follow their flight path as Soren and Rook set their sights on Adriel.

The god-like man was laying waste to everyone and everything in his path, even killing off a few of Bao-Ren's men who had gotten in his way. Jai and Baz knew if they were going to defeat him, they would have to work together.

"Find Enara," Jai ordered then ran in Adriel's direction.

Baz did not hesitate to return to where he had last seen her. However, smoke filled the field, making visibility low, and he struggled to make his way across the sea of bodies. Every few feet, he would see a face he knew, and it made his stomach tighten. There was one face he begged the Maker not to see bleeding out on the ground.

He breathed a sigh of relief when he spotted her. She was helping one of the medics drag a body over the edge of the hill. He tried waving to get her attention, but she was too focused on the task at hand.

When the medic was out of sight, she ran back down the hill, cutting diagonally across the field, when movement caught the corner of Baz's eye.

No! he screamed internally as he yelled aloud to warn her. "*Enara!*" But he was too late.

Their eyes connected for a split-second before General Corvus's winged form landed in front of Enara, cutting off their path to each other.

Baz's eyes narrowed at the creature's back, and his boots smacked hard with each step as he ran in their direction.

In moments, she was on the ground. Even her incredible skills were no match for the creature's centuries of experience.

Baz felt the pieces of his heart shatter as the general picked Enara up by her throat and began squeezing the life out of her. Enara stopped flailing, and the general threw her lifeless body aside.

Baz let out a cry filled with rage as he closed the distance between him and Enara's killer, tackling him into the ash. He pinned the creature's wings behind him, his fury only amplified when Corvus laughed in his face.

"Killing me won't bring her back," he gargled, and that was when Baz noticed the blade of Enara's staff sticking out from the side of the creature's ribs.

He lifted the half-man by his chest and slammed him back into the ground. He did this over and over again until General Corvus's skull split open on the battlefield before him and all the life left his dark eyes.

He breathed heavily from the exertion and spat on the creature before snarling, "No, but it will sure as fuck make me feel better." That said, he got to his feet and pulled Enara's lifeless form into his arms and wept.

He nuzzled into her neck, whispering, "I'm sorry. I'm so sorry," over and over again, rocking back and forth. It had only been minutes since he'd watched her fall, so heat was still rising from her body. He pressed against her chest, wishing he could switch his heart for hers so that he could take her place when he heard it.

Thump.

And then again a moment later.

Thump.

It was the single, most beautiful sound in the entire world, and hope bloomed in his chest like the wildflowers in springtime.

"I'm here," he whispered. "Come back to me, Enara."

Thump. Her heart beat again, faster this time. *Thump.*

He held her softy as he watched shallow breaths lift her ribcage and she stirred in his arms. When she finally spoke, her voice came out in a broken rasp. "Baz," was all she could manage.

"It's okay," he replied. "I know. I'm here. I'll always be here," he rushed out.

She sat up and wrapped her arms around him before getting to her feet.

"Take your time," he said, holding her elbow.

"I'm okay," she replied.

His brows furrowed when he noticed the black and purple bruises forming on her neck and wished he could bring that bastard back to life so he could kill him again.

Noticing his gaze, Enara reached forward and lifted his chin. The gold flecks in his eyes were glassy, shined to a fine polish with unshed tears. She urged him to believe her when she whispered the words again, "I'm okay."

All Baz wanted to do was to pick her up and take her away from battle. To nurse her back to health and spend the rest of their days in quiet happiness. He would not do that, though. Not yet. Enara could not leave her friends now any more than he could. So, he kissed her, pressing his forehead to hers, and said, "I love you, you know."

"I know," she rasped back then looked to where Soren and Rook were facing off with Adriel. "Let's end this."

CHAPTER THIRTY—FIVE

Soren was lifted from the ground by her arm, and she swore as she swung Quill violently, attempting to make any contact. She and Rook had cut Adriel dozens of times using their agility to their advantage, but he healed faster than they could injure.

She screamed in frustration as Adriel scowled at her, throwing her to the ground. She wanted to take her blades and dig them into the red scar on his face in an attempt to make the rest of his body match.

She coughed against the pain in her ribs, the stabbing feeling inside the cage of bones letting her know that at least two of them had been broken by the impact. Her shoulders ached, and sweat rested thick on her brow, but she stayed on the offensive.

As she was thrown to the ground, Rook took her place, ducking quickly before arcing his blades back up, the right one catching the underside of Adriel's chin.

He roared angrily and focused all of his attention on his son.

"You are no son of mine." Adriel thought the words would hurt Rook, distract him even. The boy had always craved the attention of his father, and he wanted his words to cut as deep as a blade.

"Corvus was more of a father to me than you ever were," Rook retorted, darting back in with another barrage of his blades. Adriel blocked them all with ease as the slice on the underside of his chin stitched itself back together.

Soren had gotten back on her feet and threw Quill, hoping her blade would find purchase in one of Adriel's more vital organs. Her aim was true, but as the dagger flew end over end toward the exposed space between his front and back armor plates, he turned and caught it.

Without a second thought, he whipped it back at her, and it lodged deep into the top of her thigh. Soren's scream could have shattered eardrums as she landed hard on the ashen ground.

"You'll pay for that!" Rook shouted, his nostrils flaring. He attacked his father with everything he had, this time focusing on a new target—the straps of Adriel's armor.

The rapiers sliced through the taut leather, and the breast and back plates fell to the ground, leaving his father's torso exposed. He seemed unconcerned.

"I do not need armor to break you, son," he goaded, his smile a bright white, only fueling Rook's hatred for him.

His father raised his sword, fighting back with all his skill for the first time, and Rook struggled to block the blows. The height and weight advantage took its toll, and Rook's muscles strained against the pressure his father's sword placed on his blades.

They spun and parried, and blocked and sliced, until Rook was covered in a layer of sweat and struggling to breathe. He fell to a knee, heaving, but looked to where Soren was tying a strip of fabric around her leg and forced himself to stand. He needed to win this fight for her. For them. For the future of Entheas. For this world she had taught him to love. He could do this. He would do this.

"Come on, Father," Rook spat the word out, as though it were poison on his tongue. "You can do better than that."

Rook knew his father's ego was incalculable and continued to spit insults as he took his time defending each swipe of Adriel's blade. He then saw Baz and Enara helping Soren in his peripheral.

Baz took out a few of the straggling warriors from Xian-Dao as Enara helped Soren to her feet. The blade of the dagger was embedded to the hilt, and they dared not remove it for fear of her bleeding out.

Baz stood at the ready, waiting for a moment to jump in to assist Rook, when he heard the final insult that sent Adriel spiraling.

"She never loved you!" Rook bellowed.

"*Ah!*" Adriel roared. Those words were the final crack in the god's armor, and his composure fell. His face became a grotesque mask of twisted hatred, his eyes blackening into those of an unhinged beast.

It was too late when Rook realized his mistake.

As he watched his father's face change, he had let his guard fall and was unprepared to defend himself from Adriel's next blow.

His father's sword pierced through his armor, straight into his chest. Rook's eyes bulged, and he choked on his own blood as he fell to the ground.

As he lay gurgling in a crimson pool, his eyes found Soren's. He could see her fighting against Enara's grasp to get to him.

A chill settled over him, and as his eyelids fell, he could hear Soren's voice drift across the battlegrounds.

"I love you," it whispered.

The words were like a cocoon, enveloping him in warmth as his soul left his body and drifted toward the after.

SOREN SCRATCHED AND TORE AT ENARA'S ARMS, TRYING TO GET to Rook. She watched on in horror as Adriel lifted his body and tore the armor from his back, revealing the large stab wound.

"Look what we have here," Adriel cooed. In his hands, he the held the reason for all the bloodshed—the Oculus. Rook had tucked it into a metal cavity between his armor and back plate, not wanting it to be out of arm's reach.

Adriel lifted up the object, the metal eye seeming to mock them from across the field.

"I'll kill you!" Soren screamed and sobbed into Enara's arms, her body weak from the dagger protruding from her thigh.

Adriel laughed as though she had told a joke, which only infuriated her more. This man, this beast, had taken everything from her. He'd hurt her mother, he was the reason her father was dead, and now he had killed his own son on his hunt for revenge. Revenge he wanted for losing the love of her mother.

When she looked at him now, she was no longer scared, for she saw him for what he truly was—pathetic.

"You're a monster," she continued, and he laughed again.

"Stupid girl. Monsters are beasts that stem from night-mares. I am a god."

"You may be a god," Jai's voice boomed, causing Adriel to spin, "but I am a king."

Jai swung his sword down like an axe, severing Adriel's arm from his shoulder. The appendage and the Oculus fell to the ground.

The sound that came from Adriel's mouth could have crumbled mountains into sand as he spun on the tracker. His arm stump had already healed over to an angry pink socket, the skin still so thin that Soren could make out the veins below. Veins that ran black.

Adriel swung wildly, and Baz took the opportunity to run in and assist him. His arm would take a few minutes to grow back, so this would be their last chance to take him out.

Enara looked to Soren, and they didn't need to exchange words for Soren to let Enara assist her to Rook's side.

"I'm sorry, brother," Enara said over Rook's body before she ran toward where Adriel, Jai, and Baz were battling it out. She circled the three fighters, clearing the space around them, and waited for an opening to strike.

Soren watched on, helpless. Tears fell silently down her cheeks, the clear liquid adding to the crimson pool beneath her.

"I'm so sorry," she whimpered quietly. "You deserved so much more than this." She used all of her upper body strength to pull him across her lap, crying out as the dagger shifted.

He was so cold. He had never felt this cold before. She took his hand in hers, and it felt like she was back in the city watch's office with the body of her father.

"I wish we had more time. I would have … We could have …" Her words were stuffed back down her throat by the knot of grief that tightened around her neck.

She traced the line of Rook's jaw, trying to remember how it felt while he was still alive, and turned her gaze to the sky. She let loose a banshee-like scream as her system was flooded with emotions.

It was as though every terrible memory and feeling she had experienced in her twenty-four years had decided to re-surface all at once. Fear, anger, grief, hate, heartbreak, and loss attacked her psyche, willing her to break, but she couldn't. Wouldn't.

If this was to be her last moments in this world, she would not waste them in an anxiety-induced coma. She would hold Rook tight and watch on as her friends fought to save their world, staying strong for him, for them.

Groups of fights rained across the field, and more and more bodies fell.

Soren's eyes refocused on Adriel, and she found Baz and Enara shortly after. *Where is Jai?* she thought, taking another look. *There.* He was on the ground, doubled over, an angry red line showing through a large gash in his armor. Her hope dwindled.

Enara and Baz were fighting with everything they had, but Adriel's arm was back in play. He kicked Jai in the chest, grabbing up the trackers weapon, along with his own. He dual-wielded the long swords, and Soren knew then it was over.

Coraxis went flying, and Enara was knocked to the ground. Baz tried to get to her, but Adriel's blades were relentless. Baz dodged Jai's sword, but Adriel cracked the pommel of his into his back, causing him to drop his weapon and fall to the ground at Enara's feet. They tried to reach for each other, but Adriel pulled him up by his auburn hair, holding him to the side as if he couldn't stand to be in his presence.

Enara struggled to her feet, but Adriel kicked her to the ground again, looking between them. His face grew into a saccharine grin, and he licked his lips.

"You love him, don't you?" he sneered.

"Please," Enara replied, her heart breaking. "Take me, kill me, but spare him."

Baz was struggling in Adriel's arms, trying to grasp at anything, but even his strength could not compare to a god's. Both of his hands grasped at the one Adriel had around his throat, and he strained to look at Enara.

When their eyes met, his showed no fear. The gold flecks sparkled brighter than ever, and he looked at once like the boy from school who had lent her his jacket on a cold autumn day. Her heart constricted as his eyes softened, as if to say, "*It's okay.*"

Before she had a chance to respond, Adriel said, "Let me cure you of that weakness," and then he snapped Baz's neck.

Enara heard screaming that she thought was her own then realized the cry came from Soren. She looked back to see her brother propped in Soren's lap, and then her eyes returned to where Adriel held Baz's body. He was so still that he looked like a doll she used to play with as a child.

She did not move, or cry, or scream, or even speak. Because to do any of those things would be to admit the truth of what had just happened. That Baz was dead.

Her heart cavity felt like a black hole, sucking her into the void, and her stomach twisted painfully.

Adriel dropped Baz's body then held his blade toward her. She refused to look at him and instead reached a hand toward Baz's, wanting to touch him one last time. At the sight of his lifeless body, she turned to the side and retched, earning her a *tsk* of disappointment from Adriel.

"Humans," he scoffed. "Even your stomachs are weak." He then raised both swords, crossing them in front of Enara's neck, poised to decapitate, when booms sounded from the gate and he smiled.

"You know what?" he said, lowering his weapons. "I don't want your blood sullying my blade. I think I'll let my beasts have you." He backed away a few steps, and Enara got to her feet, standing between whatever was coming and Baz's body.

Black creatures filtered in through the portal, and she readied herself. The booms kept coming, and then a horrific screech filled the sky as one of the creatures fell to the ground in front of the gate and fire flew from the archway, finishing it off.

Enara smiled. Then, before Adriel could grab her, she was running to one of the nearby bodies to take up her sword. She knew in her heart that whoever was coming through the gate was an ally. And she was right.

The Anistera rebellion was here. Luscinia and Abraxos, as well as their brothers and sisters, pushed into Irefeld and filtered over the field, snuffing out all enemies in their path.

Adriel forgot about Enara and began cutting down his brethren as he commanded his beasts to surround him.

Baz's body was left alone in the dust, though Enara mentally promised him that she would be back as she charged toward a nearby beast with fury in her eyes and love in her heart.

SOREN WAS STILL STARING INTO ROOK'S PALE FACE, HER MOUTH open in a silent scream, when she felt a hand rest on her shoulder.

"Let me help."

She wiped her eyes, recognizing the voice. "They are all dead," Soren whispered. Her heart was cut into pieces so small she wasn't sure they could be put back together.

She looked up, and her brows furrowed when she took in the sight of Luscinia. The ethereal woman was battered and bruised, and her silver hair was plastered with black and red blood.

"Luscinia," she breathed, "what happened to you?"

"Nothing that cannot be undone with time. Come; allow me to help." She gestured then kneeled to lift Rook's body from Soren's legs. Her thigh was on fire, but the rest of her felt cold, as if a mountain stream were trickling over her skin.

Luscinia took in the sight of her and reached forward, but Soren held up her hand.

"Him first," was all she could manage as the adrenaline began to wear off and the pain filtered in.

"As you wish," Luscinia replied, letting her hands drift over Rook's body.

Soren was scared to ask, but she needed to know. "Is he alive?"

Luscinia nodded, her hands glowing lightly. "He is, but only just. It will take most of my energy to heal him."

Soren's heart slammed forward so hard it nearly knocked her over. Rook was alive. However, her happiness was short-lived when Luscinia's words finally registered.

"You could die saving him," she whispered.

"Yes, I might," Luscinia replied matter-of-factly.

The selfish part of Soren wanted to sit back and let that happen. She wanted Rook alive, and breathing, and in her arms. She wanted to tell him all her secrets and protect all of his. She wanted to go on more walks and enjoy silent moments in the library by the fire. But most of all, she wanted to tell him what he meant to her.

War raged around them as Luscinia worked. From a distance, Soren could see Enara return to her position, hovering over Baztien like a mirror image of her and Rook moments ago.

Her eyes flicked to Baztien's body before she pressed them shut, willing the image away. Her heart could bear no more pain, so she encased it in ice. It could break later. Her head swam, and black dotted her vision as another wave of pain threatened to knock her out.

"It is done," Luscinia said, exhaustion clear on her face. It looked as though she had aged backward twenty years in but a few moments. The fine lines tracing the edges of her eyes were gone, and her skin held a youthful glow. "Give me a few moments, and I'll see to that leg."

"I'll be fine," Soren lied. "You said your abilities were finite. I will not ask any more of you."

"It is mine to give to whom I wish," Luscinia replied, her eyelids fluttering as though she were falling asleep.

"Rest," Soren said just as Rook's hand tightened in hers. She tried to keep her movements slow, not wanting to jostle her leg.

"Rook," she whispered, her voice breaking.

He inhaled deeply, his chest expanding, and then he opened his mouth to speak. "Hello, little bird," he said, opening his eyes and reaching a hand up to cup her cheek.

"You came back," she cried quietly, nuzzling against his hand.

"I will always come back for you, little bird." He sat up and inspected his chest through the torn material of his shirt and found that his injury had fully healed.

He folded Soren into his arms, minding her leg, and she ignored the dull ache that came from her shoulders.

"Baz is dead," she choked out, sobbing against his chest.

He scanned the field to see Enara standing over Baz's body. He knew no words would comfort her, so he settled for holding her tighter.

"Thank you," he said to Luscinia, who was struggling to regain her energy.

"Keep her safe," she replied before passing out.

"We need to protect her," Soren said, pressing away and reaching for her mother's friend. The dagger felt like a hot poker pressed to her thigh, and she bit back a cry, but her struggle did not go unnoticed.

"Let me look at you," Rook said, crouching in front of her.

"Don't," she replied, grasping his wrist that had been reaching for her leg. He was about to comment about her being stubborn, but before he could, she said, "Not before I say what I need to say."

He let out a strained breath and sat, resting his elbows on his knees. His hands shook, and he could still feel the coolness of his father's blade penetrating his chest. He itched for his rapiers that were no longer by his side, wanting to rejoin the battle, but he would give Soren this moment. Because, as beasts and men fought and fell around them, there was still only her.

"Okay, little bird," he said softly, waiting.

"I love you!" she half-cried, half-yelled then slapped her hands to her mouth.

Rook let out a whisper of a laugh before he replied, "I love you, too, little bird."

She looked at him sheepishly, wanting to elaborate. "I need you to know what I mean when I say those words," she continued. "People say *I love you* all the time, for all sorts of different reasons, and I want you to know mine."

He pressed a kiss to her knuckles. "Go on," he coaxed.

She blew out a breath and spoke again, laying her emotions on the ground before them. "When I say those words, I mean I want to start and end the day with you. Every moment with you, no matter how small, is important to me. I want to bottle your laugh. I want your every kiss and every touch to brand my skin and forsake me to all others. I want you to know that you are mine, and I am yours, and no being in Entheas or Anistera can take that from us. And when we die, I will follow you into the after to float with you amongst the stars until we cease to exist. You are it for me." She was breathless when she finished, and her heart was hammering against the cage of her ribs.

"I am yours?" Rook asked softly, testing the words on his lips.

"Yes," Soren breathed.

"And you are mine?"

"Always," she replied, and he pressed his mouth to hers.

Something happened then. As they kissed, an invisible tether took shape inside them, bonding them to each other forevermore. Their hearts were two pieces of the same flame that ignited both of their souls, their love burning hotter than a thousand stars and a thousand blazing suns. The sky seemed to rise and fall with their breaths as the bond fell into place, confirming something they had known for a long time.

They were mates, and even though fate had destined their paths to cross, it would never change the fact that their love was what truly bound them to one another.

They picked up every broken piece of each other to build something new, together. A perfectly imperfect love. A love built on broken promises and shattered dreams. On darkness and trauma. They were the light to each other's day and the sun that broke through each other's storms. They were more than mates; they were twin flames. Two pieces of the same soul searching the earth and heavens for its other half.

Maker help anyone who tried to keep them apart.

CHAPTER
THIRTY—SIX

"We can destroy him now," Rook breathed, the mating bond sizzling between them. It was then Rook noticed his armor, along with the Oculus, were gone, and Soren's hope fell.

"We have to get it back," Soren said, trying to get to her feet.

Rook had found another healing draught from a nearby med kit for her leg, but it was still weak.

"I'll get it and come back to you," Rook said, standing and moving out of her reach.

"No!" Soren cried. "I just got you back."

He leaned forward and held her chin gently. "You can't walk, little bird," he said softly.

"No"—Soren smirked—"but I can fly."

Soren lifted her bow, providing cover fire for the Anisteran rebellion. She nocked an arrow that was stolen from a dead man's quiver and let it fly. The feathered shaft cut through the air, whistling softly, before embedding through the side of Adriel's beast.

Soren cursed and readjusted her aim. She had hit her target, but not where she had wanted to.

Bows from Nuraka were designed to be used with a thumb draw. It was an archery style unfamiliar to her. That, mixed with the fact that she was flying bareback on a winged horse, hindered her accuracy further.

"Come on; let's circle again," she said sternly, nocking another arrow. This one met its mark, striking one of Adriel's followers through the chest.

She cheered silently and continued assisting from above while Rook darted from one enemy to the next, zigzagging a path toward his father. She squeezed her eyes shut, sending a prayer to the Maker to watch over him.

She had realized weeks ago that her prayers were unfounded, considering that Adriel was now the Architect of Anistera, the new god they were expected to worship, but she sent her hopes skyward, anyway. Maybe the previous leader of Anistera would somehow hear her prayers and provide assistance.

Enara was standing over Baz's body, surrounded by a ring of carnage. She was a woman possessed, and anyone who dared to get close to her was cut down with such force it made Soren flinch.

She could make out the sheen of Baz's armor from her vantage point in the clouds, and her chest felt hollow. She did now allow herself to think of all the things she would miss about the silly, sweet boy who had snuck his way into her and Enara's lives. The big guy with the even bigger heart would hold a permanent place in hers.

She pressed her eyes together, and when she opened them again, she refocused her sights on the man who had killed one of her best friends in this life and let another arrow fly.

ENARA BATHED IN THE BLOOD OF HER ENEMIES, HER ARMOR A deep shade of crimson, veined with the ichor of the beasts, made her look like a goddess of death. She snarled as wave after wave tried to get between her and Baz. Bodies already created a line in the ashes, a dark caricature of the sparring ring she had fought in only days ago.

The majority of the warriors from Xian-Dao had their blades set on her now. They saw Baz as a betrayer to them and wanted to string him up as a warning to those who did not follow Bao-Ren. Their loyalty to their leader was unwavering, and as one body fell, another took its place.

Blood and ash filled Enara's eyes, and her arms strained with every swing of Coraxis's blade. She could feel her body giving out, but she couldn't let them have him.

His body was hers to love, hers to mourn, and hers to burn and bury. Thoughts of his mothers and how she would have to break their hearts by telling them their son was lost fueled her fight. She would bring him back to them.

As metal cut into flesh and beak met bone, her heart tore itself from her chest. Breathing was laborious, and grief was clawing at the back of her throat like a demon trying to escape from hell.

There was a beauty in grief that people often overlooked. For grief only came to those who had loved and lost. To those whose hearts beat for another. To those who had been met with a benevolent hand and a warm embrace. Those who, against all odds, had found a kindred soul to whom they would be forever connected. Grief did not belong to those with hatred in their hearts, but to those who had the capacity to love and be loved in return.

Enara's shoulders screamed as Coraxis took down another body, and she clenched her teeth, the muscles in her legs straining from the effort. She did not have much more in her. She was only human, after all, and the adrenaline in her body would give out soon.

There were few Xian-Dao warriors left. Most had been killed in the first wave of the attack, being the easier targets than their Celestial allies. A few traitors had run when the rebellion had arrived. The fifteen or so left stalked around the circle of bodies, waiting for Enara to fall.

Two more jumped in, but one fell to the ground at her feet, an arrow protruding from his skull, the metal of his helmet crushing into his face on impact.

Enara flicked her eyes to the sky, tracing the arrow's trajectory. She smiled thankfully to Soren who held up her bow triumphantly from above.

She wiped the dead warrior's fresh blood from her mouth and let out a cry before slamming Coraxis into the second soldier's chest.

She was winded from the kill and took a knee, her lungs struggling to oxygenate her blood. *I can do this*, she thought. *I can finish them.* In the time it took her to struggle back to her feet, three more warriors had entered the ring, one of them sneering at her.

"The battlefield is no place for a woman," he said, his eastern accent lacing his discriminatory words. From the insignia emblazoned on his armor, she guessed he was the major general. His armor had barely a scratch. He had clearly been watching from the sidelines.

"That's an odd thing to say when it's your men's bodies at my feet," she spat.

The general's eyes darkened as he lifted his double-edge sword, his brows pressed together angrily. "And you shall join them," he threatened, lunging toward her.

His men stood by, knowing better than to join the fight when their leader was trying to prove a point.

Enara struggled against the blows of his sword, her feet catching on a hunk of severed flesh, making her trip backward, landing hard beside Baz's body. She lifted Coraxis to defend another blow, but the weapon fell from her hands, skittering to the side. Her body finally gave out.

"I will carve your tongue from your mouth so no one will hear you scream when we hang your lover's body from our leader's walls. You will beg for death, and only when his body is nothing but rotting flesh, hanging from bone, will you find your end. You will be buried on opposite sides of this earth so your souls may never be reunited in the after."

"Torture me, kill me, remove my tongue if you wish. You may be able to stop my heart from beating, but the love we have for each other can never be taken from us!"

The general did not even grace her with a response before arcing his blade down toward her, his bloodlust taking over.

She welcomed it with open arms, her thoughts drifting to Baz. *I'll see you soon.*

Enara felt heat coat her skin, and her heart warmed knowing she would soon be with him. She could almost hear his voice calling to her.

"Enara," it whispered, and she smiled when she felt his strong hands on her shoulders.

"Enara," the voice said louder this time, the grip on her arms tightening. "Sister, get up."

Rook's voice rang clear in her ears, and her lids shot open. His blue eyes assessed her, and she realized he looked just like their grandmother on her mother's side. She had passed away when Enara was just a child. She had forgotten she'd had white hair before her day, as well. She couldn't believe she hadn't noticed it before.

"Enara, are you okay?" he asked more sternly now.

She mentally gave her body a once-over and realized that the warmth she felt was the general's blood. She grimaced.

"Yeah, thanks," she replied, letting him assist her to her feet.

She looked around and noticed the last of Bao-Ren's men had been slain; a few from Soren's arrows and the rest by Rook's blade.

"We need to get to my father," Rook said, his mind back in battle mode.

"I can't leave him," Enara choked out. She turned to look at Baz's body. If she tricked her mind long enough, she could pretend he was sleeping.

Her eyes traveled over his still frame and stopped when she noticed something sticking out from the thigh plate of his armor. It was made of a metal not found in Entheas. She recognized it immediately.

She bent down and kissed his forehead, reaching a shaky hand forward to grasp the artifact. "It seems," she said, turning and handing the object to Rook with a smile, "that even in death, he had one last part to play in our story."

Rook took the Oculus into his hand, feeling the power emanating from it. The buzz that normally surrounded the artifact was gone, the mating call diminished. His grip tightened on the object, and his lips curled into the hint of a smirk.

"Please tell me you and Soren can do something of use with this," Enara said.

A true smile graced his lips now. "I think we just might."

ADRIEL COULD FEEL THE SHIFT IN THE AIR, THE TELLTALE SIGN OF a mating bond clicking into place. The field was vast, but his eyes found his son and the vile girl, Soren, across the field. He hated to admit that his heart lurched slightly at the sight. For a moment, he could remember how it felt to be back in the Architect's quarters, Celandine wrapped in his arms, their mating bond tingling between them.

The sight of his son finding his mate made him feel ill. No matter how many lifetimes he had left, he would never find that again. Celandine had effectively ruined him, and he had forsaken all others.

He brushed off the isolating thoughts and chuckled to himself. Mating bond or not, they were useless without the Oculus.

He reached down to touch the artifact for reassurance, and when he found his hand empty, he let out an angry, "*No!*"

His sword came up as two of his sisters sprinted forward on the offensive. He cut them down without even blinking, their blood joining the burned field of red.

He stared down at their faces and spat on their remains. They were traitors, and even though he had known them for centuries, he felt nothing.

This is all Luscinia's doing, he thought. He had seen her come through the gate, standing side-by-side with Abraxos, and it had made his blood boil.

He vowed in that moment to destroy all of his betrayers, and when his sword was coated in their blood, then he would kill Luscinia. She would watch each of them fall to the after before joining them, knowing that their lives had been cut short due to her treacherous actions.

She was on the ground, unmoving, and he couldn't help but feel disappointed, his thirst for revenge unquenched.

The creature to his side took an arrow to the head and slumped to the ground. He ripped it out, and the beast made a wailing sound before the wound on its head healed and it rose to its feet.

"Leave none alive," Adriel ordered, and the beast roared before charging into a group of Celestials, impaling two upon its knife-like appendages.

Adriel smirked, enjoying the bloodshed. It would be over soon, and then the rest of Entheas would burn. But he did not wish to celebrate preemptively. He would not enjoy his success until the Oculus was in his hands and his traitorous son was dead.

He could see Rook across the field, his snowy hair streaked with red and black, giving him away like a white flag demanding a ceasefire. Adriel could also see a girl with brown hair surrounded by bodies, one of which was the boy whose neck he had snapped like dried kindling. It had been a long time since he had killed with his bare hands, and he had reveled in it.

Something caught his eye, and that was when he noticed the sun glinting off an object that Rook was holding his hand over. To his disbelief, Adriel realized it was the Oculus. He watched as his son bled into the artifact, and then both him and the girl waved their hands to the sky. It was then he noticed Soren riding Obsidian.

His anger intensified as he plowed his way through the field toward his son. If Soren reached him, they could use the Oculus against him, and he couldn't have that.

He ran, his body a blur, flying across the field, fury driving him. He thought the stupid beast had died along with Celandine, but it seemed the horse's life force had connected to her daughter's upon her death.

No matter. I can amend that, he thought, using all his strength to thrust his sword toward the sky.

SOREN CAUGHT THE FLASH OF ADRIEL'S BLADE JUST BEFORE IT sank into Obsidian's side. He let out a strained whinny and began to fall.

Soren screamed as he struggled to keep them aloft, his wings flapping erratically. Blood was seeping from where the sword had embedded between the horse's eighth and ninth rib, and his chuffs were labored.

"Come on, boy; almost there," Soren coaxed as the ground grew close.

Obsidian tried to land gently, but his legs crumpled below him as he skidded to a stop, his wings disappearing into his sides.

Soren jumped off, wincing as her leg twinged. "No, no, no!" she cried when she pressed her hands to the horse's black coat only for them to come back covered in red. "I'm sorry. I'm so sorry," she whispered, wrapping her arms around the horse's neck.

The creature let out a soft whinny, straining to hug her back.

When Soren pulled away, she swore she could see tears in his eyes.

"I'll come back for you," she whispered.

His ears twitched, and he huffed in response as Soren wiped her eyes and ran toward the Oculus.

She pulled Vane from its sheath and wrapped her fist around the blade, slicing her hand in one swift movement. She then stopped as she reached Rook and Enara, who had met her halfway, and resisted the urge to look past them at Baztien's body.

Rook thrust the Oculus into Soren's hand, and she let her lifeblood flow into it.

"We have to imagine exactly what we want for it to work properly," Rook reiterated.

Soren had studied the lore of the Oculus in Rook's library but was happy for the refresher.

"Destroy all enemies?" she asked as they placed their fingers on the metal edges.

"Too vague," Rook responded.

"Let's start with your father then," Soren suggested.

Rook grimaced at the title but responded with a sharp, "Fine. Then close your eyes, little bird."

Soren pressed her eyes together tightly, putting the thought at the forefront of her mind. *Unmake Adriel.* But before the thought was fully formed, she felt a sharp impact and found her body flying sideways onto the burned ground. She struggled to regain her breath as her ribs smarted from the blow.

She turned to see what had struck them and was horrified to find Adriel standing over Enara. He held a plain blade in his hand, obviously stolen from a fallen soldier, and arced the blade down toward her friend.

Coraxis struggled against the strength of his blows, but Enara had rested for a few moments and swung back with renewed vigor. Finally, she was face-to-face with Baztien's killer.

She would show no mercy.

JAI RAN TOWARD ADRIEL, HOPING TO CATCH HIM OFF GUARD again. He raised his sword out to his side like a bird's wing and swiped toward the god's legs. Before his blade could hit its mark, however, Adriel turned to block the blow, his weaponless hand coming up and catching Jai hard in the face. He could feel bones crunch, and the sick metallic taste of blood filled his mouth.

He willed himself to push up from the ground, trying to clear the stars from his eyes. The edges of his vision were inky black, and he could barely see the fuzzy figure of Enara's bladed staff clanging against Adriel's sword.

He could just make out Rook's white hair, his arms dragging his body toward something in the dirt.

Jai pushed himself off the ground, spitting crimson from his mouth, and made his way toward where Adriel and Enara were still fighting.

Another Celestial had his eyes set on them, and Jai made to cut him off until he realized they had the same target. Hope creeped into his veins as he watched Adriel's brother join Enara in battle.

Adriel's chest was all but bare, strips of fabric from his tunic dangling from his shoulders. He was covered head to toe in dried blood, the flakes lifting off of his body to be carried away in the autumn breeze. Sweat slicked his skin, and his blue eyes were as sharp as the icicles that hung off the eaves of Thorncrest Manor. The red scar on his face seemed to pulse as his anger grew.

"*Traitor!*" Adriel roared as Abraxos's sword sliced deep into his bicep. "How dare you attack your leader?"

"You are no leader of mine," Abraxos ground out, continuing his assault.

Enara grunted and swung along with him, hacking and slicing until Adriel's chest was coated in a fresh layer of red.

"Insolent girl!" Adriel yelled as Enara sliced down his pretty face. She did so with a smile, her teeth flashing.

"Now you have another one to match."

This angered him even more, and he began swinging wildly, not caring where he landed his blows. His aggression won out, and all three fighters fell to the ground at his feet, bruised, broken, and bleeding.

A smug smile cut through his already damaged features as he cracked his neck from side to side and strode past Jai, Enara, and Abraxos, his sights set on Soren and Rook.

Soren had reached the Oculus first, struggling on her wounded leg. Rook was almost there, his body as heavy as lead. He reached forward, his fingertips stretching toward the artifact, but Adriel snatched it up from between them.

"I think we've outgrown the need for silly toys," he sneered, snapping the Oculus in half and throwing the pieces to opposite sides of the field.

"*No!*" Soren screamed, her hope cracking like a clay vase falling from a great height.

Adriel kicked her in her already damaged ribs, and she cried out.

"Do not touch her!" Rook croaked, reaching his hand toward Soren.

Adriel pressed his armored boot against it, crushing his fingers into the ground. Rook refused to voice his pain and clenched his teeth together.

"You could have been so much more than this," Adriel scolded. "I gave you everything you could ever need to succeed in this world, and you threw it all away for a stupid human."

"If you haven't noticed, *Father*," Rook said, the word as caustic as acid, "I *am* human."

Adriel's features screwed up at the comment, and he shifted his blade to Rook's neck. "You could have been a god."

"And yet, I know true happiness where you do not," Rook replied, scowling. His eyes flicked to the blade as it pressed into his neck.

"You could have lived forever," Adriel scoffed. "All these years, honing your healing abilities, and what do you have to show for it?"

"Invisible scars and internal trauma," Soren interjected, stabbing Vane into Adriel's ankle.

He roared and smacked her head to the side, her body crumpling next to Rook, who laced his arm around her waist, pulling her closer.

Adriel grabbed the dagger and ripped it from his ankle, pointing it in Soren's face. "Stupid girl, that little scratch will heal before your body hits the ground. Your efforts are wasted."

"Were they, though?" Soren asked, her face stretching into a large grin, eyes flicking past him.

He turned just as Coraxis's blade hooked around his neck and removed his head from his body.

As blood spurted from the wound, Adriel's head rolled to the side. The last image he saw was Enara's satisfied smile before his soul faded into oblivion.

CHAPTER THIRTY—SEVEN

The battle came to an abrupt end as Adriel's head fell to the ground, his persuasion over his brothers and sisters severed, along with his spinal cord.

The field went still as the Celestials dropped their weapons mid-swing, eyes blinking back years of hazy memories.

The rebellion herded the last remaining Xian-Dao warriors into a group, relieving them of their arms, as the rest of the Celestials came to terms with everything that had transpired.

"Here," Jai said, handing Soren the broken pieces of the Oculus. They hummed in her hands, and as she placed them side-by side, their edges melded together, reforming the artifact.

Enara and Jai had helped her and Rook to their feet, Adriel's head staring off into the distance from where it seeped blood on the ground.

"Should we unmake him?" Soren asked, tilting her head to where Adriel's body lay.

Rook prodded Adriel's head with his boot before responding, "Every soul deserves redemption." His voice low. "Even one as black as his."

"Are you sure?" Soren asked. "After all he has done to you? To us?"

He sighed, releasing a breath through his teeth. Then he straightened his posture, the pain fading as his body pieced itself back together, and finally confirmed, "I'm sure."

"So, what are you going to do with it?" Jai asked, looking down at the artifact.

"Well, this holds the power of all creation," Soren responded. "So, really, we could do anything with it."

"Could we bring him back?" Jai asked. They all knew whom he was referring to.

Soren resisted the urge to cry. Her eyes burned with the effort.

Enara held her breath. She knew what the answer was before Soren even spoke, but she let herself hope, anyway.

"The Oculus is not meant to be used as a means to change what has already happened. Adriel pushed the limits of its powers and look what became of him."

"Shouldn't we at least try?" Jai asked. "Consequences be damned?"

Soren's chest ached, and Rook gave her the slightest nod.

"I mean, we cou—"

"No!" Enara said, cutting her off sharply and holding up her hand to silence all of them. "We all knew the risks, Baz included." She paused for a moment to collect herself. "Let him be at peace. In time, we will find ours." A single tear drew a tiny river down her cheek and fell to the ashen ground before she bowed her head.

"Can you guys give us a minute?" Soren asked softly.

"As you wish, little bird," Rook replied, ushering Jai toward where Adaryn stood. The headstrong woman brandished a kitchen knife and was covered in soot and blood. Soren could see the relief in Jai's eyes that his lover was ok.

She laced her hand with Enara's and squeezed her fingers tightly as they hovered over Baztien's body. Soren said nothing, for there was nothing one could say when they had lost a loved one. No words could soothe the blinding pain when a life had been taken too soon.

Enara released her hand and fell to her knees, and Soren joined her, ignoring the pain it sent shooting up her thigh. Now that the battle was done, she finally allowed herself to look at him, and it broke her.

He was so still. It looked as if all the warmth and kindness had seeped out of him and into the ash. His eyelids were closed, and his normally olive complexion was unsettlingly pale. She reached for his hand, which was cold and stiff against hers. It reminded her of stone, as if his insides had turned to clay and hardened in the early morning sun. A statue resurrected in the middle of a war field.

"We won," she choked out as emotions flooded through her. The heartache was relentless, and her body shook as she grieved over him. "I'm so sorry, Baz."

Enara was stoic, her hand pressed to Baztien's chest as though she could will his heart to start beating again.

They sat in silence for a few moments longer before Enara helped Soren to her feet and they rejoined the boys.

Luscinia had regained consciousness, Abraxos's arm wrapped tightly around her waist. Soren's horse was nuzzling her hand, and they could hear Luscinia cooing at him softly as they approached.

"Ditching me for a new rider already?" Soren admonished as she walked up.

The horse chuffed as Luscinia responded in a wistful voice, "Not to worry, Soren; Obie is connected to you through blood. So, like it or not, you're stuck with him."

"Obie?" Soren asked, quirking a brow.

"Your mother named him after the Obsidian Sea that surrounds these lands," Luscinia answered, giving Obie a gentle pat on his rump.

"Obie," Soren said, testing the name.

The horse whinnied loudly, standing a little taller.

The reaction spurred a laugh from the crowd, the animal's innocence bringing a sliver of positivity to a harrowing day.

"I guess that means you're coming home with me."

Rook led Obie to join the few horses that had survived back to the corral, returning just in time to hear Jai address the group of Bao-Ren warriors who had managed to stay alive.

"You will return to your province, never to set foot beyond your borders. We have shown you mercy on this day, but do not expect us to continue to do so if we find you in our lands again. Leave with your lives and relay the same to your leader.

Let this be a lesson to you all—those who seek infinite power will ultimately drown in it."

The Celestials waited, weapons at the ready, to see what they would do. Soren was secretly hoping they would attempt an attack so she had a reason to cut them down. They had labeled Baz a traitor to his people, and the thought burrowed into her soul, sparking her anger into an inferno.

As if reading her mind, Rook whispered into her ear, "Let them go. Returning to Xian-Dao in defeat is worse than death for these people. Bao-Ren will have them executed either way."

With Soren's thirst for bloodshed quenched, she pressed her lips together and watched as, one-by-one, the warriors slipped through the gate, never to be seen again.

By the following morning, the rest of the fallen had been buried, the Celestials assisting in digging a grave for every warrior, from Estelar to Patrivah.

Jai, Erick, and King Elias had decided to label the burned fields sacred ground and a symbol of their newfound alliance. The provinces would keep their borders, but they would govern together. A democracy to lead all of Entheas. Each province would have a leader at the table, and decisions would be made by the people's vote. They would still have to speak to Shakti, the leader of Dhamtra, to confirm that they wanted to be part of the new world order, but they had high hopes. Dhamtra had always been a peaceful country, and Soren had no doubt Shakti would join them.

The next steps would involve rescue efforts for the people of the Esinian Isles, as well as cutting down crime in Thorncrest, but those things would have to wait until they could heal the wounded and form travel groups.

Jai clasped arms with Abraxos, and Soren gave Luscinia a tight hug before they slipped through the portal, heading back to Anistera. Luscinia promised to visit each month.

It was hard to say goodbye, but Soren didn't want to risk putting any more strain on Luscinia's form after she had healed Rook. She wished there was a way to use the Oculus to allow them more time together, but she would not use its powers improperly for selfish reasons.

"Goodbye, sweet Soren," Luscinia called, stepping through the gate.

After all the Celestials had returned to Anistera, those closest to Baz gathered around the pyre Jai had built. They took turns saying their goodbyes, each person sprinkling a handful of rose petals over his body.

Soren approached and let the petals fall across his still form, circling around to place her hands on his feet and pressing them to her head. If anyone deserved the conveyance of respect, it was Baztien.

Soren could hear Jai whisper, "I'll see you again soon, brother," before he grabbed a handful of flower petals.

Enara went last, leaning in close to whisper into Baztien's ear. Soren knew that wherever he was, he would hear her words and cherish them until they could meet again. However, she could not hear what was said and preferred it that way. Those words were meant for Baz, and Baz alone.

Enara placed one last kiss upon his forehead before joining Soren a safe distance away, taking her hand and repeating the word's Soren had said to her those few months ago on the hilltop.

"I'm ready."

Jai lit the pyre, releasing Baztien's soul to the after to wait for her.

THREE DAYS AFTER THE BURIALS HAD BEEN COMPLETED, EVERYone packed up to say their goodbyes. After spending nearly every day together and going through so much, they struggled to part.

"Come to visit Adaryn and I as soon as you're able," Jai said, hugging Enara and then Soren.

"We will," Soren responded.

"You better!" Adaryn commented, pulling both girls in for a big hug. "I need someone to help me make sure this guy doesn't get too big for his crown."

"Well, anytime you need him knocked down a peg, send for us," Rook replied.

It warmed Soren's heart to see him being more open with people, even if it was a select few.

They waved goodbye as Adaryn and Jai boarded the ship to Patrivah. Callan and Saoirse had left that morning, Ori and Ikei alongside them.

Soren watched as Everett said a heartfelt goodbye to Erick, planting a passionate kiss on Stelonbriar's leader in front of the entire congregation. An action that would have caused an uproar in recent times was finally seen as all it really was— an expression of love. For love came in all shapes, sizes, colors, and orientations. After seeing the world burn, they could all use a little more of it, regardless of what form it came in.

The love of a mother for her child, a husband for his wife, and even an owner for his pet. Love made their world of ash and flame burst with new life. The seeds were planted in the hopes that the future would bloom into something beautiful, something new to fight for.

When the boat pulled away from the dock and the rest of the gathered citizens had taken their leave, Soren, Rook, and Enara tightened their packs and mounted their steeds.

"Ready to go home?" Soren asked Rook as the horses found the trail leading back to Vreburn.

Home. Rook thought about what that word meant. He had spent most of his life in Thorncrest Manor and had thought he and Soren would return there after all was said and done, but as they headed East instead of North, his heart knew they had chosen the right path.

He thought of Soren's house in the woods. The sense of calm that the boards and nails imbued. The warmth that seemed to emanate from the very bones of the place. That was when he realized there was nowhere else he would rather be. Thorncrest represented everything he was, whereas Vreburn was everything he wanted to be.

He no longer wanted to be a shut-in, unwilling to open himself up to the world for fear of rejection. He had spent his entire life in cold, dark places and wanted to run directly into the sun, into the warmth that was Soren's heart, and stay there until they were old and gray, reading side-by-side until the final embers of the hearth burned out. And when their bodies finally gave out, they would join each other in the after, finding peace among the stars.

Soren cleared her throat, and he realized he had yet to respond to her question.

"Yeah," he replied, "let's go home."

CHAPTER
THIRTY—EIGHT

Soren stood in the kitchen of her father's home, breathing it all in. The smell of wood and parchment, clay and sand, filled her nostrils. She was elated to be back, though she had to admit it was slightly surreal to see Rook in a place that was so close to her heart.

Enara had decided to stay with Laraline and Alondra for a while after they had broken the news of Baztien's death. Soren was still coming to terms with it and wanted to be there for her but hadn't wanted to argue when Enara had packed up her things, gave Soren a teary-eyed hug, and then hopped onto Ellie's back, trotting back toward town.

The old man had stayed true to his word and had taken care of Ellie, Obsidian, and Enara's riding companion over the last two months and had been happy to trade Ellie back for the war horse she had been riding in exchange for his lost canoe.

"This one gave me quite a shock," he'd said, giving Obie a fond pat. "Never had an issue, almost as if he were waiting for something. Then, about a week ago, he just vanished! I searched high and low for him, but his tracks stopped mid-stride. It was the darnedest thing."

Soren and Enara had shared conspiratory smiles, not wanting to spread the news about a flying horse.

"Well, thank you for taking care of them both," Enara had said, tracing her hand down Ellie's strong neck.

"It was my pleasure. This one, in particular, is such a sweet girl."

"She is, isn't she?" Enara had responded.

They had bid the man goodbye, promising to visit again if they were in the area, and had taken Ellie home. Soren knew Baz had been smiling down on them, watching over their journey.

In the short time they had been away, Baz's mothers, along with the other townsfolk, had rebuilt the main strip in town and had been working their way outward. Luckily for Laraline and Alondra, that meant their house had been one of the first to have been mended. There had not been much left, but somehow, Baz's room had remained largely untouched by the flames. The townspeople had stopped the fire before it had spread all the way through their home.

Her heart broke for Enara, and for herself, and as she looked at Rook, she couldn't help but feel guilty that the man she loved had survived when Enara's had not.

"You okay?" Rook asked, his soft tenor breaking through her mind spiral.

"Yeah," she said, picking at her fingernails. "Just feels weird to be here again." She shifted back and forth on her feet, avoiding his eyes.

She had spent plenty of time with Rook alone but, for some reason, having him in this house—*her* house—seemed more intimate. She suddenly felt even more vulnerable as his glacier gaze slipped over her. Her skin felt hot and tight against her clothes, the leather vest seeming to cinch a few inches closer to her chest.

He held out a hand to her, and the warmth of it fought off the last of the autumn chill. Winter was coming, and the yard was filled with leaves of all shades—orange, red, and yellow. They had crunched and crackled as they'd made their way inside after their long journey.

Soren shook off the thought as Rook pulled her into his chest and nuzzled his face into her hair.

"How are you feeling?" he asked, pressing a kiss in the soft place just under her jaw.

"Like I want to crawl into bed and not come out for the foreseeable future," she answered honestly.

"I think I could arrange that for you." His voice hummed against her neck as his fingers undid the laces on her vest, his breath whispering across the shell of her ear, causing her to giggle.

"That tickles," she said.

"Good," he replied, his voice rumbling low in his chest as their lips met.

"Rook?" Soren asked against his mouth.

"Yes, little bird?" he responded between kisses, pushing the vest off her shoulders and letting it clatter to the floor.

"I hate you."

She could feel the smile that formed on his lips and pressed her body closer to him.

"I know," he replied. His skin tingled as the mating bond lit up all of his senses, urging him forward.

"Rook?" she asked again, her face flushed with desire.

"Yes?" he replied. The word was honey, sticky and sweet, seeping into her skin, warming her from the inside out.

"Make me forget," she replied, and he did.

She gasped as he lifted her into his arms. Then she wrapped her legs tightly around his waist and deepened the kiss. His tongue explored her mouth, tasting of sweet citrus from the orange he'd had earlier.

Her hands fisted in his hair, and she moaned against his mouth, his hardness pressing into her through the fabric of his trousers. He growled as the friction sent waves of pleasure to his groin and turned to sit in the wingback chair, Soren planted firmly in his lap.

She ground against him, their mouths devouring each other's, only pausing for a moment for Rook to shrug his tunic off his shoulders.

Soren reached down, fumbling with the button on his trousers, but he stilled her hands.

"Patience, little bird." His eyes glinted lustfully in the firelight. He had stoked the embers while she had brought water in from the well, and the flames danced playfully at her back.

"I want you—*now*," she ordered, and he obliged.

"Anything for you, little bird." He lifted her from his lap, leaving her to stand on unsteady feet. Then he stood, towering over her, and removed her shirt before kneeling in front of her to slide her trousers down. He tossed the pants aside and pressed his tongue to her core, his thumb circling her clit as her hands found his hair again. His fingers grasped her back-side as he devoured her, and she panted as his tongue dipped in and out of her.

"Rook … please," was all she could manage.

"Oh, not yet, little bird," he admonished before reaching a hand up to her mouth. "Suck," he growled.

She grasped his hand in hers and sucked hard, coating his fingers in her saliva.

"Good girl," he praised as she released his wrist. He inserted one finger, then a second, curling them in the way she favored.

"Maker, Rook," she moaned breathlessly. "I'm going to—"

"Ah, ah, ah," Rook said, stopping his ministrations. "Not yet, dirty bird. Today, I will take your pleasure with mine."

He stood quickly, and before she could complain, his lips were crashing against hers once more as he lifted her then slowly laid her down on the rug before the fire. His hands traced the lines of her body, and she writhed under his touch. She was wet and wanting, and her core ached so badly she could not stand it anymore.

"Rook," she ground out, "you're killing me."

He loosed a laugh that promised he was about to and lined up with her entrance. He impaled her with one swift thrust, and she cried out.

"Yes, little bird, scream for me," he groaned before taking her lips once more. His forearms rested on either side of her head, the veins straining against his skin as he ground into her. Her moans turned to whimpers as his pace quickened, her breaths coming in shallow pants.

"Rook, I'm so close. Don't stop." Her words came out broken, as the pieces of her orgasm came together. It was the first time they had coupled since their mating bond had clicked into place, and the feeling of it was overwhelming. Everything was hotter, heavier. Rook's skin buzzed against hers, every touch and thrust shooting jolts of electricity up her spine.

Her back arched, and she cried out as he moved his hips in just the right way to make her toes tingle and her breath catch, the final piece of her climax falling into place. She detonated, and he swore as her inner walls tightened around him.

"Fuck, little bird, that's it. Come for me."

Her calves ached as pleasure pulsed through her. Euphoria washed over her, wave after wave, and she cried out once more as he spilled into her.

They stayed like that for a moment, chests heaving, kissing each other lazily as the fire warmed their skin. Then Rook slid out of her and used his tunic to clean them both off before grabbing a woven blanket from the couch and stretching out beside her.

Soren turned over, pressing her cheek to his chest and wrapping her free arm up over his shoulders. "What happens now?" she asked quietly. So much had occurred since they'd met. So many secrets and lies, and healing and heartbreak, that she wasn't sure where their trauma ended and they began.

His response was so simple, and it was exactly what she needed to hear. What everyone needed to hear.

"We live."

It had been three months since they had returned from the war, and Soren had checked in on Enara nearly every day. Meanwhile, Rook had returned to Thorncrest to tie up some loose ends. He had gifted the manor to Meena and Evelyn, explaining how it was their home just as much as it was his. They had refused, of course. So, ultimately, Thorncrest had been sold to the highest bidder. The final tie connecting Rook to his father was severed.

Rook used some of the funds to purchase a home for Meena and Evelyn, refusing to take no for an answer. He had taken Soren to Eldrin to see the tree cottage he had purchased for the girls.

Eldrin had fared surprisingly well against the fires. Many of the large trees had been charred, but their core and roots were strong and stood firm. Meena and Evelyn looked so at home there, and they felt safe being up in the canopy. They wouldn't let Soren leave until she promised to visit at least once a month so they could enjoy a nice dinner together. Her heart lifted a little when she was reminded she would see them in a few days' time.

Soren pulled her fur jacket tight around her shoulders and readied herself to brave the cool winter morning when a knock sounded at her door.

Her stomach dropped, and her mouth went dry. Rook and Enara never knocked, and the last time she'd heard that sound was when she'd found out about her father's death.

She inhaled slowly, holding her breath in her lungs, and turned the knob. Her anxiety dissipated when she opened the door to find Everett standing there with a megawatt smile.

"Everett!" she exclaimed, pulling him in for a hug. "Come in, come in. It's freezing." Snow swirled around him on the front step, and some of it trailed inside, like little white shadows following his boots.

"I hope I'm not interrupting anything. You look like you were about to head out."

"No, no, it's fine. I was just about to meet Luscinia and Enara for lunch. The new tavern was finally finished today, and we promised the owner we would show."

"The Celestial who healed Rook?" he asked.

"Yeah, she visits monthly when her grace allows. It's been very cathartic, actually. She's been telling me all about my mom." Her eyes misted. "Anyway," she continued, shaking away the tears, "what brings you all the way to Draestel? Are Jai and Adaryn okay?"

"Oh, yeah!" he exclaimed. His energy was infectious, reminding her of Baztien. "Jai sent me. He has news he wanted me to deliver personally."

Soren chuckled nervously. "Should I be scared?" Her stomach twisted as her mind reeled, searching for a possible reason for the impromptu visit.

"No, no, everything is fine. Here." He handed her a letter. She broke the royal seal and read it aloud.

My dear friend Soren,

I hope this letter finds you well. Adaryn and I have missed you these last three months. Patrivah is rebuilding, and our walls are almost complete. The people are still adjusting to having Adaryn as their queen consort but, overall, the reception has been a positive one.

We wanted to formally invite you, Rook, Enara, and Baztien's mothers to the coronation ceremony in one month's time.

Each province had been allowed to vote for their new leader under the new Enthean Democratic Decree, and Jai had received ninety-three percent of the votes from his people. Under the new law, the king was allowed to take whoever he wanted for a wife, which meant him and Adaryn could officially take their rightful places as king and queen of Patrivah.

A formal invite will be sent closer to the date, but I like to think a personal invitation from the king is more official, anyway. On a more serious note, we finished combing the battlefields about a week ago, and we discovered Baztien's sword.

Soren's breath caught, her chest tightening as flashbacks from the war battered against her skull. *Blood. So much blood. Baztien lying in the dirt, lifeless.*

She pushed past the intrusive thoughts, blinked back the tears that were tugging at the edges of her eyes, and continued.

I don't know if I ever told you or Enara this, but he finally picked a name for it. "Unyielding." He named it for Enara and the strength she showed through all her adversity. Said she was as unbreakable as the blade itself. He would have wanted her to have it. Please, pass it along to her.

Everett had removed the sheathed blade from his back and laid it out on Soren's dining table. "I kept it safe, I promise," he said softly before she continued reading.

The text was blurry as the tears toppled over, the words shifting and moving like water.

The final note we have for you is happier news. Adaryn is expecting a child. Patrivah will have an heir. My heart nearly burst when her courses stopped coming. She is due in six months time, and we had rather hoped that you would be her godmother. Everett, of course, is already the godfather, but we can discuss the details further at the coronation.

We have already decided that if it is a girl, we could name her Indira Jai, after my mother and I, but if we were to have a son, he would be named Baztien Grey.

Your friend,
Jaideep Ashwood, King of Patrivah

Rook fingered the spine of the oldest book in his collection, releasing a relieved breath that all of them had made it safely to Vreburn. He stood before them, hoping they would bring him comfort, for today was a big day. Today, he would meet his mother.

He had debated if he even wanted to meet her. What if she rejected him? She had already mourned him, so he thought showing up on her doorstep might be considered cruel.

He turned his gaze downward as Soren's arms locked around his waist, her cheek pressed tightly against his back.

"Whatever happens today, I'm here, okay?" she promised.

"I know," he replied, turning to face her. He brushed a strand of hair behind her ear and kissed her softly. "I just don't want to disrupt her life. I never had a mother; I can survive without one."

Soren cupped his cheek, her eyes misting. "But you don't have to." She hugged him again, tighter this time, hoping to squeeze some confidence into him. "We don't need to just survive anymore."

She could feel him nod before he pressed a kiss to her head. He let her hold him until Enara returned from saddling the horses.

"You ready?" she asked.

"I don't really have a choice, now do I?" he quipped, shrugging on his winter cloak.

"No, but I thought I would give you the illusion that you have a choice in the matter," Enara poked.

He gave her a pointed look before heading out the door.

"Take care of him for me," Soren said, grasping Enara's hand.

"Only if he behaves," she replied, smiling.

They said their goodbyes, and then Rook and Enara rode in silence the whole way to town. If there was one thing he appreciated about his half-sister, it was that she never felt the need to fill space with unnecessary interaction.

They might not be what he would call close, but they had an understanding for one another that no one else had. They were both stubborn, so opening up to each other was an elongated process. Though, he had no doubt they would get used to the idea that they were siblings over time.

As they crossed the threshold into town, Rook's stomach tied itself into knots. Then they were dismounting their horses, giving them each a solid pat before Enara led the way to the front door of their mother's new house.

Rook winced as his half-sister knocked on the lacquered wood. Then he clenched his fists nervously as they waited for Mrs. Montgrove to answer. It felt like an age had passed when the thin woman slid the wooden lock aside, embracing Enara before letting them in.

Enara had seen her mother a handful of times, working to reconcile everything that had happened with her father, and had informed her about Rook. From his understanding, she had fainted upon receiving the information and needed some time to process it. That had been a few weeks ago, and Enara had made the plan to introduce them shortly after he had returned from Thorncrest.

Rook's posture was stiff as he entered his mother's home, unsure of how he was supposed to act. What did one say when they showed up in their birth mother's home after twenty-five years of life?

"Mom," Enara started, "this is Rook. Rook, this is Beatrice Montgrove, our mother."

"It's nice to finally meet you," Rook said formally, holding out a hand for her to shake.

The breath was nearly knocked out of him when Beatrice rushed forward and embraced him in a rib-shattering hug. Before he knew it, his mother was sobbing against his chest while Enara gave him a sympathetic look.

Beatrice pulled away, wiping her face. "I'm sorry," she apologized. "I told myself I would keep it together, but there has been so much loss … I just … I am glad you're here."

He took in the fine lines of her face, noting the similarities between them. Though the majority of his bone structure had come from his father, he could see where her genes had softened his hard exterior.

"You look so much like your grandmother," Beatrice said, gesturing for him and Enara to join her at the dining table.

"So I've been told," he replied. He wasn't trying to be short; he just had no idea how to navigate this conversation.

"Enara tells me you grew up in Thorncrest?" she asked.

"Yes, I lived there my whole life," he replied, resting his arms on the table.

"Well, I hope you know that I am happy that you have relocated to Vreburn. It will be nice to have both my children close," she said softly, as though she were testing out the words.

Something inside him fractured. Hearing her acknowledge he was her son opened a dam on feelings he hadn't realized he had hidden away. All of a sudden, his inner child screamed at him to run around the table and embrace this woman, whom he barely knew. To lie on the couch with his head in her lap as she told him stories of faraway places. To call on her in the middle of the night when the shadows seemed to be closing in on him. To spend the day baking and ruining their dinner by gorging on apple pie.

He pictured himself coming home from school, his white hair mussed from playing with the other boys, and her pulling him in for a hug. She would ask him how his day had been, and they would laugh and play, and all would be right in the world.

"It's okay," Beatrice said, reaching across the table to take his hand. To his own surprise, he let her. It was oddly comforting. "You don't have to say anything. Neither of you do," she continued, reaching her other hand over to grasp Enara's.

"I want you both to know how sorry I am for everything. You two went through things that no child should have to endure." She squeezed their hands tighter, tears spilling down her cheeks as she continued, "My silence did more damage than your father ever could, Enara, and I only hope that, in time, you will be able to forgive me. And Rook, I know I cannot make up for the years we have lost, but I want you to know that you are always welcome here."

"You already know I forgive you, Mom," Enara said, leaning her head on her mother's shoulder.

Beatrice released their hands to press her palms to Enara's cheeks. "I wish someday to be as strong as you are, sweetheart."

Rook remained silent, worried if he spoke, all his emotions would come rushing forth. He was not ready to shed tears in front of anyone but Soren.

They spoke a short while longer, sharing the few happy stories they had from their childhoods, before getting up to leave.

"I hope you'll come back soon," Beatrice said as they donned their winter gear.

"I'm sure we will," Rook answered. His simple response seemed to be exactly what she needed to hear, and his eyes misted.

She pulled him in for one last hug, and this time, he let himself relax into her arms. She smelled of rosemary and chamomile tea, and it put him at ease.

He pulled away gently, looking from his mother to Enara, and couldn't help the bit of joy that peeked out from behind his black heart. He had a family.

EPILOGUE

Enara touched her fingers to the necklace that hung from her throat and took a steadying breath. The small pendant had been fashioned from a silver alloy, the stone formed from applying immense pressure to a collection of Baztien's ashes. It was the color of fresh milk, and the white swirled with flecks of gold, just like Baztien's eyes.

After they had collected his ashes from the pyre, Saoirse had come to her later in the evening, asking if she could have some of the ashes to make something for her. She had shown Enara the ring she wore that held her grandmother's ashes, and Enara had obliged, wanting a way to keep him with her always.

When the package had arrived from Olecastor, it had brought tears to her eyes. Saoirse, being ever thoughtful, had fashioned four necklaces, all the same, apart from Enara's.

Hers was the only one that had the gold flecks. She couldn't believe Saoirse had remembered how she'd spoken about Baztian when they had dressed for Hallival.

Enara ensured the other three went to their rightful owners—Soren, Alondra, and Laraline. She had stayed with Baz's mothers for a few months after they had returned to Vreburn, and as they had mourned together, she had begun to heal. Now, it had been over a year since she'd lost the love of her life.

Every now and then, someone she knew from the institute would ask her to join them for a drink, but she always turned them down. Sometimes people were cruel and would tell her it was time to move on. They did not understand that one did not just move on from grief.

Grief was a dark passenger that latched onto your soul and never let go. Grief was the cold hand that would forever be entwined with yours. The only thing in existence that could compete with grief was time.

A relationship with grief was like experiencing exposure therapy. If you tortured yourself long enough, the pain would become more manageable. The burning of a shattered heart would dull to a low ache. The agony, a gentle reminder of those they had loved and lost.

"Hey, hon," Laraline called from farther down the beach, "it's time."

Enara gave her a wave in response and headed in her direction. Today, they would release the remainder of Baztien's ashes into the Obsidian Sea so that he could join his birth parents and be reconnected with his homeland. Then he could finally be at peace.

They had wanted to come sooner, but they had stayed to help rebuild Vreburn. Soren had wanted to join her, but

Adaryn was about to give birth to her and Jai's child any day now, so she had gone to provide her emotional support.

She waded into the water where Alondra and Laraline stood, her white dress floating on the ocean's edge like a ghost. Her skin prickled, and her feet sunk slightly into the wet sand.

Alondra held up the small, golden urn that held the rest of Baztien's remains and asked Enara, "Is there anything you want to say?"

"He knows how I feel about him," she replied softly. "Now, let's send him home."

Alondra nodded, and then they took turns sprinkling the ashes into the dark waters.

The day was relatively still, and a gentle current carried the ashes away almost as if the sea was helping him on his journey.

The three of them stood in the shallows, letting the waves lap at their feet until the ashes were out of sight. Silent tears joined the great expanse of water, each droplet finding its way back to him.

"Are you ready to go?" Laraline asked softly.

Enara nodded and wiped her tears with the pad of her thumb. "Yeah, we just have one last stop to make."

ENARA KNOCKED SOFTLY ON THE WOODEN DOOR OF THE FISHER-man's house then waited patiently as the man made his way to the door. His movements were chased by a faint knocking sound that she couldn't quite make out.

He opened the door to reveal that he was missing a leg. Baz had never mentioned that. Then again, he always saw people for who they were and spoke of them from what he knew of their hearts, a trait that seemed to have been passed down to him from his mothers.

"Can I help you?" the older man asked.

"I won't take much of your time, but I was hoping we could come in for a moment," Enara said, gesturing behind her.

The fisherman's eyes shone brightly as he recognized Laraline and Alondra. "Of course, of course, come on in!" He ushered them into the house, and they each took a seat at his table. "What brings you all to my neck of the woods? It's been … what? Must be about sixteen years ago we met," he said, scratching at his beard.

"Eighteen," Alondra replied with a sad smile.

"Yes. How have you all been? I often thought about you three. Where is that boy? I'd love to see the strapping young lad he's grown into!" he exclaimed. Then his smile faded when he saw the grave looks on the women's faces. "The boy is okay, is he not?" he asked.

Enara pressed her lips together, unable to speak the words. Even after a whole year, she struggled to say he was gone.

"He is at peace," Alondra replied, squeezing Laraline's hand. Her wife was tearing up again, and she handed her a handkerchief from her trouser pocket.

"I am sorry," the fisherman replied, bowing his head.

"Don't be," Enara replied, finding her voice. "He died protecting those he loved." Her voice cracked, and she fought to rein in her emotions.

"I hope he is well celebrated, then," the fisherman replied. "He was always such a good boy."

"It would do you well to know, then, that he became a great man," Alondra offered. "He would have wanted you to know what became of him."

The fisherman pressed his fingertips together, his elbows resting on the table as he replied, "Yes, I always imagined he would be. I am glad you've come, though I'm sorry you had to travel so far to reach me. A letter would have sufficed."

Laraline wiped her face and spoke then, "Baztien always said, if anything were to happen to him, that he wanted you to have this." She reached forward and placed a small piece of wood in the fisherman's hand.

The man's eyes misted. It was the ship he had gifted Baztien as a boy.

He turned it over between his calloused fingers, smiling fondly. "He kept this? All this time?" he asked, his gaze meeting the three women's.

"It has been on his side table since we left here," Alondra confirmed. "He wished on it every night, praying to the Maker to protect you while you were out at sea."

The fisherman swallowed down the lump in his throat before speaking, and to Enara, no truer words had ever been spoken.

"It would seem, then, that he saved us all."

ACKNOWLEDGMENTS

First and foremost, I want to give a special shoutout to my good friend, Rebecca (Bec) Edwards, for being my Lightning McQueen. When I wrote *Secrets and Songbirds*, I said, if one person loved it, I would be over the moon, and you were that person for me. So, from the bottom of my heart, thank you. Your support has meant the absolute world and has pushed me to keep going on this crazy writing journey.

Of course, major props need to go to my husband for putting up with my crazy antics and watching over our tiny human so that I may write in peace. I promise to buy you an island when I become a bestselling author.

I would like to thank my mother and father for always being supportive of my new adventures and for letting me fly, just like Soren.

Thank you to my wonderful editor, Kristin Campbell, for keeping my voice while fixing my atrocious grammar to give my readers the best book possible.

Lastly, as always, I want to thank my readers. Without your feedback and praise, *Feathers and Thorns* would not exist. So, thank you for the hours you chose to spend in my world. I hope you loved Entheas as much as I do.

ABOUT THE AUTHOR

N.J. RODMAN IS THE AUTHOR OF THE FANTASY ROMANCE DUOLOGY *The Oculus Duet*. She is a wife and mother, born and raised in Edmonton, Alberta, and has been an avid reader since childhood. She looks forward to bringing her readers into all the new worlds she has planned and can't wait to see what her future holds.

Follow the author on Tiktok and Instagram @nj.rodman and don't forget to grab the first book in the *The Oculus Duet*, *Secrets and Songbirds* to find out how the fight for Entheas started.

www.ingramcontent.com/pod-product-compliance
Lightning Source LLC
Chambersburg PA
CBHW050850210726
48290CB00004B/1157